ALWAYS PLAY THE DARK HORSE

A JESSICA MINTON MYSTERY
BOOK 3

SHARON HEALY-YANG

Relax. Read. Repeat.

ALWAYS PLAY THE DARK HORSE (A Jessica Minton Mystery, Book 3)
By Sharon Healy-Yang
Published by TouchPoint Press
Brookland, Arkansas
www.touchpointpress.com

ISBN: 978-1-952816-75-8

Editor: Kimberly Coghlan
Cover Design: Sharon Yang (concept); De-Ping Yang (compilation)

First Edition

Printed In The United States Of America

Jessica Minton Mystery Series

Bait and Switch
Letter from a Dead Man

To Mary Wilson, a "Supreme" lady who has given so much joy to people with her music, her laughter, and her support. The world shines a bit less without her; she is missed by so many.

First, I want to thank my "posse," who have plowed through many a draft of this book, helping me to figure out what to clarify, what to trim, and what to keep, as well as to avoid using "quip" too much: Ruth Haber, Kathy Healey, Amber Vayo, Yang De-Ping, and Judy Jeon-Chapman. I also want to thank all my readers who have supported my writing by reading my books, encouraging me to keep writing, and/or by spreading the word, especially Tricia Lebreton, Sue Thorne-Gagnon, the Keith Hall Girls, Patricia "Sweetpea" King, Anita Jenkins, Phil Healy, Stephanie Leccese, Kerri Phillips, Kayla Sturm, Tamara Trudeau, Diane Jepson, C.J. Kinton, Dawn Watson, Mary Kramer, Peter Chapman, Melissa Dearden, Rini Kilcoyne, and many more folks. You know who you are. I also want to thank my writer friends for their encouragement and support: Lisa Lieberman, Leslie Wheeler, Arlene Kay, Lisa Kramer, and Kate Zebrowski. I want to give a special shout-out to Connie Johnson Hambley for helping me figure out how to describe being in a barn fire, with a horse. Whatever I got wrong is on me—and woe betide the daughter of a firefighter for any errors in that department! There's also a tip of the hat to the folks at the Worcester State University library for helping me find and navigate the microfiche for full editions of the *New York Times* in 1946. Yes, people really did eat salmon and sardine sandwiches—blech! A big hug and kiss for my husband yang for all the emotional and material support he's given throughout the creation of this novel. Once more, he scores big with his cover design! If I've left anyone out, please know that I have still appreciated all you've done for me. Let me know, and I'll get you in the acknowledgments of the fourth book. Finally, thanks to the crew at TouchPoint Press for giving me my first chance and sticking with me, with a special tip of the hat to Kim Coghlan for superb and supportive editing and Sheri Williams for taking me on in the first place.

Prologue

May 1946

A dark and stormy night. What a cliché! Actually, it was more a night of fog and cold than flashes of jagged lightning, pelting rain, and lashing wind. Nevertheless, the dark lantern barely illuminated a foot in front of her on the wet lawn, her raincoat and kerchief scarcely fending off the teeth-chattering rawness from the ocean roaring ominously some distance behind, past the lawn and down the beach.

But she knew her way. She knew it too well, whether crossing the grass toward Cameron House in the brilliant morning to teach a class or slipping through the night for more clandestine, less savory, even dangerous, encounters with the secret *amoré* she was meeting tonight.

The Chapman Lighthouse down the coast let off one of its periodic mournful calls as she reached a set of French doors. The ring of keys jingled in her shaky hands. She ought to have found the right one easily after all this time but knowing how different this rendezvous promised to be made her nervous. No, afraid. The exhilaration of forbidden passion had morphed into something that shook her—but not with the old, delicious pleasure. No, hope and anticipation had become something tired, almost hopeless. Almost. But love, hope, passion had never really died, or she wouldn't have answered his note by coming here. She'd take one more chance, not quite daring to believe that this elusive love would finally be hers, but not daring to let slip any possibility to make it so.

She shut the glass doors behind her in the darkness, her lantern now closed, and slid the kerchief off her head. If there had been any light, a peeper into the reception hall would have seen a young woman of about thirty. Soft brown hair was parted in the middle, a braid coiled in a band holding back tresses curling almost to her shoulders. Her cheekbones were high, and her cheeks rounded. Her mouth was full and lipsticked a tasteful red; eyes large, brown, intelligent. But she wasn't sure now how intelligent she'd been since getting into this mess. What had she been thinking? About tonight? About the last six months? Was this really what she wanted?

The woman moved slightly to her left, her hand resting on the intricate carvings of the great fireplace's tall mahogany mantle. She'd always been early. Always the first one to arrive. Too eager, too eager. But was she eager tonight? The note had promised so much. Promised what she'd pressed for—for so long. It was what she craved, especially after the subtle, then more palpable falling off from him. So why wasn't she excited? Ecstatic? What felt wrong?

A buoy clanged warningly. Rough seas. Rough seas all around. The foghorn moaned again. Many nights, she had moaned with it, alone in her cottage after he'd left. Worse, when he'd no longer come as often, there or to their secret place. She shook herself. No, tonight she wouldn't have to lament, to ache for what couldn't be, for promises gone sour. Still, would her conscience let her enjoy this prize? Could she have what she'd grieved over for so long, without having to sell her soul? And there were his connections to fear. But hadn't the note promised that, yes, he *had* found a way for them to be happy together?

So where *was* he? That was when she heard the familiar creaking across the Great Hall of the *faux* china closet with its enormous scallop-shell headpiece. It led to a tiny room and a back pantry. She knew those hideaways oh too well.

"I'm here!" she whispered into the darkness, happily, hopefully anyway. "By the hearth!"

He needn't have hidden on a Sunday night. No one would have seen him slip in—but it was just like him to spice everything with a dash of mystery. Perhaps that's why his letter had sounded just a bit off, to unsettle her so he could sweep away all her doubts and play the gallant. A flash of the adventurous, the forbidden zest with which he'd conquered her good sense, her conscience, took hold again. The thrill of forbidden passions stolen in forbidden places. The sweetness of its return swept away almost all the ache of recent frustrations, doubts, fears–almost.

She started eagerly forward, toward their secret lair, now as dark as the great room encompassing them, as cloaked as the fogged-in lawns, campus, ocean. No, of course he wouldn't say anything to her–the silence was part of the mystery, the excitement. *She* knew her way so well. Blackness was no impediment to reaching him.

So, when the flashlight blazed her into blindness, she fumbled, shocked, surprised. But she had no time to be scared, never seeing the pistol raised and firing a shot perfectly timed to be drowned in the wail of the foghorn. Her lifeless drop to the floor was muffled within the walls of Cameron House by the silent fog and the thundering assault and retreat of the Atlantic.

Chapter One

Tuesday, June 4, 1946

The sky was that clear, rich blue, so typical of the brilliant early summer. The whole of the country might be just coming off, about to be, or *on* strike, but nothing could haunt a man striding through the Village in Manhattan this Tuesday afternoon. Not even those damned memories of France and the war. Not in this one moment.

He was tall, his lean face only starting to fill in a bit, a mustache fuller than the norm, and dark hair a tad longer. In the countryside and small villages of France, the look had blent in admirably with the rustic populace. But here, Manhattan 1946, James Crawford no longer had to worry about melting into the crush. Maybe his look did fit his life now: an academic in a tweedy jacket moving amongst Village bohemians—an *avant-garde* appearance was just the ticket.

James Crawford smiled at that thought, shifting the brown parcel of books he carried, dodging pedestrians, some casual and happy to meander through the streets, others hurrying to places they didn't want to be (judging by their expressions). Still, they weren't James's problem today. Well, maybe he *was* hurrying a bit, himself, but it was hurrying to a place he really wanted to be. What a delicious conundrum—for a change: enjoy the rest of the June sun and sky or nip back to spend time with his wife.

That was the only drawback to the afternoon: Jessica couldn't come with him. Tuesdays, a messenger delivered the script for her Friday-night broadcast. So, she had to spend all day reading, studying, reviewing, to be ready for rehearsals tomorrow. He knew better than to interrupt today's dose of concentration.

James was mightily proud of Jessica, the way she brought life to so many different roles—although some of those parts on the Wellstone Mystery Hour gave him a bit of a turn. Being married since last October to Jessica Minton had been a lifesaver for him—though he regretted it hadn't always been exactly a picnic for her.

What he'd seen, what he'd done, had to do, working with the Underground in France off and on since 1939, hadn't just wafted out of his life when he'd been sent back to the States a year ago—those unexpected flashes of temper, those nights when anxiety, even guilt, sent him away from his sleeping wife to wander the apartment, the garden behind the building, or to sit and brood in the morning grey.

But not always alone. Sometimes, Jessica slipped in, not saying a word, just sitting there reading, or watching the stars or the darkness within him. And, of course, there was also Dusty, who'd been Jessica's feline roommate long before he'd entered the picture, sitting calmly on the opposite end of the sofa, quietly blinking. Jessica now referred to Dusty as Wife #2, but they both knew Dusty ranked herself much higher.

Damascus Place loomed to his left. James glanced at his watch. Almost four o'clock, and he was nearly home. He had reached a decision about taking a teaching position at Margaret Point. Making that decision, knowing how Jessica would be thrilled for his happiness, almost put an extra spring in James Crawford's step. Almost. He knew his responsibilities to Dick Streeter in the FBI shadowed that decision, even though Jessica didn't. He wouldn't want her to know, even if it were allowed. She'd worried about him enough. But he shouldn't worry, either, according to Dick. Just do your teaching and keep your eyes and ears open for that special someone, and report back, had been his orders. *Maybe* do a little discreet sniffing around town. That was all. That was the promise. It was little enough payment, wasn't it, to be loaned back to the Yanks on the East Coast? Or was this assignment an acknowledgment that after six years in the field, he was no longer up for more than a little low-key observation.

James shoved that thought aside, instead focusing on what he really cared about now. He and Jessica could be together. The price was little enough—except he couldn't tell Jessica everything. Hell, with any luck, there'd be nothing to tell. Anyway, he wanted this teaching position. He was looking forward to Connecticut. And with the summer hiatus of her radio program, Jessica could enjoy a well-deserved vacation.

The nineteenth-century building he approached housed their flat on the first of two floors. Extending its length parallel rather than perpendicular to the street, the edifice was particularly distinct amongst New York's congregations of Brownstones. James liked that. His whole life he'd so immersed himself in trying to fit in, be inconspicuous, during the war, or even as a scholarship boy at university. Now he couldn't help relishing any opportunity to break out of the pack—only not *too* noticeably. Old habits died hard.

James shifted his parcel of books to retrieve his keys from his inside jacket pocket, smiling as he reflected that it was convenient to be able to get in the apartment by the front door. Things had been quite different when he'd first met Jessica almost three years ago. Fortunately, the package he was carrying now was a horse of a different color from the one with which he'd disrupted her life then.

The door opened into a small foyer, a dining area with a mahogany table and chairs by a window to his left. The large living room was a few steps down, beyond. To the right, a corridor led past the bedroom and opened into a bright kitchen.

Putting his parcel down on the table, James turned in mild surprise at being welcomed by Wife #2. Usually, he got the double treatment.

"Hello, puss," James returned the grey tabby's greeting, distractedly glancing into the living room. No Jessica in either the seat at the bay window or the couch across from it. Not even an empty teacup.

"Raow!"

Dusty's impatience snatched back James's attention.

"Well, puss, I know you'd rather tuck into a dish of tuna, but tell me; where is the other lady of the house?"

Dusty turned and trotted toward the kitchen, then stopped and flicked her tail commandingly, with a long-suffering blink at James. She really thought she'd trained him better!

If Jess were in the kitchen, James knew he would have heard her clattering about, or she would have heard him and at least called a greeting. She was like that, her voice always telegraphing her pleasure at his return. Yeah, she didn't even think about it but always seemed to do what made him feel he was back amongst the living–and glad of it!

So, James played a hunch and followed Dusty halfway down the corridor before breaking off to peek into the bedroom.

The bound script lay open on the bed, marked with a nearby pen. Curled up by it, closer to the head of the bed, her face buried in her arms, Jessica was asleep. Her breathing softly rose and fell beneath the folds of her white wrap dress, its hem and sleeves bordered in double stripes of smoky blue.

James smiled to himself, checking an impulse to gently wake her. No. She deserved the break, especially with her added worries over whether a strike might put her indefinitely out of work. Better just to nip into the kitchen and put on the kettle. Feeling a little peckish himself, James decided it wouldn't hurt to scramble an egg or two and even toss a few bangers into the frying pan. He could wake up Jessica later.

"Snrr! Ghgh!" reverberated from under the long waves of her dark hair.

Ah, his delicate little flower–and yet the snore that could have drowned out a Flying Fortress still hadn't woken her up.

What did the trick was Dusty leaping softly onto the bed and treating Jessica to the electric caress of her whiskers.

"Gagck!"

Jessica Minton bolted upright, shoving away the cobwebs of prickly sensation from Dusty's whisker brush. The feline culprit, barely fazed by the startled human, sidled back from the gradually less-flailing arms. Dusty was not about to go anywhere until one of these humans got on the ball, marched into the kitchen, and fed her.

"Have a nice lie-down?" James queried, leaning against the doorframe, mischief dancing in his hooded eyes and at the corners of his mouth.

It took Jessica a moment to get her bearings, but after she'd shaken the clouds out of her head, her arms went akimbo and she chided with a glint of her own, "I could have done without that heart-stopping wake-up call. And shame on you for making such an adorable feline do your dirty work, mister."

He loved the way impishness shone from those sapphire eyes and

4

shaped her smiling lips and cheeks. Pushing off from the doorframe, James sauntered over, sitting near her on the edge of the bed to continue their verbal play, "Script can't be that much of a thriller, putting you into such a sound sleep."

Jessica reclined comfortably to the side, resting on her elbow, enjoying James's noticing her legs as she tucked them in and explained, "Oh, the story is creepy enough—too creepy if you ask me! We're doing 'The Horla.'"

"Guy de Maupassant? The story you told me was the most frightening you've ever read?"

"You said it! I never should have told Mars Crandall—you know, one of the writers. He decided my history with good old Guy's tale would give my playing a special oomph! I say, if they want an oomph girl, let them hire Ann Sheridan."

"I don't know. You're still my choice for 'oomph girl,' whatever oomph *is*."

"Well, according to Ann, 'Oomph is what a fat man says when he bends over to tie his shoes in a telephone booth.' What the heck? I'm just glad Petrillo didn't call that strike yet, so we have a show to put on."

James surmised, "I'd have thought a story like 'The Horla' would put you on pins and needles not conk you out."

Jess explained, "There's loads of narration—by yours truly, of course. Very intense. I was all tuckered out just prepping myself. I hate to tell you, but this week you're going to be in for some rough sledding, between my exhaustion and my getting the willies as I immerse myself in the part."

James shook his head. "I'm still not quite past having had to check every dark room we entered for zuvembies when you did 'Pigeons from Hell.' And why did *I* always have to go in first?"

"Simple. After all those years dealing with Nazis, zuvembies should have been a piece of cake for you." Then, Jessica sank back on her elbows to observe, "You are in a good mood—not that I'm complaining. Come on now, give. What's going on in that devious master-spy mind of yours?"

"Perhaps," James answered, moving closer, "I've decided to dedicate my prodigious intellect to teaching in a private college in the lovely environs of seaside Connecticut."

Jessica's arms encircled James's neck, and she enthused, "James, I'm so happy! I know this is what you want, where your heart is. I'm so glad you're comfortable with this. It is the right thing for you to do. You deserve it–and now you won't have to worry about giving up your position at Washington Irving University when the guy who had it originally gets discharged and comes back. Not to look a gift horse in the mouth, but what finally tipped the scales?"

"Well, I had time to think today, and I realized what you said last night made a lot of sense–Don't look at the job as charity because we're friends with people at the college. Don't look at it as taking advantage of a chap's not making it back. They need someone who can teach, and whether or not Rose or David tipped the balance in my favor, I can give them their money's worth." All of which was entirely true, but James also knew he ought to add: true as far as it went. He suppressed the guilty twinge, feeling better at being able to level completely with Jess to say, "Besides, now that your program's off the air for the summer, you deserve a break. I want to take you some place where you can let your hair down."

"Raow!" impatiently interrupted them from the doorway.

Jessica grinned, "Dusty wants to take you someplace where you can let some cat food out of the can and onto her plate!"

"Then she'll just have to wait," James pronounced, a green glint in the brown of his hazel eyes, as he took Jessica in his arms. "I want to make some time with my wife."

The kiss was delicious, and James refused to think about the other responsibility sending him to the Connecticut coast. It likely would all come to nothing, so why not spare Jessica the worry?–as if Dick Streeter had given him a choice. But now he would make her happy, let himself be happy. They *were* happy, sharing each other's warmth, the tenderness of her hands, his arms cradling her. The whole world and all its problems, crises, strikes, and shortages could just go whistle for them at this moment.

The front doorbell rang.

"Criminy Dutch!" Jessica muttered against his cheek.

"Just ignore it. We're not home," James whispered. "Whoever it is will go away."

But Jessica shook her head and mourned, "No, *she* won't. She told me she was going to drop by this afternoon. She knows I'm expecting her."

James straightened, still holding Jess and questioned, a brow cocked with suspicion, "'She'? Which 'she' is that, my love?"

"Your favorite person in the whole world, next to me," Jess replied with feigned innocence.

James narrowed his eyes, then asked, "Your sister, Liz? I might have known no man could have this glorious a day without having to pay for it. You're certain we can't just play possum and hope she goes away?"

The bell shrilled determinedly, as if resenting James's suggestion.

Jessica maneuvered to sit up, her arms still linked around James's neck, and pointed out, "I think you know by now that my big sister is too good a bird dog to be buffaloed."

"Hmm, I won't argue with the canine part of your mixed metaphor. In fact, I'd be willing to carry it a little further."

"I'll just bet you would, wise guy!" Jessica teased, landing a mock slap on her husband's cheek before she bounced to her feet.

Slipping those bare tootsies into a pair of mules, Jessica moved to the door, while James "innocently" pondered, "I can't understand what your sister has against me. Most people find me a likable enough fellow."

Jessica paused at the doorway to posit, "Gee, honey, I don't know. It couldn't have anything to do with the fact that three years ago you dragged both of us into a life-threatening spy plot, nearly got her little sister killed, got *her* conked on the noggin, and *destroyed* her marriage."

"He really wasn't good enough for her, Jessica," James deadpanned. "You might say I did her a favor."

"Yeah, right. You stick with that story—see how far it gets you with Liz. But first, give Dusty and me time to dive into a bunker—an atom-bomb-proof bunker!"

With that, Jessica Minton dashed down the corridor to propitiate the impatient assertion of her doorbell. *Looks like Joe Louis and Max Smelling will be going another few rounds in my living room this afternoon. Three guesses—and the first two didn't count—who the referee will be.* That was okay, though. Jess was far too happy to be dragged down. James had made a decision that she knew would turn around his life. This work in Connecticut would set him on the right track, give him stability and a permanent focus for his energies. Plus, she could think of no better way to spend her upcoming hiatus than by taking the man she loved to the beautiful Connecticut side of the Sound, while having her own fun riding, gardening, reading, walking the beach, and catching up with her friend Rose Nyquist. Best of all, if all parties agreed, James would stay on permanently. She could easily commute by train to the city for rehearsals and broadcasts–barring that the rail line out of Grand Central didn't join the one out of Penn on strike.

As she neared the door, Jess reflected that, truth be told, she more than suspected James got something of a kick out of Liz's prickliness toward him. She knew he enjoyed needling her sister, and Jess more and more believed that he even respected Liz for challenging him back. Even crazier, Jess had the feeling that Liz, in spite of herself, got just as much of a kick out needling James—not that for one minute she believed that her sister and her husband had, as James would put it, "kissed and made friends."

Jess opened the door on a tall, slightly older, dark-haired woman dressed to the nines in a navy, nip-waisted jacket and matching pleated skirt bordered at the hem in white. She wore a white French sailor's hat, the edge of its broad brim navy and cheekily curving up. There was good reason her shrewdly stylish sister Liz was successful in designing and manufacturing mid-level women's fashions.

"Say, kiddo, are you just going to stand there admiring the view, or are you going to invite me in?" cracked Liz Minton.

"Since you put it so prettily," Jessica began, finishing with a gracious sweep of her hand, "*entrez*, Madame."

Liz shook her head as she strolled in, continuing as her sister closed the door behind her, "I thought you'd never answer the bell. What took you?"

Jessica smiled and explained, "Let's just say I was busy."

"Busy? So busy you left me standing flat-footed on the stoop for ages? You knew I was coming over after I got out of the New York Business and Professional Women's Convention. How on earth could you be so busy that . . . oh, I see that cat-who-ate-the-canary smile. His nibs is lurking around here somewhere, right?"

"That's the funny thing, Liz. When a guy lives in an apartment, his being there isn't really 'lurking.' But sorry I kept you waiting. At least the neighbors got a gander at that stunning ensemble of yours. One of your designs?"

Liz immediately brightened and answered, "You bet. $10.95 retail. I thought it would be ideal to show what I could do at the Convention. What do you think?"

"I think I wish I were still modeling for you, so I could get the first crack at these stylish little numbers." Jess smiled, not entirely joking.

"It's not out of the question, kiddo," Liz offered. "Aren't you going on break soon? We'll be doing our fall layout, so you could get the jump on the next season."

"I just hope I'm not out of work sooner," Jess returned reflectively.

"The Petrillo guy? The strike? Say, what's the story on that, anyway? I thought he was president of the musicians' union. What's that got to do with you? The whole thing seems wackier than a three-dollar bill to me," Liz shook her head.

"Well, the *Readers' Digest* version is that his union and mine, AFRA–"

"AFRA?"

"American Federation of Radio Artists. Anyway, we're kind of sister unions. The sticking point is mainly that broadcasting recorded, rather than live, music puts musicians out of work, while not paying royalties on their recordings cheats them out of their livelihood. We actors came in over the e.t.s." To Liz's bewildered expression, Jess elaborated, "Electronic transcriptions, of a broadcast, for the coast or summer repeats."

"So, this one guy can put you on the breadline if he doesn't get what he wants?"

"There could be alternatives to a full-out strike," Jess explained. "We might be called on just to stop making transcriptions, so instead of broadcasting an e.t. of our nine o'clock performance to the coast on a time difference delay, we'd broadcast the show live, again, in real-time."

"At 12:00 A.M.? Oh for the love of Mike! That's more work for you! Some of these unions sound screwy to me."

"Uh, yes and no, Liz. Petrillo's deal in Chicago, where he made a three-person staff in a tiny station go on strike, might seem that way. But, you know, most of these guys in management would be happy to pay you the minimum for a live broadcast, which they'd use to put you out of work by repeating as often as they liked. So, while you stand in the breadline, you might have the dubious pleasure of listening to yourself on the radio, with the network collecting years of cash from advertisers. Royalties aren't just a nice perk; they keep the game fair."

"I guess I'm just frustrated by all the strikes we've been having. I can't take the subway half the time, and today was the first time in two weeks the ice cream vendors were selling!"

"And those big babies over in England are crying because they'll probably have to ration flour and bread," Jessica offered in mock sympathy.

Elizabeth's eyes narrowed for, "Don't get wise. But say, kid, what will you do for cabbage if there is a strike? Doesn't Prince Charming's teaching position end this month? Are you quite sure you couldn't stand a little help, like when you modeled for me?"

Jessica hesitated. She hadn't expected to spring this on her sister quite so soon. Maybe now *was* best if it set Elizabeth's mind at ease about her finances.

"Here's the thing, Liz. I'm going to be out of town for the summer, maybe longer. James is taking the position at Margaret Point College."

"What? But what about your apartment? Dusty? *Me?*"

"Liz, I'm not moving to Siberia. Just a two-hour ride into Connecticut. Dusty can travel with us. She's stayed there before—under less congenial exigencies, as you recall."

"How about your job? The apartment?"

"Remember, I'll be on hiatus until September." Jess and Liz simultaneously knocked wood on the dining room table. Jess continued, "I think I can sublet the apartment to Lois for the summer. Then, in the fall, I can stay overnight here for the show when I have to."

"It just figures. Leave it to this guy of yours to take you away from your own sister," Liz grumped. "I won't see as much of you."

"It seems to me, Liz, that you haven't anyway since you've been seeing more of Leo McLaughlan," Jessica smiled.

"Well, that's beside the point," Elizabeth continued to grumble, knowing just as well as her sister that it wasn't.

"Look, Liz. You're entitled to some happiness in the romance department—"

"Romance? Who said anything about romance? We're just friends. Good friends."

Jessica smiled knowingly, "I saw the two of you kiss last week."

"So, we're *really* good friends," Liz shrugged. "And that was the first time."

"I bet it won't be the last!"

"Oh, enough already!" Moving down into the living room, Liz changed the subject, "Say, where is *your* Prince Charming, anyway?"

Jessica rolled her eyes and pretended to mourn, "Honestly, the two of you make me feel like Dorothy Lamour between Hope and Crosby."

Without turning, Liz cracked, "I don't think you quite measure up to Dottie when it comes to filling out a sarong, kiddo."

"I don't know about that," came a masculine voice from the corridor behind them. "I give Jessica full marks in the sarong-filling department, but I fancy I am a bit prejudiced."

Jess happily took James's arm and said to Liz, "How can a girl resist such charm—and good judgment? Besides, Dusty adores him."

"Was he feeding her Polish ham when you asked her?" Elizabeth inquired skeptically.

Jessica shook her head, while James replied, "Now, is that any way for my favorite sister-in-law to think—and after I just set a nice pot of tea brewing for us all in the kitchen?"

"Don't try to snow me with that 'favorite sister-in-law' business. I'm your only sister-in-law—what kind of tea? Any scones?"

"No scones," Jessica responded. "I was too busy with the script to bake. But I do have cookies from that bakery on Delancey Street you love."

Placated with thoughts of delectable comestibles dancing in her head, Elizabeth relented to join Jessica and James at the kitchen table for a casual tea. Jess smiled, reflecting that, like Dusty, neither Liz nor James would let any conflict keep them from a tasty afternoon treat. Heck, wasn't she just as susceptible? Anyway, she knew that sooner or later these two lunkheads would learn to get along—kind of—in spite of themselves.

The kitchen was bright. Sunshine streamed in through the windows over the sink and on the door facing them, bouncing off the white cabinets, utilities, and linoleum. The Blue Willow teapot sat in the center of the table, cups and saucers and dessert plates already in place. While Jess went to the breadbox next to the refrigerator for the cookies, then put them on a plate, James and Liz sat down across from each other. But Liz's curiosity was caught by the short stack of notebooks, with newspaper clippings on top, before the chair without a plate.

"Say, Jess," she began, "are these what I think they are? Clippings about Assault winning the Belmont Stakes on Saturday? Are you still keeping your horse racing scrapbooks?"

Liz had pulled the notebooks over and started flipping through them, as James observed, "She *is* quite the tout."

Joining them, Jess set down the plate of tempting macaroons, butter cookies, and short bread, asserting, "I'll have you two Smart Alecs know that I've been pretty darned successful 'improving the breed.' So let's can the wise cracks about my passion for playing the ponies."

"Did she tell you her ultra-scientific method for picking winners?" Liz queried James.

"She picks the black ones, or the ones who look black," James replied with a smile.

"Right on the nose," Jessica confirmed proudly. "And you can thank Helioptic for trotting home first in the Queen's County Handicap yesterday to pay for these cookies. So there!"

James nodded, "It's bats, but I have to admit it works most of the time."

"But not often enough to retire on," Liz countered.

"Often enough to keep you two in sweets and tea," Jessica pronounced.

James observed, "Sounds a little messy when you put it that way, love."

"Oh, just give me your cup." Jessica pretended to be annoyed. She accepted James's cup, but changed her mind, deciding aloud, "No, Liz is company. She's served first."

"At least you have your priorities straight," Liz agreed, continuing: "Wasn't there some tragedy about one of your favorites, earlier this year or last? Blue Larkspur?"

"Blue *Warrior*. Blue Larkspur is much older and living the life of

Riley at the Idle Hour Stock Farm in Kentucky," Jessica corrected, pausing over the fate of the unfortunate Blue Warrior before continuing. "It really was just so unfair. Blue Warrior had this great handicap season where he'd taken on everyone from Devil Diver to Lucky Draw to Stymie. Then he bowed a tendon, and they had to retire him. If that weren't bad enough, just when he was settled into retirement in Damascus, Maryland, he and his groom were killed in a flash barn fire. It still upsets me. He was a great horse. Remember, James, I told you about how excited I was when I saw him come home first in the Baxter Handicap last fall? He did a mile and an eighth in 1:48 flat–a stakes record."

"How could I forget? You also told me you missed out on a big payoff."

"Wait a minute," Liz puzzled. "He won, but you couldn't collect? How did *that* work?"

"He came in first, but he didn't win," Jess explained. At Liz's further bewilderment, Jessica sheepishly elaborated. "The judge disqualified him for roughing up another horse."

"So why do you look embarrassed? You didn't rough up anyone. The jockey did," Liz pointed out.

"Not exactly," James smiled.

"Um, it was Blue Warrior, himself," Jess explained. "When the other horse tried to pass him in the stretch, Blue Warrior bit him. The other horse backed off."

"Which bears out my not liking horses," James added.

"He was only like that on the track, in a race," Jessica protested, handing James his tea. "In the stable yard, away from the track, he would sometimes eat a sundae from a little kid."

"Did the nipper count his fingers afterward?" James inquired.

"Ha, ha," Jessica shot back. "No, believe me. Off the track, Blue Warrior was an entirely different horse. In a race, he was just as fierce as Equipoise, the Chocolate Soldier. Off the track, he was Lassie. At least that's what everyone said. I never got to see him, except from the stands during a race."

"As much as it kills me to admit it, kiddo," Liz shook her head, "I've got to go with James on this one. No way I'd risk one of these mitts with that horse. No way he'd get an ice cream sundae away from me."

"Liz, the 442d Regimental Combat Team couldn't get a sundae away from you, especially if chocolate were involved," Jessica laughed.

"Jessica," James warned, "never mock the power of chocolate."

Sitting down, Jessica glanced uneasily from her husband to her sister, commenting, "You two agree on something? Next thing you know, Truman will be waltzing with Stalin. I think I'm seeing signs of the Apocalypse."

"Raow!" added Dusty from the doorway.

"Ah," James pronounced, on his feet. "The next horrific portent: the howl of the beast. I'll take responsibility for forestalling Armageddon and feed Dusty."

After a sip of tea, Liz concurred, "I've cat-sat often enough to know all hell breaks loose if her majesty isn't fed on time. But tell me, James, how do you think Dusty will take to moving to the wilds of Connecticut?"

James turned to Jessica, a bit surprised, and asked, "You've told her already?"

"Well," Jess pointed out, "Liz was here more than five minutes before you joined us. After all this time, you don't know how good she is at worming information out of a body?"

"Except, I didn't have to do any worming, little sister," Liz corrected. "You spilled the beans all on your own."

"It's hardly a state secret, Liz. We'd talked a little about this before."

"Fine, fine, just let your husband give me the lowdown on how he's taking my baby sister away from me."

James paused from feeding an extremely impatient Dusty to remark, "I think Jessica is a bit too big to be called a baby at the ripe age of 32."

"Big? I don't like the way that came out," Jessica protested. "And I'm thirty-*one*, buster."

"Ha!" Liz smiled, helping herself to another cookie. "Someone's in the doghouse now!"

Dusty actually took time out from eating to deliver Elizabeth a baleful glare for uttering her least favorite three-letter word. James returned to the table, shaking his head.

"*Anyway*," Jessica took command, "if you really want the story, Liz, *I* will explain what we'll be doing this summer. James will be taking over an opening at Margaret Point for a guy who went off to war. He'll be teaching two courses, starting in early July—which dovetails nicely with my schedule, our last broadcast being June 21st. The summer sessions run through most of August. If James likes the school, and they're smart enough to want to keep him, it looks as if the position will be permanent."

"But what about the guy who originally had the job? What if he wants it back when he gets discharged?" Liz turned to James and asked, "Isn't that what's happening to you here at Washington Irving?"

"The Margaret Point chap is not coming back," James answered abruptly. "He went down on the *Yorktown*."

Jessica tensed. Liz hadn't deserved the cold irony of James's tone, having unintentionally hit that sore spot. But the usually fiery Liz surprised Jess with her gentle, "Ah, I'm sorry. I didn't realize."

James looked down and simply said, "No, of course not, Elizabeth."

That was Jess's cue to steer them all to less painful grounds, "It's not so very far away. You can visit, and they do have telephone service in Connecticut."

"But won't you be bored, away from the city?" Liz protested.

"To be honest, Liz, I'm really looking forward to some full-on R & R, after my first full year of the show, while still taking graduate courses at City College. It will be a dream just to relax—and have more time with James. Not to mention seeing Rose and her family."

"That's right," Liz considered. "You do have connections out that way. I'd forgotten. But come to think of it, isn't there now someone else out there you know? Someone you weren't crazy about, just recently coming back from the service. Who was that? Oh, yeah, Terry. Terry Clarke."

Jessica blinked, startled that Liz should be needling her on this subject, or was she actually taking a stab at James?

Before Jess could respond, James, clearly wondering if his taking the job would put her on the spot, queried, "Terry Clarke? Who's she?"

Liz's eyes gleamed when she answered, "Not *she*, *he*."

"Well, then, who *is* he?" James continued, curious and surprised that Jessica seemed a tad antsy.

"You mean Jessica never told you about Terry Clarke, her old flame from college? The first great love of her life?" Liz responded, ignoring the daggers Jess's eyes shot at her. Apparently, Elizabeth had expended her quota of sensitivity for the day.

"Oh, that bloke," James shook his head. "He sounded like a bit of an ass to me, running hot and cold on Jessica, turning on her when he failed at acting. He couldn't have been that bright to let a grand girl like Jessica get away."

"You're pretty confident," Liz countered, not quite so thrilled by Jessica's Cheshire Cat smile at her husband's response. "Not jealous at all?"

"When you're number one, Liz, you don't have to worry," James shrugged.

"Aren't we smug," Liz remarked.

"Not at all. I just know that Jessica and I are number one for each other." Turning to Jessica and taking her hand, he finished, "Besides, we're two grownups who've been through the mill together—and apart. What we did, felt, when we were younger, that's just kid stuff."

"Okay, okay. You two can kill the lovey-dovey malarkey," Elizabeth relented. She turned to her sister: "Still, Jess, you can't be happy having to see Terry again. There's got to be bad feelings. I know I'd like to let him have it for how he made you feel back then. I don't know how you managed to avoid him all those times you went out to see Rose at the college."

"It was a little thing called World War II," Jess replied. "He's been away since 1942, just before Rose and David were hired. Stationed in D.C. Something to do with Army Public Relations."

"No combat duty?" James reflected.

Jessica shook her head, "He came from an old Virginia family that may have become short on money but was still long on pull. He got himself a comfy berth during the war."

Liz wrinkled her nose, saying, "I never trusted the guy. I wish you hadn't, Jess."

"That's all in the past, Liz," Jess said quickly, before smoothly continuing. "To make a long story short, he returned last fall, but he's been in and out, doing research and lecturing. He may not have made it on the stage, but I'll have to give him credit as a scholar . . ."

"I still say he's a weasel," Liz interrupted. "You never knew if you were coming or going with him. It was like a mild case of *Gaslight*."

"Not quite that bad," Jessica amended, smiling. "My life and sanity were never in danger. Anyway, I have the sweetest revenge." She cocked her head in James's direction.

He smiled then feigned confusion: "I don't have to kill him, do I? Perhaps just break a bone or two? I was really hoping I was done with that sort of thing."

"No, just be your charming self," Jessica smiled. "That'll kill him. Not that I care anymore."

"But," Liz questioned, "didn't you tell me he was married, and to a knock-out, too, with plenty of Southern blue-blood?"

"Yes, that's right," Jess confirmed. "She's either Marilyn from Virginia or Virginia from Maryland. I can never remember."

"Not Carolina? Her name or her home state," James quipped.

"Who cares," Jessica replied with an expressive gesture of her hands. "Rose tells me she's an elegant, statuesque red-head who can wield that Southern charm. But when you get to know her, she's haughty and bossy. She's the kind of gal who makes students cry, literally."

"Ah," Liz pronounced, "a great showpiece but nothing you'd want to come home to after a hard day at work."

"You said it," Jess agreed. "And it doesn't make for cozy marital relations when the girl you married for her money even more than for her blue blood turns out to have had the same misconception about your Dun and Bradstreet rating."

"Ouch," winced Elizabeth. "Dorothy Parker was right. Time does wound all heels."

Folding his arms, James turned to Dusty and advised, "Sharpen your claws all you like, puss, but you'll never be a match for these two sisters."

"What can I say, James?" Jess shrugged. "Revenge *is* a dish best served cold."

"Revenge, yes," interrupted Liz. "Tea, no. You want to warm this up for me, kid?"

"And people call my Jessica a Girl Scout," James shook his head.

"Don't let this little quirk fool you, James," Liz insisted. "I'll bet Jess never mentioned this Terry was at the school because she was afraid you might not take the job if you thought Terry was there to get under her skin."

James turned to his wife, a little surprised, and questioned, concerned,

"Is Liz right, Jessica? Would being around this Clarke fellow nerve you up? I don't want to put you on the spot . . ."

"I'm fine, James. Don't worry, really. You ought to know by now I'm not about to go all to pieces from seeing some guy who gave me the runaround ten years ago. Believe me; I'm long over it. At worst, he might be a little irritating, but where can you go that you won't find a pain in the neck or two? I'm a big girl now. I vote and everything."

James seemed somewhat reassured, saying, "If you're sure." Then he turned to Elizabeth for, "Any more skeletons in the cupboard I need to know about?"

Liz shrugged. "I told you she was a Girl Scout. The old flame at the place where you're going to teach is about the size of it."

Jessica munched her cookie, thinking that Liz wasn't quite accurate: her cupboard hid spy plots, dog-napping, and even suspicion of murder– but James knew about all that. Heck, he'd been responsible for half of it!

Anyway, she'd be darned if she let some dope she hadn't seen in ten years, no matter how much of a pain in the patoot he might be, stand in the way of James's shot at work he loved.

Chapter Two

Sunday, June 30, 1946

The misty green woods slipped swiftly into meadows then coves of ocean water lapping on beaches populated only by egrets concentrating on hunting, swans supremely gliding, and gulls wheeling and diving. Jessica loved this train run up the Connecticut coast. She glanced down at the copy of Margaret Millar's *The Iron Gates* in her lap. A smile played across her features as she looked across to her husband, his face creased with concentration as he poured through Coleridge's *Biographia Literaria*. He absently flicked the pen in his hand until it moved to underline something or to shorthand comments in the margins. Once James had the bit in his teeth, it was hard to slow him down, and his enthusiasm for proving his mettle at Margaret Point was driving him full bore to prepare for classes. So, even though the intensity of his sharp features might lead a stranger to see him as a little intimidating, Jessica knew he was actually a bundle of delight with his intellectual task. She was so happy he had something enjoyably exacting to absorb his mind.

Jessica smoothed the satiny softness of her skirt, black chevrons on cream that matched her short, fitted jacket and bonnet. A glance around the car showed only a few other passengers, including a well-stuffed dead ringer for Margaret Dumont. Not many commuters on a Sunday. Good. She liked a nice, quiet ride. Not one single screaming baby behind her, either—truly, a good omen. Maybe she wouldn't even have to deal with Terry Clarke today.

She hated to admit that over the past weeks she'd come to realize she really didn't want to run into the guy—not without a car, anyway. Liz had opened a can of worms when she'd brought the whole thing to the surface. Since then, niggling irritation had swollen into downright antsiness. What was wrong with her? It was ten years ago, water long under the bridge. She was happily married, had a wonderful career; so why was it that each mile closer to Margaret Point nerved her up just a little more?

"Penny for your thoughts?"

Jess blinked herself back to reality at her husband's query. Not about to throw any cold water on James's pleasure at his new opportunity, she joked, "Only a penny, with all this inflation? My thoughts ought to cost you at least a dime."

James's eyes silently said, "You may be selling, but I'm not buying."

Jess admitted, "Okay, I guess I was just thinking about stirring up old acquaintances, awkward ones."

"Mmm," James considered, closing his book. "I thought you said that was all ancient history. I hate to see anything eat at you, Jessica."

"It's not getting to me, exactly. I mean ten years ago *is* ancient history. I don't know why seeing Terry again kind of bugs me. It's not as if I've been carrying a torch or that my life has been miserable without him. My life is great. It's just that . . . well . . . I don't get it. I mean, how would you feel, running into your Terry, that Angela? What would you do? Say?"

James smiled ruefully before answering, "That wouldn't be an issue. I wouldn't have to say—or do—anything. I'd just be a lowly scholar to her. For all intents and purposes, not even on her radar screen."

"So, I'm a dope, you think?"

"Not-a't-all. I think he gave you a pretty hard knock when you were just a kid, but you never had the chance to get off your chest how angry you were with him."

"After all this time, James? I must be some kind of a psych case."

"Look, Jessica, I've broken more than one bone over the years, and they've healed pretty well. But, you know, if a cold snap hits or I bang something just the wrong way . . ." The wince he made said it all.

"So, you think I should march up to Terry and lay him out in lavender?" Jess asked skeptically. "That would go over like the proverbial lead balloon. I'd make a swell impression for you, wouldn't I?"

James shook his head, gently responding, "I wouldn't go that far. Just face the fact that you had reason to be mad at him ten years ago and try to let it go. Don't let him get under your skin, or at least don't let him see it if he does. Remember, you have a lot of people who love you out there: me, Rose, her family. I think you might be building this up more than you need to. It's just all that unvented anger, not the chap himself, eating away at you. One look at him, seeing the person, not the memory, and I bet that anxiety will melt away. Maybe not all at once, but soon enough."

"You really think so?"

"Would I lie to you? Outside of Allied security concerns?"

"Why does that answer not entirely comfort me," Jessica remarked, though she was actually comforted. Then she added after mulling his words for a few moments, "But you know, I think you've got something there, Dr. Freud."

"Much rather be Dr. Jung. Collective unconscious and all that."

"Oh, pardon my anima!"

Out of the corner of her eye, Jess caught the Margaret Dumont lookalike smiling as she eavesdropped on them. James brought her back with the observation, "If facing your shadow fails you and Clarke continues to annoy you, I'll just give him a poke in the eye. Although," here he ran his fingers along his jawline, "after that burst of temper of yours at Belmont Park three years ago, I'm almost convinced you might be more persuasive with that mean right hook of yours."

Margaret Dumont's hat almost popped off her head.

Catching James's mischievousness, Jess couldn't help adding to their nosy neighbor's consternation. "You have to admit that you asked for it. You just don't kiss a girl out of the clear blue sky. That's the work of a masher—and I've hardly mauled you since."

"San Francisco."

"That was for your own good."

"I needed stitches."

"You did not."

At this point, Mrs. Dumont had taken refuge behind a copy of *Look*.

Modern couples were far too shocking to watch—but she could still hear just fine behind her oversized periodical.

James extended Jessica a hand and said, "Come over here with me."

Happily, Jessica accepted her husband's invitation, as he moved over to let her have the window. The train emerged from the green overshadow of trees, and they swiftly approached then passed a rangy fieldstone hall where strains of a swing band swirled around then trailed after their descent into a valley between the rocky folds, then back into the woods.

Jessica turned to James and reminisced, "Remember when you first came back to me last summer? We went here in the evening and listened to the band in that rec hall."

"I seem to vaguely recall something about a tangy salt breeze, 'Stardust' à la Glen Miller, and a dark-haired beauty in my arms."

"You certainly know how to charm a girl, mister."

James leaned in for a kiss, then added, "I aim to please."

"That you do, sir," Jess smiled, leaning back into her love's arms, enjoying the familiar flash of coastal countryside with someone so deep in her heart. What in heaven's name had she been worried about? There was no way she would allow her past to undercut her present. She was going to help James to a new start here and herself to some R & R. Nothing or no one was going to put the jinx on her plans.

By the time they pulled into the station in the town of Margaret Point, a mile or so shy of the college, Jessica was too preoccupied with not seeing Rose and David at the station to waste any time worrying about ghosts from her past.

"Gee, I'm surprised they're not here," Jessica wondered, getting up. "Usually Rose is early."

James was up also, pulling their two bags from the rack overhead, commenting, "With two children, I'm surprised she's ever able to be on time. But I will tell you, Jessica, how much I appreciate your spending the last two weekends packing and shipping our things up here. You even gave up seeing your friend Stymie run last Saturday. It was grand of you, and Liz, to arrange everything so that I could concentrate on starting my class preparations."

They were waiting to let another passenger go by, before moving down the aisle behind the Margaret Dumont lookalike, as James added, "But promise me you handled my bundles."

"Why? Don't you trust your sister-in-law?" Jess inquired innocently.

"Let's just say that I'd prefer not to find a tarantula in my shaving kit."

"Don't be silly, James. A cranky wasp, *maybe*, but nothing that has to be imported from the tropics."

The older, inquisitive matron almost took a flyer over that exchange, and James dropped his bags and adeptly caught her. The woman's acknowledgments were hurried and nervous at finding herself in the hands of one of these unstable young people. She made her way off the train with an alacrity that left James commenting *sotto voce* to Jessica, "The old girl's still got quite a bit of kick in her."

"She *was* lapping up our little exchange about fisticuffs and stitches, earlier. I guess the chit-chat about killer insects pushed her over the brink. Her tongue-in-cheek detector must be on the blink." Jessica chuckled.

"That's what she gets for eavesdropping." Then James switched gears as they were about to descend the car's steps and said, "Here, wait. It looks as if the conductor was called away by our eavesdropper. Let me go first with my bag. Then I can take that bag from you. It'll be awkward getting off."

Jess concurred, and soon they were both on the asphalt of the station, bags beside them. The tangy salt air struck Jessica forcibly, delightfully. As they moved to make way for detraining passengers, neither Rose nor David yet in sight, Jessica looked down at her empty hands and blurted, "Our books. I forgot . . . I didn't grab them. Did you?"

"Oh no," James realized aloud, already starting back onto the train. "I'll nip back on board. Be back in a jiffy."

Alone, Jess took another look around for her friends. The rail car had stopped short of the station house, a long, low building with an old New England pitched, red roof, to her left, just ahead of her. A Sunday, the commuter traffic was not what it would have been on a weekday, but there were still more than a few folks greeting each other under the lovely, blue summer sky. You could hear the wash of the ocean on the rocky strand on the other side of the train.

Jess knew from past visits that on the other side of the station ran Main Street. There were shops on both sides of the street, with a gap revealing a cafe and an antique shop across the street. No David and Rose approaching through that gap, so Jessica started to turn back toward the station, when a familiar figure stepped out of the doorway of the antique store and her past, hovering there: tall, still slim in his pin-stripe suit, waves of dark brown hair under his fedora. The trim Sir Walter Raleigh beard was new.

Jessica automatically straightened with surprise. From this distance, she couldn't see those blue crystal eyes, but she remembered them well. How long before they turned from some distant object up the street and fastened on her? Would Terry recognize her from across the street? Across the years?

A patrician man, tall but not nearly as tall as Terry Clarke, came into view from the direction in which her old chum was staring. His sharp, predatory, fine features silently acknowledged Terry. Terry Clarke returned the favor, though not cheerfully. The other man removed his hat to reveal a shaven pate and was about to speak . . ..

"Jessica!"

It was Rose Nyquist, exiting the station house, barely matching strides with her much taller, handsome, blond husband. Jessica Minton burst into a smile, thoughts of Terry Clarke shoved aside by her delight. Extending her arms to hug the woman with the honey-brown hair, comfortably garbed in navy slacks and a bright yellow jacket, Jessica exclaimed, "Rose! It's so great to see you, and David—and the girls came, too!"

Rose's two daughters, Tess (fourteen) and Kathleen (ten) trailed sulkily out of the station, their attitudes explaining the welcome party's tardiness. The older girl was tall, medium build, with a round face and a halo of curly, honey-blonde hair. Her sister, though shorter, was still tall for her age, extremely slender, with a long oval face, wide and intense brown eyes, and long, straight dark hair to die for.

"It's as contentious as the United Nations at home," David joked, cocking his head at the girls, who hung back, eyeing each other almost as if they, indeed, had been on a committee hammering out civil rights or borders or war crime punishments.

24

"Uh, oh," Jess grinned. "What was it this time?"

Rose shook her head. "Two closets full of clothes and neither one is happy unless she gets to wear my grandmother's pin to show off to you and James."

"So, who won?"

"I did!" Rose tapped the jewelry pinned to her jacket. "How do you like it?"

"You're a cruel parent, indeed," Jess laughed. "Anyway, gee, it's great to see you. For a minute, I thought someone with a warped sense of humor had sent Terry Clarke to meet us. I caught a glimpse of him over at the antique shop across the street."

Rose and David exchanged an odd look. That didn't sit well with Jess.

"You saw Terry across the street?" questioned Rose, puzzled.

"Well, sure. He was meeting someone over . . ." Jess turned her head back and saw–a closed antique shop, period. "Gee, he's, they're gone. Why are you guys looking at me like that? You'd think I'd seen a ghost or something."

David wryly explained, "Granted, there are a few people who'd like to turn him into a ghost . . ."

"Including that wife of his," Rose slipped in. "But he's out of town on a lecture this weekend. You must have been mistaken. It is kind of funny you should bring him up, though. Maybe your psychic powers picked up our brain waves."

"What's that supposed to mean, Rose?" Jess questioned, surprised.

"Well," Rose began. "Terry's created a little problem in the department. I know you've never met our Chair, Nigel Cross, but you've heard me mention him. Anyway, Nigel thinks you might be able to help us out. I don't know if you'll want to do it, though."

"Who me?" Jess questioned, not sure if she were more surprised or puzzled. Curiouser and curiouser.

"Now, what are you springing on my wife?" interjected James pleasantly as he joined them, books in hand.

"I'm afraid," began Rose, "I've been assigned to ask her if she'll give up part of her vacation and help teach a course in Shakespeare and the stage this summer."

"That doesn't sound so bad," Jessica enthused. "I'd love to do that.

I've been taking courses toward a masters' in literature, and I could combine my acting background. It's right up my alley. How could I say no?"

"We-e-ell," David warned, "Rose didn't tell you there's a little catch."

"Um, Jess, you might not want to jump in feet first," Rose cautioned. "You, uh, you see, you wouldn't be doing it alone. You'd be filling in some classes for the person originally assigned. The person who came up with the idea for the course suddenly now has some lecture dates on his new book that would keep him off campus."

Jessica regarded Rose suspiciously. Having all too good an idea of the answer, she questioned, "And exactly who is this in-demand scholar?"

"I think you know," Rose replied. "I'm sorry to spring this on you right now, Jess. I just thought since you brought Terry up already, I should open the topic now rather than let you be hit cold with it at the reception. Nigel said he wanted to have a little chat with you then. I know Terry's not your favorite person in the world, but I also know you'd love to teach Shakespeare. So, I couldn't bring myself to nip Nigel's proposal in the bud. You do what you want."

Before Jessica could say anything, Rose's daughters grabbed center stage, suddenly taking notice of her husband with, "It's James! Hi, James!"

The girls were too well brought up to usually call most adults by their first names, but Jessica had known and loved them since they were babies, fostering a special intimacy with them. James had laughed that if she were Jess, it seemed awfully stiff and pokey to be known as Mr. Crawford.

Now Tess and Kat had broken from their snits to crowd their favorite fella. His accent and sense of humor were far more fascinating to them than their injured pride. That took Jessica off the hook for the moment— but, oh brother! What a surprise!

"Ah, I see my two second most favorite ladies," James responded as the girls crushed him with hugs.

Tess paused and asked, "Second? Who's your first?"

James tipped his head in Jess's direction and inquired, "Who do you think?"

"The winner and still champion!" Jessica pronounced. "So, what about me, you two? I don't have a snazzy British accent, but I can do one! Where are my hugs?"

Rose's daughters giggled, transferring their attention to Jessica, with Tess announcing, "I heard you on the radio Friday night, Jessica. That Horla story really gave me the willies! You were a scream!"

"Sounds like the response you were looking for," James concluded.

"Mom wouldn't let me stay up that late," grumbled Kat. "She says ten is too young for your program."

"You're just a kid, Kat," Tess pronounced. "You'd have had nightmares for the next ten years."

"In ten years, I won't be a kid anymore."

"My daughter, the lawyer in training." Rose rolled her eyes, putting an arm around Kathleen.

David added, "It seems to me, Theresa, that it wasn't Kat who wouldn't go into a darkened room unless I checked for zuvembies first."

"You, too?" James queried.

"Keep it up, wise guy," Jess kidded her husband, "and I'll see about trading in your English accent for Ronald Colman's."

"Ooh, he's really dreamy," chirruped Tess.

"Kind of old," Kathleen decided.

"Ouch," James grimaced.

"What can I say," Jess laughed. "Bobby-soxers get younger every year."

"Okay, cats and kittens," David pronounced. "Let's head out so James and Jessica can get settled at the cottage. They have a big night ahead of them at the reception."

James and David took charge of the luggage, allowing Jessica and Rose to catch up as they headed through the station, then out onto the street. Kat and Tess tagged along with their Mom and her friend. The kids liked their talk about the radio program. There was usually some gossip mixed into the conversation, and Jessica did have hints for them about what they could hear on the program next fall. Or, in Kat's case, what she could only hear her sister describe to her, with suitably ghoulish embellishment.

James and David were in the process of loading the trunk of the car, the girls had drifted away to chat, and Jessica found herself staring up the street at the antique shop where she could have sworn she'd seen Terry Clarke with another man.

She asked, "Rose, who runs that antique store over there?"

Rose followed her friend's gaze and answered, "That place? Oh, I don't know. I think he deals in art in the city, too. Why? You want to do some shopping? Believe me; I can show you much better places—ones that don't charge an arm and a leg."

"Is the owner tall, shaven-head, with kind of a 'lean and hungry look'?"

Rose, surprised, took a moment to reply, "Yes. You hit the nail right on the cue-ball head. Did you see him over there, earlier?"

"Yes, I did. With Terry."

"Sorry, Jessica, as I said, that can't be. Yesterday, I saw Terry and his wife take a train at this very station for New Haven. Terry was giving one of his lectures. He's not due back until late tonight, even tomorrow. Must have been someone who looked like him."

Jessica smiled, as James came to join them, and relented, "Could be. Must be. I can't imagine Terry cutting short the opportunity to tell Yale what it's all about. Anyway, I want James to see the cottage. He doesn't know what we've done to it."

"Climb aboard, maties," David invited from the driver's seat. "We won't see anything if we stand around here jawing."

With a little hustle, they squared away the passengers in David and Rose's Chrysler Airflow—David driving, Rose and Kat up front. Jess and James sat next to each other in the back, with Tess. Rose had long learned the wisdom of separating the girls when they got too excited.

They slipped down the street, and Jess, in spite of herself, couldn't help scanning the storefront of the antique shop. Had she seen a stir within? But there wasn't time to ponder any further, for Tess was peppering her with questions and comments about the radio program, the shows she and James had seen on Broadway, and the latest hot discs. Anyway, Jessica couldn't wait to see James's reaction to the cottage. She had a fleeting, uneasy thought about seeing Terry. *How silly!* Jess gave herself over to entertaining Tess and the best pleasure of all: having James beside her.

Chapter Three

Same Day

It was ten or fifteen minutes of driving through an old Connecticut village then rolling hills, pastures, and cottages—never far from the sound of waves nor the salty scent of the ocean. The car's open window treated them to a delicious breeze, pleasantly warmed by the late June sunlight. Jess smiled, thinking she'd been happy to take the middle seat to let Tess have the window. When you were fourteen, you were a lot more willing to let the wind ravage your hair than when you were a big girl who went to the beauty parlor—especially when you knew you were going to have to put on the dog that night. They slowed, approaching the open, tall wrought-iron gates of the college's entrance. A guard stepped out of the gatekeeper's dark-green-slate roofed pavilion to acknowledge David with a wave, which all the Nyquists returned.

Amidst the chatter around her, Jess once more enjoyed the grounds of Margaret Point: the old-fashioned stone buildings, the greens all across campus, the intermittent sparkling of a fair blue ocean extending into the horizon on her right. They passed the circle that fronted a gracious, three-story manse of grey stone on their right. On the other side of the building was a flagstone terrace and balustrade, a lovely green, an extension of the stone wall encircling most of the grounds, then a rocky slope onto a narrow beach. With its terraces, stone face, bronze wall lanterns, and hedged side garden and fountain, the building was like a mini-château.

She and James briefly exchanged smiles as Tess leaned forward and cried, "Wow! Look at all those trucks and those people at the kitchen entrance!" Now pointing to the far end of the house, she went on, "Big shindig tonight, right, Mom? I wish I could go. I bet there's plenty of yummy stuff on the menu."

"Not *your* idea of yummy, munchkin," Rose smiled, turning to her daughter as they passed the commotion of kitchen staff moving boxes, chairs, tables, and decorations off the two trucks and through the side entrance.

"'Fraid not," David agreed. "No hot dogs, potato salad, or ice cream."

"Just canapés," Rose added.

"Peas! Yuck!" Kat scoffed. "They're going to make you eat canned peas? Not even the fresh ones they grow in the Victory Gardens? That's awful."

"Not canned *peas*, you banana-head, *canapés*," Tess corrected with a superior roll of her eyes.

They drove on between two buildings, with Kat complaining, "Mommy, Daddy, did you hear what Theresa called me?"

"I'll let you field this one," David told Rose. "Have to keep my mind on the road."

Rose refrained from rolling *her* eyes, though Jess knew she did mentally, and adjudicated, "I heard, I heard. I also heard you calling her a square from way back when she was practicing her Shakespeare recitation for the church benefit. I'd say the score is even."

Turning her attention to Jessica and James, Rose said, "Bet you can't wait to start a family now."

The road forked three ways, and they bore to the left, following the line of buildings, away from the water, then back to the right, nearer to the shoreline. The faculty housing was just a little further along this road, Jess knew, while the curve to the left led to the stables and the straightaway to the other livestock shed and the Victory Gardens. This progressive college took pride in being almost completely self-sustaining when it came to victualing itself. Some hills rolled up in that direction, curling back to the ocean some distance beyond. Theirs was the first cottage they came to, more a cottage in name than reality, with two stories and a good-sized floor plan.

"Here we are," David announced, down-shifting to a stop, pulling on the parking brake, then shutting off the ignition. It didn't take long for everyone to pile out. Jessica eagerly watched James take in the clapboard house, with its slate roof; comfortable front porch; and, especially, the garden that extended from the roadside picket fence to the porch. To the left, sea roses abounded, blooming vivid deep red and soft pink or white. Tall delphinium spires surged upward in delicate blue, pure white, and soft lavender over sky-colored petals. Royal-blue irises, complimented by occasional white or yellow blooms, were in full flower. Bachelor buttons, starbursts of blue, purple, magenta, or white, threaded throughout.

James turned to Jessica, genuinely delighted, and said, "You weren't up here just visiting and unpacking, were you?"

"You won the $64.00 question!" Rose pronounced.

Jessica smiled, "Rose and I, and the girls, worked our delicate little fingers to the bone weeding, digging, and planting. From the look on your face, it seems to have been worth the gamble that you'd come here."

"Do you love it, James?" burst in Kat. "The roses were already here, but we did some trimming. Jessica says you love roses."

"That I do, Kat. My Mum always managed to have one growing in a pot, somehow, back in Milton Northern when I was growing up. She said it chased away the grime and the smoke and the dirt. Of course, she usually said it in French."

"Why would she do that?" Kat puzzled.

"Hmm," James pondered solemnly before concluding, "Perhaps because she was born in France."

"Huh!" Kat snorted. "You always tease me!"

"Everyone teases you," Tess jibed. "You're such a pigeon."

"Okay, okay," Rose jumped in before she had a juvenile WWIII on her hands. "We have to get Jess and James settled. They have a big night. Besides, you want James to see what we've done inside, too, don't you?"

"Yeah!" Kat was delightedly distracted. Grabbing James's hand, she led him at a dash up the path to the porch, but not before he had grabbed Jessica's hand.

With a fake grumble that her shoes were made for style not speed, Jess found herself on the porch, by the wooden door with its marvelous Triton knocker. Then they were all in the house.

The first floor opened expansively before them. Four steps descended into the living room proper, where two couches faced each other, separated by a low coffee table. To the right, a large, dark wood-mantled fireplace, with shelving on either side, was adorned with the graceful shapes of oriental carvings. Next to it was a radio/stereo combo. Comfortable chairs and side tables completed the room, lined with built-in bookcases and a piano on the left: a room both scholarly and cozy. The hard wood floor was covered in places by rugs. The kitchen could be accessed through a narrow doorway on the far side of the fireplace, while another door on their left, near the front entrance, revealed a study. Perhaps the crowning glory was across the expansive room: sliders opened onto a patio with a beautiful view of the ocean below and beyond a stone balustrade with a gap for access to that beach.

Jessica glowed with delight when James pronounced, "Wow!"

"I think you can stop worrying if he'll like it," Rose playfully assured her friend.

"I can't believe this beautiful place could be just waiting for us," James shook his head. "With all the problems of housing shortages back in the city, waltzing into a place like this is a miracle."

"Has to do with the faculty shortages," David explained ruefully. "Some guys haven't been discharged yet. Others don't want to come back. This college isn't exactly the greatest location if you want to spend all your time in the city."

"If Miss Crane comes back, will Jessica and James have to move out?" Kat questioned, genuinely worried.

James looked quizzically at Rose, but she just said, "Not much chance of that happening."

"That's right," Jessica added, "you mentioned to me that that art teacher left. New position or something, right?"

"More or less," Rose smiled, a little quickly, before finishing. "Anyway, I set up a luncheon for you two in the kitchen. The girls can move the food out onto the terrace, if you'd prefer. Right now, David and James can bring in the rest of the luggage, while I take Jess upstairs to see if I laid out the right clothes for this evening."

Rose linked an arm through her friend's and led her to the staircase on the far left of the room, calling over her shoulder, "David, when you get back in, just leave the bags by the door. You need to show James around to the fuse box, and all the other manly house stuff."

Jessica stopped short and insisted, "Rose, you know very well that I can change a fuse. I *have* changed fuses, and so have *you*."

"Fine, but these guys won't be interested in checking on tonight's wardrobe."

"Should we expect you two ladies to burst into a rendition of 'Anything You Can Do, I Can Do Better'?" James queried.

Rose teased Jessica, "I told you not to take him to see *Annie Get Your Gun!*"

Jess raised her hands in playful surrender. "What can I say, Rose? When you live in the city, it's almost a requirement to go see all the latest hits."

They proceeded up the stairs, paneled in a lighter wood to reflect the illumination from the window on the first landing. The staircase angled to the right from the landing, leading to yet another window that faced the road and the campus beyond. To the left, a door led to one large bedroom, allotted to the smaller cottages.

When Jess had done Rose the favor of helping her partially clear out and redecorate this cottage after Miss Crane's summary exodus, she'd had no idea her good deed would so redound in her favor. The college had even sold her some pieces that Jessamyn had left behind, writing in her departure letter the school could have them. Fortunately, she and Jessica had similar tastes, so not much had been changed. Not even that rather dreadful sculpture downstairs in the living room on top of the radio console. Jess's first instinct had been to stash it in the attic, except it was sort of endearing in a homely way, like William Bendix. Besides, Rose had mentioned that it was one of Jessamyn's few attempts at plastic art, so keeping it there seemed like a kind of tribute. Though, Jess had to wonder what feelings had inspired it.

"Calling Jessica Minton and all the ships at sea!"

Rose snapped her fingers before her chum's face as they stood before the closed door to the bedroom.

"Oops, sorry, Rose. I was just thinking how lucky James and I were to get this place. I can't imagine why anyone would want to leave it. I wish I could thank your Miss Crane."

Rose didn't respond. She just stood there with a strained expression that seemed to say she wanted to tell Jessica something but couldn't figure out how,

"Rose," Jess began, canting her head with curiosity, "what are you holding back?"

Her friend glanced down the stairs behind them, then said in a lower voice, "Jess, it's not as straightforward as I said, about her leaving. This is a small campus and I think the girls get enough nasty gossip without us repeating it where they can hear. The country is *not* the utopia for raising kids that people think it is. Anyway, I'll show you the outfits for tonight, and you can tell me if I got it right."

Rose opened the door of the room, which of course stuck a little, prompting her to comment as they entered, "That's the problem with living by the shore. All this damp. It puts a curl into your papers and takes it out of your hair."

Jessica would have liked to pursue Jessamyn Crane's story further. However, now that they were in the spacious bedroom, with its wallpaper of alternated stripes in cornflower blue, white, and bands of deep pink roses, she couldn't help basking in the sunlight pouring through the large dormer windows across from the bed, a small vanity between. On that bed resided a midnight-blue crêpe, v-neck, empire-waist dress, gloves, and a white-flower-capped veil matching the dress. On the other side of the bed was a light-weight, tan men's suit.

Jess walked over to the dress, touched the veil, and pointed out, "I'm glad I decided to bring up Dusty on a later trip. Otherwise, this dress would be decorated with furry grey tufts and the veil would be in shreds." Looking up at Rose, Jessica expected a grin in response, but instead saw her friend was uncomfortable. Puzzled, she asked, "Rose, what's wrong?"

Hesitantly, Rose answered, "Jess, we need to talk, girl-to-girl."

Jessica's brow furrowed. Her next words came uncertain, even uneasy, "Okay, Rose. This sounds serious. Is this about that Jessamyn?"

"In a manner of speaking. It's really more about Terry."

"Terry? Now I really am at sea."

"Well, we are by the ocean, so I suppose this is a good place for it." Rose's attempt to be clever fell flat for both of them. She cut to the chase, "Listen, Jess, I know your problems with Terry are pretty much ancient

34

history. Still, I didn't expect anyone to ask you to work with him. I couldn't really tell Nigel it's not a great idea, not without saying too much that's probably none of his business."

Jessica tossed her purse on the bed and assured her friend, "Rose, maybe I still think that Terry gave me a raw deal, once upon a time. However, I'm a big girl; I don't intend to let him get to me *now*. The more I think about it, the more I realize I can't let something that far in the past dictate my present. There are no chicken feathers in any of my hats. Come to think about it, maybe this is something I ought to do. You know how much I loved teaching with you. Wouldn't I be crazy to give up an interesting, exciting opportunity just because someone wasn't very nice to me in the past? I'm not going to hold a grudge if it means I have to give up something I want."

Gee, that felt good! Maybe it was James's pep talk on the train, maybe it was her own determination not to miss an opportunity, maybe it was a niggling determination not to let Terry Clarke get her goat–probably all rolled together!

"Well," Rose sighed, "I got a little worried when you imagined you saw Terry. Maybe I'm being overprotective of my chum, but I wondered if maybe you were dwelling on what a heel he'd been to you."

"As if I have him on the brain?" Jessica laughed.

"It's not just you I'm thinking about," Rose pointed out. "I mean, it is you. I know you can handle yourself–but Terry's tricky."

"Don't I know that!" Jess returned with an ironic chuckle. "He had me coming and going when we were together, but things are different now."

"You mean you're 'older and wiser'?"

"That and I'm married to a great guy. I know that if someone really loves you, he wants the best for you. Anyway, you can't possibly be afraid that Terry is going to make a play for me after all these years. I would imagine having a wife would put the skids on that idea."

"I don't worry about you so much as what Terry might have up his sleeve. He's complicated," Rose said slowly. "As for the wife, well, look what happened to Jessamyn Crane."

Jessica blinked, finally saying, "Those two? Are you pulling my leg?"

"I wish I were. They were pretty careful, and the two of them were doing so well in their fields that the few who had an idea were either afraid to say anything or just wanted to look the other way. With Terry's clout, it wasn't politic to go running to the administration on him. Me, I kept my mouth shut because I felt sorry for Jessamyn and knew if the word got out, she'd would take the brunt of the opprobrium. Carolina Brent Clarke knew, too; but she had a different reason for not exposing Jessamyn. There was her pride, but, more than that, Carolina is some piece of work. She got even by torturing Jessamyn, always keeping her on edge about how much she knew and whether she'd turn her in. You don't poach that lady's territory."

"Sounds worse than *John's Other Wife*," Jessica remarked. "How come you never told me any of this before?"

"Did you need to know?" Rose responded. "I figured the less you knew about Terry, the happier you'd be. More importantly, I thought I owed it to poor Jessamyn not to air her dirty linen, even to my friend. I only found out because, well, it's a long story that I just don't want to go into. Anyway, the issue never arose until Nigel started to push for you to work with Terry."

"So, was going back to Canada an attempt to break with Terry or to escape his wife's wrath?" Jessica asked, trying to understand this scandal unexpectedly opening up before her.

Rose shrugged, "She sent a letter of resignation to President Angelovic after she'd gone away, giving some vague explanation about caring for an ill family member in Canada."

"You almost sound as if you don't buy it," Jessica posited, surprised. "*Does* she have family there?"

"I know she came from a small town near Quebec. She talked to me and Nigel a little about it. But that's not my point. I think that Carolina the Cruel made things too hot for her here. Funny thing was, all this time Terry was so chummy with Jessamyn, he was starting to act more like a human being, for a little while, anyway. A bit before she left, though, he started getting jittery. Maybe it was his book coming out. Maybe Carolina was holding his feet to fire. I don't know. I do know that I don't want the lady, and I use that term advisedly, to get a bee in her bonnet about you."

"I can take care of myself," Jessica asserted. "I mean, it's not as if I'd give this Carolina any excuse to think I'm playing footsie with her husband."

"*You* might not, but Terry's a horse of a different color," Rose grimly pointed out.

"I don't follow you, Rose."

"I wouldn't put it past Terry to play the two of you off against each other just to get at her."

"For Heaven's sake, why?"

"Natural orneriness toward Carolina, or maybe resentment against you."

"Me? What'd I do? I haven't seen him in forever—and I'm the one who has the right to be sore," Jess insisted, exasperated.

"As I said, Jess, Terry's complicated. See, the reason we're asking you is that Terry dropped a bomb before he took off for Yale this weekend, thought he'd be leaving us in the lurch over a course he was supposed to teach. He wants the department to be off-balance over whether or not he leaves. It's a nice way to parley his scholarly triumph into a financial and powerful one. So, if you're here to fill in, that kind of takes the kick out of his TNT. He'll want to neutralize you when he finds out about Nigel's brainstorm."

"My vanity liked it better when it looked like Terry was nursing regrets over what he missed," Jessica remarked ruefully. "Look, Rose, I don't want to do anything that might upset James's chances. Don't you think people are wise enough to Terry not to let him hurt James or me?"

Rose shrugged, "I have to admit he's made a lot of enemies, and our president, Wanda Angelovic, is nobody's fool. Still, some trustees are thrilled with all the acclaim Terry's gotten for his new book. That gives him clout. With some ritzy offers being dangled in his face, they may want to hold onto him for the prestige, as long as they can sweep his little shenanigans under the rug. On the other hand, if you do take the job, Nigel will be eternally grateful, certainly scoring points for James."

"Gee, thanks for making it easy for me," Jess said with a sour smile. "I'm damned if I do and damned if I don't. My guess is it wouldn't help James any if I didn't help your chair out of the spot he's in."

Rose sighed, answering slowly, "Nigel's a pretty good guy, but he's in a tough struggle with Terry. Nigel's great when he's on your side, and his judgment's usually good. But he's not someone you want to cross. Unfortunately, now that Terry has some leverage, he's not daunted by Nigel anymore."

"Wonderful. I either antagonize Terry by horning in on his class so he makes trouble for James, or I tick off your department chair by taking away his defense against Terry, also making trouble for James. It's a lose/lose situation. Is that what you're telling me, pal?"

"We-ell," Rose considered. "Terry *might* snap up one of those other offers he's been dropping hints about. Or he *might* be a perfect little angel with you, just to spite Nigel. I wouldn't put that past him!"

"I feel *so* much better," Jessica deadpanned. Then, more seriously, she pressed, "Rose, what do you think I should do?"

"Well then, as I said before, see the lay of the land with both Terry and Nigel. And whatever you decide, pal, I've got your back. I'm just sorry that I couldn't have warned you sooner, but the you-know-what only just hit the fan," Rose earnestly responded.

Jessica nodded. The hug she gave Rose went beyond words to convey her appreciation, even relief. A little relief anyway. Whatever happened, she had this friend.

Chapter Four

Same Day

The late June evening was reasonably mild as the quartet strolled along the paved road toward Cameron House. Surprisingly, not even a slight ocean breeze ruffled hair or clothes. Rose more than matched her friend for casual elegance, her honey hair gently curled away for her face and clipped into a bun, except for a wave of bangs dipping saucily across her forehead. Her dress was a fitted two-piece number, bottle green and accented by gold trim lining her cuffs and the v of her collar. Rebel that she was, Rose had thrown caution to the winds and foregone a hat. Their handsome squires also had passed on head gear but honored the occasion with their dress summer suits. David added a dash by wearing his brown and white spats.

Conversation was a congenial mélange of topics ranging from classes to house repairs. When talk came around to some of the less toxic campus gossip, Rose made sure conversation did not veer into anything anxiety-inspiring. She was still kicking herself for her earlier conversation with Jess. Seeing Jessica exhibit good spirits, Rose hoped she hadn't done much damage, after all. Then again, her friend was a good actress and prone to trying to make her friends feel better.

Rose was on the money about Jessica. The bomb she'd dropped might not have been of the atomic variety, but it had made an impression. Enough of an impression for Jess to put off discussing with James Rose's concerns. He'd been so upbeat, so cheery. How could she impinge on his good spirits tonight? There'd be time enough to talk things over once she actually had the offer in hand.

No, tonight would be a lovely reception where she'd meet the President, as well as all kinds of intelligent, stimulating people. Besides, it wasn't so long since she'd been a starving actress that she still didn't appreciate the opportunity for a free feed, with or without canned peas. My, she was a class act!

"Where has your mind wandered off to, Jessica?" David's pleasant query cut into her thoughts.

"Oh, sorry, David. I was just admiring that gorgeous view of the Sound and the beach below the wall. I've always thought the scenery so beautiful here."

That last was no lie. Breathing the salty tang, listening to the rush of the tide, no "dull sad roar" to her ears, was truly a salve to jangled nerves past and present.

"It's quite a switch for a fellow raised in a manufacturing town," James congenially added.

The road curved, they moved past two buildings, and Cameron House came into view, groups of faculty, students, and administrators converging there from different directions.

"Hmm, good turn out," David observed. "Between semesters is just about the only time people are free. President Angelovic *knows* how to schedule."

"She's a sharp cookie," Rose noted. "She started on the factory floor in a big manufacturing company, became a union steward, then eventually a respected negotiator. Even educated herself through night school. She genuinely values education, not just as job training, but as a way to make people think."

"I understand she came in a close second to Frances Perkins when Roosevelt was looking for a Secretary of Labor some years back," James added.

"Not only that. She once told off Harry Truman—and he liked it!" Rose chuckled.

"She does sound like quite a gal," Jessica agreed. "You need a person who doesn't try to turn education into a factory churning out widgets. I've had a taste of that in radio, with sponsors trying to cookie-cutter everything we do—or manage *everything* so that shows can't offend narrow-minded audiences. I mean, I know what I do isn't great art, but it can make you think, and it doesn't have to make you stupid!"

David nodded, adding, "I prefer not to create mindless drones here in the academy."

"It does seem a tad counterproductive to what 'education' should be," James elaborated. "After all, isn't that pretty much what the little man with the mustache in Berlin and his mates had in mind?"

"True," Rose chimed in. "I just wish more people were wise to the problem with that kind of thinking. There are some politicians, businesspeople, and educators who've been draping themselves in the flag and making noises that sound suspiciously familiar. To them, everyone who doesn't agree with them or asks a question is a traitorous Red."

James considered before adding, "I'm no fan of Papa Joe Stalin, that's for sure. I remember too well that Russia wasn't our bosom companion until *after* Germany turned on them. But I'm not in love with witch hunts, either. They start too easily, and they're not terribly particular about restricting themselves to persecuting guilty people."

"'Witch hunt.' That's a catchy metaphor," Rose decided, not cheerily. "Definitely appropriate for some of the campus politics I've seen in my years at different halls of ivy."

"Is there much of that sort of thing here?" James asked.

Jessica forestalled opening that can of worms by enthusing, "My goodness, look how beautiful the terrace is done up: the flower arrangements, the tables, and the bronze lanterns illuminating everything. It'll be really lovely when it gets dark. I don't think I've ever seen it so wonderful. Rose, that's Wanda Angelovic over there, in the center of the terrace, by the balustrade, right? She's beautiful. How does she do it? Union executive, negotiator, administrator—but the hair, the hat: she'd make Kay Francis green with envy."

"I think she chose to come to this school so she could walk on water on her days off," David observed, straight-faced.

Rose crinkled her nose and gave her husband a mock backhand to the chest, warning, "Don't say stuff like that. There are people around us now. Someone could take it out of context."

David shrugged, "If they say anything, it'll backfire on them. I'm only quoting the lady herself."

"Oh, and she has a sense of humor, too," Jessica shook her head. "Do I ever feel inadequate?"

Taking Jessica's hand, James pronounced, "You have brilliancies all your own, Mrs. Crawford."

"Yeah," David added. "I hear the Prez has nothing on you when comes to picking winners at the track."

"So, next time I see a slew of black horses running at Aqueduct, should I do what I can to help the Margaret Point endowment?" Jess inquired.

James grinned at her as they joined others stepping up onto the terrace. At that moment, it seemed to Jessica that maybe she and Rose had gotten all fired up earlier over nothing. She was glad she'd said nothing to impinge on James's enthusiasm.

An informal line led to the reception committee; and, in short order, Jessica found herself and James introduced to Wanda Angelovic. The woman was definitely striking: tall; fair and slender; black hair of medium length, parted in the middle and curling around her oval face under a black, lacquered-straw picture hat. Her eyes were undeniably of the sloe variety, lively and friendly, with a touch of lines at the corners. Still, there was a hint of sadness in their depths, the kind that came with seeing more than her accomplishments could entirely cancel out. That hint vanished as Wanda Angelovic visibly, sincerely brightened when Rose and David introduced their companions.

"Oh, Professor Crawford, I'm delighted that you accepted our offer," she smiled. "You are a lifesaver for the summer program. I'm looking forward to seeing how well you'll do with our students."

As she continued to speak to James in a throaty voice, with just the slightest lisp on her Rs, it struck Jessica that Angelovic had mastered the administrator's trick of saying good things to you without promising too much. Decidedly pleased James was here, Wanda Angelovic still wasn't assuring him of anything until she saw how he worked out. Well, you couldn't blame her for not wanting to buy a pig in a poke, especially since her predecessor before the war had saddled her with Terry's various issues as well as accomplishments. Jess knew from Rose that though

Terry was a popular teacher, his relations with colleagues was nothing to write home about. Nevertheless, his family background had exerted a pull on the last president, while his scholarship continued to make the trustees smile with the prestige he accrued for their school.

Those cogitations were the stuff of a split second, for Jessica still had time to enjoy Wanda Angelovic's enumerating some of the good things she'd heard about James's work, scholarly not espionage-oriented, of course.

"And, Jessica Minton," Wanda now gave Jess full attention, "I was greatly impressed with the work you and Rose have done with those underprivileged girls. I also have to admit I'm excited to meet the woman who put a few white hairs in my head Friday nights. I still can't go into a dark room without checking for zuvembies."

Jessica gave James a victorious nod, then pronounced, "See, James, I'm not the only one."

Wanda offered James a questioning expression, prompting him to explain, "She sometimes buries herself a little too deeply in her parts—so to speak. You can imagine the tense time of it I had when she played a serial poisoner."

"I did get out of cooking," Jessica added knowingly.

One of the other administrators commented, "You don't kid us, Wanda. If trying to keep up facilities, make payroll, oversee programs, and all else doesn't give you a head full of white hair, a few hobgoblins should be just a walk in the park."

"It's not just the money," Wanda elaborated. "It's manpower and materials. Most wartime restrictions are still on—and with those that have been lifted, it's a case of take a number and stand in line."

Amid nods and shrugs of agreement, Jessica's attention was caught by a dark object moving rapidly towards them down the beach.

"Oh, what a beautiful horse! Does he belong to the college? Is that someone from the school riding him?"

Only Wanda turned to follow Jess's admiring gaze at a black horse powering closer. His rider, interestingly enough, wore a Coast Guard pea-jacket and officer's cap. It was the horse, though, that held Jessica's attention.

Wanda Angelovic turned back to Jess with a sad smile and explained, "That's Sailor and Blackie."

"My guess is that 'Sailor' is the rider," James dryly concluded.

Before she picked up on the silent disapproval of the others flanking the President, Jess asked, "Who are they?"

Demonstrating far more sympathy than her colleagues, Wanda Angelovic answered, "I'm afraid Sailor's an unfortunate case. He's lived here rather quietly, almost in isolation, since he was discharged back in '43. He was torpedoed by one of those U-Boats. He survived but with physical and psychological wounds. So, they mustered him out."

"We hadn't seen much of him most of the time. Shell shock still plagues him, so he likes to keep to himself. Then around last spring, we started seeing him riding the horse along the beach. Scuttlebutt is that some relative gave the horse to him as a kind of therapy. The story goes that he used to work with horses before the war."

"I think it's disgraceful," Porlock, the portly person from public relations pronounced. "He scares the kids. Don't look at me like that, Wanda. He makes them nervous. Anyway, they don't need to see something like that."

"A fellow riding a horse?" Wanda queried.

"No, a fellow without all his marbles. What if the trustees or some of our parents see him? Enrollments and endowments aren't something you want to gamble with, Wanda. You're too smart for that."

"Pat. *I* know that Sailor doesn't bother anybody. Anyway, he's on public property. We don't have any right, legal or moral, to harass him. The only way he'll hurt anyone is if she deliberately throws herself in front of that horse. I think our students are smarter than that–and if they aren't, we'd better do something about admissions standards. Anyway, maybe Sailor is part of their education. Maybe they need to see and understand what war does to people–and develop some compassion."

Apparently, Porlock knew when to throw in the towel. He relented, "Guess you have a point there."

Tactfully, Jessica changed the subject, "I'm just happy everything worked out so James and I could come. He's so looking forward to teaching here. But I can see that we're holding up the line. We'll let you chat with the rest of the guests. So good to meet you, President Angelovic!"

"Thank you. So glad we have you here. Do go into the Great Hall, where we set up refreshments. Enjoy."

As Rose and David led their friends across the flagged terrace, a nod or a smile or a "hello" extended to acquaintances, Jessica couldn't help asking, "Tell me, did I really put my foot in a hornets' nest over that vet and his horse?"

"Yeah, it's a good thing you weren't representing us at the Yalta Conference," David decided. "We'd be at war with Russia and *England* now."

"Don't be such a wise guy, David," Rose shook her head. She turned to her friend and said, "Don't pay any attention to this lunkhead. The Sailor business is no big deal."

"Still," Jessica considered, "I'm surprised that Porlock took on the President, right in a social gathering. Isn't that the kind of thing that usually goes on behind closed doors? You know the brass always put on a smiling, solid front for the public, be they producers, advertisers, network bigwigs—or college administrators."

"Normally, you'd be on the money, Jess," David agreed, "but you've got to remember that even if many of the people around here are progressive, there are still plenty who aren't so broadminded. Too often, they're the ones holding the purse strings."

"You might say," Rose finished, "in their minds, a woman's place is in the kitchen or the bedroom but definitely not in the boardroom."

She and David sealed their agreement with simultaneous nods as the foursome reached the French doors opening into the reception hall.

David changed the subject with an expansive gesture and the invitation, "After you, esteemed guests."

Cocking an eyebrow, James deferred, "Sorry, chum, but lately, every time I've had to go first, it's because someone has been afraid of Horlas and such."

Folding her arms, Jessica pretended to lower, "You're never going to let me live that down, are you?"

James only smiled.

"That suits me just fine, mister. There's a glass of wine and a plate of *hors d' oeuvres* with my name on them in there," Jess smoothly pronounced. "So, I'm not waiting around for you!"

With mock defiance, Jessica marched into the Great Hall she knew and loved so well. White-tiled floors and high, dark-wood wainscoting above the white-washed walls greeted her. Across the room, a beautiful dark wood staircase, its rail and dowlings intricately carved, led to a railed landing that extended to the opposing wings of the building. An enormous floor-to-ceiling fireplace, with gorgeously carved wooden mantle and side shelves, rose to Jessica's right, and further in that direction, across the room, were tables laden with goodies. The washed, blue-grey light streaming through the French doors on either side of the hearth and the expansive picture windows lining the landing above was complemented by candles and a beautiful chandelier pendent from the vaulted ceiling.

Jess felt an arm link through hers and looked up at James to tease, "I thought you were afraid of 'things that go bump in the night'?"

"Rose mentioned that they had those shrimp wrapped in bacon."

"Hunger triumphs over trepidation?"

"That's about the size of it, old girl."

"Well, just remember; no matter how 'old' this 'girl' gets, you'll always be six years older."

"Ouch!" David grimaced.

"He can take it on the chin," Jessica laughed.

James allowed the ghost of a smile at their private joke.

But Rose brought them to the point with, "Enough already! Let's chow down before the guys from Physics get here. They're like locusts!"

Joining the line for the tables, Jess found herself and Rose separated slightly from the guys. She took that opportunity to query, "So, no one mentioned my subbing for you-know-who. Does that mean the deal's off?"

"No, no," Rose clarified, taking up a china plate, cutlery, and a napkin. "That wasn't exactly the plan. Wanda's leaving it up to Nigel to handle everything. She's a miracle as an administrator, actually respects our rights to govern our department. She keeps tabs on things, but she doesn't put her hand in until it's time for a final approval. Miracle of miracles, she gives her faculty credit for knowing what they're doing."

"So where is the Chair?" Jess questioned, interrupting ladening her plate to scan the clusters of people across the Great Hall.

Rose quickly surveyed the room, then shook her head, facing Jess again to say, "I wish I knew. He should have been in the reception line,

46

with the other Chairs. I expected him to be there to greet James. Knowing Nigel, though, he's probably trying to catch up on paperwork. If it's not grading, it's administrative stuff. Then there's his own scholarship. The guy works too hard, way too hard. I think he's trying to punish himself for taking two or so years off between this job and his last one at St. Barnabas College. And wouldn't you know he spent that time nursing a dying brother."

After a quick survey of the table's gustatory delights, Rose changed the subject: "Gee, there doesn't seem to be much seafood. And here we are right next door to the ocean!"

"You know with the government lifting the price controls, seafood, especially shellfish, has just gone right through the roof," Jess pointed out. "A shrimp cocktail jumped from thirty-five to fifty cents. I even read that one Brooklyn lunchroom tacked five cents onto their salmon and sardine sandwiches."

"Salmon and *sardine*?" Rose repeated, wincing.

Thinking the combination over, the two women looked at each other and uttered, "Blech!!!"

"Seriously, though, Rose," Jess began as they moved away from the table, "how much of a problem would it be if I did work with Terry? . . . Say, where's James?"

Indeed, though David was still with them, holding two plates, James Crawford seemed to have disappeared.

"That's right," Rose agreed looking around. "Where is he?"

"Relax, ladies," David reassured them. "While you two were deep in conversation, Nigel Cross apparently sent someone to bring James upstairs for a chat. See, I still have his plate."

"Nigel didn't even come down?" Rose queried.

"Sounds like a grand summons," Jessica opined. "Will James return with his head on a platter?"

Realizing that her chum wasn't entirely joking, Rose responded, "No, nothing like that. I told you the guy just can't tear himself away from his work. If you're not a jackass, Nigel is fine, pretty much."

"Gee, I *think* I'm reassured," Jessica returned. "I can hardly wait to meet the great man, myself. How does he feel about radio actors? You know we're not ranked the highest on the artistic totem pole."

Before Rose could answer, David interrupted, "Sorry, girls, I see two other guys from Mathematics. I have to talk to them about department business. We'll recombine forces later."

"I thought he had the summer off," Jess winked.

"Right. And teachers only work a few hours a week, when they're in the classroom," Rose added sarcastically.

Jessica rolled her eyes in commiseration, explaining, "I get the same malarkey about my work. Radio actors just stand around and read someone else's words for sixty minutes—oops, less with commercial breaks."

"Anyway," Rose said, "at least we get to work on this beautiful campus. Say, I see two of our best students over there: Alicia Wraxton and Lauren Fleet. Come on over and meet them. I think you'll like these girls. Bright and funny, they're not just here to earn an MRS. rather than a B.A."

"If they were, they wouldn't be bright at all. Not much opportunity to find a husband at an all-girl school."

"Oh, you'd be surprised at how clever some of these kids are at trolling for brothers and cousins," Rose apprized her friend as they crossed to the two young women dwarfed by the gorgeous fireplace.

"Alicia, Lauren," Rose called as they approached, catching the girls' attention, eliciting looks of relief at the advent of a familiar and friendly face and voice, "here's someone I want you to meet."

Rose continued as she and Jess joined the girls, "These are two of our top students, Alicia Wraxton and Lauren Fleet. They were teaching assistants last semester and will be carrying on the same duties (and drudgeries) next year. They're both taking James's seminar this session."

The girl whom Rose had introduced as Alicia nabbed Jessica's attention first: tall and slender; lush wavy black hair down to her shoulders; high cheek bones and a pert nose; brown eyes that sparkled behind possibly the longest natural lashes Jessica had ever seen, all packaged in a high-waisted, red, flared skirt and a white, eyelet peasant blouse, its square collar bordered with a threading of blue and red ribbon. The eyes, the hair, the dress: all Jessica could think of was a fiery gypsy. Lauren Fleet was a study in contrast: soft brown hair cut in a chin-length bob, slender frame and features, but enormous, alert eyes. Lauren struck Jess as kind of a tyro Bette Davis, albeit a milder version, in her pale-yellow, two-piece linen dress.

Surprisingly, it was the gentler seeming of the two who burst out, "Oh swell! You're the radio actress, right? Gee, it's grand to meet you! We all crowd around the radio in the dorm to listen to your program. It's the limit! Your show scares the pants off of us!"

"I'll take that as a compliment," Jessica smiled. "I'm really happy to meet you girls."

"Take Lauren with a grain of salt," the other girl, Alicia, explained knowingly. "She has a V-8 charged imagination."

"Okay, smarty," Lauren countered, "but you still made us check the wardrobe for Horlas last week."

As Alicia blushed, Jessica laughed, "I guess we're doing our job right on the show: reducing dorm rooms full of teenagers to jelly!"

"Maybe you could put together an acting class," Lauren eagerly proposed.

While Jessica registered surprise at the unexpected suggestion, Rose pointed out, "Lauren, you ought to know by now that nobody just throws together a class on the spur of the moment."

"Lauren, it would be superfluous," Alicia stated. "You ought to know that. After all, we're both in Dr. Clarke's Shakespeare: Stage and Page class."

"But, Alicia, no one really knows for sure if the class is going to run, with him doing all those lectures on his book," Lauren disagreed. Then turning to the two older women, she asked, "Professor Nyquist, do you have any inside dope, I mean, information?"

Jess watched her friend take time to think before answering, "I don't believe the class will be canceled. We're trying to find some way to avoid that. I'll let you know when I get the official word."

Rose was not about to give too much away about command decisions to the kids, let alone start conjectures snowballing before any decisions had been made, Jess decided. Besides, Rose was too much of a pal to put Jess on the spot before she'd even been officially asked to pitch in, never mind made a decision.

Lauren proceeded to knock all that caution into a cocked hat, proposing, "Say, Miss Minton might be able to fill in. I mean she hasn't done only radio work. My parents saw her on the stage—and you've done Shakespeare, too, right? I saw that picture of you as Ariel that Professor Nyquist has in her office."

Alicia immediately took center stage: "Dr. Clarke did Shakespeare when he was in college and in summer stock, too. He still does Shakespearean readings. And *he* is a renowned scholar. You can't just replace him with anyone."

Jess only allowed herself a faint smile at Alicia's loyalty, feeling not so much slighted by the girl's comparison as mildly amused by her idealization of Terry. Well, she had been even blinder at the same age.

Rose's loyalty to her friend took over: "Girls, you don't realize that Jessica has almost completed a masters' in English and was wonderful teaching with me in our Saturday program at the New York Public Library. In fact, I bet you didn't know that when Dr. Clarke was doing Shakespeare in college, he was on stage with Jessica Minton."

The girls blinked in surprise at finding unrelated phenomena actually coexisting in the same sphere. That didn't exactly sit well with Jessica. Of course, what's past was past and no big deal in the first place. But she couldn't quite dismiss the vague awkwardness at her personal life coming up for strangers' perusal. She could also see that Rose sensed her disquiet and was inwardly kicking herself. So, Jessica put those shadows of discomfort to rest. If she didn't make a big deal of the past, then it wouldn't be one.

"That's right. He was my Orlando when I played Rosalind in *As You Like It*. I was Paulina when he was Leontes in *The Winter's Tale*," Jess pointed out brightly.

She tactfully didn't mention that there had been times that Leontes' immature egotism provoking Paulina's criticism had cut very close to the bone in her relations with Terry. Something she wished she'd figured out back when she'd mistakenly believed she was a warm, wise Rosalind guiding a rough-around-the-edges Orlando.

"So," concluded Alicia, "you stayed with acting, and he stayed with scholarship."

"Mmm-hmm," Jessica nodded. "We just went where our hearts led us."

It would have been more satisfying to say, "Terry just didn't have the stick-to-itiveness to succeed in acting. For him, academia cost him less effort, was less of a challenge to his ego and kept his family approval." But why tear down the guy in front of his admiring students just to score points off him?

Lauren laughed, "Kind of like: 'to each her own said the old lady as she kissed the cow!'"

Alicia rolled her eyes, while Rose commented, "How do you like that, Jess? Both our noble professions are reduced to the level of smooching bovines!"

"I think that this is still a grand place to be—as a student or a teacher," Jessica replied, moving the conversation to a field *sans* land mines. "The view is beautiful. The buildings are exquisite, except maybe for that wooden board replacing a pane in the French doors over there. What—what did I say?"

Jessica's observation of the damaged glass had provoked startled expressions on both students.

Rose tried to shift the subject with, "You remember what President Angelovic was saying about the scarcity of materials."

The girls did not follow Rose's lead, though. Lauren started off, "That showed up the day after Miss Crane disappeared. I mean, they think it happened the night she disappeared."

"So, you think she was so ashamed of breaking a window that she flew the coop?" Jess quipped.

"No," Lauren persisted solemnly. "There's a rumor that there was a bullet hole in the window."

Jessica started, not just at Lauren's revelation but at the sharpness of Rose's response: "That's enough, Lauren. You know better than to spread irresponsible rumors. We all know that Miss Crane sent a letter to the President explaining her sudden resignation."

"But they say it wasn't hand-signed," Lauren persisted, trying to justify herself in Rose's eyes by virtue of more detail.

"And who are 'they,' Lauren?" Rose questioned pointedly. "Did you even see what 'they' described?"

"I, no, I'm sorry. I just . . ."

Alicia broke in, "Maybe it's time big mouth and I circulated. You can see who else you can offend, Lauren."

Lauren looked wounded, so Rose immediately explained, "Look, girls, I'm not really angry. You're young, Lauren, and you need to learn that spreading rumors has consequences. Think how a rumor about murder on campus undermines all the hard work Dr. Angelovic and the rest of us are doing to give you an education that means something instead of just serving up a candy-coated finishing school. What if parents pull their children, donors turn off their funding, all because of phony rumors? There's a lot at stake here."

"Yes," Lauren allowed. "Some people are even pointing fingers at Sailor. He's never done anything but ride his horse."

"Good thinking," Rose commended her. "Anyway, go mingle. Get another plate of food. If Professor Cross ever lets him free, maybe we can introduce you to Jessica's husband, your teacher, Professor Crawford."

After the girls left, Jessica turned to her pal and observed ironically, "I thought I was coming here to get away from murder and mayhem, real and theatrical."

Rolling her eyes, Rose said, "Wait a minute." She snagged a glass of wine for each of them off a passing waiter's tray, then asked, "What was it your mother used to say? 'Enough rumors/roomers to start a boarding house?'"

"Never mind quoting my illustrious ancestors. What's the lowdown on that 'bullet hole' in the glass and the 'unsigned' letter of resignation?"

Rose shrugged, "All I ever saw was the glass pane replaced by a wood panel, and the president is hardly going to ask me to take a gander at someone's letter of resignation. Who knows where the stories started? Just don't get any nonsense about murder into your head. And don't go giving the girls any ideas."

Jessica assured her chum, "Don't worry about me, sister. I've had enough real drama to last a lifetime. Still, I'll tell you, Rose, it's beginning to sound as if you have more soap operas and thrillers here than we do on the air all week."

"Relax, Jessica. It's not like this all the time. No more contentious than some of your theatre groups. Maybe not even as bad."

Jessica smiled and relaxed, taking a sip of wine before joining Rose to enjoy a survey of the room in the deepening dusk and candlelight. To their left was a door leading to a stone gallery and circular garden outside, while further down the line of the hall were broad doorways leading into the seminar rooms, rich in dark wood paneling and hearth mantles carved with Renaissance and Medieval figures, both human and supernatural. But what caught Jess's attention back between the two rooms was a small cluster of men talking over their drinks, amongst them James—his features tight. Before Jess could get a better look, her attention was snatched by Rose almost choking on her drink.

"Rose, are you all ri—?"

"Too late to beat it out the door. She's seen us and she'd heading right this way. Damn, she wasn't supposed to be here tonight."

"Who? What?" Jessica puzzled, her eyes following Rose's to an absolutely magnificent female striding toward them, a strange smile shaping her features. Statuesque, the woman's curves were flattered by a jewel-tone green two-piece dress, its sweetheart neckline highlighted by the strands of a coral necklace. Her lustrous copper hair was coiled in a French role, accentuated by a rakish green cap that matched her dress and was complimented by a wave of coral feathers curving along her cheek. Her jaw line was strong and square, her eyes a piercing green.

"Rig for impact," Rose muttered softly. "Here comes the *Battleship Carolina*, or maybe I should say *Destroyer*? Just don't lose your temper, Jessica, no matter what she says, and you'll be fine—probably."

Jessica shot her friend a sharp, leery glance, then quickly channeled charm into her features. She didn't like the way this Carolina's green eyes glinted like the emeralds of the bracelet on her coral gauntlet gloves. Would the lady be throwing down one tonight? Had Terry said anything about Jess to her?

"Rose Nyquist, you scamp, hoarding our guest Miss Jessica Minton all to yourself over here like a sly little squirrel."

Hoarding me like a squirrel? Does that make me some kind of a nut? Down, girl. Jessica inwardly cautioned herself. *Don't go on the defensive, yet.*

"Hello, there, Carolina," Rose smiled, reservedly. "I didn't expect to see you here tonight. I thought you'd still be in New Haven with Terry."

"Well, I was," Carolina explained, her accent an intriguing mid-Atlantic with the faintly lingering honey of something south of Mason-Dixon. "But I just couldn't stay there and be smothered by those old fogies. Not when I could meet our two new arrivals and see how they fit in. So, aren't you going to introduce us, Rose?"

"Yes, sure. Carolina, this is my long-time friend Jessica Minton. Jessica, this is Carolina Brent Clarke. She teaches and is an artist in residence, a sculptor. And, of course, she's married to Terry Clarke in my department."

Jess hadn't really expected Rose to mention anything about her and Terry to his wife. But it was a relief just the same to have that part of her past–if you could call it a "past"–elided. And if Carolina knew anything, she wasn't exactly spilling the beans. Not exactly.

"Yes, we're all proud of my husband," Carolina fairly preened. "Terry is quite the superb scholar, with his new book. My husband rushes in and brushes away all the academic cobwebs. I'm positive that some of those old fossils at Yale will just be having heart attacks over what he has to say about Shakespeare and psychoanalysis, while the young Turks there will be embracing him. Rose, you have told her all about my Terry and his impressive work, haven't you?"

"To tell the truth, Carolina, Jess and I really don't have any call to talk about Terry. We just have too much going on in our lives," Rose smiled sweetly, past experience having taught her that an early shot across the bow always came in handy for signaling Carolina to keep her claws retracted.

Zing! thought Jess, striving not to let the reaction creep into her expression.

Carolina, however, didn't miss a beat: "Well of course not. Why would you? Jessica here is an actress, on, um, the *radio.* (A shadow of a smirk on the word?) We can't expect her to be interested in scholarly matters." Still, such a sweet smile. "Never the twain shall meet–except with Terry. You know, he's teaching a course this summer about Shakespeare and the stage, the modern stage. What a pity he'll have to cancel some sessions, what with his book lectures and all."

"Truly," Jessica concurred pleasantly, not giving Carolina the satisfaction of reacting to her snub. Playing it cool was the way to go just now.

However, Rose couldn't let Carolina get away with even a veiled dig at her chum: "You know, Carolina, you're not completely right about Jessica's academic *bona fides.* Her undergraduate degree is as solid as

Terry's, and she's been completing a master's while working as an actress. I've seen the wonderful insights she brings to teaching literature when we were working with underprivileged girls. Not to mention that her performing on the stage gives her a deeper understanding of plays—you know, a more professional version of Terry's acting experience."

Jessica shifted uneasily. Rose's tone might have been perfectly reasonable, but her actual words hadn't exactly followed her own advice. Worse, even if only indirectly, Rose had opened the door on Jess's old romance with Terry by bringing up their college days. Jessica would have much preferred no one set off that A-Bomb of a topic.

Carolina smiled and walked right through that door: "That's right, isn't it? You and my Terry were in college together?" Oddly enough, the formidable woman almost beamed, adding, "You were his leading lady, weren't you?"

Wasn't that cagily put, Jessica reflected. Leading lady on or off stage? Hmm, this really *ought* to be a simple conversation. After all, she had nothing to hide, no scandal from the past, no ulterior motives for the future. Yet a chat with this slick chick was about as simple as tip-toeing through a mine field.

Jessica wasn't about to start anything, but she also was *not* going to be intimidated. Nonchalantly, she explained, "We appeared in a few shows together back in the day. The artistic director thought we handled the classic comedies well: Shakespeare, Moliere, Shaw, Goldsmith. I'm sure the names are familiar to you. Terry was a nice little actor. I had a bit of trouble when it came to the tragedies, I will admit. I couldn't be passive enough for Ophelia nor vicious enough for Lady Macbeth. I've greatly expanded my range since, except for the passive."

It was clear in Carolina's eyes that Jessica's countermove, deft with charming assurance had taken her by surprise. But only for a moment. A glint slowly sparked in those green eyes.

Rose popped in, as if cutting the detonation wire on a bomb just in time: "So, Carolina, I haven't had a chance to hear about your latest work, your sculpting. Isn't it supposed to tie in with Terry's studies? Something about the inner psychology of Shakespeare's characters?"

Carolina paused, the appeal to expound on her own artistry distracting her from calculating a sortie against Jessica. Pride won out, and Carolina explained, "Rose, darling, it's fascinating work but so darned frustrating! I know I perfectly captured the burning drive and tortured guilt of Claudius, but I just can't seem to capture Gertrude. I mean, what motivates the woman to cling to her man, but keep switching that man? She just won't see what's going on in front of her. No woman is that stupid. So maybe she does see. Maybe Gertrude's the smartest of them all: marrying a king, provoking his virile younger brother to do him in when he gets old, tricking her son into trusting his secret with her, then taking the big sleep in the end when it all falls apart. I just can't make up my mind, and it's destroying my work. I start something, then smash it to bits. I feel like such a failure. You ladies just can't conceive of the sensation. Oh no, wait. Jessica, Terry, and I saw you in a production of *Darkness Falls* a few years back. You must know *exactly* how I feel about failing after your performance in *that* disaster."

Whoa! That was sure one bean ball! However, a girl didn't spend as many years as she did in the business without learning to think on her feet when disaster loomed. Jess smiled her most sympathetically and answered, "Truthfully, Carolina, with a play the blame often goes around–actors, directors, playwrights. But you, as a sculptress, you have no one to blame but yourself. I am sorry. My heart goes out to you."

Jess wasn't sure, but she could have sworn that Rose choked back a chuckle. Surprisingly, Carolina Clarke only gave her a fleeting, skeptical look. No explosion. Good.

Still, Jess wasn't quite sure how to read her flame-haired nemesis's next tactic: "You know, Jessica, I am dying to meet that charming husband of yours. Now, just where is he?"

"He's upstairs in conference with Nigel," Rose supplied. "That means he'll be down sometime in November."

"Rose, you're such a card. You know I always say to Terry that you have just the snappiest sense of humor."

"That's me," Rose quipped. "The Fred Allen of the English Department. I keep 'em all in stitches–students and profs, alike."

"Maybe Mr. Crawford will take that title away from you, Rose. What do you say, Jessica?"

Jess was just glad she was the only one who'd noticed James had come down from his meeting with the Chair. Diplomatically, she smiled and replied, "I say that the department has room enough for more than two sharp wits. And I'm sure Terry could give them a run for their money."

The words were no sooner out of her mouth, than Jessica wondered if she'd made a slip. Would Carolina wonder how she knew Terry was a clever boy or just think she was trying to make nice now?

"Well, thank you, Jessica. I have to say my husband is downright talented with seeing irony and delivering his *bon mots* with exactly the right timing. That's one reason he's such a great teacher. He can give these girls great truths but not put them to sleep doing it. I'm afraid, though, he doesn't have that charming English accent your husband does. I think the girls will adore it. I know I did."

Jessica blinked her surprise and asked, "Wait, you've met James? I thought you just got here?"

It was no fun for Jess to see how calmly Carolina Brent Clarke seemed to enjoy taking her off guard. "I did, but I saw him talking with some other fellows in the foyer. He was pointed out to me. You better keep an eye on him. He's going to turn a few heads. He's a nice-looking fellow, in a Bohemian sort of way. I guess we both appreciate that kind of charm, don't we? Just think about Terry's Elizabethan beard and mustache. Yes, I guess we both love the same look in a man. But you lucky girl. Yours has that charming English accent to boot. I guess you're one up on me for now."

For now? Was Terry's wife speaking in terms of the present with James or the past with Terry? Either way, the intent wasn't friendly, no matter how playful the tone. Before Jessica or Rose could respond, Carolina was preparing her departure with, "Ah, there's President Angelovic. I must go over and say hello to Wanda. Do take care, ladies. Lovely to meet you, and my best to your husband, Jessica—and yours, too, Rose."

"Back at you," Rose smiled, and as soon as Carolina was gone, she turned to Jessica and said, "How do you like our resident southern belle."

"*Is* that what you call her? Not something a little more canine?" Jessica inquired. Then she put her real concern into words, "Rose, she spent an awful lot of time dwelling on James and dropping 'subtle' hints that Terry was all hers. Do you think she knows I went out with him once and resents it? You said she could be a troublemaker. I don't want to see James hurt or harassed in any way because she thinks she's got a bone to pick with me. Maybe I'd better steer away from working with Terry. I wouldn't back away from trouble, but I don't want to deliberately stir it up, either."

Rose thought a bit before saying, "Well, what did James say when you talked it over with him? How does he feel about the situation?"

Jessica shook her head and explained, "Who had time? We were busy getting settled, then getting ready. Anyway, he's been so happy and excited today, I couldn't throw cold water on him, especially for something that hasn't even happened yet. So, do I need to keep a low profile to prevent anyone from making waves for him? And *would* Terry be so overjoyed to work with me, let alone see me take over his class, even temporarily? I don't think your Professor Cross realizes I'm not quite the high card he was hoping to use against Terry. I can't help wondering if my history, such as it is, with Terry is going to give your Chair a headache, no matter what I decide. I don't want to put James in Dutch with him."

"I understand, Jess," Rose sympathized. "Tell you what. I see Nigel over at the bar. I wanted to introduce you to him, anyway. How about we swoop down on Professor Cross and quietly lay all our cards on the table? He's good at sorting out messes, and when we know where he stands, we can better figure out where we should. Sound good to you?"

"Oh, he's going to just love me waltzing over and saying: Nice to meet you, Doc. By the way, I'm here to start WW III in your department."

"Don't be a schlemiel," Rose ordered. "So, snap it up. Put aside that plate and your glass, and let's see Nigel.

Chapter Five

They hadn't covered more than half the way before Jessica put a hand on Rose's arm and stopped her friend with, "Rose, I think we better hold our horses a minute."

Rose paused and quizzed, "Sure. What's eating you?"

"Just this. I can't go over there and say: 'Hi, I'd love to take your offer, but Terry and his wife are picking on me.'"

"I didn't intend to put it that way," Rose responded.

"I know, I know. But that's how it'll sound, don't you think?"

"I suppose you do have something there."

Jess could see Rose gave her words some deep thought, especially when she finally said, "And progressive as this place is, there are still too many people around here–Terry included–who would love to dismiss any woman's complaint as just some nonsense from a whiney female."

"We certainly can't afford to let anyone cast us as all catfights and irrational emotions," Jessica confirmed.

"So, what *do* you want to do, oh Swami of Suffragettes?"

"How about this? Let's go over and see your Chair. You have to introduce me, anyway. The two of you have to make the official offer, too. Let me handle presenting the problem. I think I know how I can swing it." Jessica proposed.

"Okay. Let's see how you handle academic politics. You've got to get your feet wet sometime, especially if you and James plan to stick around. Let's go," Rose decided.

Jessica nodded. She had a plan all right. Nothing quite as elaborate

59

as storming Normandy Beach, but maybe her past experience finessing disagreements with producers and directors would pay off now. After all, she had James's interests to look out for as well as her own. A quick glance back where she'd last seen him, a disappointing result, and she found herself wondering where he had gone. Well, she only had time for the briefest of musings on that question.

Rose guided Jessica over to the bar, where, unsurprisingly, there was a crowd. Free liquor always seemed to elicit that response, everywhere. So, which gent *was* Nigel Cross?

"Nigel, I have someone here you want to meet," Rose said, pointing Jessica toward a man sipping a blood-red wine. His appearance was more than a little startling.

It wasn't that he didn't look intellectual, in his almost *de riguer* academic tweeds and turtleneck (even in summer!), with his neatly cropped white-blond hair, and the probing intelligence in his dark eyes. He was just, so, well, formidable.

Nigel Cross easily stood six foot four. Though his form was trim, his shoulders were extremely broad. His face was long and lean, his forehead high, his lips full, and his eyes and mouth intelligent, revealing mental power as strong and broad as those shoulders. His eyes seemed to say, fine, try to snow me, impress me, intimidate me. It will be such a bore if I have to take the time to crush you, but I will. Jessica couldn't help gulping, just a little, as Nigel Cross zeroed in on her.

Well, Rose seems to like him, so maybe he uses his powers for good not evil. Still, Jess pictured Nigel Cross far more at home in the *Inferno* than the *Paradiso*.

At least there was a light of interest, not predation in his eyes, when he spoke: "Ah, I don't have to strain my intellectual powers to recognize this new face. Jessica Minton, the actress. A pleasure. I'm Rose's, now your husband's, fearless leader, Nigel Cross."

Jessica forced herself not to hesitate in accepting his hand, nor to wince at the strength of his grip, but to smile as she responded, "A pleasure to meet you, as well. I'm sure, Professor Cross, that you don't recognize my face from my latest work."

There was only a minuscule missed beat before Cross calculated her irony and smiled, then said, "But you wouldn't know that I'd seen you on the stage before your radio work. Such a pity that you had those bad breaks with *Ill Met by Moonlight* and the one where that marvelous character actor Frederick Bromfield met his unfortunate demise."

"I couldn't agree with you more, Professor Cross," Jessica responded, leaving out "You don't know the half of it, bud!" What she did say was, "I was beginning to feel like a jinx for a time—but this radio program seems to have put that curse to rest. Now if you'll just give me some wood to knock . . ."

"I'm rather glad the hoodoo seems to have freed you from stage commitments, as I imagine Rose has told you already that we could use your help filling in for Terence Clarke. Ah, but I am being remiss. May I get you a drink, Miss Minton, or should I say Mrs. Crawford?"

"Jessica is just fine—and, no, I'll pass on the drink just now, but thank you, Professor Cross."

She wanted her wits decidedly unpickled for dealing with this gentleman, though she did find herself rather liking him.

"No need to be so formal. Nigel is fine. We're one big family here in the Literature Department."

"Notice he didn't say 'happy family,'" Rose wryly pointed out.

"Funny you should both bring up that point," Jessica began casually but carefully. "I am interested in accepting your offer. It dovetails beautifully with the work I've done on the stage and the studies that I've been pursuing."

"I know," Nigel smoothly informed her. "R.K. Knutsford speaks highly of you."

"That was very kind," Jessica replied. "But to cut to the chase, Nigel, Terry Clarke might not be terribly fond of *me* being the one to save his class."

To Cross's interested "Oh?" Jessica continued, "I'm sure this has never come up. By and large, there would be no reason it should, but Terry and I knew each other as college students. Our 'friendship' did not end amicably, exactly. It's all water under the bridge, a decade or so under the bridge, as far as I'm concerned. It's probably the same for Terry. It ought to be. But from what I've heard from Rose, it seems that Terry is as temperamental as ever. I just thought you'd like a heads up before you chanced setting off any fireworks."

Nigel Cross calmly took a drink of that very red wine before smiling faintly and noting, "Very tactfully put, Jessica Minton. As I see it, however, Dr. Clarke made his own bed, quite poorly I might add, and doesn't have much choice about how comfortable his nap is."

Jessica nodded, then just as carefully added, "I met his wife, Carolina, a moment ago. I'm not sure she likes my being here."

"How unfortunate for Mrs. Brent Clarke. But she does not direct my department."

Jess concluded that she could really like this guy, if he were on the level.

Rose shook her head and decided, "I'm not sure what I'm even doing here. You two seemed to have worked things out just dandy without me. Maybe you could both pop down to Washington and help Truman with labor relations."

"Not Machiavellian enough for me, Rose," Nigel returned. "After dancing between academics and trustees for fifteen years, I'm afraid I'd find politics far too facile to be interesting."

Jessica added, "I know Woodrow Wilson said he had an easier time of it in the State House and the White House than as the President of Princeton."

"Oh, perfect for Terry," Rose decided. "Isn't that one of the places supposed to be dangling a position before him?"

"Bully for Princeton," Nigel evaded the question. Then he turned to Jessica and said, "I rather enjoyed my chat with your husband. He's a young man in love with his work. I was also delighted to realize that we had traveled to some of the same spots on the Continent, though not recently, of course."

"Of course," Jessica agreed, hoping smoothly. She feared being overly sensitive about keeping James's work in the SOE and the Resistance under her hat. Maybe the war was over, but his superiors had made clear that that information was to stay on the q.t. Jess continued, "James is so excited about this opportunity. He belongs at a place that values teaching as well as scholarship. He loves to dig into literature and bring it alive. He has a way of challenging you and inspiring you that's . . . well, I guess I am going on a bit. I suppose I'm more than a little biased in his favor."

Nigel Cross smiled. Jess wasn't sure how to characterize that smile.

Still, she liked his words, "I might say the two of you are charter members of a mutual admiration society. He had quite a bit to say about your abilities as an actress—and I agreed with him."

Jess couldn't help beaming at those words.

"That's kudos you can take to the bank," Rose pronounced. "Nigel does *not* hand out bouquets every day!"

"I appreciate those words, Nigel," Jessica responded. "There's quite a bit of snobbery towards radio. People forget it's not all soap operas and talent shows. We have some wonderful writers who craft the scripts to the new medium. I could go on and on about the actors, directors, sound people, too, but I won't. I'll just say 'thanks' for appreciating what we do. And the program even gave me the opportunity to work with Claude Rains, in a show to raise funds for British war relief."

"Ah yes. I remember that broadcast!" Nigel Cross's eyes actually lit up. "Tell me, Jessica, did Rose let slip that I adore Mr. Rains?"

Jessica glanced at her friend and brightly answered, "No. Maybe I should have led with that tidbit! I'm so pleased that you recall that show."

"I was most impressed with one dramatic pause you played after his character threatened you."

"That wasn't acting. He scared me silly. The man is intense. The only thing that brought me back was that I was more terrified of what our director would do to me if I left them with any more dead air!"

That seemed to relax them all, and the talk continued. Still, the mention of James started Jessica wondering where her husband had gotten to. She hardly wanted him on a leash, but she definitely needed to sit down with him and compare notes, particularly about Terry and Carolina.

Nigel Cross mentioned last seeing James when the conversation of the group they were with had skewed toward a sensational murder by a group of young punks, who were also vets. Nigel remarked that he'd had his fill of war back in 1915, and Jess remembered that Rose had once mentioned he'd been a POW. He added that he'd noticed James had seemed inclined to stay, almost compelled. So, Nigel had left her husband there.

That information gave Jessica a quiver of concern, so she made her goodbyes to search out her guy. Though not before she'd promised to think over Nigel's proposal and give him an answer within two weeks.

How good was it for James to be on the outside looking in on others' views of the war's atrocities? It would have been one thing if he could have spoken of his own experiences, gotten it off his chest, but he was still under orders to keep his role under wraps. Worse, his cover story of being 4-F, or whatever the British equivalent was, left people thinking he'd sat out the war in a cozy classroom. He not only had to suppress the shards of his memories but deal with the disparagement, subtle and not so subtle, of exactly the people who truly ought to understand his own little personal hell. And Jessica couldn't see him anywhere right now.

She had wandered into one of the seminar rooms, moonlight washing pure the white plaster walls, setting in stark, ominous contrast the tall, dark wainscoting and Medieval and Renaissance carven figures and faces now seeming to sneer at her from the ornate mantel piece. Standing by the long, heavy dark-wood seminar table, Jess was almost glad not to find James in this room of grotesque mockers if he were in the mood she suspected.

Maybe she was making a mountain out of a mole hill. James had toughed out pursuit by Nazis, aided saboteurs, and rescued downed flyers. Maybe only her imagination turned this room into a haunted carnival. It was just that she was seldom sure when James's demons would surface. Now that he wasn't on the run. Now that the adrenaline had stopped turbo-charging his heart, and he had a chance to remember, to think about what he remembered, that's when the trouble set in. He tried to hide it from her most of the time, protect her—or himself—from what she might think of him if she knew too much.

A curl of smoke drifted up into the night within the circling hedges in the garden beyond the bay window before her. Jessica crossed the room, stopping at the window, her fingertips softly resting on the pane, as if gently trying to bring James back to her. If a person were sitting within the mini-labyrinth, you couldn't see him; but Jessica's heart told her who brooded there. Yet even as she turned to leave the room and join her husband, she paused, a little afraid. Not of James, of course, but of her own inadequacy.

How could she understand what he'd seen and done? What could she possibly say or do that would matter? She was only an actress who'd been safe and sound in the U.S. throughout the war—mostly. But she knew that the gambit with the package, the adventure in San Francisco, were like rides on Coney Island compared to James Crawford's war years. Nevertheless, Jess knew that she couldn't, she wouldn't abandon her husband to his darker thoughts. Even if he sent her away, she had to let him know she'd come when he wanted her.

Leaving the room, moving back out into the great hall to take the side entrance to the garden, Jessica was vaguely aware of Carolina Brent Clarke giving her the once-over behind her smile. *What bright, Max Factor lips you have, Grandma!* fleeted through Jess's mind. But bigger concerns commandeered her thoughts.

Smoking and thinking in the light that floated in from the terrace, he didn't seem to notice her. Sitting in the heart of the labyrinth, he leaned forward, forearms on his thighs, a position so typical when something was eating him. The lantern light washed his face pale, seeming even paler in contrast with his dark mustache and hair ruffled by the breeze that had sprung up. Not so distant, a buoy clanged. Jess could feel her flowered cap's veil wavering in the salty air from the ocean pounding beyond the hedges, the lawn, the stone wall. How did those lines from Matthew Arnold go?

James quoted to her without looking up, "'A melancholy, long withdrawing roar,/ Retreating, to the breath/ Of the night wind, down the vast edges drear/ And naked shingle of the world.'"

Sometimes when he read her mind like that it almost gave her the willies. But Jess only commented, "That bad? What a pity. I thought things started off rather well tonight."

James tossed away the cigarette, unfinished—whether in unhappiness or in deference to her sensitivity to too much smoke, Jessica couldn't tell. Then he faced her, his features wry, sardonic, and brooding all at once. He said, "You ought to have your head examined for marrying a bloke like me."

His tone was tired, even weary, but she also knew he was hoping she'd contradict him.

Jessica aimed to please.

"What's not to love?" she gestured extravagantly as she spoke. "A guy who can quote Arnold at the drop of a hat. Handsome as all get out—and you annoy the hell out of my big sister. Dusty would never have forgiven me if I'd let you get away."

The hint of a smile played on his lips, even if his eyes still held some darkness. He looked away but gestured to a space beside him on the stone bench.

Jess wasn't quite sure what predominated: relief at his drawing her in or uneasiness at what he might let her in for. Regardless, she took the place next to him and only with great difficulty kept herself from taking his hand sympathetically. Only when he was ready.

James didn't look at Jess when he started, "We were talking, Cross and I, and joined some chaps. Conversation took a turn toward war and he vanished. I should have, too. It's an untenable position that back story of mine puts me in, but there you are. And I couldn't keep away, even to hear that someone else knows what I've been through. Anyway, it was a sensational story. Some young thugs ganged up and murdered one chap, then the next day killed another and raped his girlfriend. There was some chatter about war destroying a man, which I know far too well. Then some Prof from Chemistry, I think, said something I'd seen more than once: war doesn't make a hero out of a punk. If you go in a hooligan, nine times out of ten you come out a hooligan, with better killing skills."

"There's something you don't see on recruiting posters," Jessica remarked.

James's mouth twisted upward, but the expression was pretty much mirthless, leaving Jess unsure if she'd sounded too flip.

He went on, "The trouble is, Jessica, maybe he's right as far as those bastards in the news story go. But that shouldn't give anyone an excuse to dismiss the decent guy who's seen and done more than any man should if he wants to stay human. And I can't say a damned thing without sounding like some bloody armchair warrior. But I came close, damn close, and that really scared me. Maybe I can't hide who I've been any longer. Maybe I'm too tired; I've lost my edge."

"But you aren't involved in actual espionage anymore," Jessica protested. "Why do you need an edge?"

James hesitated, then made a decision. Whether it showed his "edge" still working, Jessica couldn't say.

"It's not just a case of efficacy on the job. The war may be over, but no one knows what else lies over the horizon. Methods, contacts, whatall, too much knowledge that I could have to put back into practice. I've only told you this much because you've already been involved to some extent."

Fear knifed through her, and Jessica blurted, "James, are they going to, um, 'reactivate' you, send you off against the Soviets?"

This time, James's smile was *almost* untinged with irony, and he took one of her hands, squeezed it, to say, "Now, love, how much Russian do I speak? What do I know about the nooks and crannies of Mother Russia? The reasons I was recruited during the war was that I learned to speak French like a native from my mum and I'd traveled all over the country while at university. I admit, I might be able to pick out a few Nazi occupiers, but it's the French background that made me valuable. So, unless de Gaulle sells out to the Russians, I'm off the hook on overseas duty."

Jessica smiled down at James's hand holding hers. Finally, she said, "It can't be easy, I know, never entirely free to be yourself. And I'm probably not much help. What do I know, what could I possibly say, to help, to take away what's eating you?"

James's other hand turned Jessica's face to him, and he said quietly, "You don't have to say anything."

The kiss he shared with her made Jess feel as if, for that moment, they were together alone, almost beyond the rest of the world. Their foreheads were now pressed close, their hands entwined. If only this moment in the lantern light could last forever. The pettiness, doubts, and concerns that had plagued Jessica that day sank away into the oblivion of insignificance.

Chapter Six

Sunday, Next Day

The kitchen in the cottage was smaller than the one in Jess's apartment. Well, that only meant she didn't have as far to go when she bustled about putting together a hearty breakfast for James. Jess had been up early and left him sleeping, finally. James wasn't the only one who'd spent a restless night, though. While he'd tossed all night, she'd stared at the stars through the windows across from the bed, wondering how to navigate the reefs of school politics. No, not reefs: two large, spherical, spikey, black water mines, with Terry's and Carolina Clarke's faces. She hadn't given Nigel Cross a definite answer, yet. She could still say, "No." But did she want to? She liked teaching, and the thought that lending Nigel a hand might help James was a powerful incentive. Equally powerful was the realization that she didn't like to think Carolina and Terry could scare her off. On the other hand, *did* she want to poke her head into what might be a hornets' nest? And *could* she be certain the Clarkes wouldn't make waves for James? Maybe Nigel had promised support, but he wasn't the final word. She knew all too well from Rose that administrators and trustees had a lot of power, and that the Clarkes had influence. Would that she could have sat down and talked this over with James last night. That was their normal m.o. when troubles arose, but his restlessness had signaled that then wasn't the time.

James had finally drifted off. Unfortunately for Jess, his drifting off involved his sawing wood to shake the rafters, until she literally took matters into her own hands and shoved him over on his side. That wasn't adding to his worries, just shifting his position. At last, she'd been able to get a little shut-eye. Now, it was a new day, with time to talk things out after breakfast.

Jess stopped to survey the table she'd set for two. Toast with steak and eggs set out on Blue Willow china. Thank goodness she'd given Rose some money to fill the larder the day before they arrived. Milk in the creamer and coffee perking on the stove. She'd have to call James in a little bit; he wanted to continue working on his class preps today. So she'd let him sleep until 9:00 if he didn't bestir himself sooner.

Untying and removing the full apron she'd worn over her white, short-sleeved sweater and black and white hounds-tooth checked slacks, Jess tried to figure out what she'd forgotten. Tugging pensively on the edge of the black snood encompassing her dark hair, she felt that something seemed to be missing. Of course, flowers! Wouldn't the perfect homey touch for the first meal she'd made them here be a bunch of sea roses from their garden–even a lovely reminder of James's mother's tradition?

Taking up a pair of scissors, a mat to kneel on, and sunglasses against the startling seaside morning sun, Jessica left the kitchen to move through the garden. The salty air stirred the taller flowers into swaying and bowing greetings to her, but predominating was the sweet scent from peony bushes; lilies of the valley; and the roses near the road. The rose bushes were laden with blossoms: deep, velvety red; pale pink, almost white; and softly pure white. Putting down her mat, Jess knelt and began clipping flowers for her table, only to hesitate at the bush of white sea roses.

"Hmm, why do the icky insects all seem to prefer vanilla?"

She carefully pulled apart branches on the bush to discover the least nibbled or infested blossoms. Nothing killed the appetite like a pincer bug meandering past your steak and eggs–unless he meandered *across* them.

"Ah ha!" Jess pronounced triumphantly, finally finding an untouched cluster of white sea roses. She was too intent on clipping her prize to hear the crunch of gravel beneath approaching feet.

"Well, well, it looks as if Rosalind is back in the pastoral realm."

Jessica didn't look up immediately. For a split second, she couldn't move, except for the slight trembling of her hand holding the roses. Too much rushed through her brain on instantly recognizing the subtle honey of a West Virginia drawl. Absurdly, the last thought to settle in her head was a long-buried recollection of how much Terry Clarke sounded like Vincent Price.

Jessica's eyes went up, way up. Terry Clarke was a long, cool drink of water, easily 6'4". *How had they ever danced? Hugged?* The expression in his eyes, clear blue crystal, still seemed to lie in the no-man's-land between mischievous and sarcastic. Trying to read them was always like trying to figure out exactly where seemingly solid ice would crack and plunge you into dark waters. *Oh for Pete's sake! Stop being so melodramatic. He's an old boyfriend, not Count Dracula.* Still, Jess was glad sunglasses hid her eyes.

Jessica was on her feet with the tactful, "It's been a long time."
Gee, that was original.

Terry Clarke smiled his trademark long, slow, knowing smile. She'd almost forgotten that. Yes, he was just as aware as she how trite her response was. Well, what did he expect this early in the morning, Noel Coward?

"I'll be frank, Jessie. I didn't think you'd be too happy to see me."

That sounded like an invitation to get loads off her chest. Except, Terry Clarke's tone hadn't been conciliatory, even apologetic. It was, actually, a little smug. Yep, Terry Clarke was a good-looking guy, but he was smug. *He'd* be damned before she admitted to him that he'd hurt her way back when. But, and this only sank in now, she *didn't* need to give him a piece of her mind. She could, and did, honestly reply, "Really, Terry, you're talking about ancient history. To tell you the truth, I'm too busy to hold a grudge over something that happened that long ago. You weren't worried, were you?"

Terry looked downright surprised. Apparently, nonchalance was the last thing he expected from a former girlfriend. But that chink in his poise was only momentary. He took a different tact, saying, "Not at all. We were just kids. How could anyone take puppy love seriously?"

"Couldn't agree with you more," Jessica smiled, but thought, *You were never any puppy, you wolf.* Instead, she elected to kill him with kindness, continuing, "So, I understand from Rose that you're having loads of success with your book. I haven't read . . ."

"As a matter of fact, yes," Terry interrupted. "I've been lecturing around the Northeast. That's why I couldn't make the reception last night. I was at Yale. I definitely believe I made the right choice to put aside that acting bug for the academy. So much more rewarding, intellectually stimulating. I don't know if you can understand that, Jessie."

Jessica refused to take the bait, instead observing pleasantly, "That's a funny thing for you to say, Terry. I mean, with your doing a course on Shakespeare on the stage and in the text, the way you use performance to teach, it looks to me that you haven't put aside the acting bug at all."

That charming smile of his was followed by, "You're wiser than you know, Jessie. Thank you for pointing out how I've found a way to create the best from both worlds. But what about you? Is performing on the radio enough now that you haven't been on the stage for a while? Don't you miss the intellectual stimulation we enjoyed when we were in college? You were so bright and funny in the classroom."

"I'm bright and funny everywhere, Terry. Just ask my husband," Jessica volleyed easily. This was also the Terry Clarke she remembered; the part she didn't like.

"Ah yes, James Crawford. Nigel Cross's new special discovery. Well, who knows, Jessie, perhaps if I do make the jump to Yale, there'll be a spot for your husband in these little halls of learning—maybe even for you. I heard that you were working towards a master's degree, finally. That's nice."

Of course, he left unsaid that he was one of the elite new breed with a Ph.D. They both knew it—and he knew she knew it. He used to pull this kind of little trick back in their college days: you either got the dig and squirmed or you didn't, and he enjoyed laughing up his sleeve at you. He'd only tried it once on her back in the old days and she'd quashed it. She'd never liked it when he did it to others. Was that how far she'd fallen in his eyes, thinking he could pull that malarkey on her now? Well, she wasn't about to play his game and simply changed the subject.

"I met your wife Carolina last night."

"Did you? Of course, at the reception," his eyes were speculative, but Jess wasn't sure what he was thinking. Hoping she was jealous? Hoping she wouldn't comment on what a live grenade he was wedded to?

Terry finally pointed out, "She's quite a woman. Brilliant, creative . . ."

"And beautiful," Jessica finished, stealing his thunder, while dismissing any possibility of jealousy on her part.

"You do think so?" Terry smiled. Again, Jessica wasn't sure what that smile meant. He continued, "Some people can be intimidated by a woman with brains and beauty."

"I know that for a fact," Jessica parried. "Oh, but you meant your wife. Relax, Terry; I didn't find her intimidating in the least."

Jess couldn't help pleasantly tossing off that quiet little zinger. For heaven's sake, she was only human. As for Terry, his smile tightened a trace, unable to completely hide that he'd taken a hit.

Still, he wasn't about to fold. But Jess didn't really want to make him. She just wanted to nip a bad attitude in the bud and not give him any excuse to make trouble for James. Anyway, why should *he* be acting as if he had an ax to grind?

Cutting to the chase, Jessica proposed, "Terry, let's put our cards on the table. You're trying to get under my skin and there's no reason for it. What is your beef with me?"

"Jessie, there you are—as forthright as ever. I don't know how you expect to survive here if you don't learn to play politics, be more subtle."

He was smooth now, trying to divert her, even put her on the spot. No dice, as far as Jessica was concerned.

"Terry, I learned politics from Harry Truman. The buck stops here. Come clean with me. Petty sarcasm isn't becoming to you."

"My, my, the kitten has teeth. I don't remember you being quite *this* feisty."

"Then your memory needs a good jogging. Is that what's ruffling your feathers? You're remembering that I left you behind?"

Jessica's tone was calm but not superior. However, Terry clearly didn't like what she had to say. He answered coldly, "Lay our cards on the table and be direct? By all means, then. This isn't the place for you. You have your world, out there in acting. You're not dedicated to scholarship like me. You and your husband can't just waltz in here and take over . . ."

His voice trailed off, as if he'd realized he'd given away too much. The blue eyes glared at Jess in a way she'd never seen before.

Taking a moment to overcome her surprise, Jessica questioned, "Terry, what in Sam Hill are you talking about? Take over what?"

"'Take over what?' Don't play innocent with me, Jessica. Nigel Cross had a talk with me this morning. I ran into him when I stopped by my office. First, they bring your husband in, then Nigel tells me you'll be taking over my summer class. The two of you think you can undercut me in the classroom, even in the department. With your friend Rose, you'd like to form a nice little bloc against me."

"What?!" Jessica's eyes almost popped out of her head. She stared at Terry. Yes, there was the same wavy brown hair, the well-shaped long, square jaw, the piercing blue eyes, but the fierceness in those eyes, the cruel sarcasm souring what had once been devilish humor proved to her that he was far different from the young fellow she'd been smitten with years ago. The Terry she'd known hadn't been perfect, but never this defensive, angry cynic. She found her voice again: "Are you kidding me? Where are you getting these half-baked ideas? Have you been spending so much time teaching the Renaissance that you're beginning to think like a Machiavellian?"

"I see. So you're trying to tell me that you and Rose and Nigel didn't cook up a little plot to steal my summer class out from under me?"

Jessica realized that for everybody's sakes she'd better straighten Terry out, let him see all he had was a will o' wisp of angry imaginings.

"Now you listen to me, Terry Clarke, all I was offered was an opportunity to take over a few classes when you were out of town with your book lectures. I'm just pinch-hitting. That hardly makes this *The Tempest* and me casting you off in a 'leaky bark' so that I can take over Milan." Then, thinking a minute, Jess added, "Anyway, I thought you were planning to fly the coop for headier intellectual climes."

Oddly enough, Terry flinched at her last comment. However, he didn't offer any clues as to why when he warned, "Just don't get too high on yourself or this place. You and your husband may not be the fair-haired children you think."

Jess had no idea what that comment meant, but before she could question Terry further (or at least point out that she and James were actually both brunettes), he smiled sardonically, looking past her toward the house, and observed, "Speak of the wolf and who walks in."

Brow furrowed, Jessica turned around and sighted James sauntering up through the garden. The knot in her brain from contending with Terry Clarke unraveled. *Here comes the cavalry!*

James raised a hand in greeting, offered an affable, "Good morning," to them both, but she could also see, whether Terry could or not, something speculative in his eyes. Terry was being sized up.

She couldn't help a quick glance at Terry, who momentarily revealed uneasiness before masking it with one of his most charming smiles and a friendly nod in greeting.

"Up at last?" Jessica teased, as James joined them, his arm sliding over her shoulder, giving it a squeeze as her own arm slipped around his waist.

"James Crawford," he introduced himself, extending a hand, which Terry took quickly enough, offering his own name along with it.

"I'm sorry," Jess joined in. "I should have made the introductions. I guess I'll have to give back that charm school diploma."

"Nonsense," James kidded. "You're charming enough for me. So, Terry," his attention startling Clarke a little. "You're an old friend of Jessica's. She's told me so much about you. And you and I will be colleagues this summer. I don't suppose I'll see much of you, with your lectures and all that. Don't worry; I'm sure we can all hold down the fort, while you let the Ivies in on some first-rate intellectual illumination. Perhaps one day you might try and dazzle some of my old Oxbridge cohorts."

If Terry hadn't been asking for it, Jessica would have felt sorry for his disquiet at being unable to read her husband. James had the sweetest, friendliest smile, the most affable of tones, but Jess could see from that flicker in Terry's eyes, the calculation before he spoke, his brief stroke of that Elizabethan beard, that James's words left him worrying precisely what Jessica had said about him—and was that some kind of slight, James bringing up *his* Oxbridge background?

Terry managed a politic, "Of course, we've all heard fine things about you, sir."

"James, call me James, Terry. We're all very matey, aren't we?"

"It makes life smoother when we are," Terry agreed, now back in form, turning on the old charm. "I'm sorry I missed you last night at the reception. When I was talking to Nigel this morning, he said he was quite impressed with you, James. Here's hoping you live up to his high standards. He can be a heart-breaker."

"A chap can only do his best," James replied easily, ignoring Terry's implied challenge.

"Your best is pretty darn good," Jessica interjected, "and don't you forget it."

But Terry unexpectedly interrupted Jess and James's camaraderie with, "I think you should know, if you don't already, that Nigel hopes Jessica will be my assistant for a summer session. Two old college pals back together. We'll be sharing Shakespeare as it's played and as it's read, how the theatre of the mind and the stage interact and diverge. You know your wife and I played together quite a bit in college. She was Rosalind to my Orlando."

Jessica had an uneasy feeling about where this was going, until James responded, "Oh, in college, yes? You must know that she played Rosalind on the professional stage, in New York. I saw her; of course, it was before we officially met. I think I fell in love with her then and didn't know it. Too bad you didn't get to see her then. But it's lovely that you trained with her, way back when. Did he do a nice job, love?"

"We both got good reviews," Jessica answered noncommittally. James was doing just fine neutralizing Terry without any help from her. She could tell that by how Terry's smile had hardened.

"Right, then," James said. "School paper, was it? So, Terry, I know you're enjoying this lovely Monday morning before your holiday."

"*My* holiday?" Terry puzzled.

"Where I come from, July Fourth is hardly a great day for celebration," James smiled before affably dismissing the other man, "So, we'll be seeing you around campus, I'm sure." Hand extended. "Splendid to meet you, Terry. Don't let us keep you."

Shaking hands, Terry's expression vaguely seemed to hint an appreciation of how deftly he'd been given the brush. Yet before leaving, he turned to Jessica and put to her, "I hope you consider what I said about our working together."

Her former beau's earlier hostility flooded back on Jessica in such a rush that she couldn't answer for a moment. James, observing, squeezed her shoulder and stepped in: "Jessica's the sort to mull things over. I think we both know her decisions are solid. Again, don't let us keep you, Terry."

Terry's smile was of the Mona Lisa variety. Then he was striding off down the road.

Jess's eyes followed the tall, lanky figure, her thoughts troubled. She felt another squeeze of her shoulder and looked up at James.

"Charming fellow," her husband commented.

Jessica shook her head while watching Terry head down the road, then looked up at James again and explained, "He *really* doesn't want me to work with him on this class. You wouldn't believe it, but he talked as if I were plotting to do him out of his job. Who needs that kind of hostility?" She paused before continuing, "But, I just, well this teaching gig did sound really interesting, blending literature and the stage. You know how much I enjoyed working with Rose, but Terry . . . Still, truth be told, I just loathe that he might think he could scare me off."

"Jessica, I know you can do whatever you set your mind to. Just be sure you're setting your mind to something you truly want, that you're not just trying to prove a point."

"I know, I know. You're right. I just need to think a little more."

"When will you have to tell Nigel?"

"Well, he's going away the 6th and 7th. So, by the time he gets back."

"All right. That's a nice bit of time but take my advice and don't drag it out. I'd hate to see you brooding for days when you only need to brood an hour."

Jess smiled, and James continued, "Would it make you feel better if I disabled him for you? Nothing fatal, nothing that shows—just painful enough to set a chap thinking."

"I thought you were supposed to be semi-retired, or at least keeping your special talents under wraps?"

"Yes, of course, but it's a shame to let all that training in hand-to-hand go to waste. And a chap needs to stay in practice, just in case."

"Just aren't enough Nazis left to grapple with anymore, eh?" Jessica surmised sympathetically.

"You might say that."

"Well, I don't think I'll need to take you up on that kind offer, Mr. Crawford. But I do appreciate the thought," she smiled. Jess looked off after Terry Clarke, then shook her head and turned back to James to say, "I just wish I knew what's eating him. He seemed so antagonistic, angry, towards me. He was never like that before. Why should he have been so paranoid, almost, about me helping with the course?"

James shrugged, before suggesting, "Maybe he realized what he was missing."

"My ego thanks you, kind sir, but I don't think so. That's not the impression I got. He said Nigel Cross told him about me only this morning. But why should that threaten him? Do you think Cross put it to him as if he were using me as a Dane Clark to his Humphrey Bogart?"

That analogy evoked a truly quizzical expression from James.

"Oh, okay, it's like this," Jessica elaborated. "They say that Warner Brothers hired Dane Clark so they could trot him out as a threat any time Bogie got difficult."

"Did it work?"

"Not really."

"Then, I think you're wrong about Nigel Cross. From what I've seen of him, I'd say he's a fellow who knows how to win a chess match. He wouldn't use a club. And I have to say that if he ever did try to use you as a pawn, it would put me off staying here."

"Oh, I don't think that," Jess responded quickly. "I would never have brought any of this up if I'd thought you'd feel as if you had to choose between me and the position. No, let's skip it. I'm not going to be working with Terry. It's all moot now."

James studied Jess, trying to be certain her heart was in her words. Finally, he said, "As long as that's the way you want it. Say, what are you doing out here, anyway? Especially when I can still smell that steak and eggs and coffee back in the kitchen. Aren't you starving?"

"Oh! My roses!" Jess burst out, remembering her original mission. While James again found himself looking quizzical, Jess knelt down by her clippings and gathered them up, saying, "I wanted a floral centerpiece for our first breakfast here. I know you love roses; they remind you of your Mom's trying to make your home nice. I thought it would be the perfect way to make the cottage seem like home to you. I really want you to be happy here."

James was kneeling, helping her with the roses, meeting her eyes with his smiling eyes, then kissing her.

As they both got up, he decided, "You're a good scout, you."

Jess smiled up at his brown, green-flecked eyes and opined, "You're not so bad yourself, mister. And thanks for giving Terry a little verbal kick in the pants."

"My pleasure—not that I doubt for a minute that you can't take care of yourself. Allies have to stick together." Then, with a bit of the devil in his tone, he finished: "I also know your temper, so I thought I'd better get out here before you gave him a poke in that pseudo-Elizabethan beard of his."

"Oh, yes, the fringe on his chin," Jess chuckled. "It is not flattering, if you ask me. He looked much better back when I knew him clean-shaven . . . Oh, my gosh. I *did* see him yesterday!"

"Yesterday?"

"Yes, across the street from us when we were at the station. You were getting our books off the train. Rose and David didn't believe me. They said he was out of town. You came in on the tail end of our conversation."

"All right, but what's this sudden brain wave about a beard? Why so excited?"

"I'm excited because I didn't imagine something—and the deal with the beard is that the last time I saw Terry he was clean-shaven. If I imagined seeing him yesterday, I wouldn't have pictured him with a beard I'd never seen before," she explained, pleased with herself.

"So, he lied about when he got into town," James mused. "Do you really care if he has a secret life?"

"No, of course not. I . . . A secret life? What kind of secret life? Maybe it has something to do with that tall, creepy bald guy with the hawklike face. Hmm."

"What creepy chap?" James was curious now. "Bald and predatory looking?"

"Yes, yes. He was definitely predatory-looking—that's a much better description than creepy. Come to think of it, he wasn't so much bald as shaven-head, headed. His head was shaved. They were standing in the doorway of the antique store. Kind of lurking."

"Lurking?"

"Lurking."

James thought a moment, then shrugged and said, "Again, I don't see anything to get excited about. So, you saw Terry Clarke? Being at an antique shop on a Sunday is no crime. It's not as if you saw him and his mate fleeing a bank with guns and bags of money in hand. And so he lied about his whereabouts. What's it to us? Do you really care?"

Jess decided, "No I suppose not. It's just that you know I can't resist unraveling a mystery."

"That's done so well for you in the past," James observed dryly.

"It got me you, handsome," Jess outplayed her husband.

James threw up his hands and relented, "You win! But seriously, Jessica, you've been saying this Terry chap is bad news. Do you really want to tangle yourself up in his misadventures just out of curiosity? Stay out of this one. And be careful not to drag Rose in by telling her what you just figured out. Take it from a man who's had more than his share of politics in academia."

"Okay," Jess agreed. "I'm intrigued, but I don't believe in poking a hornets' nest with a stick."

"Or with *anything* for that matter," James added. "Now, let's tuck into that breakfast before it gets cold."

"You're darned tootin'! I didn't slave over a hot stove for nothing!"

James took her hand, and they headed back to the cottage through warm seaside sunshine, talking about their plans for the day: his class prep, her jaunt around campus with Rose. Thoughts of Terry's mysterious antique store visitation and this morning's hostility were almost completely forgotten. Almost.

Chapter Seven

Same Day

The white-tiled and painted kitchen of Cameron House was brilliant with the July sunshine streaming through windows facing the glittering sea. Rose had brought Jessica there for a quick lunch on the prior evening's leftovers before picking up some papers in her office and taking her friend to visit her favorite horses in the stable. At a table just left of the doorway were the two students Jessica had met last night. The girls looked up, surprised then delighted, to see Jessica and Rose. Both ladies were dressed for comfort, with Jess having slipped into a cooler soft pink silk blouse and deep rose slacks and Rose in a pale yellow cotton blouse and chocolate brown trousers.

"Hi there, Professor Nyquist!" chirped Lauren.

"You brought your friend. Great!" welcomed Alicia.

Rose questioned in mock sternness, "Don't they feed you kids in the dining hall? Isn't this place off-limits to students now? Not that I plan on turning you in."

"It's copacetic," Lauren assured Rose. "We have permission."

"Oh?" Rose queried, strolling over to the refrigerator across from Jess, who took off her sun hat and hung it on a peg in the mudroom behind her.

"Sure," Alicia answered. "We were helping Professor Clarke. He had us making handouts for his class."

Rose asked casually, "So the good Professor is in the building?"

Jess was annoyed with herself for hanging a bit on their answer, but she really preferred not to run into Terry so soon after their unpleasant interchange.

Digging into her potato salad, Alicia replied, "No. He left us to finish up."

"He had an appointment in town," Lauren elaborated. "He does that a lot, goes into town. I don't think he likes it on campus."

"He's a brilliant man, Lauren," Alicia patiently explained. "It's boring here for him. He needs intellectual stimulation."

"In Margaret Point? Intellectual stimulation?" Lauren snorted.

"It's not the hind end of Siberia," Rose pointed out, amused. "And we've got one or two good minds here on campus."

"I think he likes to 'get away from' more than 'go to' something," Lauren clarified, "especially now that his wife is on campus more."

"Lauren," Rose warned. "Didn't I talk to you about making innuendos last night? I'd hate to think the trust and responsibility that the faculty has given you has bred the contempt of familiarity."

Jessica was decidedly silent through all this. She felt sorry for Lauren, but she knew better than to undermine Rose's warning about shooting off your mouth without considering the consequences for others—or yourself. She was actually a bit sorry for Terry. Even if she was humanly curious about Lauren's implications concerning his marriage, it was sad his personal life had become fodder for gossip. From what she'd seen of Carolina Brent Clarke, she was sure he'd have to pay for any humiliation he caused her. What a mess his life must have become. Maybe she could be a little more charitable about his attitude toward her, but only a little.

Alicia's voice broke into Jessica's thoughts: "Honestly, Lauren. You ought to have your head examined. Have some respect, some propriety, before you talk yourself out of your assistantship. And think how you must make Miss Minton feel. Remember, Professor Nyquist told us that she and Professor Clarke were friends in college. Right, Miss Minton?"

Jessica only nodded, deciding to give that topic short shrift. She wasn't about to let herself get sucked into the whirlpool of rumors swirling about Terry. Lauren had other ideas.

"That's right!" the girl nodded emphatically. "Tell us, Miss Minton, what was he like to act with? He's wonderful in the classroom, when he performs all the parts for us. I can't wait for his class next week to start."

"That's *if* it runs," Alicia tossed cold water on her friend.

"Oh, that's right," Lauren frowned. Turning to Jessica, she suggested hopefully, "But maybe there's a chance you might fill in for him, or work with him, like we talked about last night. It would be a crying shame for all the girls if we had to give up that class."

"I thought we covered this topic last night, too?" Rose warned.

The kid looked so crestfallen that Jessica couldn't help trying to save her face. Leaning against the door frame, she said, "No pressure, Lauren? I'll tell you what. It's really not kosher for me to say anything to you before I straighten things out with the Chair. Besides, Professor Clarke might not want someone else involved in his course."

Was that tactful enough? To tell the truth, thinking about the spot the kids would be in if Terry's class didn't run kind of took the edge off her reluctance to work with him. Still, if he didn't want her, the whole situation was out of the question. Yet she couldn't come right out and tell the kids Terry would probably only let her in his classroom over his dead body–no, he'd prefer it be over hers.

Alicia seemed to mull over Jessica's words before settling the question with, "You know she's right, Lauren. You can be such a chowder head about shooting off your mouth at times. Anyway, we'll still have the class with her husband, Professor Crawford. I can't wait for that. You know Miss Minton, I read your husband's article on Keats in the *Nichols University Review*. It gave me loads to think about. He's quite a smart guy, isn't he?"

"I like to think so," Jessica beamed, "but then, I'm prejudiced."

Both girls grinned, and all four were soon settled down at the kitchen table for a feast of leftovers. To Jessica's relief, the conversation meandered from movies to life in New York to working in radio to the best places for riding, walking, and swimming on campus. At one point, the conversation drifted onto the existence of an off-limits "haunted" wreck, cast up on shore a year or so ago during a violent storm, more than a mile down the beach. Lauren and Alicia both lamented that the harsh punishment Coast Guard patrols, on the alert for saboteur landings, had meted out to anyone daring to trespass had left both town and gown afraid for some time now of risking getting caught there. Anyway, they'd related, most people knew much better places to gather firewood, indulge in beach parties, or just plain poke around than a spot with a steep, rugged rock perimeter strung with barbed wire and implacable guardians.

Finishing lunch first, Alicia and Lauren made to clean up, but Rose told them: "Don't worry, kids. We'll take care of the dishes. We're going to be the last ones here, anyhow. Go on. Get out of here."

"We can't let you do that," Alicia protested.

"Yes, you can," Rose insisted. Jess suspected her friend felt a little bad about coming down so hard on Lauren earlier. *The old softie.*

"Don't look a gift horse in the mouth," Jess advised with a smile. "She'll be glad to do all our dishes."

"Not so fast, smart guy," Rose shot back. "I was talking about both of us, and you know it."

"Oh well, there goes my manicure," Jess conceded, holding up her lacquered nails.

"Jeepers, that's a hot color!" Lauren blurted out. "Where can I get some of that?"

"Down, tigress," Alicia patted her friend's shoulder. "That's just for the big girls. Not until you're ready to vote." Turning back to Rose and Jessica, she finished, "Thanks a bunch."

After the girls left, Jessica concluded, "They seem like bright kids, nice kids."

"Mmm," Rose agreed, scraping up the last of her potato salad. "They are. Lauren's a little too effusive; I think you saw. She sees a lot, discerns a lot, but doesn't always know when to keep it to herself. She's not malicious, just . . ."

"Over eager?"

"Nicely put."

Jess noted, "I could see that Alicia seemed more in charge. Have they been friends for a long time?"

Rose nodded, gathering up the plates while explaining, "Since they started here. They latched onto each other right at freshman orientation and have been a dynamic duo ever since."

"I think that Lauren is lucky to have Alicia to steady her," Jess concluded.

"And vice versa," Rose said. "Alicia came here a little bit in a shell, a little too distant. Her parents died when she was ten–tragically. The mother was killed in a car crash and the father committed suicide afterward. The kid was raised by an aunt and uncle. One of the reasons she's here is that her father left her a legacy to study at Margaret Point– not that she doesn't belong. Lauren understood her because she was adopted when she was quite young. Anyway, Lauren's good nature and genuineness brought Alicia out of her shell."

"So, they complement each other perfectly," Jessica summed up. Then she added, "Still, that's a lot of grief for anyone so young to bear. Makes me realize how lucky I've been."

"I just wish they didn't pick up so much gossip," Rose considered. "And between you, me, and the lamp post," she lowered her voice, "I'd prefer they spent less time with Terry."

Jessica raised her brows and began carefully, "Rose, I can't believe you're implying . . . I can't believe Terry would . . . well, you know . . ."

Rose looked out the windows facing the ocean, gathering her words carefully before clarifying, "I'm not saying there's any funny business going on, not really. But I do think that Terry thrives a little too much on the adoration of his students. It's not healthy, the hero worship he encourages. I'm just afraid that one day someone is going to take him too seriously. He's not popular amongst the faculty, so an overly protective kid could get herself in hot water if she went to bat for him too vociferously. Or she might exhibit her devotion a little too noticeably to suit Carolina or one of the deans. Either way, it would be a real mess for her. Terry would go unscathed by playing innocent victim and leave her out on a limb."

Rose turned back and surprised Jessica with, "That's why now I think it wouldn't be such a bad idea for you to accept Nigel's proposal."

"Honestly?"

"Look: it's not only that I think you could keep an eye out for trouble or even use your grace and wit to nip it in the bud. I really believe you might prove a nice alternative for the girls, a role model. They can see a professional woman who isn't 'wowed' by Terry's charm. Kind of like kryptonite for phony hero worship."

"Rose, that's all well and good," Jessica now picked her words carefully, "but you seem to be forgetting that Terry would give a warmer welcome to a two-by-four off the top of his head than to me coming into his class."

"Okay, I read you," Rose gave in. "Sorry. Here you are, supposed to be having a break, and I'm throwing you smack dab into the middle of a tornado. Forgive a misguided friend?"

"In a sec," Jessica smiled quietly. "But you know, I do feel bad for the kids if they miss a class they need—but not bad enough stir up trouble. It's too bad Terry has gone so sour. I'm sorry to see what's happened to him. He could have turned out so much better."

Rose smiled wanly and observed, "Stop being such an old softie. Terry made his bed with a thousand choices over the years. We all do. That's how we end up where we are."

"I guess," Jessica agreed a little sadly. Then she tapped the table with her hands and pronounced, "Enough with the tear-stained philosophy. Let's get to those dishes. I'm dying to hit the stables and see the horses again. Do you think Domino still remembers me?"

"Filch a lump of sugar from the bowl in the cabinet. He never forgets the treat, even if he gets a little sketchy about the human," Rose grinned.

8:00 That Evening

Twilight quietly descending, the sky was softening to dreamy blue-grey, with the ocean silvery. The breeze off the waters played with Jessica Minton's long, dark hair as she sat atop the wall separating the terrace of her home from the slope down to the beach. Even from this distance, she could discern sandpipers dashing at then dodging from the waves. It was good here, in this moment. It really was. No one could take that away from her.

Having James with her right now would have been especially nice, but there was a whole summer for that. He'd left a note saying that he was taking the bus into town and would grab a late one home; she needn't worry about him getting a lift. That note had been taped to the closed door of the study, so she'd see it when she looked for him at her return. He knew she'd make a beeline for him there when she got back.

James knew her so well. That made things comfortable, put her at ease—for the most part. She wished she could read James as easily. Oh, she knew the man he was inside. And sometimes unexpected revelations of his hidden talents or knowledge proved exciting, even funny, surprises. Still, there was so much that he kept hidden. Protecting her or afraid of shocking her? Six and a half dozen of the other. Maybe if James didn't think she should know, she didn't want to. Convenient? Sort of.

After all, the deeper he buried what haunted him, the longer it festered and the deeper it ate into him. Was she buying her peace of mind at his expense? Was this what other women were going through with the men they welcomed back from the war? Once the fighting was over, shouldn't the casualties stop mounting and the wounded souls start healing? If only she knew someone to talk to about this.

There was Rose, whose David had come back wounded early in the war, but Rose never talked about what it had been like four years ago. And Jessica couldn't bring herself to try to pierce her friend's silence if she didn't want to say anything. It was just so hard to figure out the right thing to do.

Jess was pulled from her concerns by the rhythm of hoof beats gradually growing louder. There, coming up the beach toward her, was the much remarked upon Sailor and his black horse. What a beautiful animal! Finely muscled, sleek with graceful action that devoured the ground and sent clods of sand flying. Mane and tail whipped bannerlike, as the horse ran with his head and neck extended like a racehorse. He must have Thoroughbred blood in him, with that tall, tight frame. Not in racing trim but still sleek and built for speed, Jess concluded.

His rider's build put the kibosh on all that racehorse imagery. He was no slim, well-muscled jockey, but tall and rangy. As horse and rider drew closer, Jessica could better see the rider's craggy features and dark hair under the officer's cap. She was too far away to read the expression in his eyes, but Jessica could see in his face a kind of release from darkness in his oneness with his horse in flight. Sometimes she saw that in James's face.

Automatically, Jess waved to them both as they moved almost directly across from her. Maybe it was silly of her. The man was probably too intent on his ride to notice. Then, his expression seemed to reveal a kind of guarded surprise, almost pleasure, and he waved back before his mount sped them past, leaving Jess to turn her head and shoulders to follow man and horse down through the surf.

"Can't leave you for a minute and you're flirting with some other chap."

Jessica just managed not to jump out of her skin at her husband's jibe out of nowhere. She emphatically straightened her spine and swiveled to face James as he covered the distance between them from the cottage. Fixing him with a mock-baleful eye that would have done Dusty proud, Jess demanded in her best Ethel Barrymore tones, "*Must* you sneak up on me and scare ten years off my life?"

"Sorry, love, force of habit, you know," he smiled.

"Well, you'll just have to remember that I'm your beloved spouse, not a Nazi or a collaborator or something."

It was good that right now the past was something they could mock.

"I'll do my best," James conceded as he came over and kissed her forehead. Sitting on the wall with her, he echoed her earlier thoughts, "It's nice here, isn't it? I had a walk about the village and a bit of a look at some of the shops. Didn't buy anything. Everything's pretty much shuttered up on a Sunday."

"How about supper?" Jess asked. "Did you grab a bite?"

"At a little diner in town. What about you?"

"I had hefty lunch in the kitchen of Cameron House with Rose and two students. I don't know if you met them, Alicia Wraxton and Lauren Fleet?"

James shook his head, so Jess added, "You will. They're in your summer course, and they're all excited about it, even before they got to see how truly charming you are. Just don't sneak up on your whole class and give them a group coronary."

"You must admit that it's a handy talent for patrolling during a test."

"Mmm hmm. Well, I've always maintained that you're a man of many talents. How about demonstrating one more of them and making us a smashing pot of tea?"

"Sounds like a good idea," James agreed with a smile, getting up, still holding her hand. Looking down at Jess in the deepening twilight, he added, "I can't tell you how much I enjoyed working on my notes today, thinking about being back in the classroom. And coming home to you. I'm glad."

"I'm glad, too, James," Jessica assured him. Then she gave him a little push and teased, "Now, go in and make us that tea, you big lug."

"What exactly *is* a lug?"

"I don't know, but it beats being called a big baboon, right?" Jessica laughed, popping to her feet.

"Unless you're another baboon."

"Are you getting personal, wise guy?"

He shrugged innocently, then sauntered into the house. Jessica sat back down on the wall, contented. She scanned the beach. The horse and rider were long gone, but the memory of that supposedly dangerous man's tentative wave lingered. It was good to know that sometimes you could drive away the darkness. Those were the times to savor. Too bad Terry Clarke didn't seem to know that.

Chapter Eight

July 3rd, Evening

It was dark, well after 9:00, and on the beach, three bonfires glowed with camaraderie as well as heat, encircled by Margaret Point College celebrants. Before one fire, by an ocean shimmering under a nearly half-moon, James Crawford played an introduction to "Shenandoah" on his clarinet, accompanied by David Nyquist's guitar. Beside James, on an overturned wooden box, Jessica sat with arms clasped around her knees, her head tilted toward her husband as he and David now harmonized over the wistfully romantic lyrics. The ocean's rhythmic wash provided soft accompaniment. To Jess, it was like drifting away to Debussy in the moonglow or reading Keats by candlelight, all on a dark, romantic summer's eve as the ocean breeze played with her hair and caressed her skin. Not running on the sharp wind of the north but wafting.

What a wonderful Eve of the Fourth celebration! Good food, good company, even cooperative weather. By now, hamburgers, hot dogs, corn on the cob, clams, and crabs had been consumed. Only the young still had the stomach space or fortitude for marshmallows toasted over the bonfires, though a few of their elders were now indulging in coffee (no alcohol with minors about!). Now was time for music.

Earlier, they'd been drawn into a calypso number by one of the Biology profs from Jamaica, Dr. Smythe. Next, all bounded through "Old Buttermilk Sky" and "Spirit of New Orleans." James had given them a French tune he'd learned from his mother, and Judy Ricardo from World

Languages had joined in. One sadistic or foolhardy soul had tried to start a round of "Mairzy Doats" but was quickly foiled by threats of being toasted with the marshmallows or dumped into Long Island Sound. That threat likely forestalled any requests for the equally excruciating "Three Little Fishies/Itty Bitty Boo."

The clarinet haunted them with a melancholy coda, solo except for the tide rushing in behind them. Silence followed the fading music, until a horn moaned out to sea.

"Perfect timing!" David pronounced to everyone's laughter.

James quietly smiled, and Jess leaned over to give him a peck on the cheek.

"Aw," teased David.

"What's next?!" blurted out Kat and Tess in unison. "When are the fireworks?"

Enjoying James's arm about her, Jess listened to the chatter around the fire over who had or hadn't brought the fireworks down to the beach. Finally, Dr. Zach Smythe lamented, "Drat! I don't think anyone did bring the fireworks. I'll check with Sam and Alphonse from facilities, the next bonfire over. Maybe someone else should do something about more firewood, too."

Meanwhile, Rose asked Jess and James, "Are you two still on for the cookout at our place tomorrow?"

"We may need someone to wheel us over after tonight," Jessica joked.

"Mom says you're making apple pie," Tess put in. Turning to James, she asked, "Does she make a tasty pie, James?"

"She bakes a beautiful pie," he solemnly answered. "Particularly if you put vanilla ice cream on it."

Before discussion of Jessica Minton Crawford's cookery could go any further, Smythe returned to inform the crowd that the pyrotechnics had been left up at Cameron House after all, and volunteers were needed to bring them to the beach.

Still in newly-wed mode, James hesitated a moment, but his ever-helpful nature triumphed, and he asked Jess, "I could stand to stretch my legs. Think you could spare me for a bit while I help, old girl?"

"'Old girl'? What am I, your grandma?" Jessica shot back with mock indignation that made Kat and Tess giggle. "Sure, go ahead, grandpa, just don't strain yourself. Remember those knees of yours aren't what they used to be."

James and David had no sooner gone, than Kat and Tess spied Lauren and Alicia at another bonfire. With the quickest of "so longs," they were off to shoot the breeze with companions closer to their own ages.

"Was it something I said?" Jess feigned perplexity.

"Face it, sister," Rose returned playfully. "You might be a big-time radio actress, but you're still from way back. You're friends with a *parent* for Pete's sake!"

Chuckling, Jess admitted, "Okay, okay. My ego's deflated, but I think I'll survive. So, since we've been temporarily abandoned by spouses and off-spring, what say you and I take a stroll down the beach–walk off some of the poundage we've acquired tonight."

Rose brightened, on the verge of agreeing, but a quick check on her daughters changed her mind. "Maybe I'd better not. Even in the moonlight, Kat looks awfully green. I need to rustle up a bromo while there's still time. You go ahead."

"Oh no, I can't leave you guys in the lurch."

"Jess, the only lurch may be Kat's tummy–and I can handle that just fine. Besides, I know how green around the gills seeing someone else's heave-ho leaves you. So, go ahead."

Jess started to protest, but Rose convinced her with, "Look, it's much easier for me to deal with just one person's tummy troubles. Anyway, remember Zach Smythe said we needed more firewood. Why don't you rustle up some on your stroll? Then you'd be making yourself useful."

"Okay, Rose," Jessica gave her friend a smile. "You don't have to twist my arm."

"Nope, all it took was a little Catholic-school guilt. Now take a hike, literally, while I see to my offspring."

Tucking her hands in the pockets of the dark pea coat she wore over her dungarees and white blouse, Jessica started down the beach away from the direction James had taken with the others. It would have been swell to have him with her, moving along just beyond the reach of the tide that raced for her before precipitously retreating in scalloped swirls.

Still, solitude in the moonlight was something to treasure, with the sands slapping under her shoes and the wind dancing off her cheek. Jess paused and turned her eyes to the stars. The war-time blackout over, ambient light dimmed the Milky Way, but she could still pick out the Big Dipper and . . ..

"Her feet are on the ground, but she can't make up her mind between the sea and the sky."

The tone was playful, almost admiring, like a mortal bemused by Ariel. The accent was not British, though. It had the hint of a West Virginia honey drawl.

Jessica whirled on Terry Clarke. What the dickens was he doing here? And why so friendly now? What was Terry up to? If it hadn't been for their last meeting, she could have smiled back at those unexpectedly gentle, bemused features. *This* was the guy she'd known ten years ago.

"Sorry, Jessie, I didn't realize I'd startle you. Once again, I'm off on the wrong foot."

"No one calls me Jessie anymore," she corrected Terry calmly. *So, he did realize he'd been out of line at their last meeting?* Jessica still didn't trust him, but she *was* curious. More important, even if she was leery of his olive branch, hitting him over the head with it wasn't exactly advisable.

"There I go, putting my foot in it again. But you can't blame me for that, getting the name wrong, Jess . . . ica. I haven't seen you since you *were* Jessie."

"Except for Sunday morning," she corrected, not hostile but not warm, either.

Terry ducked his head and smoothed down the waves of dark hair at the back of his head before admitting, "Yes, well, that's why I'm here." He hesitated, took out a pack of cigarettes and offered her one.

"Terry, you know I don't smoke," she frowned. "In fact, I'm almost allergic to smoke now."

"Oh?" Oddly enough, he seemed genuinely surprised. "Guess I'd better not, then. Sorry."

"Forget it," Jessica replied, adding, "We're outside now. Just don't let it blow in my face."

What the heck, she could afford to be gracious—and doing Terry a favor made her feel one up on him. She almost felt guilty about that smidge of cattiness. Almost.

After cupping a hand over his lighter to ignite his cigarette, Terry was careful to stand so the ocean winds blew the smoke away from them. He smiled, again sheepish, before saying, "Thanks. Calms me down."

One long drag and an exhale.

Jessica wasn't quite gracious enough not to question, "So, what's this all about, Terry? After our last encounter, I have a hard time believing you're here because you enjoy the pleasure of my company."

That sheepish look again. The cigarette came down, furling smoke by his side; he began, "Yes, well, that's why I'm here. That's why I followed you, to explain, to square things with you. Take it on the chin from you if I have to."

Terry? Admitting he was wrong? Not trying to finesse his way out of a jam by charming you into thinking that he was an innocent soul, and you were all mixed up? The temperature in hell must have just dropped precipitously.

"Excuse me," Jess questioned skeptically. "Who are you and what did you do with the Terry Clarke I knew?"

A careful draw on his cigarette and then a quiet, "The Jessica Minton I knew would have forgiven a stupid mistake, especially if a guy admitted he'd been wrong."

"That Jessica Minton stopped forgiving you and took a powder for bigger and better things," she calmly parried.

"And she was right."

Jess was glad neither a tern nor a sea gull had dropped a feather on her because it would have knocked her over.

"The old Terry Clarke wouldn't admit he'd been wrong, as I'm doing now, Jessica," he pressed earnestly. "Won't you give me a break, another chance?"

"Chance? To do what?"

Where in Sam Hill was this going? Who was this guy standing there actually seeming to level with her?

"A chance to apologize and explain what a heel I was Sunday." Another draw on the cigarette, an awkward embarrassed pause, then Terry continued: "I can't tell you how ashamed I am that I let things get to me, and I took them out on you. I gave you a raw deal just because I'd gotten some kicks in the pants that I couldn't handle. I'm really sorry for how I acted. I want a chance to square things with you."

Far too many thoughts whirled and collided in Jessica's head. This guy who'd basically tried to drive her off four days ago was now practically choking on humble pie? It was an avenger's dream. Yet a kindness in her soul wanted to reward and comfort even this hint of a good heart. Finally, skepticism predominated over all the soft soap she'd had to rinse away over years past, though her forgiving side wasn't *entirely* quashed. *What exactly was Terry Clarke up to here?*

"Aren't you going to say anything?" Terry prompted.

Jessica allowed herself a determined little sigh before finally replying, "Terry, why this conversation *now*?"

"Life, Jessica, life. I saw a lot when I was in the service."

"You were in D. C., with the OWI producing propaganda," she pointed out, unimpressed.

"You have to know what's going on in order to know how to rewrite it. You have to know the whole truth in order to edit it. What I saw wasn't pretty."

Living it was even uglier, Jess thought, reflecting on James's dark moments. However, she didn't say anything, just folded her arms and let Terry forge on, "It put things in perspective: my ambitions, my frustrations, my marriage."

His marriage, huh? Now there's a pit of quicksand I don't dare poke my foot anywhere near, as juicy a topic as it might seem.

"And that's why I'm apologizing now, Jessica, trying to explain," he continued. "I'm not going to let you feel bad because of my stupidity. I've changed that much."

Before Jessica could protest that he hadn't hurt her, Terry went on, "This is humiliating for me to admit, Jessica, but at Yale they *killed* me. No one bothered to listen to me. The traditionalists attacked me for being new-fangled and the New Critics went after me for not being their kind of new-fangled. Here I thought I was a brilliant young Turk, but I found out I was nothing more than a football tossed around by two teams at war. They just played with me to get at each other."

In spite of herself, Jess felt more than a little sympathy for both Terry's comeuppance and what it cost to admit it to her. Before she knew it, she was consoling, "Maybe it wasn't as bad as all that."

"No. It was worse; believe me."

Jess almost put a reassuring hand on his arm but checked herself. Still, she knew her expression showed the compassion her skepticism couldn't quite bury.

Terry took another pull on his cigarette, then exhaled the smoke away from them, up into the dark skies, before saying, "So, when Nigel told me about you and the course, my course, I saw red. I felt humiliated all over again, in so many ways."

"Why? How?" Jessica puzzled, curiosity spicing her pity.

"Jessica, you don't know how wounded I was when I couldn't make it on the stage—especially after all my battles with the family. Then, for you to succeed after we broke up, it was kind of a slap in the face, even a punishment. Still, I had my scholarship—and I was good at it—damned good. It justified me. You had your world; I had mine. But, after Saturday, it didn't feel as if I had mine anymore. And here you were back on the scene and ready to horn in on what little I thought I had left."

Jessica's sympathy notably dipped as his phrasing seemed to shift blame onto her. Sternly she set him straight, "Look, Terry, I would have been helping you not 'horning in.' You better get that straight."

"I know. I know, now," Terry assured her quickly. "But at that moment, that morning you had everything I didn't, acting, teaching, a great marriage. I was a grade-A jackass. I admit it. Can't you appreciate that I'm leading with my chin here? You don't have to be my pal, just accept this apology. And I *would be* happy to have you help me out with the class. What do you say?"

Jessica was aware that her mouth hung open in shock. Terry apologizing and asking her to work with him? Admitting he'd been a jackass? Only a saint wouldn't have savored all this just a little. But Terry's troubled, earnest expression tugged at her. Nevertheless, her skepticism was muted not silenced.

Finally, Jessica put her doubts into words, "All this breast-baring just so I'll work with you? This bill of goods is hard to buy, Terry."

"No, Jessica," he explained intently. "The class, working together, and maybe even having some fun, that's a small attempt to square things with you. It's not much, but it would be good for both of us."

"*Both* of us?" Jessica puzzled.

Terry was so close now that they almost touched, not a proximity Jessica relished. Yet she was determined to stand her ground and not let him think he disquieted or intimidated her. Terry responded, "Yes, *both* of us. I won't lie. I definitely profit from keeping this course running. It makes me look good here and to other places interested in me. But there's a perk for you, too. You get experience and you score points for your husband by being useful. You know that getting a permanent position here isn't a shoo-in."

"Just what do you mean by that?" *Was Terry trying to use James to manipulate her?*

"Nothing sinister. Just that between finances and politics, nothing's a sure thing till you sign the contract. However, if Nigel can say what a help both of you are around here, he can tickle the fancies of the bean counters. That strengthens your case, and you know it."

"Well, yes, I guess," Jess hesitated.

It made sense. They had made a good team once upon a time; and, with no romance in the picture, a lot of their conflicts could disappear. But a red light blinked in the back of her mind.

"And it's not just about us. It's about the students," Terry cut into her thoughts.

"How's that?" Jess demanded, resenting the twinge of guilt he'd evoked.

"I mean that if this class is canceled, some will lose credits. It could take them longer to graduate. In fact, some of the scholarship kids will be in a real bind if they lose this class. They'll be stuck for the summer with no income."

"But Rose said there wouldn't be a problem," Jessica insisted. "They could be reshuffled into other classes."

"Rose would say that, to keep the pressure off you. She's your friend, and she doesn't know *everything* that goes on around here. For instance, there may not even be room for them in a class they could use toward graduation . . ."

"I'm sure James would find room for them in his class . . ."

"I'm sure he would, if he could, Jessica. He seems like a right guy. But not all the girls who would be out in the cold are eligible for his class. It's only for advanced students, and there are some intermediates on scholarship. I checked this out thoroughly before I brought it up to you. Believe me; I wouldn't have made this proposal otherwise, knowing how hard it might be for you to work with me."

Jess's first instinct was to counter, "I'm not afraid to work with you," but she caught herself. Terry hadn't said she was *afraid*. Having put *that* spin on his words was an unsettling self-revelation. She only replied, "I didn't know. I wouldn't want any scholarship kids to suffer because you and I had some bad blood."

"In the past, Jessica. In the past," Terry insisted.

He took a quick pull on his cigarette and expelled it just as swiftly, waiting for Jessica's response. But Jessica's attention was piqued by a sound removed from them, the pound of hooves on sand, then splashing through the waves and back onto the sand again. Her eyes shifted from Terry to the dark horse charging nearer from the direction from which she'd originally come. She knew she ought to answer Terry, but she couldn't help grabbing at the reprieve brought by the approaching horse and rider.

Though moving with speed, the horse was holding his head high, reminding her of Stymie's trademark arched neck before he set sail from behind to surge up in the final strides for victory. Then the black horse stretched out his long neck, seemingly determined to nose out some imaginary competitor. Almost upon them, the rider appeared to perceive her love and admiration for his mount. For a moment, his craggy features hovered around a smile, until they settled on Terry. He turned away. Jessica raised a hand in greeting, anyway. The horse's blowing, his hooves tearing through the sand made her smile as he thundered past. Only his pricked ears told her that he wasn't in the least extended. Oh, to one day ride that gorgeous animal–if she could control him!

The rider surprised her by glancing back, but only at her. His expression didn't change, but his eyes telegraphed their brief bond over his horse. Still, it was rather dark. Maybe she had imagined it. Maybe not.

"He shouldn't be out here, racing that thing around people," came Terry's irritated voice.

Jess turned back to Terry, surprised at how annoyed he was with the rider. Curiously, she questioned him, "Why shouldn't he? The school doesn't own that part of the beach. It's public; and, since he did more than his share in the war, I'd say he's a particularly deserving part of that public."

Terry backtracked with, "No, no. I just meant that it could be dangerous, riding so fast, on the beach. What if he trampled a child?"

Jessica turned back to the receding figure and disagreed, "I don't see any children on the beach now, do you? Anyway, I heard he usually doesn't ride when people are around. Gosh, what a beautiful horse. He must have Thoroughbred blood, don't you think? Look at his action, his confirmation."

"Oh, come now, Jessica," Terry good-naturedly snorted, tossing away his cigarette, joining her to watch the disappearing horse and rider. "What would a racehorse be doing galloping around here, under a vet with battle fatigue?"

"Terry," Jess set him straight, "not all Thoroughbreds are racehorses. He could even be from an Army cavalry station. Maybe he just got his discharge papers. Or he could have been a washout at the track. We're surrounded by four states with racetracks. He just got lucky and didn't end up in a can of dog food or a bottle of glue."

"I might have known that when it came to horses, you'd have an answer," Terry shook his head, with a slight grin. "You were off riding all the time at school. I just wished you hadn't been such a confirmed equestrienne that you actually took care of them in the stables. Things could get a little ripe at times, as I remember."

"Hey, if you want to do things right, you have to commit yourself to the whole package, buster. Besides, my scholarship only covered so much. At least I could earn my keep doing something I liked," Jessica laughed. "Not all of us had a wealthy family to put them through school, you know."

As soon as she'd spoken those last words, Jess wanted to bite her tongue. She'd been joking, but she suddenly realized the joke might not be so funny to a guy whose family no longer had the dough that once made his life so easy.

Terry surprised her by not taking offense. Instead, he reflected, "That situation screeched to a halt not long after I graduated. You probably know that, though. But," he switched to a more upbeat tone, "I found my

98

place as a scholar. I like it. I may have had to hock the old silver spoon, but I'm doing all right. In spite of what happened at Yale, I have hopes of doing better, one way or another. So, what do you say, Jessica? I stuck my neck out to apologize. I promise to be on my best behavior. You won't even have to work with me much. We'll do the first class together, one or two more later, then you can sub for me when I have to take off for a lecture. You may sit in on some classes, to keep in sync with what we're doing, but only if you want to. So, how about helping these kids, especially the ones on scholarship. You remember what it was like to worry about money for your education."

He really did know how to hit her where she lived. How could she, in good conscience, put her discomfort ahead of some kids' educations? Hadn't quite a few people gone out on a limb to make sure she could enjoy one? And tonight's Terry was a far cry from the stinker who'd ticked her off Sunday. Maybe he *had* had a God-awful weekend. His apology seemed sincere. It wasn't exactly as if he were asking her to marry him! She was sorely tempted by the prospect of teaching. Once she'd started working with Rose and those kids at the NYPL, she'd been bitten by the bug.

As if a mind reader, Terry added, "I heard what an excellent job you did with Rose last summer. With our stage experience, we could have a lot of fun enacting the scenes with the students, making them think about how staging creates the art. And, as I said before, it couldn't hurt your husband's chances."

Was this guy psychic or what?!

"C'mon, Jessica. Maybe this way I can square things with you for Sunday, for the past."

Terry's words, his heartfelt expression held Jess. *Maybe it was time to bury the hatchet—and not in Terry's chest.*

"Aren't you two afraid of missing the fireworks?"

James's query broke the spell, and Jessica turned abruptly to him. Why, she wasn't sure, but it suddenly felt terribly awkward to be standing alone on the beach with both men.

Terry, however, felt no such awkwardness, leaping into the breach with charm and camaraderie: "James Crawford, grand to see you. I was just trying to persuade your wife to let bygones be bygones by working with me so my course can still run. She'd be just the ticket to spark the students, and I've heard that she loves to teach. It's a win-win situation."

James was standing beside Jessica now, to her left, almost between her and Terry. He shot Jess a quick, appraising glance. He didn't seem thrilled to read in her face a weakening to Terry's proposal. James turned to Terry and neutrally said, "I understood that my wife had decided against the proposition–and that you weren't too keen on it either."

"Let's just say I've come to my senses," Terry smiled, refusing not to be endearing. "I explained to her what a rough time I'd had recently. And I apologized. After that, she seemed quite receptive, interested."

"I don't think that she changes her mind at the drop of a hat," James countered, eminently pleasant, civilized, and firm. "I don't think that she's about to put herself in a position that could easily go sour."

"Why, she wouldn't be doing that at all," Terry persisted, charm still at 100%. "I am convinced that nothing of the kind will happen. I think she would love another chance to teach and work with these kids. I think . . ."

"*I* think," Jessica asserted, "that *she's* right here and can speak for herself, boys."

At least James and Terry both had the sense to look sheepish at being taken to task.

"Now, fellas, here's how things are going to shake down. Terry, I will seriously consider working with you. I don't have to tell Nigel until Friday morning. So, I'll tell you what I decide tomorrow. If it's yes, you can meet me at Cameron House to work out our plans for the class. If my answer is no, then, obviously, we don't need to confab. Either way, no hard feelings. Can you live with that?"

Terry took a quick glance at James, whose expression gave little away, then replied, "You've got a deal. I hope you'll come on board." He turned to James and said, "Good to see you again, Crawford. I'm sure we'll be running into each other around campus."

"I'm sure," James concurred quietly. He wasn't hostile, but there was nothing in his tone indicating he was exactly looking forward to the prospect.

"Enjoy the fireworks, you two," was Terry's farewell. There was a hint in his eye that he wanted to avoid the fireworks he anticipated between Jessica and James.

As soon as Terry was out of earshot, James turned to Jessica with an expression of displeased skepticism she hadn't seen in some time. She was not daunted, however.

"This is a bit of an eleventh-hour twist, isn't it, Jessica? You two seemed surprisingly matey after last Sunday," he observed thoughtfully.

Jessica simply answered, "He came to apologize."

"More than that, from the sound of things."

"Yes, it was," Jessica agreed, equal to James. "He explained that he'd had some pretty rough sledding at Yale, that he realized it was no excuse for his behavior, and that he was determined not to be a jerk anymore."

"Something like Saul on the road to Damascus?"

"Are you just going to be sarcastic, or are you going to listen to me, James?" Jessica questioned levelly.

James thought over the justice of his wife's words, then admitted, "Sorry, Jessica. He's the one on whom I'd like to use the sarcasm. I just worry that you're too forgiving and that he may have sold you a bill of goods. I know that you're no fool, but you still must admit you do seem to have made a drastic about-face."

Jessica nodded, allowing, "I know. But, James, if you had been here to hear him out, you'd probably agree that what we saw Sunday morning is not the whole Terry Clarke. Don't get me wrong. I still think the greatest love in Terry Clarke's life is Terry Clarke. I have no illusions about the guy. But I also see that he's not Hitler, Tojo, and Stalin all rolled into one."

James shook his head and warned, "You are too tenderhearted, Jessica. It's not your job to straighten out his messes . . ."

"I agree 100%," Jess set her husband straight. "That's not at all my intention. I'm not doing this to save Terry; I'm doing this for me."

Surprised, James countered, "That I don't follow."

"Don't you see, James? If I spend my time avoiding Terry, it just keeps up my resentment and builds him into some kind of Boogie Man. If I do work with him, and everything goes fine, then all that anger and bitterness diffuses. If he acts like a jackass, he shoots himself in the foot and I'm the good sport. Anyway, the bottom line is that unless I live as if I'm not bitter about or afraid of the past, I will be. You can understand that, can't you, James?"

He thought, studying the sands, before relenting, "Yes, yes I can, Jessica. But I think the man's a bad apple, deep down. I have a bad feeling about him."

"No," Jessica disagreed. "I don't see anything about Terry that I can't handle. Besides, after the fivers and gangsters I've been up against, Terry has got be a piece of cake."

"I wouldn't be too flip," James warned quietly.

"No, okay, but there's more to consider, James. Some students'll have problems with their scholarships if they can't take this class. You and I both know what it's like to be on a scholarship. How could either of us deny someone else the kind of help that pulled us through?"

She saw James's mouth twist slightly beneath his mustache, acknowledging she'd hit home. Still, Jess wasn't about to let James know that she was doing this for him as well. She knew he'd rather cut off his right arm than use her as a chip to get a job. It wasn't fun, not being completely on the level with him, but she couldn't see any other way. Instead, Jess pressed her point home.

"Anyway, James, I really would love to try my hand teaching this class. I had a ball when I did something similar with Rose. Yes, I know Terry is a far cry from Rose, but I think we can still make this a wonderful class. I can also help those kids while I'm enjoying myself."

"Well," James relented, "it looks as if you've made up your mind. But I have to say I really wish you wouldn't do it."

"After all I've said and explained?" Jessica puzzled.

"Yes, even so," James answered thoughtfully. "I'm concerned. Can't you just trust me on this one?"

Jess studied her husband, trying to understand what was up with him. It would have been flattering to read him as jealous, but she could see that wasn't the case. Well, no reason she couldn't just ask him.

"James, is there something you know, something you're not telling me about Terry?"

"What could I know?" James returned, sounding affable. "He's *your* old chum. No, I just see him as a bit of a dark horse. I don't want you mixed up in any trouble he might get himself into."

"Not much chance of that," Jess assured. "I'm only going to work a few sessions with him, then take over a few classes on my own. I'll need to do some preparations, which reminds me. I may need to run some practice lessons by you. Could you help a bit?"

"So, you ignore my advice, but you expect me to abet you while you're at it?" James queried, some of his humor coming back.

"Something like that."

James shook his head, took her hand, and promised, "Anything for my lady." He paused, though, and warned seriously, "Just don't get too chummy with Clarke. Don't trust him or confide in him. And don't let him tangle you up in his problems, no matter how sorry you feel for him."

"Are you kidding? No way! I had my share of going round the mulberry bush with him years ago. And I certainly don't want to do anything that will put me in range of that wife of his."

"She does seem a bit of a Tartar," James observed.

"You said it! Believe me; my connection to Terry Clarke will be strictly professional. I can forgive someone without turning into a sap."

"Right, then. How about we go back and enjoy the fireworks with our friends? I should be able to point out the Catherine Wheel that you were asking me about."

James seemed cheery, his hand holding hers as they strolled back, and he listened to her description of the gorgeous black horse—even though he did crack wise about his aversion to the equine species. Yet Jess sensed that he was still concerned about Terry, as if he knew something he wouldn't, couldn't, for some reason, reveal. How ridiculous! She really needed to put away the pall of mysteries, murder, and mayhem from her radio show. Whatever the case, she was woman enough to handle whatever Terry might throw at her.

Chapter Nine

Wednesday, July 17

From the stone bench before Cameron House, Jessica looked across the slate-flagged terrace and beyond the lawn to the silvery blue ocean. The morning breeze raced up from the waters, forcing her to hold down the brim of her white, wide-brimmed hat. Jessica kicked off a pair of walking shoes she'd worn for the long stroll from her cottage and slipped on the black and white spectator pumps that she's pulled from a roomy bag next to her. A student or two trotted across the terrace and into the building. James waited by her and acknowledged the ones he'd met before, one hand attempting to slide his longish dark hair back into place against the intrusive breeze.

"We'll both need a good brushing once we're indoors, or we'll look as if we battled a monsoon to get here," Jessica laughed to her husband as she stowed her shoes in her bag. "You've already met with your class, but I'm not about to make a first impression as an unkempt frump."

"Not to worry. You're perfectly kempt."

"You could have disputed the frump part, too, you know," Jessica bantered, rising and smoothing her fitted black linen dress with the flared skirt, key-hole neckline, and white scalloped collar. Her tone expressed more confidence than she felt.

"Then I might add you're a bit of a knock-out in that dress," James observed with a twinkle. "Maybe too nice around a fellow like Terry Clarke. I wouldn't want to have to come into class and give your chum a thrashing."

Jessica kidded back, "Don't worry. I'm perfectly capable of decking any guy who makes like a wolf. Though, to be perfectly honest, I hardly think Terry is about to risk his wife's ire by making a pass at me. Anyway, I've worn this dress before without causing a commotion. It's not as if I'm going in like Sally Rand missing one of her fans. What would *you* have me wear?"

"You wouldn't have a potato sack, maybe with a bit of twine as a belt. I can concede that much to fashion," James suggested.

"What a wise guy," Jess pretended annoyance. "I don't know how flattering it is that you're not even the tiniest bit jealous."

"Ah," James surmised, "it's jealously you're looking for not a reasonable, trusting husband? Sorry, love, no time for any of that. As I recall, you were the one who wanted to get here a bit early, to settle in. So, shall we?"

Briefcase in hand, one arm proffered to Jess, James made her grin as she linked her arm with his. He leaned down to her and said, "And if anyone gives you a hard time of it, just remember what a whiz you are with a banana-cream pie."

Unable to suppress a giggle at his allusion to how she'd once disarmed a fifth columnist, Jessica added, "Right in the kisser?"

"Precisely."

They entered the Great Hall and crossed its sun-brightened expanse. A few summer students, a professor or so, a secretary or two were crisscrossing around them, but Jessica barely noticed. At last, D-Day. In about fifteen minutes, she'd join Terry to get this show on the road. At least all she had to do today was play the scene. So, in a way, it wasn't even Jessica and Terry but Rosalind and Orlando from *As You Like It*. And Rosalind had the upper hand.

"Ah, you've quite the-cat-that-ate-the canary smile, Mrs. Crawford. What's going through that devious mind of yours?"

They'd stopped by the open double doors to the empty seminar room, and Jessica grinned, "It's just nice to know that the scene we play puts me in the catbird's seat."

"Hmm, I wonder who picked it," James pondered ironically.

"We both did, smarty."

James's expression showed his pleasure at the lightness of Jessica's mood now. He told her, "Anyway, I'm glad to see you feeling more chipper. You'll be fine. You've already charmed those two, Alicia and Lauren. I'll wager you'll have the rest of them eating out of your hand in no time. Just be yourself."

"Not everyone finds me as irresistible as you do, James," Jessica pointed out lightly.

"Then shame on them. Anyway, I've got to nip off to my class." A quick peek at the ornate paneling and seminar table of Jessica's classroom, and James lamented, "I ought to be jealous. Here I am an accomplished scholar, but I'm assigned a small classroom on the third floor, somewhere left of the Hebrides. Here you are, holding class in this finely appointed chamber."

"Think again," Jess corrected her husband. "This is Terry Clarke's classroom. I'm just along for the ride."

"Well, if your ride does get a little bumpy, which I'm sure it won't, spur Clarke on with some of that sharp wit of yours, but just a touch."

"Or I could go direct to the banana-cream pie–if I'm thinking in terms of Rosalind, Orlando, and Curley."

"You'll be splendid. And don't forget; I'll be by after your class to take you for lunch in the dining hall."

Jess nodded. James, after making a swift survey to ensure no one could see, ducked under the brim of her hat and gave her a quick kiss. Jess had to try *very* hard not to chuckle when he, moving away with his eyes still on her, nearly hit the wall behind him.

"Reflexes of a cat," she solemnly observed.

James smiled sheepishly, then was off into the great hall to take the main stairs to the next floor. This time without hitting anything.

Jess strolled happily into the room, the warmth and fun of their parting driving off her earlier anxiety. No one here yet, so she decided to check on the staging she and Terry had set up yesterday. A large table predominated the room to her left, with desks facing it. Directly across from Jessica, French doors opened into the terrace that curved around the side of the edifice. Just beyond was the garden where she and James had talked so deeply two weeks back. Remembering that talk, James's ghosts, kept her piddling anxieties in perspective.

Jess dropped her bag on the table, before carefully pulling the hat pin out of her chapeau and taking it off. She turned to the area between the table and the French doors to survey the setup for their performance: a desk with a chair atop it and a step ladder to its right. She and Terry had hung a good-sized Maxfield Parrish landscape, *sans* figures, on the wall, left of the desk.

Yep, everything looked ready to go—as long as Terry remembered to bring the books they'd mocked up with overlarge titles. As if on cue, Terry Clarke waltzed in earlier than was his habit. But promptness wasn't his only surprise.

"Terry, you're early. But my goodness," Jessica burst out, "What happened to the distinguished fringe on your chin?"

The trim Elizabethan beard was gone.

Terry's eyes sparkled and he asked, a hand to his chin, "Don't you approve?"

"I wouldn't say that. This is the way I remembered you. What prompted a shift to the past?"

"Not nostalgia," Terry replied, putting his briefcase on the table. "More like a fresh new leaf. I told you I was planning to be a new man. So, *do* you like it?"

"It doesn't matter if *I* like it. What does your wife say? I got the impression she thought the dashing Elizabethan look was just her cup of tea."

"I'll let you in on a little secret," Terry explained, leaning forward after shooting a feigned glance of secrecy over his shoulder. "I think she never really liked it. A few times I caught her muttering that my neatly trimmed whiskers scratched. My bride has very tender skin."

Jessica chuckled, "Well, as I said. This is how I remember you. But what will your students say? Aren't you tarnishing your carefully crafted image?"

"Don't worry about that, Jessica. I have the teaching chops to keep them in the palm of my hand."

"Which palm? Left or the right?"

Amused, Terry observed, "Still with the wise cracks. I can see I'm going to have to stay on my toes with you in the room."

"Not too high on those toes, friend. You are 6'4". Stretch out much more and your head will go through the ceiling."

"Then we won't have to worry whether I can teach without my beard."

Jessica shook her head, smiling. She'd forgotten how much fun Terry could be. Well, there had to be some good reason she'd been attracted to him in the past. Maybe this could work out after all.

"There's that smile, Jessica. You still have that million-dollar smile."

How to take that comment? Jess finally answered thoughtfully, honestly, "That's because I have some swell people in my corner, Terry, especially James."

Would Terry take that as an attempt at one-upmanship? She hadn't meant it that way. *Not exactly.*

But Terry responded gently, "I know. I can see that. He seems like a stand-up guy. I'm glad it worked out for you. It's darned lucky you didn't lose him in France or someplace like that during the war."

"Yes, well," she stumbled a bit, as lying never made her comfortable, "he couldn't serve. Heart issue. So, don't sneak up behind him and yell 'Boo!' I'm too young to be a widow."

James's warning about not spilling too much about their personal life to Terry sounded a faint klaxon in her head. But she did have to keep his cover story in play till his superiors said otherwise. Anyway, maybe the humor went a long way to cover her awkwardness. She hoped.

Must have worked, for Terry continued, "Oh, well, I know that he's fluent in French. He was in France, right? Maybe in the '30s? I thought I heard that he lived there at one time."

"His mother emigrated from France. Maybe Rose mentioned it."

At least that much was the God's honest truth, as far as it went. Glancing at her watch, Jess changed the subject: "Our little scholars should be skipping in any minute now. We'd better make sure all our ducks are in a row. I checked out our 'set' just now. How about you? Bring the books?"

Terry patted his briefcase and answered, "Right here. I gave seating arrangements a lot of thought. You and I should bracket the girls on either end of the table. I'll take the side by the French doors. Why don't you stay right here, at the other end?"

"It's fine with me."

"Professor Clarke, where's your beard?!" came Lauren Fleet's shocked voice. Alicia, from her friend's side, only appeared mildly surprised.

Terry put a hand to his chin and uttered, "Good Lord, where did it go this time?!"

Jessica couldn't help smiling, thinking that things certainly were far less formal here than in any school she'd ever studied, but maybe that wasn't such a bad thing at all.

"Lauren, we can always depend on you to blurt out the first thing that comes into your mind," Alicia said, setting her Shakespeare and her notebook down on a desk.

Lauren rolled her eyes, pointing out as she put down her own books, "*This* is my best friend. With friends like her . . ."

Alicia refused to acknowledge the playful jibe, instead turning to Terry for, "Do you need us to go to your office to get the handouts, Professor Clarke?"

"I'm way ahead of you, Alicia," Terry answered easily, opening his briefcase and pulling out the material in question.

Lauren faced Jessica and grinned, "This is the easiest assistantship we've ever had."

"Is it then?" Terry mused with an arched brow. "Be grateful, because I promise to keep you hopping with reading, writing, and thinking in class. And if that's still not enough, I can always dream up some challenging extra assignments for you."

"You had to open your big mouth," Alicia kidded her friend.

"Oh, don't worry," Lauren countered. "He won't make us do extra work."

"And why not?" Terry questioned in a tone one might expect from Richard III.

"Because then you'll have extra work grading our extra work," Lauren grinned knowingly.

"She has you there," Jessica noted.

Terry threw up his hands in surrender, then advised his students, "Fine. Now, why don't you two make like scholars while I discuss some final plans with my esteemed colleague."

Terry crooked a finger to lead Jessica away for their confab. She cocked her head skeptically at the secrecy implied by that gesture, then shrugged and circumambulated the table to join him. Other students were now entering in clumps as Jessica pondered what her "esteemed colleague" had up his sleeve. Terry took her by the arm and guided her over to the French doors. He certainly was making a WPA Project out of this—and why had Alicia paused to study them carefully?

In a quiet voice, Terry informed her, "I just want to firm up with you the structure of today's class before we started. Make sure we're on the same page."

"You had to drag me over here for that?" Jessica whispered. "I thought you were going to reveal some murderer's name to me."

"No one gets murdered at Margaret Point, Jessica," Terry corrected her a bit impatiently. "Now, are you ready to get down to business?"

"Sorry, Terry. I'm all ears," Jess promised. Hmm, maybe Terry got just as jittery before he went on his stage as she did for hers.

"All right, then. I'll introduce you. Give them some background on the course, plays, era, stage environment—ask them to think about what they bring to the play, as an audience, then we'll break."

"Check," Jess concurred. They'd discussed it all before, but she understood the need to psych oneself up for a performance, on stage or in a classroom.

"After the break, we'll go into our act, then both do the questions and answers with them on how we shaped the play with our staging and performance and how *they* created the play with what they bring to it." Terry's expression was intense.

"Double check. Let's hit the boards."

"Okay. Break a leg, Jessica," Terry broke into a grin of anticipation.

They turned back to the students, buzzing with eager, bright young voices. The excitement she'd known whenever she had started a class as a student, combined with that of hitting the boards, took over all Jessica's thoughts. Now Terry was introducing her and explaining her role in the class. There were far too many new faces and names to learn so fast, too many personalities to read from this herd of twelve eager, bright bobby-soxers.

Back at her end of the table, Jessica watched Terry take over. Impressive. He had that great sense of humor, all that charm, but he was definitely in charge—not because he was a tyrant but because his knowledge and his challenging questions held the students' respect. Yes, Terry really had found his métier in this marvelous, stimulating interchange with his class, his audience. It was a crying shame he didn't appreciate what he had, instead of pining for more prestige.

All this was neither here nor there, though, as they rounded toward the break. Terry's background on the original plays had subtly shifted from an interesting history to an intriguing prompting of the girls to figure out for themselves how stagings and interpretations shifted to reflect the times that produced them. Jess couldn't help her delight when Lauren pointed out they'd been talking about some of these same ideas in Professor Crawford's class. Turning to Jess so no one else could see, Terry gave her a wink.

Break time came faster than anyone expected, with Terry asking the students to think over what they, 20th-century children of the atom age, two world wars, and Frank Sinatra, might bring to a play about a green forest, isolated from a civilization reft by tyranny and usurpation. When he asked for any questions before breaking, Lauren poked her hand in the air.

"Professor Clarke, what is all that stuff piled over there? What does it have to do with *As You Like It*? A table with a chair on it?"

"And a step ladder?" added another girl. Murmured queries followed from the rest of the class.

"That," Terry smiled devilishly, "is for Miss Minton and I to know, and you to figure out—when we get back."

Twelve pairs of questioning eyes turned to Jessica, hoping she'd be a soft touch.

"No dice, kids," Jessica stood firm. "I'm not giving up anything."

That answer elicited a few chuckles, then the young women were getting up, stretching, and strolling off to take advantage of the next fifteen minutes.

"Remember, ladies," Terry warned. "Fifteen minutes is fifteen minutes. If you come back and the doors are closed, that's all she wrote for you. And you know that I mean business."

Jess got up, stretching her own arms in front of her. Terry strolled over to her, to ask, "How do you like it so far?"

"I like it fine, Terry, not that I've done anything yet."

"I don't know. You fielded those curious, pleading gazes nicely. I think we make a good team."

"I'm thrilled you're so optimistic, Terry. As for me, ask me again after we put on our show."

"You'll be a smash, and should worst come to worst, I'll carry you," he teased.

Jessica warned impishly, "Just take care of yourself, lad. You never carried me before, and we aren't going to start now."

"I knew once I got your dander up, you'd be fine."

"Oh, sure. That's it. You were just trying to *help* me with that smart remark."

"Well, if you are feeling a little jittery, how about we take a quick jaunt to the kitchen for a cup of coffee?"

"Right, *caffeine* to soothe my nerves. Anyway, I'm just fine and dandy. But I was thinking of popping upstairs to see James."

"Won't do you any good. I saw him walk out with Nigel a little while ago. Your back was to the door."

"Oh," Jess couldn't help the twinge of disappointment. Before she could indulge that feeling any further, though, Terry had her arm and guided her to the door with, "Never mind the coffee. I'll make you some tea. I remember what a maniac you are for a cup of tea, even in boiling July weather. And if you want to tell me what a master of pedagogy I am in the meantime, I won't object."

"Why doesn't that last proposal surprise me?" Jessica queried archly as they crossed the Great Hall.

"How about, after that, I tell you what an astounding thespian you are."

"Oh, well then, you've got a deal," Jessica agreed. Terry might have been a lousy boyfriend, but he wasn't half bad as a colleague. At least not at the moment.

The scene began with Jessica/Rosalind leaning casually against the desk, bidding a mocking adieu to an imaginary Jaques, the professional cynic.

While she spoke, Terry/Orlando wandered in through the French doors, his nose alternately buried in either of two books, one held open in each hand. The titles *The Courtier* and *The Art of Love* identified each in oversized letters. Rosalind had barely finished dismissing "Monsieur Melancholy," when the preoccupied Orlando bumped into her and knocked her down.

While Orlando stood befuddled, Rosalind sprang to her feet, dusting herself off and irritably demanding, "Why how now, Orlando, where have you been all this while? You a lover? And you serve me such a trick," index finger stabbing his chest, "never come more in my sight."

Quite a few giggles erupted as Orlando was forced to back down by the petite but feisty Rosalind over whom he towered. His reaction a mixture of anguish and horror, he dove back into his books to pull out a "prize" rejoinder: "My fair, Rosalind, I come within an hour of my promise."

This Rosalind wagged a finger and warned her Orlando that the response was *not* a winning one. Once more he dived into his book, emerging pleased with the less than mordant, "Pardon me, dear, Rosalind."

And so they proceeded, Rosalind, mocking Orlando's attempts to idealize his love; Orlando gallantly trying to deny her humor and steer her back into the channels of the virtuous courtly lady's requisite behavior, frequently reverting to his books for a comeback or guidance when his own wit couldn't match hers. Then, when suddenly changing her mood and urging Orlando to "woo" her because she was "like enough to consent," Rosalind required him to hand her up the step ladder so she could sit on the chair and preside over him. Still, he insisted on trying to find answers in his books on love, while she continued to chide him mischievously for it. The class cracked up when Rosalind mockingly acted out "the very Patterns of love" that Orlando kept pulling from his books—especially when she mimed Leander not drowning while trying to reach his love but ungallantly being "taken with a cramp." The girls burst into guffaws when Rosalind later promised that she would have Orlando, and "and twenty such." If he is as "good" as he claims, "can one desire too much of a good thing?"

Orlando's finally starting to smile at the sallies, set off a few whispers from the students of "Oh, now he's getting it." As the couple's repartee proceeded, Orlando stopped turning to his books, even wittily parrying his companion's gibes. Once this "very Rosalind" found him responding to her rather than spouting clichés, she softened her tone and gradually came off the chair to sit on the desk. As he sat on the step ladder, putting them on the same level, their banter became tender. Unexpectedly, Orlando bounced to his feet, as if this tenderness were too awkward and confusing–he did think he was wooing a boy impersonating Rosalind to "cure" him of love–and announced, "For these two hours, I will leave thee."

This Rosalind's "Alas dear love, I cannot lack thee two hours" was breathtakingly quiet. So, they parted with jests and turned away, but when certain the other could not see, each cast a longing look back. Alone, "on stage," Rosalind swung her leg pensively, her eyes surveying the Forest of Arden before her, eyes winsome yet amused at her own longing. Jessica could feel the quiet of her audience. She almost saw their faces, but too much of her was still Rosalind.

"And curtain!" came Terry's voice, as he poked his head and shoulders through the double doors.

The spell broken, the students laughed and applauded. Hearing "That was swell!" "Wow!" and "Jeepers!" tickled Jessica no end as she bounced onto her feet. Terry, was beside her, taking her hand, leading her into a bow, saying, "Anyone who gives us a standing ovation gets an automatic A–Sorry, just kidding."

Jess knew she was beaming. How grand this moment felt! The girls had loved it! Terry gave her shoulder a pat and guided her to sit on the edge of the desk with him, each taking an opposite corner.

"All right, scholars," Terry began. "Let's get down to cases. What did you see here that reflects what we've been saying about the stage's ability to create the play: stage business, sets, costumes, the acting itself. Where do we start?"

"I have a question," came from a red-haired girl, her face overwhelmed by freckles. "About the books. What's *The Art of Love* and *The Courtier*? Are they modern or old books from back then?"

"Good question," Terry confirmed. "Anybody recognize the titles?"

Alicia Wraxton spoke out, "*The Courtier* was a Renaissance book about how to be a noble man. There's a big chapter in it on how to be a courtly lover and what's expected of the lady beloved. *The Art of Love* is a kind of Bible for romance for medieval and Renaissance upper-class young men. I read some excerpts from them in another class."

"Good," Terry confirmed. "So, what does it say about Orlando? Think about how he's using the two books."

"Oh," Lauren leaped in. "They're a crutch. He kept turning to them for help to win the girl."

"Didn't do him much good," asserted an olive-skinned girl with a short, curly bob. "Rosalind cleaned up the floor with him every time he opened his mouth. She wasn't buying any of his banana oil."

They all laughed, and Terry summed up, "So, Orlando's a dope, and Rosalind wouldn't give him the time of day?"

"No! No!" came protests.

"Oh, why not?" Terry asked innocently, as if playing devil's advocate were the last thing on his mind.

"Lots of swell guys act really goony around a girl they like," Lauren pointed out. "It's like someone stole half their brain! You should see my brother when he had a crush on this girl from Smith. And he goes to M.I.T."

"So, what makes Orlando M.I.T. material, not just 'goony'?" Terry pressed. "What did you see?"

"He threw away the books when they weren't working!" one girl declared.

"*He* decided when to leave," the red-haired girl added.

"At one point, when she took away one of his books," Alicia carefully pointed out, "she was above him. However, when they started to *exchange* quips, after he gave up the books, and began thinking for himself, he and Rosalind were on the same level, equal."

There was nodding and murmuring assent amongst the students. Now, Jessica decided it was time to put in her two cents worth: "Hey, what about Rosalind? Let's not give Orlando all the attention. What kind of a gal is she? What do you think *she* thinks about Orlando?"

"Good question, Miss Minton," Terry pronounced.

Jessica nodded a thank-you, pleased at a commendation from him, in spite of herself. Then her attention was swept up in the students' discussions. Did Rosalind think Orlando was an L-7 from Squaresville, reading from old books rather than making like Errol Flynn or Tyrone

Power? Was she just flirting with him like the smart-talking gals did in the movies today? Maybe she thought love was the bunk?

Alicia pulled everything together, "You people don't get it. Rosalind's not cynical. It's not love that's the bunk to her; it's all the old clichés. She sees beneath the surface, and she's right because she gets Orlando to give the brush to all the old saws about love in those dusty books. The way you two played it, he didn't want to leave her, and she didn't want him to go, once they were on the same level."

Impressed, Jessica thought, *This girl is sharp! What a detective she'd make!*

Terry summed up, "So, listening to you ladies, I'm seeing that how you understood the play comes as much from your experience as from our staging. Anyone want to take that ball and run with it?"

Run these girls did, covering everything from Lauren's brother, their own rocky romances (those who'd had any), the bantering couples of movies and radio, and so much more. Jess had a ball joining in, happy to find Terry actually encouraging her. Anyway, this wonderful experience brought home to her that she would do almost anything to ensure James wouldn't lose his opportunity to have such exhilarating work permanently.

Finally, Terry wrapped up the class, closing with instructions to take what they'd learned today and carry it into *Macbeth*, to think about how audiences and stage productions interpret and create a play in light of living through a World War.

"That should keep the little darlings busy," Terry whispered to Jess as their scholars packed up to leave.

Jess would have bantered back, but she was now surrounded by girls who *had* to tell her how exciting the scene had been, how wonderful she'd played it. Relaxing into the moment, Jess wondered why she'd ever been nervous. Of course, she hadn't run the class all by herself, merely been a supporting player. Oh, who cared! It was just so swell to see these kids' enthusiasm, to laugh with them, to share ideas with them. She couldn't wait to tell James. He'd be so delighted to see her happy.

The group of students having moved off, at last, Jessica looked about to see Terry conferring with Alicia and Lauren at the far side of the seminar table. She joined them, beaming, and inquired, "Getting all squared away for the next class?"

"Natch," grinned Lauren. "Professor Clarke sure keeps us on our toes. You should see the list of props he's assigned us to dig up for *Macbeth*."

"Ah ha," Jessica chuckled, "will I be seeing a dagger before me?"

"Perhaps something a bit more twentieth century," Terry promised devilishly.

"Hmm," Jessica speculated, "A tommy gun? Flame thrower? Off to physics for an atom bomb?"

"Don't be ridiculous," Terry chided. "An A-bomb would wipe out the entire cast. There wouldn't be any Macbeth, let alone Duncan or Banquo."

"That would certainly be overkill," Alicia deadpanned.

"Terry," Jess mischievously chided. "Is this a girl's college or a training school for Fred Allen replacements?"

"Sometimes I have my suspicions," Terry replied. "Not that I expect many chuckles from *Macbeth*."

Lauren turned to Jessica and asked, "Will you be back with us, Miss Minton?"

"Oh," Jessica hesitated. The question had taken her by surprise, as did Lauren's genuine enthusiasm. It was a nice surprise, though. "I'm not sure, Lauren. We're not doing a scene."

Terry offered, "It's up to you, Jessica. It's not required, but if you think you could get a better feel for the course that way, if you think you'll enjoy it, you're welcome."

"Oh, say yes," Lauren urged. Alicia didn't speak, but her expression implied she liked the idea.

"Well," Jessica temporized. This was such an extraordinary turnaround from Terry's attitude two weeks ago! And yet, after the past two weeks working together, after today's class, maybe a turnaround made perfect sense. Perhaps, he had been completely sincere in his apology, after all. She finished, "Let me think. I don't have anything planned, and I know James is busy. So is Rose. Okay, why not, if my being here isn't going to gum up the works."

"Great!" Terry agreed, smiling down at her and shaking her hand to seal the bargain. "It's a deal."

"Oh, isn't this just lovely," came a woman's voice from the doorway behind Jessica. "Two old chums clasping hands in amity."

Before Jessica could turn, she saw Terry tense. He dropped her hand like the proverbial hot potato. Both Alicia and Lauren looked as if they wished to be *anywhere* else.

Jessica took her time turning around. Carolina Brent Clarke. She was truly a gorgeous woman. Those luscious red lips, piercing green eyes, Technicolor red locks framing her face in glowing waves almost to her shoulders. And of course her outfit was perfection: white silk dress, fitted bodice, flared skirt, and a splash of turquoise, coral, and Kelly flowers printed along the left of her square-cut neckline. The picture hat dipped strategically over her face, just enough to lend elegance without obscuring her fine features. A silver and turquoise necklace provided an exquisite highlight to the design on her dress. Clearly, the lady was as much an artist of wardrobe as of sculpture.

Lauren and Alicia had quietly stepped back, away from their elders. Jessica could feel those earlier doubts about working with Terry snaking back.

"Don't let me interrupt," Carolina smiled pleasantly, joining Jessica and Terry, standing between them. "Are you two wrapping up some final details?"

"Something like that," Terry answered attempting to be casual but *not* relishing the moment.

"We had a delightful class," Jessica tried to smooth the waters. This gal was not going to ruin her morning's experience.

"I'm sure you did, Mrs. Crawford–Oh, I forgot, Jessica. My husband is a marvelous teacher. Everyone admires him. Students are just mad to take a class with him." Turning her head to Lauren and Alicia who now stood by the cold hearth, she added, "Don't you agree, girls?"

Lauren and Alicia didn't exactly shuffle and mumble their assent, but it was clear they'd rather *not* be on Carolina's radar. For just a sec, Jess thought she caught a tinge of irony in Alicia's eyes as soon as Carolina turned away. *Were these two amongst the contingent of students whom Carolina at one point made cry?*

Sympathetic to Terry's and the students' discomfort, Jessica graciously said, "Terry certainly is a wonderful teacher. I enjoyed today's class so much. You should be proud of him."

Carolina linked an arm through Terry's and smiled, "I am. I wouldn't give him up for all the diamonds in Africa."

Terry did not seem to be enjoying any of this, saying lightly, yet a little too quickly, "Thanks for the fan club, ladies, but I need to pack my briefcase if Carolina and I don't want to miss our lunch reservation at the inn. I still have to give Alicia and Lauren instructions to make sure all our props get back where they belong."

Terry deftly disentangled his arm from Carolina's, sparking only a temporary gleam of something unpleasant in her eye. He somehow managed not to look as if he were scampering to relative safety when he moved to the other side of the room.

That was also the Terry Jessica remembered. Metaphorically speaking, he always would be the first one to "swim away for help" the minute the sharks started circling.

"Oh, Jessica," Carolina caught Jess's attention in a surprisingly soft voice. "Now that Terry and the students are occupied, perhaps I should give you some advice."

"Advice?"

Jessica was genuinely perplexed; she had to admit trepidation entered into the equation as well.

"Yes, about that dress."

"This . . . *my* dress?"

Jess didn't have time to figure out if she were more annoyed or stumped at the remark before Carolina continued, "Yes. I'm sure that sort of frock may go over well enough with show people; but here, in the classroom, you really oughtn't to wear something, so, well, décolleté, do you think?"

Of course, James's kidding her on how good she looked today annoyingly came to mind, but Jessica was not about to let Carolina Brent Clarke get her goat. Besides, Madame Clarke was hardly dressed like one of the Sisters of Charity of St. Joseph. The irony in Jess's expression barely peeped through her charm when she gave Carolina's outfit a speculative once-over before returning pleasantly, "Oh, Carolina, now how can you stand there in that stylish frock and say such things? And relax, I don't think my dress bothered a single one of the girls. They were too busy with our class even to notice my outfit. They're too smart and independent for that. That's what you're worried about, right, how I'll affect the girls?"

Steam didn't come out of Carolina's ears, but she definitely was steamed, and searching for a comeback. However, she smiled and explained, "I think you have me wrong, my dear. I'd hate to see you make the wrong impression here. I wouldn't want you to inadvertently do something that could, well, disturb your husband."

"My husband?" Jessica repeated doubtfully. "Why would James be 'disturbed' by my looking nice? As a matter of fact, he told me that I looked lovely today. So, you have nothing to worry about. Don't you feel better? I'm just sorry that *you* think a husband would feel threatened when his wife looks good."

Oops. The glare in Carolina's hell-cat eyes told Jessica she'd overplayed her hand. Even if Carolina had been asking for it, Jess didn't feel any better about scoring a hit that could rebound against her and someone she loved.

That was when Terry, suddenly there, cut in, seeming to have sprinted over. Maybe this little tête à tête hadn't been conducted quietly enough not to carry across the room.

"Okay, Carolina," he began a little too cheerily. "We don't want to miss our reservation."

Carolina almost pulled her arm from her husband's hand, but she thought better of it and only gave Jessica a smile so honied she thought diabetes might set in, saying, "Isn't he just a dear? He's so eager for us to be off together."

It occurred to Jessica that amiability in the face of antagonism was the best comeback with a person like Carolina: "Then, please, don't let me hold you up. I know the inn's restaurant is delightful."

Terry smiled quickly (gratefully?) at Jess, snatched up his briefcase, and hustled his lovely wife out the door.

Jessica folded her arms as she watched the two leave. *If ever there was a gal who needed a kick in the pants. Poor Terry—or had he given Carolina reason over the years not to trust him? What about Jessamyn Crane?* She'd almost forgotten her in the excitement and fun of the class's camaraderie. And what had Terry said about her to Carolina? He must have said something. Or had she not been as important to him as she'd thought? Hmm, whatever the case, Carolina did not want her getting too chummy with her husband. Maybe coming to class on Friday wasn't such a hot idea, after all. It was a little early in the game to be making waves for anybody.

"She really is a stinker."

It was Lauren. The two girls had surrounded Jess and were regarding her sympathetically. As much as she appreciated their moral support, Jessica knew she had to tread delicately around students.

"It's nice of you girls to be so concerned, but everything's fine. They're just in a hurry," Jess responded casually.

"She's always in a hurry to keep him away from the people who like him," came, surprisingly, from Alicia.

"Alicia," Jess began carefully. "I can see you have a good heart. I appreciate your sympathy but be careful what you say. Don't get yourself mixed up in other people's conflicts, especially when you don't know the whole story. You could really get yourself in Dutch—or make an awkward situation worse for the person you intended to help."

Alicia bit back something, finally promising, "I won't do anything to put you in the middle, Miss Minton."

"Well, that's not exactly what I meant, but thanks."

Lauren jumped in, "You really add a lot to the class. Professor Clarke kinda shines when he plays off you. You have neat things to say, too. You will come back on Friday? You won't let Mrs. Clarke scare you off?"

"Scared? I'm not scared," slipped out of Jess. However, she added more neutrally, "We'll see what's on my schedule for Friday."

"I didn't mean to say you were scared," Lauren apologized.

Before Jess could reassure the girl, James sauntered in and inquired, "Scared? What would my lovely bride have to fear around here? Marauding horseshoe crabs?"

James's entrance seemed to signal the girls that they'd gone too far. Their words hadn't been intended for any ears but Jessica's, even if those other ears might belong to her husband.

"Oh, hello, Professor Crawford," Lauren piped up, puzzling James with her uncertain tone and uneasy expression.

"We have to put away the props from the play before we can go to lunch," Alicia smiled a little nervously. "C'mon, Lauren."

As the two all but scurried off, a bemused James turned to Jess and observed, "Usually I have to return grades before I get that kind of reaction from students. Do you know what's going on?"

Jess gave a quick little nod, glanced at the girls, and explained in a low voice, "Yes, I'm afraid I do. C'mon, let's talk somewhere else—and, no, it's not you."

"That's a relief—except if it's not me, is it you? Everything go all right in class today?"

Jessica calmed her husband's concern as she beamed, "Oh, class was wonderful. I had a ball. The students and even Terry, everything, was just grand."

"Everything?"

Jessica glanced at the busy Alicia and Lauren. Busy but not oblivious to her conversation with James, though not blatantly eavesdropping.

"Lauren, Alicia," she called, causing them to look up. "We're going to lunch. Do you need my help breaking down the set or with anything else before I go?"

Lauren looked ready to ask a question, until silenced by a little poke from Alicia. It was Alicia who wished them a happy lunch.

After getting her hat and pocketbook, Jess slipped her arm through James's and guided him out into the Great Hall, quietly advising, "Let's talk outside, by the front entrance, where nobody's around to overhear."

Moving to their left, past an almost "secret" spiral staircase to the upper floors, then into the shadows under the grand staircase and landing above, Jessica guided James through the heavy wooden double doors leading outside, even as he was asking, concerned, "Was it something Terry did or said?"

"No, Terry was fine. Great to work with. No, it was another member of the Clarke clan, after class."

"His wife?"

"You nailed it, ace."

They were standing in the shade of the grey granite building. Above them, one of the Gothic framed lanterns, elegantly balanced on the tail of the traditional curling "dolphin," extruded from the wall. Not the July sun, any passersby, or even an open window pressed in on their conversation.

"So, what happened?" James asked carefully.

"Let's just say no fur flew but fangs and claws were definitely bared," Jessica responded, not exactly happy recalling the interchange.

"Hmm, how bad was it? I didn't notice any bloodstains or shattered furniture. Your dress isn't in tatters."

Hmph, he would have to bring up the dress. At least James didn't seem too concerned, though. Maybe I'm making a mountain out of a molehill. Well, let's see what my better half has to say about that exchange—editing out Carolina's cracks about this dress.

"She just sashayed in and was a little too emphatic asserting her territorial rights over Terry—as if I had any interest. So, I set her straight in a fairly ladylike way," Jessica explained, trying not to burn with the memory.

"That doesn't sound so bad, especially since you were 'ladylike' when you set her straight."

Was there a tinge of irony in James's tone?

Concern colored his words when he read her expression: "What's the problem, love?"

"Well, I," Jess groped. "I just resent her insinuations that she *had* to assert her rights. As if *I* could be on the prowl. It's insulting, really, James. And Alicia and Lauren were still in the room. I feel, I don't know . . . besmirched!"

James pretended to rub something off Jessica's nose, then smiled amiably, "Right. Now you're unsmirched."

"You don't take this very seriously, do you?" Jessica observed, not immune to her husband's humor. Still, she insisted, "It's just that I'm concerned that if she goes around spreading rumors, maybe it will reflect on you, somehow. Make us seem undesirable to have around. I don't want to make any waves for you."

James shrugged and explained, "You're forgetting, I'm an old hand at university politics. There isn't much I haven't seen. Take my word for it; Carolina Brent Clarke is small beer—and her reputation around here isn't exactly sterling. She's made a great many enemies. Truthfully, her bad opinion could work in our favor. And remember, I can take care of myself. Didn't I defeat heaps of Nazis, undo quislings by the score, and win the last war?"

"I think you had a little help, my friend."

"Maybe a little. But I want you to buck up. Remember, any time you let her dirty cracks get to you, she wins a round."

"You really know how to appeal to my weak spots, don't you?" Jessica smiled. "Maybe you're right. Anyway, looking back, it's almost a laugh the way Terry had to hustle her out the door. I think he was terrified of what she was going to say next. I'd almost feel sorry for him. I mean, she can't be an angel to live with if she's that suspicious. Of course, if he's given her reason to be that way . . ."

"A marriage made in the first book of the *Divine Comedy*," James concluded. "Just don't let them suck you into the maelstrom they've created for themselves."

"Thanks, mister. I feel better," Jess said. Then, after taking a quick look around to make sure they were still alone, she tilted her hat and leaned in to give James a quick kiss.

"Here now, Miss Minton," James remonstrated. "What are you up to? What will happen when this gets back to Mrs. Crawford?"

"As the hep cats say, it's copacetic," Jessica grinned. "She gave me the green light."

"Progressive gal, this wife of mine," James smiled.

"Only with me, buster. So don't get any smart ideas."

"Right, General," James saluted her. "So, are you ready to join David at the dining hall to tuck into a nice lunch?"

"Sure thing," Jess agreed as James slipped his arm through hers and they started off. She went on, "And you've helped me make up my mind about something. I'm going to sit in on Terry's class Friday, and any day I see fit. I'm not going to let Carolina Brent Clarke's nasty little mind keep me from doing my job and enjoying it."

James stopped them both and warned, "Look, Jessica, I said don't let her get to you. I don't think you should poke her in the eye, though."

"That's not what I meant, James," Jessica protested, adding, "though if anyone deserves a good eye-poking . . ."

"No argument from me there," James agreed. "And her husband could probably stand one as well. But that's not your job. I just don't think you should spend too much time with Terry Clarke. You have a tender heart, and I'm afraid he might spin a few poor mouth stories for you and . . ."

"And what?" Jessica questioned, not exactly sure where this was going but pretty sure it wasn't in any direction she'd like.

"I haven't changed my opinion of him. He's a dark horse, untrustworthy. I wouldn't put it past him to get chummy with you while making his wife believe you were more than chums."

"That's ridiculous! No, it's horrible!"

But Jess had to admit to herself that supposition was not far afield from other aspects of Terry Clarke's character she'd dealt with before. The past few days had gone so well, she'd almost forgotten. James's expression told her that he was reading her thoughts quite clearly.

Jess agreed, "Okay, I see your point. Anyway, I wasn't planning to attend as a social activity. I really do need to see where Terry's going with his class, if I'm going to fill in for him."

James nodded and said, "I know you're enjoying bringing together acting and teaching. I don't begrudge you that. Just don't let Clarke get too matey, that's all. He's not really your friend. He doesn't need to know your business, and you want to steer clear of his."

"I agree with that wholeheartedly. I've absolutely no intention of becoming his pigeon," Jessica vigorously reassured James. "Anyway, I have to be there Friday. I can't let Carolina think she made me afraid to show my face."

Realizing he'd pushed Jess as far as he ought to, James let the argument go and said, "All right. So, is that all out of your system? Ready to sit down to a relaxing lunch?"

"Sure—well, there is *one* other thing?"

"Not about the Clarkes?" James queried, feigning exasperation.

"No, wise guy. About my shoes. I need to switch into my walking shoes. You may have been made for me, but these roads were *not* made for spectator pumps."

Chapter Ten

Friday, July 19

The Sound stretched under a hazy mist before Jessica Minton, Long Island's bumpy line on the horizon blotted out. A dreamy day to sit on the sand and watch the waves roll in then dash back out. Sandpipers and other long-legged birds skittered in and out after the waves, piping abruptly to each other. The foghorn moaned through the grey, buoys clanged in melancholy melody, while gulls wheeled and sharply wailed overhead in a sky the sun seemed to have abandoned.

Jessica, arms clasped around her knees, actually smiled. Perfect setting for a Romantic poet brooding over lost inspiration, love, or nature's bond–a fall of humanity or a prayer for madness. James could have brought his students for a field trip, especially if they were delving into the dreamy musings of Keats's "Ode to Melancholy." No, that long-neglected gal, Charlotte Smith said it better:

O'er the dark waves the winds tempestuous howl;
The screaming sea bird quits the troubled sea:
But the wild, gloomy scene has charms for me,
And suits the mournful temper of my soul.

Yet this Friday afternoon, Jessica Minton was hardly mournful, sitting amidst the seashore life, her dungarees and black pea coat fortifying her against an unexpectedly cold, damp day in July. True, it would have been better if James could have shared it with her. However, he was at a department meeting; the reason her second choice, Rose Nyquist, couldn't join her, either.

Her roam down the beach, beyond sight of the campus with the bends, rocks, and inlets obscuring her, wasn't entirely aimless. It was her job to accumulate some driftwood for the bonfire she and James would share with the Nyquists tomorrow night—unless the brewing storm rolling fog around the coast scotched those plans.

As much as Jess enjoyed stretching out with Dusty while having a cup of tea and reading, she just couldn't sit still in the cottage today. For one thing, Dusty had discovered a mouse colony subletting the cellar. Consequently, the grey tabby was far more interested in big-game mouse hunting than dozing with her human roommate. On top of that, today's class had gone so well, with no awkward intrusions, Jessica was far too keyed up to stay indoors. So, with a note tacked to the front door telling James she'd gone beachcombing, she'd been off.

A glance at her watch told Jessica she'd better snap to collecting that wood. But this meander was about more than gathering kindling. Rose had clued her in on the q.t. that the Coast Guard had recently, unobtrusively stepped down then discontinued patrols. So today was perfect for taking a sneak peek at Margaret Point's closest thing to the haunted world: that beached ship. *But just a peek, only to the top of the rock wall and away from the barbed wire. Surely that wouldn't violate any strictures. No one would see, anyway.*

Up on her feet, Jess dusted the sand from her dungarees, picked up her canvas duffle bag for carrying wood, and moved off to her left, toward the arm of rocks reaching into the sea. Fortunately, this was hardly an Everest-like climb, just high enough to block her view of the cove beyond. A path of packed sand wound up, through the rocks, and flattened surfaces took over where the path disappeared. There was that barbed wire strung along the wall of rock that, along with those Coast Guard patrols, had kept so many of the curious out for so long. However, Jess blinked in surprise. A clearly fresh rockslide had opened up a sufficiently large gap to let a person through the wire without fear of being snagged. Today, anyway, a person limber and dressed for the occasion could manage the climb and scramble through the tumbled rocks to the cove below. Should she? *No more patrols to fear. Well, looking down into the cove and seeing what lay below couldn't hurt.*

The damp in the air left the rocks slick and requiring some attention. So, Jess was all the way to the top before she could divert her eyes from the path into the cove for her first sight of the legendary hulk.

It lurched into the sand, perpendicular to a wall of rocks about a quarter-mile opposite the height where she stood. The cove was enclosed by this fortress of rugged, ocean-aged stone. With the tide only starting to return, there was a sliver of beach between the grey Sound and the battered remains. It must have been some storm to drive that hulk this far up the beach. Jess studied the blurring of sky into sea. Maybe she shouldn't hang around too long, with the fog creeping in and the storm lurking out in the Atlantic. In fact, searching for firewood seemed rather a waste now. It increasingly looked as if there would be no bonfire on the beach tomorrow night. More like candles against power outages, although candles *were* romantic. Just James and her—and Dusty, and the mice. *What more could a girl ask for?*

Curiosity drew Jessica's eyes back to the hulk. After a morning immersed in *Macbeth*, this cove haunted by the wreck looked the perfect setting for the Three Witches. That suggestion evoked an irresistible temptation to take a gander at the ship.

Jessica really had intended just to stand up here and look over the wreck. She'd had no intention of violating campus rules to stay out of the cove; but all alone, getting a good read on the sands beneath her, Jess couldn't help thinking that it wouldn't hurt just to visit below. She'd never do something half-baked like go into the wreck. *That* would be dangerous. The cove, though, was simply a safe beach. There was even a path down through the rocks, not *exactly* dangerous to navigate. Why, she could see plenty of driftwood down there, which they could always use in their fireplace if the weather kept her and James in. Besides, no one was around: no students to see a bad example, no authority to scold her off.

Jessica carefully picked her way down the slope, surrounded by rock turned grey, green, brown in the damp. Yes, there was a path, but you still had to watch your step. At last, the packed sand of the cove was under her feet, and Jessica crossed toward the lowering form. Halfway there, she stopped. The mist crept in. A foghorn moaned, lost in the grey of the sea. The only other perceptible noise was the pound of the ocean echoing around the cove—until a lone gull wheeled low and pierced the opaque of sight and sound with his lament. Maybe this place was too eerie and deserted for even the Three Witches.

A shiver rattled up Jessica's spine. Right, then, it was all just too much beyond the pale for her. What kind of a bright idea had brought her here, alone, on a day like this? The old derelict seemed to menace like a beached sea beast, weakened but not quite dead or even incapacitated.

Oh, for Pete's sake! What was with her? No one, nothing, was here to menace her. She couldn't allow her imagination to run away like this. No reason to be chicken. She was supposed to be taking a vacation from all this spook malarkey. Anyway, Jess told herself as she propelled herself across the sands sliding underfoot, it wasn't as if she were planning to go inside that old wreck. All she wanted was to take a look at the outside, a little closer look.

Approaching the old ship, its metal hull rusted and battered, Jess's emotions shifted, sadness and pity enveloping her. How many men had been lost on the ship? It had been fatally wounded during a storm, at least not by a U-Boat. How much consolation was *that* to its crew? To their widows and children?

The ship listed toward the ocean, as if longing to return to its natural element, to escape exile in this alien landscape. Jess moved to her left, the landward side, for her perusal, unmindful she had unfastened her watch and was nervously tapping it against her palm as she moved along the vessel.

So far, nothing specific to elicit additional shivers, Jess assured herself. A glance back at the cliffs. No one to spy her trespass, either. Vaguely, she noticed a cleft in the rock wall opposite the broadside of the derelict. Passing along the rusted metal sides, pausing to try to peer in through a porthole, Jessica picked her way carefully around some old beams, weathered and covered and re-covered by sand. *How had this cove not been stripped of firewood ages ago? Maybe the ghosts of the wreck preserved the ship's lumber? More like campus security, no, more likely, the fear of God implanted by the Coast Guard. Lucky for her, none of them were here now.*

Up ahead, Jessica noticed, for the first time, a gap in the side of this ship. *Had anyone been daring enough to take shelter there? It wouldn't hurt to just take a peek.* She certainly had no intention of entering this dead hulk. *Just take a peek.* Her watch was now tapping to the wash of the waves.

The opening wasn't so much a gap as an old hatchway long ripped way, now sleeping somewhere in Davy Jones' locker. There was enough light from the hatch and two port holes to see inside. It was the light of twilight, and what Jess saw surprised her.

She leaned through the gape in the ship's side, still careful not to enter. Quite the little getaway met her eyes. Not exactly the Waldorf Astoria but not the Wreck of the Hesperus, either. The floor still appeared fairly solid; an old rug had been thrown down on it. A hammock stretched across the narrow chamber, to the right, cushions piled against one end, as if awaiting an occupant. A bottle of some kind of wine and two glasses lay before the hammock on the floor. To the left was a battered, built-in desk. Candles, affixed by their own melted wax, and a box of matches waited there. A book of some sort also rested near them on the desk. A chair was tucked in, mismatched. The setup seemed to be waiting for an assignation that would never be; for dust, rust, moldiness, and despair were everywhere.

Someone had *found a way around the Coast Guard and the barbed wire. Maybe there was a hidden entrance to the cove? So, who had been responsible for setting this up? Why hadn't the meeting come off?* There was a touch of sophistication here that belied the involvement of students. *So, who? Well, do you really have to ask that question? Who were the secret lovers Rose told you about?* Still, Terry and Jessamyn Crane might not be the only people on campus carrying on clandestinely.

Jess gave the room another survey. *Hmm,* would *it really hurt just to take a closer look? No, none of your business!* She forced herself away abruptly, too abruptly, lost her footing, and went down, half in the room. In shock, Jess's hand sprang open, sending her watch flying somewhere into the chamber!

Jessica shook her head to clear it and recapture the wind knocked out of her. Her first thought: *Swell, now I have to go in there to find my watch.* She pulled herself up but hesitated. *Was the floor sound enough?*

It had to be if some couple had been meeting here for extracurricular activities, right?

Her first steps were tentative, but they carried her well into the chamber. There was a faint smell of, what, patchouli? *Here?* Jess moved over to the desk, knowing full well her watch would not be sitting atop it amongst the candles, matches, pouch of incense, cigarettes, and the book.

Her fingertips rested on the cigarettes. "Le Chat Noir." Not a brand she recognized. And the book? Jess held it, musty from its stay in this wreck. An unfamiliar name. She flipped through it. Poetry. In French, though a bit different from the Parisian she learned at school. One page opened naturally, betraying its unknown reader's preoccupations in lines of longing, passion, even despair. *Someone was certainly an unhappy camper when it came to love.* Jess flipped to the publication information in the front of the volume: Québec. *Hmm, French cigarettes, wine, and Québecois poetry. Far too highbrow for an undergraduate or most locals.* Somehow, she doubted it belonged to the happily married Judy Ricardo of World Languages, either. She had no such doubts about a Canadian artist and teacher like Jessamyn Crane, however.

Of course, she didn't know for certain whom Jessamyn Crane was meeting here, who drove her to immerse herself in poetry of love's pain, but she certainly could make a good guess. Maybe she could almost feel sorry for Carolina. *Nope, no dice!* But maybe she felt a twinge of understanding of why the other woman might be so suspicious and mean. Oh, she wanted to get the heck out of here!

Where the devil was that watch? How do I get myself into these things? "Curiosity killed the cat," snaked into her brain. *Bad thought for this lair. How about "Information brought her back?"* Jessica had far more information than she wanted at this point. The only information she wanted was where to find her watch!

Unexpectedly, under the desk, something gold caught her attention, and she snatched it up, even as her grasp told her its size and shape were all wrong. Then she saw it, over to the other side, her watch, and Jessica absently dropped the other object into her pocket, before picking up and inspecting her time piece. *Great, at least the crystal isn't broken, and the watch is still running! Boy, could I ever use some fresh air about now!*

The fog was beginning to drift into the cove as Jessica sat down on an old beam, a little ways from the lovers' lair, and caught her breath. She knew she ought to be scurrying around, gathering wood, but she just couldn't push herself to work. Something was mesmerizing about the dark, rounded, grooved and wind-blasted rocks; the sand; and the ocean pounding insistently beyond the derelict. She didn't really want to think about what she'd found in that wreck behind her, especially since she'd started, almost, to like Terry again. But who was she to judge? Maybe he deserved sympathy. Maybe Jessamyn Crane had been a blessed relief from Carolina—except that chamber in the wreck wasn't blessed; it was so forlorn. And Jessamyn had left. *Why?*

Because she had a sick relative to care for. That was the only reason Jessica had a right to think about it. Besides, she didn't know for certain that Terry was whom the woman was meeting. The mantra "it's none of your business" droned in her brain. With a big sigh, Jess tried to clear her mind of all these sordid personal complications, plunging her hands into her pockets against the chilling damp. Her fingers brushed something hard. Oh yes, the shiny object she'd initially mistaken for her watch.

Pulling the thing from her pocket, she examined it and puzzled aloud, "A tie clip? Initials? N. B. C.?"

She seriously doubted the entire National Broadcasting Company had been rendezvousing with Jessamyn Crane. So, whom did she know . . . ?

"Oh, good grief! Nigel . . . Cross. Nigel Cross? And Jessamyn Crane? Whoa, boy, this is way over my head!"

But maybe the tie clip wasn't Nigel's. It wasn't impossible for someone else around here to have these initials. And she didn't know that his middle initial was "B."

Jessica stuck the tie clip back in her pocket, thinking how much she wanted to be out of here. She was on her feet but stopped. Hadn't she better bring back some firewood—the "real" reason to be out here? She'd better make it snappy, too. James would probably be home any time now. Mightn't he start to worry if he thought she was out too late in the kind of weather that would give Edgar Allen Poe the willies?

Jessica was snapping up driftwood, zig-zagging her way around the cove, still never too far from the hulk. She neared the edge of the wrecked ship, now moving in closer, concentrating so intently on her task that her unpleasant earlier conjectures were temporarily buried. She barely even noticed the funny plopping sound that slipped through the wash of waves. Unfortunate. Jess reached the end of the hulk and came face to face with the biggest, blackest horse she had ever seen! Or at least it seemed so in the first second of their abrupt encounter.

Who was more startled? That was a toss-up. Jessica jumped back, tripped, and went down hard on her keister, her burden scattering around her. The riderless horse, under full tack, snorted and pranced backward, then stuck out his neck toward her to whinny an equine equivalent to, "What in Sam Hill do you think you're doing, Lady?!"

It seemed an eternity before her hair didn't feel as if it were standing at attention and her eyes went from saucer to normal shape. Then, Jessica laughed.

The horse shook his head, snorted again, stepped forward, and gave her a friendly head butt in the chest. With that, he trotted off toward the far wall of the cove behind her, seemingly satisfied all was well.

Jessica gave her head a clearing shake, muttering, "Well, I'll be . . ." and rose up enough so she could gather her booty. She watched the horse dash about and kick up his heels like a sailor on liberty, but still ever careful not to put a step wrong. All of which led Jessica to hunker into a crouch to do some tall thinking. A horse didn't just tack himself up and go for a gallop. Where was his rider, the lone sailor? She quite clearly recognized the gorgeous black horse. Had "Sailor" been thrown? Injured?

"Are you all right?"

The voice answered Jessica's question, as she looked up at the tall, lanky uniformed man who had suddenly appeared around the hulk and was staring down at her. For the briefest moment, Jess had an uneasy twinge, startled to confront the resident man of mystery, but not for long. His craggy features were worn more by care or anguish than age, and the eyes were concerned, genuinely concerned.

Before she could answer, he pressed, "He didn't knock you down, hurt you, did he?"

Jessica good-naturedly answered, "Nothing fractured but my dignity."

She really liked his answering smile as he put out his hand to help her up, while he explained, "He's a horse who likes to run by himself, sometimes. There's never anybody here. It's supposed to be off-limits. So, I let him have some fun—I didn't think he'd be causing any trouble."

"No trouble," Jessica assured him. "I've been wanting to get a good look at him since the first time I saw you ride by, but this wasn't exactly how I'd planned it."

Her companion nodded. "I know who you are. You're in Jessamyn Crane's cottage. You're married to that new teacher at the school. Aren't you an actress, too, on the radio—Jessica Minton?"

"Do you work for the FBI or something?" Jessica kidded. "That's some low down you have on me. I don't even have the foggiest what your name is. Only that you have that beautiful horse."

"I think you've probably heard a few stories about Blackie and me," he replied, maybe a little bitterly. Then he lightened and extended his hand, "They like to call me Sailor, but I have a name. Phil, Phil Novack."

"Pleased to meet you, Mr. Novack," Jessica smiled, shifting her burden to shake his hand. Out of the corner of her eye, she could see Blackie trotting back to them.

"So," Phil Novack regained her attention. "Like I said before, this place is usually off-limits. What are you doing out here?"

Jessica glanced down at her bundle, then back at Novack and quipped, "Shopping for shoes."

Novack smiled briefly, then more broadly as Blackie came over to him. He put up one hand to pat the horse's neck and took the reins with the other, all while pretending to grumble, "Stay out of trouble, you."

Novack turned back to Jessica and observed, "Those kinds of 'shoes' are much easier to come by closer to your cottage—and a lot easier to bring home. What takes you all the way out here?"

He was still perfectly affable, but Jess sensed that he didn't think her being here was quite according to Hoyle. Maybe if she came clean, it would clear things up. "Okay, you got me. It's a long way to go for firewood. I have to admit that I heard a lot about this wreck, and I was curious."

"Curious, huh?" he didn't disapprove, *exactly*. "So, did you satisfy your curiosity? Find anything here to intrigue you?"

Jessica hesitated. She wasn't about to chew the fat about other people's shenanigans, but maybe she could still manage to be honest without being a gossip.

"It's sad and lost here, isn't it, Mr. Novack? I mean this ship; its life is over. Stuck on a beach, close enough to feel the water but never be able to reach it. This wreck, it's like a ghost and this cove is a graveyard of lost dreams, lost hope."

"Poetic kind of a gal, aren't you?" the weathered man posited, observing Jess keenly.

She shrugged and returned, "You asked me. That's what I feel here."

"Do you also feel like a grave robber?"

Jessica jerked her head in surprise and blurted, "Me? What do you mean?"

"Some of these planks you're holding came off ships. Maybe this one here, maybe some of the thousands of tons that U-Boats torpedoed in the Sound or the Atlantic. You're making what's left of someone's sunken coffin into a little campfire for warming your feet or toasting marshmallows."

"Now who's poetic?" Jessica posited in a quiet voice.

"Yeah, I'm a regular Elizabeth Barrett Browning," he tossed off as he watched Blackie nuzzle his hand, now clenched.

Yet Jessica wasn't afraid, alone in the fog and sea damp with this man now grown haunted. She knew that look in Novack's eyes; she'd seen it often enough in James. She understood.

Lowering her kindling to the ground, Jess said, "I'm sorry. I didn't realize. I'm not one to show disrespect for the dead. I have a few ghosts of my own."

He looked sharply at her, as if seeing her for the first time, then relented, "Skip it, lady. I guess there's a reason no one wants to spend time around me. I don't like being around most people. Maybe, though, I should give some people a chance."

"Maybe," Jessica agreed, smiling gently. "Tell you what. I'd really appreciate it if you gave me the chance to pet your horse. I've been dying to. He won't take my hand off or anything?"

Novack broke into a broad grin at the chance for an unfreighted conversation, especially about his horse, answering, "Blackie bite? No chance. This fella's a sweetheart. A kid could pet him. Go ahead."

Jessica slowly put her hand out for Blackie to sniff, not nervous but ready to act fast should the horse decide to make a liar out of Novack.

The muzzle was like velvet. His forehead soft, his eyes friendly. He even gave Jessica a sociable little whicker. She almost felt she knew him.

The humans both chuckled, and Novack concluded, "I guess you must be A-okay if Blackie likes you."

Jess smiled, rubbing the horse's chin, and said, "I wish I had some apples or carrots for him."

"And he'd eat 'em. But this fella's got a real sweet tooth. He'd love a nice lump of sugar. Wouldn't you, Blackie?"

"Now, I can't get over that you have this magnificent horse, but you call him by such a pedestrian name. I know you have some poetry in you, Mr. Novack. You mean to tell me you couldn't come up with something more elegant?"

"He's black, isn't he? It suits him. His real name is a little more regal, but . . ."

"His real name? You're telling me this guy is traveling under an alias? Is he on the lam for hay burglary? Heisting sugar lumps during rationing?" Jess laughed.

"Not exactly," Novack answered, stroking the tall horse's neck. "My brother Val used to train horses at Rockingham Park in New Hampshire. He claimed this guy up there. Anyway, the horse came up lame on him. Since he couldn't afford to keep a horse that can't pay his way, he sent him to me. Figured it was better than turning him into dog food. Said they called him Blackie around the stables, so that was good enough for me. Anyway, I guess he figured two broken-down veterans belonged together. The best kind of pals."

Jess beamed at them and opened up, "I suspected he was a Thoroughbred or had Thoroughbred blood in him. He has the long, clean legs and body. He's big, too. At least sixteen hands, and just a touch of the original Arab, with those ears that turn in slightly and the dished face. Even though he's filled out a bit in his 'retirement,' he's still quite a beauty."

"You sound like an improver of the breed. Maybe you had a dollar or two on his nose back in the day. The New England circuit has plenty of tracks. Who knows where he was running before my brother claimed him."

"Who knows?" Jessica shared a smile with Novack and wondered if this guy might hit it off with James.

It was Novack who broke the spell with a look around them, followed by the assessment, "Cripes, this fog is bad. You better get back home, especially before the storm breaks."

Jessica surveyed the cove and was shocked to realize suddenly how the fog had shrouded them in: "Good grief, I never even noticed! This is miserable. James will be so worried. I've got to get back."

"Your husband doesn't know you're here?"

Jess wasn't quite sure if Novack's tone was concerned or curious.

"No," she replied, amending, "I mean, yes, he knows. I left him a note, but he'll be worried if I'm not back. I really have to go."

"The way you came? Over those rocks?" Novack jerked his head in that direction.

Jess nodded, uncertain where her companion was going with his questions.

He shook his head and warned, "Think again. In this fog, if you don't slip and break your neck on the rocks, you'll get washed out in the high tide."

Jessica was startled into anxiously insisting, "Well, I can't stay here, that's for sure."

"No, but you can let me guide you out of here. Hardly anyone knows about it, but there's a cleft straight ahead in the rocks leading out. It's a little tricky, but Blackie and me can get you through."

Jess remembered noting the cleft earlier, so she asked, "Then what? I don't know my way from there."

"Then me and Blackie ride you home once we get to the road. If you're worried your husband might try to come after you in this mess, we can stop at my cabin, and you can call him. Let him know you're all right, or I can even tell him our route back so he can meet us. How about it?"

Jessica hesitated. How smart, let alone proper, was it to go off alone to a man's cabin–a man you didn't even know, a man some people had plenty of doubts about, to boot? Still, her instincts said Phil Novack was on the square, and staying here or trying to scramble back the way she had come felt far more dangerous. If she didn't accept his offer, she was in a tight fix.

Novack read her hesitation but didn't take offense, saying, "Okay, look, I know you don't know me from Adam. But we both know you can't exactly stay here, or you'll have to swim home. Why don't you at least let me guide you out of the cove? I could ride you home or set you on your way and go back to my cabin to make a call for you. But to be honest, lady, I don't like your chances with cars on the road in this fog."

Jessica bit her lip, considering, but before she could decide, they were both startled by a male voice cutting into their discussion.

"Jessica! Jessica Minton!"

Terry Clarke. Having just emerged from the cleft in the rock wall, he was striding across the beach toward them, his face growing grimmer the closer he drew.

"Stay right there, Jessica. Don't move!" Terry ordered. "You shouldn't be here. This is no place for you. Everyone knows this is off-limits."

Jess expected Phil Novack to ask her what was the deal with this guy. Instead, he took a tighter grip on Blackie's bridle and turned impassive. Blackie, however, was far from impassive. After sniffing the air, the nearer Terry came, the more he fidgeted. *Was it Terry's tone or Terry himself that bothered the horse?* Jess wasn't sure which riled *her* more just then.

"Friend of yours?" Novack asked neutrally, as if he'd decided he ought to say something.

"It's a question I've often asked myself," Jess answered, not sure if she were puzzled or annoyed at Terry's intrusion. Novack appraised her with slightly amused curiosity.

Terry drew close enough for Jessica to question at normal volume: "Terry, what on earth are *you* doing here? Why are you so upset?"

He joined them, a little breathless, shot Novack a quick, disapproving look, then repeated, "I know you must have been warned about this place. It's dangerous. That rusty old heap behind you could collapse any time. And in this God-awful weather, what were you thinking?"

Then he turned to Novack and accused, "How could you let her? You know this beach better than anyone, if rumors are true. You should have been the first to put a stop to her wandering into a death trap."

Blackie snorted ominously in response. Jess and Novack both automatically gave the horse a steadying pat. It was Novack who pointed out, "I didn't see her wandering anywhere but on the beach, buddy. Hey, she's over twenty-one. What's it to you? *You're* not her husband."

Stymied, Terry floundered for a moment before saying, "She's an old friend, and I just don't want to see her getting into trouble because she doesn't know the score."

Terry seemed genuinely chastened. Jess kicked the sand in front of her before saying, "Look, Terry, I appreciate your concern, but I'm fine. In fact, Mr. Novack was actually looking out for me." *Did Novack shoot Terry a quick look of amused triumph? No, couldn't be.* Jessica went on curiously, "Anyway, Terry, what made you come out here looking for me?"

"You left some papers in the classroom. I went to your house to drop them off," he explained matter-of-factly. "No one seemed to be home, and I saw the note you left Crawford. You said where you were going . . ."

"You read my letter to James?!" Jessica flared.

Blackie jerked his head and snorted.

"It's all right. I sealed it up again and put it back on the door," Terry assured her, as if not throwing away the private note made everything according to Hoyle.

"How dare you!" Jessica lowered in a quietly threatening voice, more mindful of Blackie's nerves.

"What's the fuss?" Terry challenged. "I put it back. And it's a blessed good thing I did read it. Look at you, stuck out in this fog with no quick, safe way home–with a Nor'easter in the offing! You ought to thank me."

"I ought to let you have it," Jessica grumbled.

"Okay, okay," Novack cut off Terry's rejoinder. "Both of you simmer down. Not in front of the horse. He's sensitive. The real issue is to send the little lady home safe and sound. So, first, let's get off this beach."

Terry gave Novack an impatient look, but he couldn't dispute his logic. Jess wasn't sure she liked being dubbed "the little lady," but she knew she didn't want to dog paddle her way home, so she only said, "Okay, yes. I'm for that."

"Fine," agreed Terry. "My auto's just over the ridge, beyond all the rocks, on the road."

Jess was not pleased to be dependent on Terry to get home, but Novack headed off any protest with, "That's your best bet. He can run you home faster than I can. That'll save that husband of yours a heap of worry. If you give me your number, I'll call him up to say you're on your way."

James's peace of mind outweighed her annoyance with Terry, so Jessica smiled her appreciation and said, "Thanks, Novack. You're all right."

Not pleased with this chumminess, Terry gave Novack a hard, disapproving look before turning to Jessica and advising, "If you're really worried about your husband, you'll cut the chit chat and come back with me. The sooner the better."

Jessica started to zing Terry verbally for his highhandedness. However, Novack, who had just retrieved selected firewood for her, put a calming hand on Jess's shoulder. Turning to Terry, he instructed, "Here, Galahad, take some of this firewood for the lady. A gallant guy like you wouldn't expect her to tote it all by herself."

Before Terry could resist, let alone protest, Novack had dropped half the load into his arms and walked past him, calling to Jessica, "Lady, grab Blackie's reins. I have my hands full, and I think he's taken enough of a shine to you to let you lead him. But keep him clear of your pal here. I don't think Blackie's too fond of him."

Jess leaped at the opportunity to be with the horse, though she secretly wished she might leap into the saddle and ride him home. Maybe that would be a *little* too forward. She contented herself with leading the dark stallion with one hand and giving his neck an occasional stroke with the other, as she followed Novack across the sands and through the growing wisps of fog toward the cleft. Terry brought up the rear; she could feel his scowl burning through her and scorching at Novack.

Jess knew that Terry was doing her a big favor, going out of his way to find her and drive her home in this mess. Didn't it show a concern that she hadn't thought he possessed for anyone but himself? So, why did he have to act like such a stinker in the process? Just as well she didn't have to look at Terry now. But the car ride home would prove a doozy. This wasn't exactly what James had in mind when he'd told her not to get mixed up too much with her old chum.

Chapter Eleven

Silently, Terry held the door while Jess got into the car. He didn't even say a word after he had gotten into the car and put them on the road. As they crept along the fog-muffled route, Jess stared straight ahead, her forehead cradled by a hand and arm propped against the side window. Silence suited her just fine, even if it meant waiting for the other shoe to drop. What should she say, feel, right now? She did owe Terry big time for saving her a trudge through this God-awful murk, but his tone to both her and Novack–bro-*ther*, was she steamed! So, what to go with: gratitude or anger?

Terry finally broke the silence, his voice controlled, his eyes concentrating on the road: "You know, Jessie, you really take the cake. I thought you might have grown up since college, but there you are–impulsive as ever. What the devil were you thinking, traipsing off on a day like this? You know the college has designated that wreck unsafe, off-limits. And cavorting with that Sailor guy? Everybody knows he's not all there."

Not about to confirm Terry's assessment of her by flying off the handle, Jessica resolutely avoided the powerful temptation to shove him out of the car and drive herself home.

Instead, Jessica coolly rebutted, "First of all, as I told you before, no one has called me 'Jessie' since 1936. Second, the weather was a little gloomy but hardly ominous when I left home. Third, the man's name is Phil Novack, not 'that Sailor guy,' and I was hardly 'cavorting.' In case you can't differentiate, there's a huge gap between talking and

Bacchanalian revels. And as for his being 'not all there,' I found him quite reasonable and considerate. He certainly behaved better toward you than you did to him."

"I was concerned about you, seeing you alone with him in the fog, isolated."

"We weren't alone. Blackie was there," Jessica corrected, shifting her attention to what she could discern of stone walls and deserted meadows in the mist.

"I suppose you think you're pretty cute, don't you?" Terry returned, his tone serious. "This is no joke. I live here. I know what people say about the guy. Some people are more than a little afraid of him."

"Some people are bigoted and nasty," Jessica snapped back, thinking not only of Phil Novack but of James and other vets she knew who'd been through hell. "I met the man and talked to him. He's an okay Joe. He's fine. Even your President Wanda Angelovic stuck up for him."

"A Roosevelt lefty. The kind who won't crack down on anybody but successful businesses."

"Don't change the subject. This isn't about politics. Anyway, since when have you ever been worried about my well-being? Even when we dated . . ."

"Not so," Terry disagreed. "Remember that time you were sick, and I brought you chicken soup from Chez Jalbert? That wasn't concern?"

"Sure, I remember," Jessica agreed doubtfully. "I also recall that you told me not to read too much into it at the time. I also remember that you were still more than a little chummy with other girls. I never knew whether I was coming or going with you. I still don't. Why this deep concern about my wellbeing, Terry?"

"Maybe I just don't want to see an old friend get into trouble. Give me a little credit. I'm not exactly Lex Luthor."

"No, I'll give you that," Jessica allowed. "You certainly have more hair. But aren't you afraid of getting yourself into trouble with Carolina? We both know that she is *not* my biggest fan. I don't need a crystal ball to see she's going to hit the roof when she finds out you've been playing Sir Galahad for *me*."

"She's not going to know," Terry calmly replied. "There's a great deal she doesn't tell me, and I return the favor."

Jessica was quiet as this indication of the sorry state of Terry's marriage sank in. Did she feel a twinge of pity? *Skip it.* But she wouldn't skip over the fact that she was now in a position to spark even more hostility from Carolina Brent Clarke.

"Terry, she's certainly going to wonder where you disappeared to for all this time. Are you going to lie to her?"

"I don't have to. She went into the city with an art dealer from town for a gallery showing. In her book, I'm out of sight, out of mind."

Jessica couldn't say she minded avoiding antagonizing Terry's wife. However, Terry wasn't the only one with a spouse who could be concerned right about now. In this weather, James would be uneasy, even though she'd left him a note. *Good grief! Would he try to go looking for her, in this soup?!*

"Terry, can't we go any faster than a crawl?" she anxiously asked.

"Are you kidding? Take a look out there! Anyway, are you in that much of a hurry to get away from me?"

Jess wasn't about to waste time on the last question, answering, "I don't want James to worry. And I *don't* want him to go looking for me in this weather."

"Ah, so maybe you shouldn't have traipsed off to the wreck? Maybe I have a point?"

Jess shot Terry a sharp look, but she felt more anguish than anger. It wasn't that he might be right and she wrong; she just didn't want to have worried James.

Terry seemed to read her concern and surprised Jessica by softening, "Hey, take it easy. Before I taped your note back up, I added something about my going to find you and that he should sit tight."

Anguish slipped into annoyance, then relief for James's sake. Still, she couldn't keep some sarcasm out of her response: "Oh, that will go over really well with James—your reading *his* letter and telling him *you're* going to take care of his wife for *him.*"

"What gives here?" Terry retorted, surprised, a little affronted. "I'm doing him a favor and he's going to get sore? Maybe if he were around for you . . ."

"He was at a department meeting, which shouldn't you have been at, too?"

"The subject didn't interest me," Terry answered shortly. "And lucky for you I was free."

He had something there, Jessica had to admit, but only to herself. She also bit back commenting on the irony of *Terry* charging a husband with neglecting his wife. That was one sleeping Doberman she would *definitely* let lie.

All Jess said was, "Terry, I'm tired, and you need to concentrate on the road. Let's just maintain radio silence till we get home. Deal?"

Terry hesitated, as if he had more to say, but he only nodded. So, they crawled down the murky road, and Jess silently brooded over what she would say to James when Terry delivered her home. Relying on Terry's taxi service was a far cry from her promise not to get too chummy with him. But had there been any choice today?

Finally pulling up towards the cottage did not turn out to be the relief Jessica had expected, and she observed, "That's odd."

"No lights," Terry elaborated as he parked the car on the wrong side of the road before her house.

"What do you make of it?" Jess worried, her hand already pushing on the car-door handle.

"Only one way to find out," Terry pronounced shoving open his own door.

Both of them in front of the car, Jess looked at her front door and observed, "The note's still there. That means . . ."

"Department meeting should have let out a long time ago, Jess . . . ica. I don't think your James has even been home. I guess I'm not the only one with a spouse who's hard to keep track of."

"Do you *try* to be a pain in the neck?" Jessica snapped, even though she could see that Terry had been merely tactless not antagonistic, this time.

Where *was* James? She hated realizing she had no idea, and on the kind of night Dracula should have been meeting the Wolfman. Coldly, she changed the subject, "My firewood's in the trunk. Please help me get it out."

"I'll carry it to the door for you."

"That's not necessary."

Maybe Terry was repentant, but Jessica just didn't like the thought of being in his debt any more than was necessary, even if she knew she was being rude.

"Nonsense," he disagreed, heading for the trunk, unlocking it, and pushing up the hood as he continued, "If I'm going to play the gentleman, I'm going full throttle."

Jessica softened, "All right. Thank you."

But her eyes were on the cottage, the empty cottage. Where had James disappeared to? She did not like the thought of him out on the road. Nevertheless, Jessica forced herself to turn and help Terry. Anything to keep from considering dark possibilities. She was leaning into the trunk, gathering up kindling, when through the fog she heard her name called by a voice that made her heart sing.

"James!" she exclaimed. She shamelessly shoved her wood into Terry's arms and left him flat-footed to rush into the arms of James, who had trudged up the road toward them from the direction of the campus.

"Oh, I was so worried when I got back in all this mess and you weren't here," she breathed, stepping back, then giving her husband an impulsive squeeze.

"Sorry, love, I didn't mean to worry you. I took the bus into town after the meeting. I was sure we'd be back ages ago, but I didn't anticipate this fog. We moved like a tortoise the whole trip. But 'got back'? You just got back from...?"

"The hulk out in Joseph's Cove," came Terry's voice as he stepped around the car into view, still laden with firewood. "Your girl was about ready to have kittens when we got back, and you weren't home."

James did not appear at all happy to recognize Terry. He looked from Clarke to Jess, and she could read in his eyes, "*This* is what you call keeping it purely on a professional basis?"

Jess hadn't expected so strong a reaction. She didn't know what to say. It was not what she'd come to expect from James.

"So," asked James carefully, "you took my wife out to that dangerous derelict to collect firewood?"

"Good heavens, no!" Terry protested. "That was her own bright idea. I came by to drop off some papers, saw the note she left you on the door, and went after her, knowing what a mess it was going to be getting back."

"You read *my* note?" James's controlled tone was not at all friendly.

"Your wife already read me the riot act for that *faux pas*," Terry tried cheerily to placate James. "Look, I'm sorry. But the truth is, she needed a ride home. You wouldn't want her walking in this fog, would you? Didn't it work out for the best, all things considered?"

James gave Terry a measured look, finally saying, "Yeah. All right. Thanks for giving my wife a lift." He moved over to Jessica and handed her his briefcase as he said, "I'll take the firewood, Clarke. You must be anxious to get back to your wife. I imagine she must be concerned."

"Yeah," Terry simply replied, shooting Jessica a rueful glance.

"Thanks, Terry. Drive carefully," was all Jessica said, uncomfortable in acknowledging what he'd revealed about his marriage.

Terry nodded and got in his car. Watching him pull away, Jessica and James stood together just inside the gate. Her hands warming in her pockets and James's briefcase tucked under her arm, Jessica said without turning, "You know, I didn't plan any of this. And you wouldn't want me to hike home through this pea soup, in the dark, would you?"

James replied tiredly, "No, no, I wouldn't. I just don't trust that Terry Clarke."

Jess turned and looked up at James to ask, "Don't trust him? What do you mean? You think he'll make a pass at me or something?"

James wanly smiled and said, "It's not inconceivable." Then he thought and added, "But that's not it, exactly. I said it before; I always have the feeling he's up to something, but I can't quite put my finger on it yet."

"Well, quit worrying. I'm not about to let him get me mixed up in anything shady, of any ilk. You can take that to the bank."

James slightly shifted the subject by asking, "So, when he gets home, what do you think he'll say to his wife. I don't want them dragging you into any sordid business."

"Mrs. Brent Clarke is off to New York City with a village art dealer."

"Sophisticated company she keeps. Who's the chap?"

Jessica shrugged, "Terry didn't say. Anyway, it sounds as if she and Terry don't do much talking, so she probably won't even hear about the rescue of this fair maiden."

"Unless he gets jealous of the art dealer fellow or annoyed with her and throws it in her face," James considered quietly.

"Oh, James, I never thought of that!" Jess blurted, her stomach sinking. "But what could I do? It seemed the fastest, safest way home."

Hands full, James nudged Jessica toward the cottage with his elbow and comforted her, "I know. No matter where you go, there's always something. I wish I'd never gone into town today. If I'd come home earlier, I could have ridden in on my white steed and rescued you myself."

"You? On a horse? There's one for the books," Jessica chuckled.

"All right, then. I could have walked up in my Oxfords—maybe not on the beach. How about in my brogues?"

"Eminently more practical," Jessica affirmed as they neared the porch. "And speaking of 'in,' let's get out of this fog and drizzle. Now that we have this wood, I could really go for a fire in the hearth. If you take care of that, I'll put on the kettle and rustle us up some vittles."

"Excellent idea, madame. Your husband is ravenous."

"Fine," Jess grinned, warming to James's better spirits. "And when we get settled, I have a horse tale to tell you about a pony named Blackie."

James's hands full, Jessica took care of unlocking the front door and flipping on some lights once they were inside. They were both rather surprised not to be greeted, or even chastised, by Dusty after being absent so long. Jessica conjectured to her husband that perhaps a safari for mice in the wilds of their cellar was more important to Dusty right now than righteous feline indignation.

James set down the wood by the fireplace, holding it in reserve until it had dried off a bit. Jessica took both their coats, damp with mist, into the kitchen and set the kettle on for tea, while James occupied himself building the fire.

By the time Jess returned, her husband had already ignited some newspaper and was feeding kindling to the flames until the fire was strong enough to devour the logs.

"So, what were you up to in town?" Jess inquired, leaning against the mantle.

"I got word that my new camera had arrived at the shop, so I popped in to pick it up. Remind me to get it out of my brief case later, would you? Afterward, I explored some of the shops. Your antique store was closed, on a Friday, too. Funny, eh?"

"It's not *my* antique store. I just saw Terry there that time. Say, did you see Nigel in town, too? I remember when I ran into him on the train, bringing Dusty back, that he remarked he always seemed to see you poking around the town," Jess went on, now looking out at the opaqueness beyond the sliders.

"Did he now?" James remarked casually without glancing up. "What did you say?"

Turning back to him, Jess answered, "Oh, just that you liked to wander around like that when you were thinking, preparing for classes. He said something about 'great minds,' blah, blah, blah. Apparently, he does the same thing. Say, that fire's looking like a honey. Good work, old chap."

James looked up and smiled, then admitted, "I rather wished I'd foresworn my wanderings today, all things considered. But I did want to get my camera, and there were some papers I wanted to pick up, too."

As James returned his attention to keeping the fire going, Jess silently mused whether those papers were wrapped around tobacco. James had been trying hard to quit cigarettes, concerned with Jessica's allergy to too much smoke, but it was a difficult habit to break. So, even if she could still whiff the tobacco after James believed he'd secretly enjoyed his "vice," Jess kept her lip buttoned. The guy had enough on his mind without her shutting down this release.

"Mmm," Jessica agreed. "Maybe I didn't pick the best day to go exploring. Although I'm happy I made the acquaintance of Phil Novack. The one they call Sailor, with that beautiful black horse. He seemed like a right guy."

"And his having a lovely horse didn't blacken your impression of him, either," James concluded.

"Don't get wise, mister. Anyway, you're not going to pull a Terry on me—start warning me about getting into trouble by consorting with strange men, are you?"

"Worried about you and strange men? Isn't that how we met?"

"You're being awfully flip over this. Seems to me you must know something that I don't. No holding out on your lovely wife. Come on, give."

"Well, lovely wife," James explained, tossing more kindling in at well-judged intervals. "As a matter of fact, I called in a favor with Dick Streeter and had a check run on this chap's records through the War Department. He came up clean. Acceptable war record, invalided out of the Coast Guard after a U-Boat took out his ship. No arrests, no family left to speak of."

"He has a brother who trains thoroughbreds on the New England circuit," Jess playfully one-upped her husband.

"Had," James corrected her with equal impishness. "Vladimir Novack died of a heart attack."

Jessica cocked her head and observed, "Do you check up on all my acquaintances like this? I don't know if that's flattering or creepy."

James sat back on his heels and answered easily, "Just good policy in this case. The chap did have a bit of a spotty reputation around here. I could see you might be getting chummy with that horse in the picture. I thought you'd like to have the facts so you could make a smart decision. I just didn't expect you to be making friends quite so fast."

"What can I say? I'm a charming gal. Anyway, I do like the guy. He tried to help me with the firewood, even to get me home, and he did let me pat his horse. Talking with him, I could see he has a sense of responsibility, and humor. I think he likes to be alone because he doesn't have the patience to deal with jerks, especially after all he's been through. I will tell you one thing: he *does not* like Terry. They didn't seem to know each other, but Novack enjoyed getting Terry's goat."

"Really?" Pretty much finished with the fire, James stood up and continued, leaning against the mantle, "Well, your chum Clarke does present a tempting target for anyone who abhors an inflated ego."

"Let's forget about Terry Clarke," Jessica proposed, slipping her arms around James's waist, "You and I are here, together, warm and cozy. All that *Sturm und Drang* (literal and figurative) is outside. What more could we ask for?"

"Dinner?" James proposed hopefully.

Jessica heaved a sigh and chided, "That's *not* very romantic, you know?"

"What can I say? A bloke has to keep up his strength, doesn't he? And at this point, I've surpassed peckish and have cruised full speed into ravenous. Do we have something that's quick?"

"All right, all right. I'll go throw together a couple of sandwiches to go with the tea. The kettle should be singing any second now." A glance behind James, across the floor, and Jessica smiled with devilish sweetness. "Oh, look. You might not have to wait. Dusty's bringing you an *hors d'oeuvre.*"

James cocked an eyebrow and stated, "I can do without snacking on anything with four paws, a long skinny tail, and big ears."

Jessica made a funny face before replying, "Well, all four paws are there. There is a long tail. But it's hard to tell about the ears, what with the head missing. Oops, there's the kettle! *Bon appétit!*"

Their romantic evening drove away any of Jessica's desire to relate what she'd found inside the hulk. None of that sordidness was going to taint their sweet time together. Besides, she could go forever without James pointing out she was becoming as much of nosey Parker as her sister.

Chapter Twelve

Saturday, July 20

It truly was a dark and stormy night, but Jessica Minton didn't mind at all. Wind and rain may have lashed the cottage, but the kitchen was warm with steam from boiling potatoes and another pot cooking peas. While baking the ham, the oven helped drive away the outside chill. For once, Jessica was glad they had a gas stove rather than one of those new electric jobs. The power and the telephone lines were down, and she didn't mind at all. Candles on the table and an oil lamp on the counter set the room glowing romantically.

Jessica stirred the potatoes and skimmed away the starchy froth, a full apron over her long-sleeved cream dress. Dusty dozed on one of the kitchen chairs, her presence there rather than under a couch indicated that the thunder and lightning had passed. The house did creak under the furious howls and moans of the wind, but a day spent playing cards and snuggling with James undercut any sinister intimations of those sounds. Rather, Jessica softly sang, humming when she forgot the words, "I've Got It Bad and That Ain't Good." *Wait a minute; I really do have it good!* She cheerfully switched to "Arthur Murray Taught Me Dancing in a Hurry."

The door to the mudroom banged shut, Dusty cocked an ear and opened her eyes, while Jess turned to the kitchen door opening under James's hand. His slicker now hanging in the mudroom and his brogues sitting on the floor, James stepped into his slippers and announced, "It's a little wet out there."

"Really? I hadn't noticed," Jessica dryly replied. "So, how are the windows?"

"Holding up."

"How is my garden?"

She knew James had perceived her concern, for he temporized, "I couldn't really tell, love. A few things may have been flattened, but the roses look pretty tough."

"Well," Jessica sighed. "I can't fight Mother Nature. Oh, what about the ocean? Any danger from a storm surge?"

James shook his head, walking over to scratch Dusty's neck before explaining, "We're quite some distance from the water, and then the slope from the house down to the beach is a bit of a drop. I don't think that Dusty's in any danger of having to do the cat paddle."

"That makes sense," Jessica agreed, wiping her hands on her apron. "The cottage was built after the hurricane of '38. I imagine someone from campus security would have gotten word to us if there were anything to worry about."

The timer on the oven dinged, and James asked brightly, "Time to eat?"

"Almost. If you could just grab a loaf from the bread box and put it on the table, I'll get the ham out of the oven. Then I have to mash the potatoes . . ."

"Oh, do let me," James volunteered gallantly, retrieving the bread and setting it on the table. "Potato mashing was my favorite tutorial at university."

Jessica's only reply was to shake her head as she opened the oven to check on the ham. Deeming it fit for consumption, she removed and set its pan on trivets atop the counter.

So, potatoes mashed, ham sliced, bread retrieved, and peas ensconced in a blue-willow bowl, all was ready for the Crawfords to sit down to a cozy dinner, safe from the lashing wet outside. Even Dusty feigned peacefulness, though slitted eyes studied the ham, while flicking ears did radar duty in hopes of detecting an offering of human comestibles.

James was just about to tuck into a slice of buttered bread and Jess was serving herself some potatoes, when a pounding at the mudroom door stopped both cold. They exchanged expressions that clearly said,

"What the dickens!" Dusty skedaddled with high dudgeon off into the living room as the pounding continued.

Signaling Jess to sit, James was on his feet, saying, "No, I'll get it. You stay here where it's warm and dry."

Jessica swiveled in her chair, following James with her eyes and the words, "Who would be screwy enough to be out on a night like this? My goodness, I hope there's no emergency."

"We'll see," James called over his shoulder as he disappeared into the mudroom. "You never know. Maybe a car broke down."

Jessica frowned her concern, listening to the sound of voices in the mudroom. *Had security come to warn them about some storm-caused emergency?*

Then, a tall male form cloaked in a Mac and rain-battered dark hat preceded James into the kitchen. As he moved into the light Jess blurted before James could announce their guest, "Nigel Cross! Are you all right? Are we all right? The storm hasn't . . ."

"Everything is fine, Jessica," James calmed her.

Cross gave her one of his half-smiles and observed, "I didn't expect my presence to cause such a stir."

A little embarrassed, but only a little, Jessica explained, "It's not the sort of night anyone would expect a social call. I was just saying to James that I was a bit concerned about flooding."

"And you thought I was here to row you to safety? No, it's not quite like that," Nigel answered. Now noticing the dinner-laden table, he began to apologize, "However, I didn't expect to interrupt your meal. Perhaps, this isn't the best moment . . ."

"Nonsense. Let me take your rain gear. Sit down," James heartily offered. "Join us."

"Yes, do," Jess chimed in, guiding Nigel to a chair facing James's and the doorway to the living room. "There's plenty. I can set you a place in a jiffy. And if you've already eaten, I can make you some tea or coffee. What do you say?"

"Well, yes. All right, then," he relented. But he was still not entirely at ease, not an emotion Jessica expected in him. *What was his story?*

"I'm afraid it's nothing fancy," James explained. "But on a night like this, anything warm sits well with a chap, doesn't it?"

"Thanks for the ringing endorsement, dear," Jessica commented as she got Nigel a place setting.

Cross smiled slightly as James managed, "Oops, that didn't come out quite right. She is a good cook, Nigel."

"I've no doubt," Nigel Cross agreed. "And I have no doubt your wife knows exactly what you did mean."

"He'd better hope so," Jessica playfully warned. "Or the scones I baked earlier will be just for you and me, Nigel. And, James, I put currants and walnuts in this batch."

James offered Nigel a platter of sliced ham and commented, "You see what a cruel temptress I've married."

Nigel just smiled slightly, selecting a slice and transferring it to his plate.

"Gentlemen, you can take that to the bank," Jessica grinned. "Now dig in!"

They both followed Jessica's direction. Nigel, at one point, congratulated Jessica on her superb mashed potatoes. At James's knowing smile, she acknowledged the true maestro of the spuds.

As James buttered his bread, he inquired, "So, Nigel, what does bring you here on such a foul eve? It must be something important."

Nigel Cross paused, then glanced from one of his hosts to the other before answering, "I'm afraid it's a bit awkward. Something I have to speak to both of you about."

That statement gave Jessica and James pause. Nigel had even dangled a preposition. Jessica knew that her uneasiness stemmed from a different reason than her husband's. He didn't know about a tie clip from a mysterious trysting place.

"Awkward?" James asked slowly, genuinely puzzled. "It's not about my work, is it?"

"No, not at all, James. Quite the contrary," Nigel quickly reassured him. "Your work is more than satisfactory. That's one of the reasons I felt I needed to come here without delay, tonight."

Jessica wasn't sure whether she or James had the more furrowed brow trying to figure out that one. Abruptly, her puzzlement turned to cold dismay when Nigel turned to her and elaborated, "No, I'm afraid the issue is with you, Jessica."

"Me?" she blinked in surprise.

James's tone was skeptical: "Jessica? Seriously?"

Jess and James both looked at each other, thoughts of Terry running through their minds. It was Jessica who took the bull by the horns and prompted carefully, "I don't get it. I haven't been taking bribes from students or selling black market cigarettes."

"It's not your relations with the students," Nigel clarified, not harshly.

"Then what, Nigel?" James asked calmly, but with sparks beginning to fleck his hazel eyes. "I can't imagine Jessica having done anything untoward here."

"I'd say 'unwise' rather than 'untoward,'" Nigel tactfully corrected. "I'm referring to a rather imprudent expedition I was told she made to the derelict in Joseph's Cove yesterday."

Jessica let out a long sigh of relief, though James still regarded Nigel speculatively. She could see it was her place to smooth things over.

"Is that all, Nigel? I walked over to an old boat? You came out in a major storm about that?" Jessica shook her head. "What's the big deal?"

"The big deal is that we have designated that area off-limits to students, for their own safety," Nigel levelly informed her. "You may not realize it, but you might not merely have put yourself at risk but any students who decide that if the people higher up in the hierarchy can ignore the rules, so can they. If we don't abide by our own rules, we've little hope that the students will."

Jessica frowned. She'd never been one to accept a lecture placidly, especially from a guest in her own home. *Even if the home belonged to the college? Skip that.* Nigel's having a point rankled even more.

As she tried to master her mixed emotions, Nigel Cross soothed her somewhat, "It's not my intention to scold you, Jessica. Truth be told, that old wreck is not safe. I wouldn't want to see anything happen to you. I do need you to promise me that you won't go there again."

Jess felt James's eyes on her, calculating how she was going to react to being told what to do. She took a deep interest in the mashed potatoes on her plate while she thought this one through. It wouldn't exactly be smart to tell her husband's superior where to get off, particularly since she could see his point. Hadn't she known from the start that she shouldn't have gone there? Hadn't the result of her gamble been to uncover some secrets she really wished had stayed buried?

"Nigel," Jessica began, "I've been there once and that was enough for me. Not much to see but a broken-down old boat. Anyway, it's not as if there's no other beach for me to walk on."

James didn't give a sigh of relief, but he did go back to his peas, a trace of amusement under his mustache.

Nigel nodded. "Good. Ah, well, that's all settled, then, and very reasonable of you, Jessica."

"Something that does strike me odd, Nigel," Jessica began casually, "is that you charged out in a monster of a storm to have this chat with me. Couldn't you have waited till tomorrow, or even Monday?"

James continued to eat, but knowing him so well, Jess could detect he was paying careful attention to Nigel's answer. Wondering if it might touch off her temper, after all?

"I'm afraid I couldn't wait. By Monday, maybe even tomorrow, if the phones are back in service, I might need a ready answer, the one you just gave me."

"Answer?" James queried, finally joining in. "Answer for whom?"

"Ah, there's the rub," Nigel smiled sardonically. "I do miss being a mere professor, not having to run the gauntlet of irate and ignorant administrators and trustees."

"I thought Wanda Angelovic was a pretty square gal, someone who listens to reason," Jessica protested.

"Indeed, she is, Jessica Minton. And if she were the only power with whom I dealt, if she didn't have to answer to . . . others, this whole issue wouldn't even be an issue. But too many people exert influence over the decisions I make for my department. The less I antagonize them, the less inclined they feel to get involved.

"And, my dear James, that's where Jessica's behavior affects you. From what I've seen so far, I'd like to recommend our keeping you. Unfortunately, if someone with clout takes a dislike to your wife as a troublemaker or bad influence on the students . . ."

"I'd hardly call Jessica a 'bad influence' or a 'troublemaker,'" James corrected Nigel reasonably.

"Perhaps I wouldn't, either," Nigel concurred. "But I think if we need to fight the powers above us, we'd better save it for something more important than where your wife takes her walks. You need to build up your capital. Don't make me try to negotiate from a deficit. You've been around. You know the politics of power."

"Indeed I do," James replied coolly, and Jess could see in his eyes that he was considering whether he was selling her out in order to preserve his position. So, she put a hand on his arm while telling Nigel, "No big deal. I had my look at the wreck, and I've no interest in going back. I don't lose anything, James doesn't lose anything, and your worry warts at the top are happy. I have to say, though, if the ship is such a death trap, why is it still there?"

Nigel answered, "It takes a lot of money to get rid of a thing like that—and the ownership rights are complicated. At any rate, the best bet all around is to stay away. I especially wouldn't want your undeterred visit there to tip off any of the curious that the Coast Guard had stopped patrolling. Now that you've had your look at it and you understand the situation, you will be steering clear?"

"You have my word on that," Jessica replied, pleased with the positive results of not losing her temper. "To tell you the truth. It wasn't much to look at, all beaten up."

"You didn't go inside, did you?" Nigel's tone betrayed alarm. He must have seen Jessica and James's surprise, for he added, "I hate to think of you in such a dangerous place. I know the trustees would be far from pleased . . ."

Jessica considered leveling with Nigel about going inside the hulk, but only briefly. He was so disturbed at that possibility, she couldn't bring herself to confirm his uneasiness. Anyway, recalling the initials on the tie pin, the romantic implications of the trysting-place, she wondered if Nigel was less afraid of the trustees than that she might have discovered something sordid about him, Jessamyn Crane, and Terry Clarke. Better to leave him in blissful ignorance.

"I'm adventurous, not a dope, Nigel," she tried to kid him out of his anxiety.

James, however, had a question of his own, casually put but still capable of stirring things up, "Just out of curiosity, Nigel, how did you know Jessica was at the wreck yesterday?"

Nigel leaned back, taking a sip of his water before replying casually, "Is that really important?"

"I'm just curious about who's tattling against my wife."

James's tone was calm enough, but there was enough steel in it to give Nigel another pause.

Jess jumped in with, "It doesn't matter, James. I think we should drop the issue."

James smiled a bit sardonically, before concluding, "Of the two gents you ran into there, Jessica, I think we both know which one was more likely to . . ."

"Two gents?" Nigel interrupted, taken by surprise. "Who . . . ?"

"Terry Clarke and Phil Novack," Jessica automatically supplied.

"Novack? You *talked* to Novack there? What did he say?" Nigel questioned sharply.

"You recognize the name?" James asked with interest.

"The fellow everyone calls 'Sailor,'" Nigel replied impatiently, still focused on Jessica. Her, he questioned, "What did he say to you about the place?"

"Why, he, he just seemed to see himself as its guardian, almost," Jess found herself answering. "He told me not to show disrespect for the dead by grabbing the planks from sunken ships. I understand what that means, his having been shipwrecked. Oh, and his horse, we talked about the horse mostly. Why? What's the problem?"

"The horse," Nigel absently considered. "He would talk about that horse."

"I'm not surprised at that," James pointed out. "It appears to be all he has."

Nigel straightened, looking from Jess to James. That sharp eye gave Jess a shiver, so to break the spell, she proffered the nearest plate: "Bread?"

The gesture seemed to release Nigel, and he said pleasantly, "Yes, thank you. Maybe one more for the road."

"Are you sure you want to dash off into that typhoon?" James asked, as if there had never been a tense moment, assuring Nigel all was well.

Nigel Cross decided to play the same game, answering pleasantly enough, "I doubt the storm is going to break before late tonight, and I don't want to wear out my welcome."

Jess and James both smiled, but neither countered Nigel's statement, either.

The meal wrapped up, with Nigel declining Jessica's offer of coffee or tea. Strangely enough, James did try to urge him to stay for scones, perhaps regretting provoking Nigel earlier, now that their visitor had turned pleasant, almost contrite. Maybe that was why James hadn't pushed Nigel to admit that Terry had ratted her out.

While James saw Nigel out through the mudroom, Jessica cleared the table and set up the tea and scones. *Hmm, those two seemed to be taking a long time chatting. What now? At least their voices weren't raised.* Jess sat down, and, yes, she was listening! *Darn it, they were too quiet, and the winds were too insistent.* At last, James came slowly into the kitchen. He raised his eyebrows at her and inquired, "So, what do you make of all that, Mrs. Crawford?"

Jess shrugged and answered, "You got me. I'll tell you one thing; we didn't need the radio tonight. Plenty of drama and suspense right here at the table."

At that point, Dusty trotted in and proudly dropped a mouse on the floor before James.

"Even murder?" James intoned in his best *Inner Sanctum* voice.

The mouse unexpectedly leaped up and scurried for cover while Dusty was distracted by the scent and sight of ham on the countertop.

"Only attempted murder," Jessica beamed, clasping her hands in mock delight.

The kettle surged into a full-blast whistle, so James turned down the flame and took away the boiling water while repeating, "So, what *do* you make of Nigel?"

Jessica raised her hands in surrender and admitted, "I don't know. A decent guy trying to tread softly around bureaucrats without giving away too much to them? One good thing, though, he said he liked your work. That must take a load off your mind, hon."

"Ye-es," agreed James slowly, almost hesitantly.

Surprised, Jessica pressed, "James, what's wrong? I thought you liked it here."

"I do, I do," he assured Jess as he poured the water into the tea pot on the counter. Facing her, James finished, "I just wonder if this is the right place for you."

"Me? Are you serious? What's the problem for me?"

Sitting down, James continued, "What about tonight? What about Terry? Carolina? I don't want you to feel constricted or to be constantly bumping up against hostile sorts."

"James Crawford, you know very well that I'm no sissy. Why, I've worked with directors that make Carolina Brent Clarke look like Shirley Temple. As for Terry, I can handle him quite nicely, thank you very much. And constricting me, well, Nigel didn't ask me to refrain from doing anything more unreasonable than not play with nitroglycerin. To be honest, I'd also concluded that I didn't need to go back to the derelict. Didn't *you* want me to steer clear, too?"

"True," James allowed. "I guess I'm more worried about Terry. He's always running hot and cold. One minute he's saving you from treacherous ocean fogs; the next he's trying to get you into Nigel's bad books."

"As much as I hate to make excuses for Terry, he might not have been trying to get me into trouble. Maybe, in his own cock-eyed, I-know-what's-best-for-everybody way he thought he was actually trying to protect me. Though I'll be the first to agree that he'd be better off concentrating on his own mixed-up excuse for a life."

James sat back and asked, "Do you really buy that, yourself?"

"It's possible," Jessica insisted, not entirely convinced.

"Look, Jessica," James began, leaning forward, "when Nigel talked to me in the mudroom just now, he said that there was a strong chance Terry wouldn't be here in the fall, and his wife would be going with him. Do you think it might be better if, until he's gone, you go back to the city? You can come back after he's left."

"What? You want me to leave you for the summer!?" Jessica was flabbergasted.

"It's not all summer. I could train into town on weekends . . ."

"And I could run yelping back to the city like a scalded pup? Wouldn't Mrs. Clarke just love that scenario? Honestly? Do you know me at all?" Jessica couldn't decide if she were more shocked or irritated.

James put both hands on her arms, his fingers pressed down with unexpected strength. He seemed to debate exactly what to tell her next, settling on, "I only want to be sure you're all right."

"James, I'm fine, really," Jess reassured her husband, touched by the genuine concern she read on his face. "Besides, you're forgetting that I made a promise to help with that class. I don't go back on my word. You know that. Anyway, everything worked out just fine tonight. No hard feelings with Nigel, right?"

"Right," James relented, not too enthusiastically. But *something* else was still eating him.

Jess began slowly, "James, it's not that you don't want me here, is it? Have I made things difficult for you? Because of Terry? I thought that you'd seemed so much less restless, lately. Am I making it worse for you, the war nerves?"

That got to him, and James insisted, "No, no, Good Lord, just the opposite. Even when I can't sleep, those nights, knowing you're still here . . ."

"Then, I need to stay," Jess decided. "I want to stay. And Dusty can't take care of you by herself."

"I guess I would get tired of mouse every night for tea," he admitted with a crooked smile.

The humans seeming more at peace, Dusty deemed it prudent to keep them soothed by curling affectionately against James, first, then against Jessica.

"So, it's all right? You're fine with my staying?" Jess ventured.

James nodded, easing the worry in her eyes with, "I'm sure I want to have you with me."

"All right, then. But," here Jess hesitated, before determinedly pushing on, "there is something I think I ought to tell you about yesterday, at the derelict. I didn't say anything earlier because I felt a little as if I'd be telling tales out of school; and, frankly, I wanted to put all that unpleasantness behind me."

"Go on," James urged quietly, maybe a touch uneasily.

"Now, don't look so worried," Jess tried to ease his concern. "It's nothing about me and you, nothing catastrophic. It has to do with Nigel, and maybe Terry."

"That's an odd combination," James observed, not exactly humorously.

"I'll say. Anyway, I'm afraid I've been a little disingenuous. I did go inside the wreck, by accident; I tripped. Don't look at me like that. Nothing happened to me. It was safe enough. It's just that I made some odd, um, discoveries."

"Discoveries?" James repeated, clearly not looking forward to hearing what she'd found.

"Yes, discoveries, about Terry and Nigel, and even Jessamyn Crane."

"Everything but the kitchen sink," James concluded.

"Maybe, maybe. At any rate, I found the inside done up like a trysting place: candles, a bottle of wine, hammock, book of Québecois love poetry . . ."

"The Canadian poetry, that's where you think Jessamyn Crane comes in," James surmised, surprising Jessica by appearing a bit relieved at this revelation.

"You pegged it."

"So, Terry was cheating with this Miss Crane," James pondered. "That doesn't surprise me, as far as your old friend is concerned; but I'd thought Crane had a better reputation than that. Still, I can buy that Terry might have seduced her into secret trysts in the wreck. But Nigel? You've got me stumped on how he fits in."

"You wouldn't be stumped if I showed you the tie clip I found in there with the initials N.B.C.–Nigel Cross?"

James mulled over that tidbit before asking, "You know for certain that Nigel's middle initial is 'B'?"

"Well, uh, no, but how many people on campus have those initials?"

"I can't say, but the answer might knock your theory into a cocked hat, if you pursued it–which I do not recommend," James knowingly cautioned.

Jessica frowned, until she reflected, "Except, Nigel did seem awfully jittery about the possibility of my being inside the old ship. I think he was concerned about more than my personal safety, not to mention that he wasn't too happy about Phil Novack hanging around there. Maybe he was afraid Novack might tumble to something about him or have seen something in the past."

James smiled, "Quite the detective, aren't we, Mrs. Crawford?"

"Over the past three years, I've had more than enough experience in that department between you and your fifth columnists and Liz and her shady business associates. Kind of jades a girl, don't you think, *Mr.* Crawford?"

She was happy to see amusement flicker in James's eyes. But those eyes went serious, and he cautioned, "If I were you, Jessica, I shouldn't mention the tie clip or the room to anyone, especially Cross. I'll wager he wouldn't relish you or anyone else knowing about it."

"James, I read you loud and clear. No need to embarrass the man. But tell me, what *do* you think? Was it he or Terry meeting Jessamyn there? Do you think he was an unrequited lover, and perhaps he went there to put a stop to her and Terry? Still, that doesn't exactly explain how he lost the tie clip."

"Tossed it to the floor in a fit of fury when Jessamyn refused to give up the irresistible Terry Clarke," James suggested, tongue firmly in cheek.

"You're kidding, aren't you?"

"Yes, I am."

Jess sighed. "James Crawford, you are no help whatsoever. Aren't you the least little bit intrigued? Maybe this all has something to do with Jessamyn Crane's leaving so abruptly. And I still don't get how Phil Novack is mixed up in this soap opera. What do you think?"

"I think I'm where Moses was when the lights went out."

Jessica narrowed her eyes and joined James in completing the old saw she'd learned from him: "In the dark."

Pouring out the tea, Jessica admitted, "I guess it's all really none of my business."

"That's true," James concurred. When Jess shot him a dirty look, he added, "But I admit that it's a bit too much temptation not to wonder."

Jess smiled and affectionately squeezed James's arm before pulling back the towel covering the scones and keeping them warm. Graciously popping a particularly plump and currant-laden delectable onto her husband's plate, she pronounced, "For that kind admission, sir, a thousand thanks and the prize scone of the litter."

"Litter, eh? You couldn't have come up with a tad more appetizing collective noun, love?"

"I can take it back, the scone not the collective noun, smart guy."

"You wouldn't dare! And remember, I'm a combat veteran."

"Sure, sure, but let's see you survive a scramble for nylons in Macy's basement, tough guy!"

So, their after-dinner scones and tea proceeded amiably, the only real excitement being Dusty's thunderous pursuit of her former murine POW into the kitchen, across the floor, around the table, and back into the living room. A skidding of claws on wood and an emphatic thump followed. Jess's only response was, "I *don't* want to know." The dejected and mouseless Dusty, on her return to the kitchen, was treated to a compensatory snack of baked ham. And this was what led to the cat's great awakening that losing mice might be a better policy in the future.

Chapter Thirteen

Sunday, July 21

Jessica Minton stood on the terrace behind her cottage, leaning into the balustrade. The gale that had driven off the storm last night was now merely a gentle wind whipping her white peasant blouse, her full skirt of tangerine swirled on white, and her long dark hair, held off her face with an encircling white scarf. The morning was truly gorgeous, bright and fresh. Who would have thought this pellucid blue above her, dashed with wisps of white mares' tails, could have been grey with gauzy fog then dark with savagely pelting rain? Wheeling gulls, crying exultantly, were turning the sky into an aerial circus with their swooping acrobatics. Still, the seaweed and driftwood abandoned by yesterday's waves testified to what had been.

The awkwardness of Nigel Cross's visit seemed almost washed away by the lovely evening passed with her husband. They'd retired to the living room, and she'd persuaded James to play and sing for her–old songs from home (his mother's as well as his father's) and some of his own. Those were the ones she loved best, the ones that took her into his heart: his joy, his struggle against the past, his hope for the future. Of course, the concert had concluded with some serious married-people's necking on the couch by hearth light. Jess smiled with the memory, scrunching her shoulder blades in contentment.

A glance back at the house. James was still inside, loading his camera in a dark place so as not to expose the film. He'd had a swell idea: since the day was so splendid and they'd been cooped up all yesterday (pleasant coop though it was), they ought to go out for a long walk on the beach. Yet Jessica's content dimmed as she glanced down and noticed the scrap of a cigarette butt almost obscured by the base of the balustrade. Apparently, it hadn't been all happy dreams for James, as this relic of a late night/predawn smoke revealed. And she hadn't been there to lend him moral support: slept right through it. *Damn.* But maybe he'd wanted to be alone? Needed to be, sometimes? He hadn't wanted her to know, clearly, since he'd been careful not to wake her or to say anything.

Those thoughts were displaced, though, by curiosity as she caught sight of a form rapidly advancing up the beach to her left—or rather a form of two in one. Phil Novack on Blackie! Jess waved excitedly, realizing that they weren't just traveling in her general direction but making for the path that led up the slope to her house.

"Good morning, stranger," Jessica greeted when Novack pulled up his horse on the other side of the stone barrier between them.

"Morning to you," Novack smiled, leaning forward as Blackie sniffed at Jess, happily, and received her rub on his nose. "Good to see you weren't washed away."

"Not at all. We were snug as the two proverbial bugs in their equally proverbial rug—even with the power out."

"Power out, huh? That's why, if you're on the ball, you rely on a generator like me. Light, power, the works. That little sun shower barely even touched me," he returned, rubbing Blackie's neck.

"That's an idea," Jessica considered. "I'll talk it over with James."

"Oh, the absent husband. I was a little worried about you when I called and nobody answered Friday. Then the telephone lines went down. I thought you'd probably be okay, but I figured, hey, why not just take a look? Can't afford to let anything happen to Blackie's pal."

"Well, as you can see, we're still here. But speaking of Blackie," she reached into her skirt pocket and pulled out a wax-paper-wrapped packet, "I prepared this little treat just in case we ran into you two on our beach walk. Apples. It's okay if I feed him?"

"Sure." Phil Novack nodded. "Go ahead. So, anyway, your friend Clarke there, he got you home okay? No problems?"

Jess looked up from Blackie to Phil, echoing, "Problems?"

"The two of you weren't exactly holding hands when you left."

"We'd better not be," Jessica dryly answered, returning her attention to Blackie, "seeing as we're both married to other people. No, I got home just fine."

"And your husband? He got home okay?"

"Sure," Jess stroked Blackie's forehead, now that he had made quick work of the apple pieces. "He came home right as Terry dropped me off."

"Kind of ironic," Phil concluded. "You worried about your husband worrying about you, and him not even home. Gallivanting?"

"Gallivanting?!" laughed Jessica. "I'd hardly say dropping into the village on an errand could be called gallivanting. Not even cavorting."

"Oh, just in the village? So, that explains why I couldn't get him on the horn. Hey, he got back safe and sound, that's all that matters—though you'd think he wouldn't pick such a God-awful day to do errands."

"I guess it wasn't that bad when he hopped the bus. And, you know, if you have to do something, you can't just wait until the sun shines."

"Oh, yeah, important business can't wait, I guess," Novack smiled down at Jess. "I'll tell you, it would have taken a Second Coming to get me that far from home Friday."

"Hardly that portentous," Jessica answered. "Anyway, look who's talking. I ran into you out on the beach in the same weather."

With a gleam in his eyes, Phil explained, "That's different. That stretch of beach, these rocks and hills, they're like my backyard, I ride them so often. Heck, I could do it with my eyes closed."

"Big deal," Jess joked, tapping Blackie's forehead. "You don't need eyes when you have this pair right here."

"A seeing-eye horse?"

"You said it!"

Novack, still smiling, nodded towards the cottage and said, "Looks like the master of the house wants in on our confab. This must be your husband."

Jess turned to see James, having exited the side door, moving toward them, his attention still intent on some last-minute adjustments to the camera hanging from a strap around his neck, a knapsack on his back. He looked up and stopped short at the sight of Blackie and Phil, then gave Jessica an inquiring look. Maybe even a slightly disquieted one, taking in the very large Blackie.

"James," Jessica began, "this is Phil Novack, the fellow I told you I met on the beach Friday. He tried to help me get home."

Novack had dismounted as Jess spoke. Extending his hand when James reached them, he said, "Crawford, glad to meet you."

James took Novack's hand, subtly but decidedly careful to steer clear of Blackie's shaking head, and offered the succinct greeting, "Novack. Glad to meet a chap who does Jessica a good turn."

"My pleasure. Couldn't leave a damsel in distress." A pause, then, "Don't worry about Blackie. He doesn't bite, unless you provoke him."

"There's the rub," James remarked skeptically. "I don't know what provokes him."

"Well, he certainly seems to have taken a shine to your wife," Novack noted as Blackie lowered his fine head and tried to nuzzle Jessica's hand.

"I think he actually took a shine to the apples," Jessica playfully disagreed. Rubbing his dark velvet nose, she told the horse, "Sorry, buster, I'm all out."

Blackie snorted and pulled back, opting to study something far off, down the beach.

"Afraid he's not the most gracious of gents," Novack apologized good-naturedly. "Once I saw him go to take a chunk off a guy who was trying to play fast and loose with him and a lump of sugar to dope him up."

James put a hand on Jessica's arm, as if to pull her away from the savage beast, but Novack assured him, "Hey, don't worry about her. He smelled something in that lump. Blackie's a good judge of character. He knows the score."

James didn't say anything, but Jessica didn't have to be psychic to know he'd prefer she donned iron-mail gloves before putting her mitts near Blackie. However, she knew enough about reading a horse to play it right. She also knew James well enough not to make an issue of his unnecessary concern.

"Anyway," Phil steered the conversation to less "fraught" waters, "I'm glad to see everyone got back home in one piece. It was a bast . . . pip of a storm. I guess I got a little rattled when I couldn't reach you, Crawford, so knowing that you and Clarke were both English teachers, I called your boss to let him know the score. I figured he'd know how to get to you if I didn't. You know that Cross guy . . ."

"*You* told Nigel Cross I was at the wreck?" Jessica broke in, surprised.

"Yeah, sure," Phil responded, puzzled by Jessica's reaction. "Did I do something wrong? Get you in Dutch?"

"No, no," James smoothly stepped in. "Neither of us expected you to be so matey with the Department Chair."

Now it was Novack's turn to seem surprised, even a little defensive, and he responded, "'Matey.' Eh? No, I wouldn't say that. But I do know how to call the operator and tell her to connect me. I just wanted to let you know your wife was safe and sound. I thought you'd be worried. Looks to me, though, that you left her just as worried about you."

Jess looked from man to man; their expressions told her this little chit chat had decidedly gone south. Trying to get things back on track, she soothed, "Anyway, gents, all's well that ends well. No one was washed out to sea. Now the power and the phones are working, the sun is shining, and it looks like a grand day for the beach. Are you doing a long, ride, Phil?"

Oddly enough, Jess noticed that while she spoke, Phil might have faced her, but the corner of his eye was on James. Novack hesitated only the briefest of beats before answering, "Down the beach, almost to town, not all the way. Don't like it there. Neither does Blackie. Too many people," he paused, as if remembering something then continued, "Probably back up the beach, then into the hills near my cabin."

"Past the old wreck?" James asked casually.

Novack surprised them both with an ironic smile and his answer, "No one's riding past that wreck anymore. Mother Nature fixed that. Smashed the whole damned thing to smithereens."

What really bothered Jessica was Phil's looking so darned pleased, whether at their reactions or the fate of the derelict, she wasn't sure.

James was speaking now, questioning, "How do you know that? You saw it?"

"What's left of it, when I rode by along the cliffs. A lot of the cove is still submerged, but you can see she's been pounded apart."

"If you don't mind me saying so," James observed. "You seem oddly well-pleased about the destruction of an old vessel. That's a bit of a surprise for me to hear from a Navy man."

"Not Navy, Coast Guard," Phil corrected, pausing to appraise whether James could understand what he was about to say. Novack reached a hand under Blackie's jaw to stroke the horse's cheek before continuing, "Your wife might get it. I told her about it Friday, when she was grabbing firewood. That ship's a monument to all the guys who died on her or to what died in the survivors, to all the guys and ships that were lost. Yeah, I think you do get it. I can see it in the back of your eyes. You try to bury it, but you can't always . . ."

"Sorry, you're mistaken," James cut off Novack. "And it's rather a sore spot with me, not having been allowed to serve. So, if you don't mind, let's change the subject."

Jess looked down, not wanting Phil Novack to see how much she felt for James's having to parade a cover story that often brought him unjust dismissal even disapproval.

However, the disapproval, dismay, or vague discomfort that James's cover usually evoked didn't come from Phil Novack. Fleetingly, he seemed ready to press James for more explanation. Instead, he only said, "Aah, what it all comes down to is that there'll be no more poking around the old ship's bones. There's nothing left to snoop into."

"*Was* there anything there to poke into?" James queried affably. "Did you ever explore her?"

Novack hesitated, then surprised them by joking, "I've seen enough of ships afloat to last me a lifetime. What'd I want to look at a beached one for? Nostalgia? Anyway, why not ask your wife what was inside. She was there."

"You saw me *at* the boat not *in* it," Jessica insisted, sticking to the letter if not the spirit of the truth. The fewer people, no matter how tight-lipped, who knew she's seen the trysting-place, the less chance of her getting mixed up in campus scandals. Thank goodness James directed the conversation into less perilous channels.

"Enough nattering about ghosts and ocean sepulchers. On a splendid morning like this, we need to be thinking about the living."

"You got that right, Crawford," Novack agreed. "I guess I'll be hitting the road now. Time's a-wasting." He swung adeptly into the saddle.

James raised his camera and suggested, "Say, how about letting me try out my new camera with a snap of you on your mighty steed?"

Almost before James finished speaking, Novack had turned Blackie around. He twisted himself back to them and explained lightly, "Nope, Blackie's camera shy. The click sets him off–hates the sound, spooks him. My brother said it had something to do with his time at the track. Last thing I need to do is have him bolt on these rocks. See you two."

"I'll always keep some apples or carrots in my pocket for Blackie if I'm on the beach," Jess called as Novack started his horse down the trail. The rider raised his hand in acknowledgment.

Jess turned cheerily back to James, whom she was a little surprised to see thinking about something.

"Penny for your thoughts, mister?" she queried, hands clasped behind her back.

His attention immediately returned to her. Arching an eyebrow, James observed, "You attract the rummest sorts, you know."

Jessica smiled "sweetly" and returned, "Of course, Liz would probably make the same observation about *our* getting together."

"Yes, indeed, she would," James agreed, putting an arm around Jessica's shoulder. "Still, I've never tried to cast my horse as the Greta Garbo of the equine set. You know about racehorses. Is that true, about the click setting a horse off?"

"Sure, why not?" Jessica answered, looking up at her husband. "Horses have *long* memories. If Blackie heard a click similar to the sound a camera makes and something bad happened to him at that time, especially if it happened more than once, he'd 'learn' to associate the click with bad news. So, it's very likely. Why do you ask?"

James shrugged, looking out to sea, "I was just wondering. Sounded queer to me, that's all."

"Well, you'll just have to get used to not looking for trouble every time something sounds funny," Jessica teased. "You're almost retired, and I doubt the *horse* is some kind of fifth columnist. The *Abwehr* wasn't *that* good with disguises."

"No, not a'tall," James smiled back. He rubbed her shoulder thoughtfully, then began slowly, "I don't want you to get upset when I say this, Jess."

"Uh, oh, this doesn't sound good," she tried to keep it light.

"No, no, nothing bad. It's just that you have a good heart, but you can't solve all the world's problems. I think your friend Novack is a man who's been through a lot and he's not done yet. I don't want you getting in over your head. Maybe you oughtn't to get *too* chummy with him."

"He's got a really nice horse," Jess protested, trying to diffuse James's concern.

"As you know, love, that trait's not a huge plus for me. At any rate, I'd hate to think you were cultivating the poor fellow just to get to his horse."

Jess playfully chided James, "Don't be such a Smart Alec. But seriously, about Novack, something just tells me he's a decent Joe. I don't want to be like Terry and that administrator at the reception, looking at Novack as if he were some kind of dangerous nut case."

"That's right, you did say Clarke didn't like him. The feeling was mutual, I gathered from our little chat. And on such short acquaintance."

Jessica stepped back and gave James a speculative look, before saying, "Are you being ironic? You think they *do* know each other? Really?"

James shrugged, theorizing, "Let's just say it's interesting that Novack had a bee in his bonnet about people nosing about the wreck, the very place where your old friend seems to have been rendezvousing with Jessamyn Crane."

"Good grief! This gets more tangled by the minute! I guess he would have it in for Terry if he thought he was 'profaning' the wreck. But what about Nigel? Novack didn't seem to have any problems phoning him, even though that tie clip suggests Nigel was there, too, at some point. What do you think about that, James? You're the master spy, even if you are supposed to be semi-retired."

"Whoa," said James taking Jess in his arms, making her laugh. "I think that we've gone far enough in turning a pleasant summer into *The Thirty-Nine Steps*. If we're smart, we'll stop poking our noses into other people's business before someone nips them right off. What say we forget about campus intrigues and enjoy this glorious day?"

Sometime later, the sky rose a pure blue over the incoming rush of waves. Nary a wisp of white vapor in the sky now. You'd hardly think last night had been possessed by such a rip-snorting storm. The sun, hot and bright, forced Jessica to squint as she sat on the blanket next to James at the edge of a ridge of sand, tall marsh grass behind them. Sandpipers chased "on printless foot" "the ebbing Neptune and did fly when he came back at them." Jessica smiled to herself, noting that James had remembered to bring everything but a pup tent in his knapsack: canteen of water, the blanket, towels, and some fruit to snack on. *She* hadn't even remembered to bring her sunglasses. It was easy to tell which one of them had had to survive on the run and undercover in war-torn France. Well, sunglasses always made the world look way too dark. Right now Jessica wanted to be sunny.

Enjoying the view, himself, James wordlessly offered Jessica the canteen, which she took with a smile, surprised to realize once the water passed her lips how thirsty the July sun had rendered her. Sips turned into gulps.

"Whoa, there," James cautioned good-naturedly. "Save some for your old husband. Maybe I should have brought a few extra liters."

"Don't get cute, mister," Jess returned lightly. "It's not as if we're stranded in the Sahara."

As James quenched his own thirst, Jess realized that he was automatically moderating his intake, conserving his supply for maximum efficiency, like a man who didn't know where his next resupply would come from, if at all. Force of habit?

She turned her eyes to the Sound beyond them, instinctively offering him something happy: "I'm so glad that you love the ocean, too. We've already made some lovely memories here, but today—it's just wonderful. I'm so happy this is something I can share with you."

Following Jess's gaze into the glitter and shimmer of rolling turquoise and green, James nodded. "It's something all right, especially for a kid who grew up in Milton Northern, the industrial North. We were right in the middle of the country, not like Leeds, where you could hop a train and end up at Whitby."

"Whitby?" Jess piped eagerly. "That's where the ruined abbey is, the one in *Dracula*."

James gave his dark head a disbelieving shake and teased, "You're quite the character, you are. I mention one of the most famous seaside resorts in my country and all you can talk about is vampires. I think you needed a holiday from that gruesome program of yours more than you realized, Jessica Minton Crawford."

"Oh, why don't go take another picture of a sea gull," Jessica feigned indignation, releasing James's arm and tossing her head in her best Maureen O'Hara mode.

"Why don't I take a picture of my gorgeous wife," James countered appealingly, getting up and drawing Jess by the hand after him. "How about over there? Stand on the block so I can get a full-length shot."

"Fine. Play to my vanity," Jess said airily as James brought her over to and handed her onto one of the stone markers that studded the beach. "Who am I to argue?"

"Thought you might say that," James returned as he stepped back almost to the sea grass, looking into the viewfinder of his Brownie to get a better shot.

"So," Jessica proposed as she hiked her skirt up over her knee and curved her leg forward, "How about a little cheesecake?"

Looking through the viewfinder of his camera, James mischievously commented, "Too bad I never got a chance to do this kind of recon photo in France."

"Never mind that. I'm much happier thinking about you photographing secret installations and documents and troop movements than one of those French *Mademoiselles*. Especially since you're half-French, anyway. I don't like the thought of you parlez-ing any pick-up lines."

"Even in the line of duty?" James inquired innocently, looking up.

"Especially in the line of duty. So just make sure that the only gams you pay attention to from now on are *mine*."

"Agreed," James smiled. "I'll even close my eyes any time Betty Grable comes on the screen at the flicks."

"See that you do!" Jessica laughed as James took another shot.

She was just about to hop down, when James stopped her with, "Wait! I want a more serious shot."

"Okay. How about if I tilt my head up, as if I'm looking out to sea, waiting for your return."

"The ocean's behind you."

"Well, yes, but the sun gets in my eyes if I look that way. I squint and get all those little crow's feet . . ."

Chuckling, James acquiesced, so Jess tilted her head up and pretended to peer across stormy seas–by staring into the marsh grass.

Well, she was an actress, wasn't she? Angling her head and craning her neck, Jess blinked at what caught her eye. *What was a mannequin's hand and arm doing draped over that sea-crusted log? Mannequin? On the beach?*

"Oh my Lord!" escaped Jessica, her knees wobbling with shock.

Jess found herself now sitting on the block. James rushed over, kneeling by her, asking something about the sun, the heat. Forcing herself to come back to him, Jessica faced her husband and managed, "James, in the grass. A body. It looks like a body. I saw an arm. Over there, to the left, in the grass."

James's features went from surprise to hard determination. He stood up, all business, questioning, "Jessica, are you absolutely sure?"

She swallowed, hard, and nodded, then said, "I know how crazy it sounds, but . . ."

Turning to the area Jess had indicated, James speculated, "Could have been a boating accident last night." Turning back to her, he said, "I'll check it out. Just sit tight, all right? Stay here."

Jessica nodded, saying, "Don't worry. I've already seen more corpses than I care to in my life. And this doesn't promise to be pretty."

James's eyes told her he knew far too well how she felt, knew *worse* things than she did, but that passed even before he promised, "I'll be right back. You'll be all right."

Jessica watched James move swiftly into the marsh grass on the ridge. She couldn't help being relieved she didn't have to go with him, even as she wanted to kick herself for sending him up to that horror. *Who could it be? What had happened to him or her? Of course it must have been an accident, as James had conjectured. But who was it?* Now that she thought back, she had the impression it was a woman's hand and arm. *Not* an image was she wanted in her mind. An image of whom, though? A terrible possibility seized her. No, it couldn't be. There was no reason to believe this was the remains of a woman supposed to have left some time ago for Canada.

James was coming down the slop, his features set with trouble. His eyes met hers and, though he didn't need to say it, he told her, "It doesn't look good. Someone murdered that woman."

Jessica shot to her feet. She knew James wouldn't have spoken if he'd had any doubts, but she couldn't help questioning, "Murdered? James, are you absolutely positive? A minute ago, you said she'd probably been killed in the storm."

Clearly not happy to confront her with the gruesome facts, James answered, "The storm brought her in all right, swept the poor thing up the beach like the log she's wrapped around. But a storm wouldn't put two bullet holes in her."

A murder here, on this sleepy beachside campus?! Maybe some hanky-panky, but not murder! Then the realization that she'd dragged James into this kind of mess, even accidentally, stabbed Jess. Grabbing at straws, she resisted, "How can you be sure it's murder? Maybe those are just fish bites or punctures from debris?"

James shook his head and told her reluctantly, "Honey, it's not just the wounds—although I know a bullet wound when I see one, even with this much time in the water."

"What else, then?"

James paused, debating whether Jessica could take what he had to say. He seemed to decide it might be worse, in the long run, to keep her in the dark and hear the story enhanced in gory detail by local gossips. So, James carefully explained, "It looks as if she was murdered, then her body chained to something heavy and dropped in the ocean. Between decomposition and the storm action, her body must have snapped free last night and been washed up on shore. I'm not sure how long she's been in there. She might have been covered with something to keep the fish from tearing her loose. Sorry, love. I won't say any more."

"No, no," Jess reassured him. "I'm okay, if you're okay."

James hesitated, glancing back behind him, finally adding, "There is one more thing. Not really gruesome. It's just that I think I know who it is."

"Yes," Jess responded, drawing out the word, thinking she knew, too. "Go on."

"I can make out a marking on her shoulder, I'm pretty sure it's a tattoo. It's an odd, *avant-garde* design. Like the shape of that God-awful sculpture on top of our console."

Jessica nodded slowly, finally saying, "I had a feeling it would turn out to be Jessamyn Crane. That whole story about her sudden disappearance was way too fishy. Sorry, I didn't mean to make such a miserable pun. Oh, James, I really am so sorry I plunked you in the middle of this horrible crime. I wanted to get you away from death."

James came over, putting his hands on Jessica's shoulders and comforted her, "Here now. I'm rather a big boy. Don't you think I can take care of myself? If anybody should be feeling guilty, it's I. It seems that even when I'm not trying, I drag you smack into a bloody mess."

Jess hugged James close. *Didn't this just take the cake?* she thought. *Here we are competing over who has more right to feel guilty about jinxing the other's life. Gee, isn't love grand?*

That's when another, more disturbing thought struck Jessica. Jerking her head up, she questioned, "If this is Jessamyn Crane, James, who killed her? What does that say about Terry, Carolina, or Nigel?"

"Even your friend, Phil? He's a chap who doesn't like people debasing his shrine."

"That's too much of a stretch," Jess protested. "Next thing you know, you'll be asking Blackie for an alibi. But never mind; what do we do now?"

James began wearily, "Well, fortunately, our only responsibility here is to report what we've found. But someone needs to stay to make sure no scavengers get at it or no people stumble onto it."

Jess wondered if he also meant so no one tried to re-dispose of the remains, but it seemed best to let that disturbing thought slide. She said, "I volunteer you for the staying behind and me for the hotfooting it to the campus police."

"Under this July sun, I don't want you passing out from heat stroke," James gently warned. "I wish you'd brought a hat, but, here, take the water. So, once you get there, have the guard ring up the local constable to meet us here. Just tell him that we found the body of a woman washed up from the storm and that I'm staying here to keep an eye on things. I wouldn't say it was Jessamyn Crane. We don't know for certain it *is* she." His expression said he suspected otherwise, but James was a cautious man. "You might be better off not mentioning she's been shot unless you have to. I'd rather see the police approach this thing with a clean slate, and I'd be just as happy if I didn't have to explain how I know a bullet hole when I see one. One more thing, keep this whole thing under your hat until the police can get here. We don't want anyone interfering with the investigation."

The last instruction struck a chord of concern in Jessica, so she pressed, "James, you'll be all right all alone here, won't you? Are you thinking that I might accidentally tip off the murderer, who'll come back and . . ."

James assured her with a faint smile, "Don't worry about that. No one's going to dash over here, do me in, then have to dispose of *two* bodies."

"All right, all right, don't get smart." But her sarcasm was weak. Jess hung on to his parting hug longer than she should have, regretting leaving him alone, hating the deadly turn their stay at Margaret Point had taken. Maybe it wasn't Jessamyn Crane. That was possible. But would a different identity for the remains really make things much better? It might clear the people she knew–but it still might not.

Chapter Fourteen

Same Day

Jessica could feel, almost see, the waves of heat roiling up from the asphalt. Where the road dropped off a little ahead, water seemed to shimmer over it. Thank heavens she had her sandals on; otherwise, her bare tootsies would be charbroiled. Her blouse clung to her back. Pushing damp, matted hair away from her neck offered little relief. Thank the Almighty that on a Sunday morning no one seemed to be around to ask her any questions. Walking at this clip, Jess began seeing spots, so she slowed: she'd be little help to James if she passed out from heat exhaustion.

It was a battle not to dwell on the vision of what was left of Jessamyn Crane. Not to let wild conjectures about the perpetrator get the better of her. But how could she keep from wondering, worrying? Carolina, Terry, and Nigel might all be said to have typical murder motives: jealousy, unrequited love, fear of exposure, or an unholy mixture of the three. Still, could any one of them be that vicious? No! Yet she'd been mistaken about others' murderous capabilities before.

Was any one of them clever enough to mask the crime by disposing of the body gangland style? Now there was a thought: gangland style. Maybe those three *were* all in the clear—some hoods had murdered Jessamyn Crane. A fine kettle of fish, feeling relieved that murderous gangsters might prowl your neighborhood!

Struggling with her maddening conjectures, Jess didn't hear the footsteps hustling up behind her. A hand grabbed her arm, whirling her around and making her cry out, "Aiee! What the devil!"

Jessica jerked that arm free and raised the other defensively, to stare up at a startled Terry Clarke.

"Okay! Okay!" Terry lifted his hands in mock protection. "I surrender! I'm sorry! Are you still that sore? What does a guy have to do to square things?"

Jess closed her eyes and let out a long, steadying sigh. *You need a clear head to get out of this one, kiddo.* She definitely wanted to expel her suspicion of Terry now that facing him in the flesh made it seem downright screwy.

But before she could speak, Terry was reasoning aloud, "Say, wait a minute, you're not mad at all. You're really rattled. Under that sunburn, you're white as a–God I hate clichés–but ghost it is. Jessie, what's wrong? Are you all right? Where's your husband? Is he all right?"

Terry's concern made Jess really feel like a heel. Good grief! She was suspecting him of murder, and here he was worried about James! Still, even as guilt started to eat at her, Jess recognized a bigger problem. She couldn't let Terry's insistence pry out of her that horrible discovery on the beach. For too many reasons, that was a terrible idea.

Jess took a deep breath before beginning, "Terry, I'm all right. James is all right, but I have to get to the guard station. I can't stop to explain. You have to let me go . . ."

"I don't think so," Terry cut her off, his hands now on her arms. "You're not going anywhere."

Jessica looked anxiously down at the hands gripping her, then back at Terry. Maybe she *should* feel leery of him.

Before she could move, Terry cautioned, "Look at you, Jessica, shaking like an aspen. You're going to have heat stroke if you don't calm down and catch your breath. Let me help."

That was when Jessica realized Terry was not so much holding her back as holding her up. She closed her eyes against the heat as well as her anxiety. Gathering her thoughts, Jess began again, "Terry, I know I'm asking a lot of you. I appreciate your trying to help me, but please don't ask any questions. Just let me go. You've got to trust me on this one. Please."

The tall man, seeming so very tall to Jess now, gave her a long, studied look, mulled her words, then finally answered, releasing her, "All right. Okay. Suit yourself. But I want to talk with you later. After you've settled your mysterious mission. Deal?"

"Deal." Jess swallowed, relieved. "And thanks, Terry."

Jess smiled quickly, but it was a smile she meant, and she was off. Behind her, she heard Terry call, "Slow down before you blow a gasket!"

Jessica powered on, but soon discovered that Terry was right. Queasiness started its assault even as she sighted the small stone building housing college security. As much as it killed her, Jess forced herself to slow down and remembered to take a drink from the canteen James had insisted she carry. Well, at least she was almost home.

Now standing in the doorway, Jess found the guard station a surprisingly pleasant relief from the outside, what with the stone exterior, the lowered Venetian blinds over the recessed windows, and a couple of standing fans fluttering papers pinned down by the odd weighty object. Unfortunately, the cooling stone also gave off a dankness that mingled oddly with the scents of powdered doughnuts, cigarettes, and old coffee. *Such a help to a queasy stomach. Tough it out, kid! You won't help James much if you pass out or pass back your lunch.*

Across the room, a blond young man in a grey campus-police uniform leaned on a filing cabinet, poking in an open drawer, his back to her. Registering Jess's presence, he turned and, before Jessica could say anything, smiled, "Hi. Jessica Minton, isn't it? Say, you look beat. You better sit down and tell me what's up."

He crossed toward her, and Jessica recognized Chris Mitchell, a new guy who'd started about the time she and James had arrived.

"I'm all right, Chris," Jess assured him, meeting him halfway into the small room. "It's the heat, and I had to hoof it here in a hurry."

"My Gosh, is anybody hurt?!"

"I'm afraid she's beyond hurt," Jessica answered bleakly. "My husband and I found a body, of a woman, in the marsh grass, about a mile back, towards the cottages. We think she was washed up in the storm."

"Here, sit down at the desk," Chris offered. Jessica accepted with a nod, putting the canteen on the desk next to her. He conjectured,

"Someone from a boating accident? I'll check with the Coast Guard and the Sherriff's office in town. See if someone's missing from last night."

"No, no," Jessica insisted. "My husband got a better look than I did. He said it looked as if she'd been in the water some time." She added quickly, at Chris's curious expression, "I mean, he's no coroner, but he said the decomposition was pretty bad. That doesn't happen overnight."

Chris Mitchell nodded and questioned, "Anything else remarkable about the body?"

Jess hesitated. James had told her not to say too much, but Chris was asking. It'd be odd to hold out on the guy investigating.

"Yes, well, James said she has two, kind of odd holes, uh, maybe like bullet holes. And, well, her feet were torn off at the ankles, as if she'd been weighted down in the water then pulled free, probably by the storm."

"Oh," Chris replied a bit faintly. He also gulped. *Definitely new to the job.*

"Chris, are you all right?" Jessica asked, concerned. "You're looking kind of green around the gills. Can I get you a glass of water or something?"

"No, it's just that, this will be the first, ah, body I've had to deal with. They stationed me in New Jersey during the war."

"I guess you wouldn't expect to stumble across a murder," Jess inwardly cringed on that "M" word, "at an all-girls' college."

"Murder," Chris repeated thoughtfully.

"Murder!" echoed the horrified voice of Terry Clarke through the open window by the door. "*Who* was murdered?"

"What are you doing here?" Jessica blurted.

Ignoring Jessica, Chris tried to placate Terry with, "That looks like something for the sheriff to work out. I'm basically just a security guard with a nice uniform."

Terry hadn't seemed to hear, for he came in and demanded of Jessica, "Is that what you were in such a lather about? But why couldn't you tell me?"

Okay, Jess told herself. *Touchy ground here. Think carefully.*

"Terry," Jess began, "There was really no reason to tell you, to alarm you. It would have taken too long, anyway, to explain. But, say, why *did* you follow me?"

Terry's intrusive inquisitiveness raised unwelcome suspicions in Jess, but those suspicions abruptly turned to guilt when he answered, "I was concerned about you. I wanted to make sure you got where you were headed all right."

Chris Mitchell took control of the situation, though he came off as uncertain about how much authority a security guard with a nice uniform actually had: "Okay, you two can hash out who was right or wrong later. Right now, I've got to put in a call to the sheriff's office and tell them to get the coroner and meet us out at the site. If you could just give me directions, Jessica. Oh, and I could use a description, as specific as you can get, of the, ah, your discovery. After, I'll run you back to your husband, and when the guys from the sheriff's office get there you two can go home. So, fill me in."

Jessica hesitated, determinedly not facing Terry, dreading when he'd put two and two together and come up with the same sum as she and James had on the victim's identity. Maybe it hadn't been kosher for Terry to play around on his wife; but, if he had genuinely cared for Jessamyn at all, realizing what had become of her would be a rotten blow.

"Now remember, all I saw was a hand and part of an arm. James saw the actual victim. He could clearly tell it was a woman." She would not look at Terry, though she felt his eyes on her. "He conjectured she was older than the students, though her, her condition made it difficult to determine. And," here Jess really struggled to go on, knowing this detail might be a clincher for Terry, "well, James said had she a peculiar kind of tattoo on her shoulder. An odd design. It's hard to describe. You'll have to see it for yourself."

Jessica had barely finished with that last tidbit when Terry's sharp intake of breath signaled she'd hit home. All Terry said was a subdued, "How long had she been in the water?"

Jess couldn't turn to Terry. She even winced when Chris Mitchell enthused, "Say, that's a great question, Professor Clarke."

Terry didn't comment. Again, Jess felt his eyes pressing on her, waiting. Did Terry realize her hesitation stemmed from knowing about his relationship with Jessamyn? The quiet intensity of his repeated question seemed to tell her he didn't care.

"How long?"

Jessica could only answer the question by addressing Chris, all the while trying not to let her pity show, "James seemed to think it might have been some months, from the state of the body. But there seemed to be some kind of covering still attached . . ."

"So that's why the fish hadn't chomped it up," Chris reflected, oblivious to Terry, who sat down hard at that gruesome extrapolation.

"Say, Professor," Chris was on his feet, concerned. "What's wrong . . . ?" He caught Jessica's warning eyes, then light dawned on his marble head, and he apologized, "Oh, sorry about that. I forgot, you intellectual types probably aren't used to this kind of talk, the gritty side of life."

Terry fired back with an iciness that could have frosted a volcano, "When you were swatting flies, stationed in New Jersey, I was in OWI, reviewing photos of the worst carnage in two theatres of war. I was in propaganda, and I decided what was too gruesome and what was safe for the rest of you to see."

Chris Mitchell didn't say anything, just stared down at his paperwork under Terry Clarke's hard, blue stare.

As much as Jess compassionated Terry's pain, she wanted to get back to the beach and relieve James. This standoff was *not* making things move any faster. She plunged in with, "That's all I can tell you, Chris. Put in your call to the sheriff and take me back to my husband."

"I'm going with you," Terry decided.

Chris blinked, surprised. Jessica wasn't. Terry's reactions fairly screamed, to her anyway, that the poor battered corpse belonged to Jessamyn Crane. Jess had never been a fan of adultery, but she'd seen enough of Terry in the past two weeks to realize that he was fighting to control deep feelings for the lost woman. She wouldn't wish the pain she sensed behind his eyes on anybody. *Well, maybe that barracuda of a wife of his. No, not even her.*

Chris Mitchell broke the silence: "Gee, Professor Clarke, I don't think . . ."

"No, Mitchell, you don't," Terry cut him off. But then he caught the young man's and Jessica's shocked expressions at his rudeness and apologized, "Sorry, it's just that I suspect I know who this unfortunate is."

"Really?" Chris blurted, genuinely surprised.

"Yes, really. It's that tattoo. I know someone with one, a woman—and the type of woman who'd have a tattoo isn't what you think. She's an artist. She liked to break traditional molds. She had a shape copied by a Greenwich Village friend from one of her own *avant-garde* works. She's a good family friend. She told my, ah, wife about it. It's Jessamyn Crane."

Jessica sat amazed that Terry had gotten all of that out in such a calm, level voice. His calling Jessamyn a "family friend," making her his wife's pal, was a neat save. Jessica wasn't sure how she felt about Terry's sidestepping the truth, though. Then again, was she in a position to judge, considering the compromises she'd had to make over the last three years?

Mitchell protested Terry's claim, going on about Jessamyn being in Canada, and Terry was testily insisting on the stupidity of people buying the "fishiness" of that story: an argument that Jess could see going on till the cows, chickens, and every other animal on Old McDonald's farm came home. Well, Terry might be working out his anguish and trying to tap dance around an awkward situation, but she had James to think about. Standing guard over a festering corpse in the hot July sun was nobody's idea of a picnic. She needed to get this show on the road.

"Okay, you two, knock it off. While you're arguing, my husband's stuck back on the beach with . . . an extremely unpleasant situation." She had enough heart to spare Terry from more gruesome phrasing. "Chris, get on the horn to the sheriff. Then you can run both Terry and me back to James. Maybe he can help make an identification. But let's snap it up."

She didn't add, "And this way, we can keep Terry from spreading the word about the murder to the wrong ears before the sheriff can get started." But it was on her mind.

So, Terry gave her a faint but grateful smile, Chris put in his call to the sheriff, and then the three of them were on their way in a campus patrol car. Not surprisingly, the ride was grim, Jess up front with Chris, Terry brooding in the back. She couldn't help an occasional sympathetic glance back at Terry in the rear-view mirror. One of those times, his eyes caught hers and she read an anger there she had never seen before in him. Her flustered gaze shot to the seaside. That anger didn't seem directed at her, but at whom? *Had* Terry some idea who was responsible?

Jess had no time for further reflections for she soon needed to instruct Chris to pull over by the side of the road, near the footpath that had led her off the beach.

"Okay, Mrs. Crawford," Chris began, shoving his car keys into his shirt pocket. "Just tell us where to go from here and we'll take over. You should stay here out of the sun. There's no reason for you to go back down there."

"Now wait just a minute. I'm not made of wax. I can lead you to James. You can't expect me to just sit here and twiddle my thumbs," Jessica protested.

Unexpectedly, Jess felt Terry's hand on her shoulder as he leaned forward to say, "Take it easy, Jessica, you've done your part. Let us handle things now."

"Sure, just tell us how far he is from the path, and we'll take it from there," Chris promised.

Jess started to argue, but Terry made her think better of it with, "We need someone to tell the sheriff where to find us when he arrives."

She knew they were right. Chris was the security guard; Terry could make an identification, but there was no practical reason for her to go. Truth be told, she wanted to see how James was doing. Still, she knew he couldn't be in any real danger; the fiddler crabs weren't that savage

"Okay, okay," Jessica agreed. "Follow the path down the beach, then bear left along the grass. You should see James standing there. He's 5'10" of hard to miss." She put her hand over the one Terry had rested on her shoulder and asked, "What about you, Terry? Are you going to be all right?"

He gave her the kind of rueful smile she hadn't seen on him in years, before answering, "I'm tougher than you think, Jessica. I can take it."

Before Jess could say anything else, Terry had shoved open the car door and swung his lanky form into the hot July sun, saying, "Shake a leg, Mitchell. I want to get this over with."

Slightly surprised, Chris Mitchell hesitated before he jumped out of the car, calling after Terry to wait up. Their heads disappeared beneath the ridge before their voices. Jessica leaned back against the seat and muttered, "Jeepers, what a hell of a day!"

A glance at her watch told her it was only just after one. The day was fairly young, so what other disasters could spring up? Putting a hand over her closed eyes, Jess decided that she didn't want to think about it. She certainly didn't want to think about what would go on inside Terry when he had to look at the terrible remains of a person he'd once cared for. Still cared for, judging by what she'd seen roiling inside him today.

And after all this got out, what would happen between Terry and Carolina? Would this be the deal-breaker in their marriage? Would it turn out that Terry had loved Jessamyn enough to throw everything to the wind and marry her? Not a prospect someone like Carolina would take lying down, but would she have been angry enough to kill? Still, the logistics of getting rid of a body seemed a bit out of the woman's league. She'd likely break a nail or soil a dress in the process. Nigel Cross, however, was strong and smart and likely not so very fastidious about his manicure. Could Terry's pushing him out of the picture with Jessamyn have pushed Nigel over the edge with jealousy?

That was powerful anger she'd seen in Terry Clarke's eyes—as if he knew who deserved it for killing the woman he loved. God! She'd seen Joan Crawford movies with fewer sordid intrigues. Now, the lovely Connecticut seaside campus felt about as safe and secure as Transylvania when the wolf's bane was in bloom and the werewolves in tune.

"Jessica?"

Jess managed not to end up hanging from the car's ceiling like Sylvester the cat in a Warner Brothers cartoon—but it was a close one.

James, leaning through the passenger side window, inquired "innocently," "Did I startle you?"

"This really isn't the day to be a Wise Alec," Jessica warned, though she was actually grateful for his attempt to lighten the mood.

"I wanted to pop up and see how you were," he explained, "and to let you know what's going on."

"Well, you can see my reflexes are still good. But what about you? How are you doing, out here all this time? I hope we didn't take too long."

"It's all right." He looked away for a moment, reflecting, "I thought I was used to this sort of thing. I guess no one is, not completely." Then he turned back to Jess, changing the subject: "Would you like to come out? You look jumpy, cooped up in there."

"Good idea. You must be psychic."

When James opened the door and handed her out, Jess smiled slightly to comment, "Quite the gent, under any circumstances, aren't we?"

"Even a chap from the wrong side of the factory yard knows how to treat a lady. It's what makes us Brits so charming."

Jessica gave James a sidelong look, then leaned back against the car, next to him. They both fell silent, unable to fully shake the bleak mood, even with the turquoise sparkle of the Sound before them. Finally, Jessica glanced up at James and said, "I'm sorry about Terry. I tried to keep him out of it, but he walked in when I was explaining to Chris Mitchell. I don't know what else I could have done."

"That's all right," James assured her. "Actually, to some extent, it rather works out for the best. He was able to make a positive identification."

"It really is Jessamyn Crane?"

"Yes."

"Poor Terry. How dreadful for him. How did he take it? Is he all right?"

James smiled at her concern and said, "You're a bit of a good scout, you know that? Well, let's say it was a real shock to him—and it's no longer any secret what he had for breakfast. Even I feel sorry for him."

Jess raised her brows and questioned, "All that in front of Chris Mitchell? Was it a dead giveaway about what was going on between him and that poor Crane woman?"

James shook his head, "No, not actually. Any fellow might react to that sight the way he did. And he talked about her as a family friend. He played it pretty cagey, emphasizing she was his wife's friend. Lot of nerve there, making your paramour your wife's chum."

"He kind of has to do that, don't you think? Even with his pull, if the trustees got *proof* of any hanky-panky going on . . . well, that's all she wrote," Jess pointed out. She thought a moment before adding, "To tell the truth, I feel worse about Terry finding a woman he loved murdered than I do about him betraying his wife with their 'family friend.'"

"That's because Terry may be something of a horse's neck, but Carolina Brent Clarke is a dreadful person," James calmly noted.

"Poor Jessamyn," Jessica shook her head. "She's whom my heart really goes out to. Getting mixed up with an unfaithful husband, then getting murdered and, to top it off, dumped in the ocean."

"I think being murdered is enough of a topper," James observed, though not callously. "And you had better stop tying yourself up in knots over people and circumstances you don't really know about. There's nothing you can do to change things. They got themselves into these jams. Now it's time for the authorities to come in and straighten things out; your duty is done. The police should be here any time now, so Mitchell should be able to run you home presently."

"Run *me* home? What about you?" Jessica puzzled.

"I have to stick around to answer the constable's questions firsthand. But there's no need for you to stay, Jessica. You've already given your statement to Mitchell. Call it a day."

"I can't just leave you here," Jessica insisted. "We're in this together. How can I go back to a nice comfy home and a tender-hearted cat and leave you out here, sweltering away with a goofy security guard and a guy on the verge of a nervous breakdown?"

"Now, I'm truly wounded," James tried to kid away her worry. "After all these years I spent outfoxing Nazis, you think another half hour with those two is going to break me?"

"That's not what I meant," Jess countered. "I just don't want you to shoulder all the trouble."

"Tell you what, Jessica, if you have a pot of tea and some fresh scones waiting for me, I'll call it a good bargain."

"Oh, I see," Jess folded her arms in front of her, feigning affront. "My main value is as Suzy Homemaker."

James shook his head with amusement, then answered seriously, "Really, Jessica, there's no need for you to stay, and I'd feel better knowing I'd gotten you away from this dog's dinner of a day. I've enmeshed you in more than enough tough situations since we've been together. Let me keep you out of at least one."

"Weeell, okay," Jessica relented, tongue in cheek. "If it makes you feel better to know that I'm home, out of the heat, taking a refreshing shower, slipping into something comfortable, maybe having a light snack, playing with our adorable little assassin of mice, who am I to deny you?"

"I appreciate your altruism," James returned. He slipped an arm around Jessica's waist, pulling her close, kissed the top of her head, then looked out to sea with her.

Her head nestled against James, Jess asked, "So, Mr. Former-Espionage-Whiz, who do you think done the poor girl in?"

James looked down at her to answer, "I was never Sherlock Holmes, love. My job wasn't to track your garden-variety murderer."

"True," Jess agreed without looking up, "but you did need good deductive skills."

"I suppose, but none of *this* is any of my business, is it? Let's leave this one alone, Jessica."

Jess blinked at the unexpected seriousness of James's tone, in the green flecked eyes she was now studying. He turned away, looking down the road on hearing an approaching car.

"Right then, that must be the constable," he decided. However, as the car came closer, he amended his conclusion, "No, not a police car. But isn't that Rose? Hmm, this may work out even better."

James left Jess to flag down the slowly approaching vehicle. As the auto pulled up behind Mitchell's, James turned to Jess and quickly suggested, "We shouldn't tell Rose too much. Only enough to make sense. It wouldn't be fair to impose the worst of this ghastly business on her and then not let her be able to get it off her chest with anyone else. I doubt the constable wants too many details to get out, even to someone as dependable as Rose, before he's had a chance to investigate. Will you follow my lead, Jessica?"

Pulling the wool over her chum's eyes was far from her first choice, but what James said had merit, especially the bit about sparing Rose from the nightmare Jess knew she, herself, was having trouble keeping out of her thoughts. She nodded to her husband and said, "I won't lie, but okay, I won't be too forthcoming, either."

His smile was a little sad. James knew what he was asking her. He slipped an arm around her shoulder as they approached Rose's car.

"Hey, you two, what's cooking?" Rose called as she leaned out the open window. "Did security catch you necking on the beach?" She surveyed the road and cracked, "I don't see a guard around. What'd you do, bump him off and dump the body in the ocean?"

That brought both Jess and James to an immediate halt, and she muttered *sotto voce* to her husband, "I told you she was even more psychic than Liz."

James guided Jessica over to their friend to begin slowly, "Funny you should say that, Rose."

Rose shrugged her long brown hair over the shoulder of her olive blouse. Looking suspiciously from one friend to the other, she asked, "Funny like *The Jack Benny Show* or funny like our Republican Congress trying to hold hearings on Pearl Harbor against a dead president who won the war and just happened to be a Democrat?"

They both had to calculate that one a moment, with James finally replying, "The second, I'm afraid. Someone washed up in the marsh grass. Poor soul was dead."

"Holy Smoke," Rose muttered, shaking her head. "We've never had something like this happen, at least not since I've been here. But I suppose that was one humdinger of a storm last night. Someone was bound to be drowned—although why anyone would be fool enough to go out on a night like that . . ." Then a thought struck, and Rose demanded, "It wasn't anyone we know, was it?"

"It wasn't anyone I've ever met," James replied simply.

Jessica looked thoughtfully at James. A perfect example of the truth as misdirection. She loved him, but she hated he could do that so deftly. Old skills, again. She also hated not leveling with Rose, but even more, she hated the thought of needlessly alarming her friend, especially if she owed it to the investigation to play things close to the vest.

"I guess it doesn't really matter whether we knew the person," Rose reconsidered. "It's still awful to be drowned by that storm."

That much certainly was true, and maybe Jess was glad she didn't have to expose her friend to how much worse the situation actually was.

James was speaking now, "Rose, would you do us a favor? Chris Mitchell wants me to stay until the constable gets here. You know, he always does routine checks in these sorts of situations. Would you mind riding my lovely bride home, so she doesn't have to stick around? I have to answer some questions about what we found, but there's no reason for Jessica to have to suffer. If it's not out of your way."

Rose was in the midst of assuring them that giving Jessica a lift would be no problem, when Terry's voice interrupted: "Rose? Rose, is that you? Did they tell you?"

All three turned to see Terry circling the security vehicle as he spoke.

Rose gave Jessica a shocked look and questioned her, "What's Terry doing here? What's he talking about?"

As James started toward Terry, clearly planning to keep him away from the women to forestall any revelations, the other man nixed that plan by declaring, "It's Jessamyn. They found Jessamyn, down there! Did they tell you she's been . . ."

"That's enough, Clarke," James cut him off, calmly but forcefully. "Do you want to upset Rose and Jessica?"

Terry leveled a furious glare on James and retorted, "Do I want to upset . . . ? They should be upset. We all should be upset. Jessamyn, she's been . . ."

"Terry," Jess cut in, more to soothe than silence him, "get a hold of yourself. Please. Calm down."

"Calm down my Aunt Fanny!" Rose barged in. "What the dickens is going on here? What's this got to do with Jessamyn? Good grief, she's *not* in Canada, is she? She's down there in the marsh grass." Rose fixed James with a piercing look and accused, "'You never met' the dead person—nice one, pal." Then, turning to Jessica, "But you, Jess, you're my friend, for how many years? And you wouldn't level with me? That's not playing it square."

Jess was hit hard. She dropped her eyes and said, "I'm sorry, Rose. Really sorry." Looking up, she finished, "We didn't want to upset you, and we'd promised Mitchell not to say anything to *anyone,* so as not to interfere with the investigation."

"Rose," James added, "Don't blame Jessica. I talked her into staying mum. She didn't want to, believe me. And she was thinking of you. She didn't want you stewing over any of this, waiting for the authorities to nick their man."

"Well, I don't want to keep this under wraps," Terry insisted. "I want everyone to know what a horrible thing was done to that sweet woman, so they'll get on the stick and catch those bastards who murdered her gangland style. You go spread the word, Rose. We need to be on our guard if gangsters have been prowling our little enclave."

"Gangsters?" James questioned, curiously. "What makes you so certain, Clarke?"

Terry seemed a bit startled, even disturbed at being questioned, replying not quite so assertively, "Dumping a body in the Sound. Tying the feet to something heavy. Sounds textbook to me. Carolina and I warned her about the rough sorts she sometimes chummed with in the city. It must have caught up with her. They probably cooked up a phony resignation, to quell suspicion when she disappeared."

Rose shot Jess a look that said, "Jessamyn? Gangsters? Huh?"

James regarded Terry pensively before saying, "It sounds as if you've been giving this a lot of thought. You seem to have some unusually intimate insight into the woman's secret life, Terry."

That assessment unnerved Terry. He fired back, "I told you people. Everyone knows that she's a close family friend. Of course I'm upset. Wouldn't you be if someone murdered Rose and sank her body in the Sound?"

"Oh, great example," Rose cracked. "Thanks, pal."

Jess stepped in to make peace: "Point taken, Terry. Say, you really look beat. Maybe you should take five in the patrol car—cool down."

Terry nodded, and apologized, "Sorry, Rose. I didn't mean to lose my head. I don't know what got into me. I guess I couldn't stand the thought of anyone getting away with the murder of a nice girl like Jessamyn."

"Skip it, Terry," Rose forgave him.

Jess wasn't sure if she was the only one to notice that Terry's offending comment really hadn't answered James's question about the source of his insight. But that ship seemed to have sailed, and it wouldn't pay in terms of peace of mind to drag it back right now. There would always be time to talk with James later.

As Terry moved off to the patrol car, he and James briefly locked eyes in a way that prompted Rose to whisper to her friend, "Get a load of those two. You could strap on blades and go skating on that look."

Jess nodded, thinking James had been harder on Terry than she would have expected. But now James was with Rose and Jess again, saying "So, Rose is all forgiven? Would you be willing to run my lovely but heat-prostrated wife home?"

Rose smiled, "Well, I could say that, at the moment, my idea of running her home is to have Jess out front of my Chrysler here doing sixty."

"It would probably be less exhausting than what I've been going through the past fifteen minutes with the *three* of you," Jessica grumped.

"Okay, you've suffered enough. Hop in, kiddo," Rose chuckled, jerking her thumb at the passenger seat.

Once Jess was in the front seat, James closed the door for her, then leaned through the window and tried to lighten the mood with, "No cavorting you two. Stay out of the pool halls and go straight home."

"Will do, chief," Rose promised, trying to keep up James's attempt but not entirely succeeding.

"You're sure you don't mind being here, waiting?" Jess cut through the humor. "I hate leaving you, in this heat."

"I can always sit in the shade of the other auto," James assured her.

Jess's glance ahead took in the back of Terry's head. She turned to James and asked warningly, "Do you think you two can play nice?"

James quirked a smile, kissed Jess quickly, then promised, "I think I can pull it over." He gave the roof of the car two raps, as if sending soldiers off to battle, and said, "Right, then, off you go, my ladies."

James had stepped back from the car and waved them off as Rose had the vehicle running and in gear. With a quick survey of the road behind her, she pulled out. Jess turned, looking back at her husband, even as Rose was leaving him behind. His smile was fading into weariness. She felt as if she were abandoning him. What a fine mess, and he had to wait for the sheriff in the July sun while that *prima donna* Terry hogged the car. This circumstance decidedly diminished her pity for Terry.

"Buck and a quarter for your thoughts?" Rose queried.

"Post-war inflation is worse than I thought," Jess surmised. But she couldn't bring herself to smile. In fact, another glance back left her frowning over the exhausted stance of James's figure, growing smaller every moment.

Chapter Fifteen

About twenty minutes later, Jessica Minton, in a cool, short-sleeved, lemon-yellow linen dress, was in her kitchen pouring hot water into a tea pot. After a refreshing shower, she might not attest that Lux soap could make a feisty gal feel dainty, as the ads claimed, but she certainly felt as if she'd washed away a ton of grit and stress. Maybe hot tea wouldn't exactly keep her cool as a cucumber, but it would go a long way to relaxing her. Still, Jess knew what would really set her mind at rest was having James home. She'd know he was all right, and they could discuss whether the tie clip she'd found in the derelict meant anything to the murder.

A sigh longer than a war time line-up for nylons escaped her. In the living room, Dusty, stretched down the spine of her couch, responded with a sharply flicked ear. Jess weakly smiled at her cat's reaction, while dunking the ball-shaped infuser by its chain into the tea pot to speed up the brewing. Too bad she couldn't speed James's return as well. Going to the cabinet for a cup and saucer, Jess considered what she wouldn't have given to have her big sister here for advice. Maybe she'd even get some Dutch uncle action out of Leo McLaughlan. But if she didn't have the right to talk to Rose, how could she justify talking to either Liz or Leo?

Jess removed the infuser from the tea pot and set it in a dish, still stewing over whether the love nest and its visitors were relevant to the case or information that would only humiliate those involved, especially that poor dead girl. Was it up to the sheriff to decide? Funny, James hadn't thought of that when he'd sent her home. Maybe he had too much

195

on his mind or maybe he hadn't wanted her to say what she knew in front of Terry. What was the point, anyway, since last night's storm had nixed any chance of corroborating her story? Or maybe James was just tired. Sharp cookie that he was, could she honestly expect him to think of everything under these dreadful circumstances? Right now, she'd have given all the tea in China never to have indulged her half-baked idea of checking out the old wreck. But not what was in the cup she'd just poured for herself. She needed it!

An abrupt knock on the kitchen door startled Jess from her thoughts. *Who in Sam Hill could that be?* James certainly wouldn't be knocking on his own door. Most people would go to the front, anyway; and she wasn't expecting a delivery around back.

The knock repeated, more peremptory. Dusty raised her head, peering over her shoulder, and almost glared through sleep-lidded eyes, "Are you going to get that or not?"

"Sorry, Dusty," Jess called back, crossing to the mudroom. "I know you're exhausted from scouting out that ideal place to sleep."

Probably James had ordered something from town but forgotten to tell her. Absolutely *no* reason to worry about being alone here—she hoped.

Jessica pulled the back door open on Phil Novack, his hand raised to knock again, his features creased with worry.

"Phil? You look awfully upset. Is everything all right? Can I help?"

Not sure where to begin, Novack hesitated, but then seemed to relax at Jessica's concern. He replied, "No, I'm okay. Funny thing is, I came to see if you and your husband were all right."

"Us? I don't follow."

Novack jerked his head toward the beach, elaborating, "Yeah. I was riding back when I saw a knot of people. It was hard to get a straight answer from them, but I heard something about you two and a body washed up by the storm. Some clown even seemed to think one of you was dead, then some other Joe was gassing about it being a teacher who was supposed to have blown town some time ago, that artist woman. So, I said to myself, maybe I better ride over and get the straight dope—make sure the two of you are okay."

Jessica could see Novack's genuine concern. Her heart warmed to him, and she reassured, "We're fine, Phil, honestly. Well, fine as anyone can be after coming across the remains of someone left out to sea that long."

"So it *was* that teacher? Crane? The other one who was nice to Blackie."

His questioning was a little sharper than Jessica expected. Then again, dealing with more death couldn't have been any picnic for the veteran. Nevertheless, she had to think about how to answer him without giving away anything the sheriff would prefer kept mum. Well, you couldn't *give away* information if someone already had it.

"Yes, I'm afraid that's who they think it is. Professor Clarke identified her . . ."

"Clarke? Terry Clarke? The guy who came charging after you Friday? I might have known."

As he spoke, Phil Novack's features went hard and his eyes cold—until he saw Jessica's startled response. He looked down and smiled bitterly, finally saying, "So, I'm giving even you the willies. Sorry about that. I just don't like to see . . . Oh, skip it. I've gotta get going. Blackie'll be wanting a nice bale or two of hay."

Jessica felt like a heel at the possibility Phil thought she might have turned on him, too. But, luckily, a chance to rectify the awkwardness flashed to mind.

"Blackie! My favorite hayburner. If you wait a sec, Phil, I have a basket of apples here in the mudroom. Give me a chance to grab a couple to tide him over till you get home."

"How about grabbing me one, too?" Phil smiled quietly, letting Jessica know that everything was square between them.

"Can do!"

Before returning from the mudroom, Jess pulled a broad-brimmed yellow straw hat from a peg on the wall—something she wished she'd had for her earlier cross-campus trek. Apples in the front pockets of her dress, she strolled with Novack toward Blackie, tied up on the other side of the balustrade. Seeing them, the horse pricked up his ears and whickered.

Novack actually grinned when he noted, "Looks like your friend is happy to see you, or maybe he can make out those apples in your pockets."

"He's a regular Sherlock Horse, isn't he?" Jess punned, with Novack wincing comically in response.

Jess reached the black horse, who extended his neck over the stonework to nuzzle her hand. As she rubbed his nose, she promised, "Blackie, old boy, have I ever got a treat for you."

Blackie, however, was way ahead of her, trying to poke into her pocket and grab an apple for himself. Jess laughed and chided, "Hold your horses, buster!"

"So to speak," Novack added, straight-faced.

Jess turned her head to smile at her companion's humor, but wondered to see his mouth smiling, but his eyes tense. She returned her attention to Blackie, taking out the apple, letting him munch it (not minding the horse slobber one wit). Yet, even though there was something so familiar, so comforting about her equine chum, she couldn't help being more preoccupied with what was bothering Phil Novack. Something he just couldn't come out with. How could she help him?

Novack surprised her by addressing that silent question: "Sorry, I've been so jumpy. This girl's murder really gets to me. I've seen death before, and I've seen it ugly. But I knew why. It was war. This, this is just wrong, happening to a nice girl like her."

"You knew her?" Jess was a little surprised.

"Not exactly. I'd see her around on the beach, collecting her driftwood. But she was friendly–like you. She even had apples or carrots for Blackie if we rode by here. She didn't deserve this. I just wish I could have said something to her to prevent what happened. Maybe I should say something this time and keep *you* out of trouble."

"Me?" Jessica was taken aback. So much so that she forgot her confusion about how little Novack's outpouring jibed with Jessamyn's activities at the wreck. Instead, she pressed him with a question closer to home, "Exactly what kind of trouble do you see me getting into, Phil?"

Novack didn't answer right away, but when he came to a decision, he warned in a subdued voice, "The two of you, you've both been chummy with that Clarke character."

That statement stunned her. Did he think she had the same deal going with Terry that Jessamyn Crane had? No, not stunned, embarrassed, then infuriated. Jess couldn't help firing back, "Now wait just one minute. I only work with the guy. That's it. Period. If you think for one minute that . . ."

"It might not matter what's true, just how it looks to someone. Someone dangerous," Novack replied intently.

"Someone? Dangerous? Who? Hold on, are you telling me that you think Carolina got jealous? Or Terry got angry with Jessamyn?"

"I didn't say that," Novack stopped Jessica. Blackie jerked up his head, flicking his ears and pawing nervously at the raised voices.

As Novack reached to put a soothing hand on his horse, Jessica demanded, "Then what *did* you say, exactly? I can't believe you'd accuse either of those two of being involved in murder. That's just nuts . . ."

The word was out of her mouth and Jessica wanted to kick herself for uttering figuratively what so many were saying literally, hurtfully.

But Phil Novack didn't have time to be offended. He smiled grimly and repeated, "Nuts? You tell me. I'm just warning you: don't go getting yourself into a tight spot you can't get out of. A fancy degree doesn't put a guy on the side of the angels."

Jessica turned back to Blackie, slowly taking out and offering him the other apple. As Blackie's mouth closed on it, she finally figured out what to say. Not looking up to Phil till she'd finished speaking, Jessica started, "If you just don't like Terry, which I totally understand, you have to let this go. You can't let it eat you up inside. But, Phil," her voice grew more intense, "if you *know* something, *really* know something solid, more than gossip or conjecture, you *have* to tell the sheriff. Not just because it's the law or for even Jessamyn Crane's sake, but for your own. Don't you think the guilt of letting that poor woman's murderer get off scot-free will destroy you? You've got to help if you have something legit to tell."

"It's really all that simple for you, isn't it?" he smiled bitterly.

"No, I could tell you some things—but that's neither here nor there. It's not about me. It's about not running away or letting others get away with . . ."

"You just don't get it," he insisted. "Do you really think anyone would take my word over someone with the clout of the Clarkes? People already think I'm not playing with a full deck."

"Believe me; Phil, Terry, and his wife are not all that popular. If you had some solid evidence, if you saw something . . ."

"It's more complicated than that," Novack cut her off, adding, "I'd better get out of here before I stir up more trouble than either of us can handle."

He swung over the wall, and, as he untied Blackie, warned, "You'd better not go all noble and start shooting off your mouth about what I told you today." When Jess started to protest, he doubled-down, "I'll deny everything, say you were all upset and misunderstood me. Then we'll see who sounds like the nutcase."

Those last words silenced Jessica like a blow. After Phil had quickly mounted Blackie, he turned and saw what he'd done. He weakened. It took him a moment of inner struggle, but Novack relented this much: "Look, girlie, it's for your own good. You're in way over your head; and so am I. I'm just telling you, steer clear of Clarke as much as you can. You don't want him turning you into his confidante by a long shot. That's what cooked the other one's goose. And if you're really worried about me, drop the whole deal. Forget everything I said except about staying clear of Clarke and his wife."

Recalling the manner of Jessamyn's "disposal," Jessica pressed, "Are you telling me that Terry and Carolina have mob connections? That they killed Jessamyn because she knew too much?"

"You don't listen, do you? I'm telling you to drop the whole subject. I'm telling you to keep your distance from those two. And," here he hesitated, as if it cost him, "maybe you better steer clear of Blackie and me. I don't seem to have brought anyone much luck, lately. What I wouldn't give to go back and start this year over." With those words, Novack sent his mount trotting down the slope.

Whew! Jess found herself leaning forward against the balustrade. What did all this mean? What was she going to do? It wasn't as if she could hightail it across campus to the sheriff and spill that she'd heard second-hand, from the local mysterious eccentric, that Terry and Carolina might be responsible for Jessamyn's death. That wouldn't fly, especially when Novack denied everything she said and painted her as some kind of hysterical female.

Jessica turned, sinking back against the stone barrier. The calls of wheeling gulls seemed more taunting than mournful now. *How trustworthy was Phil Novack's judgment about Terry and Carolina?*

Terry's surprise and grief had seemed genuine enough. Of course, he had been an actor. Could Phil be so embittered by his war wounds, physical and psychological, that his accusations had welled up from a reservoir of resentment at a snooty guy who'd desk-jockeyed his way through the war? Jessica started back to the cottage, not exactly feeling better, but not quite so shaken by *that* possibility.

So, what *should* she think about Phil? He had scared her, put her between a rock and a hard place over what to tell the sheriff, but he had been worried about her. He wanted to protect her, in *his* mind at least. There was something about this guy she genuinely liked; and, despite the turn he'd given her today, she knew she'd miss both him and Blackie. Would that James had been here to help her make sense of all this. They usually did all right for themselves once they put their heads together. Then again, would Phil have spilled to her if her husband had been here? His warning was for *her.*

Chapter Sixteen

That evening

Jessica blinked awake in James's comfy chair behind the desk in the study. Last thing she remembered was reading *Home Sweet Homicide*, probably not the most distracting selection under the circumstances– Craig Rice's playful humor notwithstanding. What *had* pulled her from a doze in this corner of the house? She'd shut the blinds against the afternoon sun, but the grayness of the room made her realize it must be much later now. A glance at her watch. *Almost nine o'clock!* She'd been conked out that long? Still, was it so surprising she'd been keeping company with the Sandman after today's events?

Jess sat up suddenly, realizing, *This late and where is James?* It seemed so quiet in the house. *Had he peeked in, seen her sleeping, and decided to let her rest?* Uneasy, Jess wasn't quite convinced. Even more uneasy, she wondered what would have kept him away *this* long. *Come to think of it, why hadn't Dusty swatted her awake for supper?* That was when she picked up the vague sounds of movement from the other side of the house. The kitchen. Of course, she'd heard someone in the kitchen.

Slowly, Jess rose, telling herself that it had to be James. *I was asleep when he checked in on me and he didn't want to wake me.* Making her way to the doorway of the study, Jessica started to call out to her husband. But she hesitated. Did *I lock the back door? Where* is *Dusty?*

Maybe it wouldn't be such a bad idea to sneak back into the study, close the door, and wait . . . for what? Was she ever being a dope! She certainly was *not* about to let the horror of the morning or Novack's unsupported insinuations get the better of her!

It wasn't as if anyone had any reason to sneak in for nefarious purposes. Who would know Phil Novack had let slip something he shouldn't have? For Pete's sake, it wasn't as if Phil would come back to make sure she didn't do any blabbing.

Still, Jess proceeded quietly, cautiously into the twilight of the living room—until a preoccupied James stepped out of the kitchen, looked up, and nearly jumped at the sight of her.

Jessica, too relieved to admit to herself, chuckled, "I thought I usually looked *better* after I took a shower and slipped into a new frock. Don't tell me I'm losing my magic already."

James's expression raced swiftly through surprise, worry, and ended in a wan smile. If she hadn't known her husband so well, Jess might have missed that second of conflicted tension in his eyes. It troubled her, even though James tried to brush it off: "Sorry, love. I never thought I'd say this, but a few hours with your chum Terry Clarke makes me miss my days in occupied France. He really gives me a pain in the neck."

James didn't come forward for a hug, though. Just sat down on the couch by the fireplace.

Jessica compressed her lips. Definitely, this was not an opportune moment to start in about Phil Novack. Instead, she went to James, put a hand on his shoulder, and said, "You look beat. How about a glass of water—no, maybe you'd like something with more octane."

James looked up at her. There was love in his eyes, along with something else that Jess couldn't quite read: Uncertainty? Worry? Guilt? All three? For a moment, she thought James might tell her, but he seemed to lose his nerve and instead looked away, putting his hand over hers and saying, "Yeah, Jessica, that'd be fine."

Jessica deeply wanted to be there for James, but she knew her guy. He would only tell her when he was good and ready. *Drat!* So, she went into the kitchen, took down a bottle of scotch from the cupboard, and poured some into a highball glass. She'd just have to play her cards so that he decided to open up sooner rather than later. James might be thinking it was his job to shield her, but it was her job to help him get something nasty off his chest.

Jess returned to James, who barely noticed her until she handed him the scotch. He smiled briefly and thanked her but didn't say else anything right away. While her husband seemed more interested in staring into his glass than drinking, Jessica pulled up a hassock to sit facing him. His continued, brooding silence led Jess to conclude that maybe a little wise-alecking might be in order.

"So, mister, are you going to tell me what's bothering you, or am I going to have to slap you around?"

That technique seemed to do the trick, for James looked up at her, smiling crookedly before opening up enough to comment, "The SOE trained me quite thoroughly on resisting enemy interrogation. In fact, I trained your OSS agents."

"True," Jessica nodded, "but I know your two worst fears, horses and ghosts. So, unless you want me to break out the Ouija board and conjure up the spirit of Exterminator, you'll come clean."

James's smile lingered, but then he abruptly went dead serious to say, "Jessica, you know how much I love you, that I'd never ask anything of you that I didn't think was in your best interest–no matter how much it might cost me."

Jess wrinkled her forehead, not knowing where this was going, only that it was somewhere she probably wouldn't want to be. But she nodded.

"Do you trust me, Jessica?"

Even in the growing twilight, she could perceive his recently sun-burned features tighten. *This is not good,* she thought; but she said, "Of course I trust you. Of course I know how much you love me. But, James, what's going on here? I haven't seen you like in a long time."

"Just listen, love," James answered quietly, putting aside his glass, taking both her hands in his. "What we uncovered today tells me this is not the place for you. I'd feel loads better if you went back to New York till my stint here was over."

"What?!" Jessica started in disbelief. "You're not making any sense. Why on earth don't you think I belong here? Wait, are you saying I'm not safe here? If you think this murder has something to do with me, you need to spell it out."

James hesitated, working out how to proceed. The nature of Phil

Novack's warning came uneasily to Jess's mind. She had to get to the bottom of this.

"Look, James, you're asking a heck of a lot of me, to trot back to the city with no questions asked. I know you, though, Mr. Crawford, and I know you're not about to go off half-cocked, so if there's some important detail that you're leaving out, you'd better come clean. *Is* there some link between me and the dead girl? Is it Terry, Carolina, something I saw at the hulk? Is Phil Novack involved?"

James paused and gave her a strange look before questioning, "Novack? Why bring Novack into this?"

"Never mind that," Jess countered, determined her husband wouldn't escape her interrogation. She thought better, though, and amended, "Tell you what. I'll spill my info if you spill yours."

Oops, wrong tactic, Jess thought as James grew annoyed at her words and said tightly, "This isn't a game, Jessica."

She nodded. "No, I know it's not. I can see how worried you are. But you ought to know by now that you can give it to me straight, no matter what 'it' is. Haven't I proven that? So, tell me why you're so afraid this murder means trouble for me."

James struggled with his thoughts before admitting, "That's not exactly it. It's not Jessamyn Crane's murder, *per se*, that has me worried for you. That's just the thin edge of the wedge. Her death is part of a bigger picture, related to why I'm here."

Jessica tilted her head, confused, before saying, "I don't follow. You're here to teach, to do what you love."

"Ye-es," James hesitantly agreed. "That's part of it." A pause, then, "Jessica, didn't you ever wonder why I was allowed to come back here so soon, so conveniently for us to marry?"

"You were injured. You're supposed to be on a kind of inactive duty. You couldn't go running after Nazis with those bum knees. Wait a minute, what Nazis? We won. The war is done."

"Is it?"

"What? James, what's this all about?"

"Jess, you've read about war criminals being hunted down in Germany and France."

"Well, yes, sure."

"And didn't you wonder why my superiors didn't keep me in Europe to help finish the job, especially in France?"

"I don't think I like where I think this is going," was all Jessica could manage.

"Nor do I, but here we are. The bitter truth is that there are still some fivers left *here*. Not everyone was rounded up by the FBI, and they can do a great deal of damage. They don't believe they've really lost. They're waiting here and in South America to set up a return match. Someone has to find them and bring them to justice before they can take us all back to hell."

Jessica was so stunned, so horrified she couldn't speak—until another realization came creeping up the "foul and muddy" "shore" of her consciousness. Eyes narrowed with hurt anger, Jess pressed her husband, "Just one minute. Do you mean to tell me that all this time you've been lying to me? Letting me believe you were through with the cloak and dagger business—inactive duty my eye! You didn't trust me enough to level with me?"

"No," James protested. "You've got it all wrong. I haven't been running secret missions behind your back for the past year. The deal was assigning me to the States to be on call. You knew that much. There was a good chance that I wouldn't be needed. Up until now, the gamble paid off. I took the offer so we could be together; otherwise, you'd still be waiting for me."

Jessica frowned and allowed, "I really hate it when you have a point. Except for one thing: why couldn't you have told me the whole story? How could you keep this from me, especially after all we've been through together?"

James sighed. "I know. You have every right to be upset. But try to understand, Jessica, it's a complicated situation. I think because of all we've been through I didn't want you constantly worrying about if or when I'd be called up. I played it down. Hell, *I* didn't really expect it to happen. I took a gamble and I lost. I'm sorry. And then there was the brass to deal with. They didn't want you to know anything for fear you might let something slip and make me useless for working undercover. I had to fight to get you in the loop on a need-to-know basis, and none of the bright boys giving me orders thinks you need to know right now— even taking into consideration all you've done in the past."

Jessica tapped her fingers impatiently on her knees. She'd have been furious for being kept in the dark, except she knew James was punishing himself enough for both of them, probably had been for some time. That conclusion calmed her down enough for her to look for more explanation.

"All right," Jessica began slowly. "Let's say, for argument's sake, I'm not going to crown you with a frying pan. We'll suppose your intentions were noble. But what the devil are you doing looking for Nazi fifth columnists in this sleepy little college berg? How does any of this connect to Jessamyn Crane? Do you think she was one of them or that *they* iced her? And I still can't see what any of this has to do with me?"

That last statement wasn't entirely true, though, because her husband's revelations were beginning to make sense of Phil Novack's warnings. Playing out the connections more, Jessica blurted, "Good Lord, is it Terry you're after? He was some kind of mole hidden in the OWI? That's why they called you up when you were coming to this campus? Well, I certainly could picture Carolina as a Nazi, but Terry? I don't think he has the killer instinct, or that he's a good enough actor to make me just *think* he doesn't."

James shook his head, "You're getting ahead of me, Jessica. Maybe I'd better start from the beginning. There's a much bigger picture than you're aware of. We're up against an enemy far cleverer than Clarke. You're just seeing the thin edge of the wedge."

"Okay, then, Mr. Buddha, enlighten me."

"I will if you promise to take seriously what I say."

"I'm listening," Jess promised, becoming grave. "But you have to level with me *completely*, and then we'll figure out the next step together. Deal?"

"Deal." James paused before saying, "I am sorry about not being completely square with you, Jessica. It's not that I don't trust or respect you . . ."

"It seems to me I've heard that song before but go on with your story."

"Right, then. I have to do a bit of a back story, so here goes. In the early 1940s, the FBI became aware of this chap running several shows out of a small town in the Midwest. Murder, espionage, sabotage—all under his direction. Quite a shark, actually, known for the brutal and efficient way he could liquidate anyone in his way—even if you worked for him."

"Sounds like a real prince," Jessica remarked.

James nodded, then continued, "Chap is clever as the devil. No one could pin anything on him for some years. We found out later, he'd been working under another identity even earlier and disappeared when things got hot. But they all slip up eventually. He had someone in his organization who was more enamored of gold and a get-out-of-the-nick-free card than he was afraid of the big man's reach."

"But the big man got away anyhow?" Jess questioned. "I mean that's the reason you're here, right?"

"Again, it's a bit more complicated."

"It figures. Okay, onward, Macduff." But Jessica's heart wasn't really in her smart talk. Funny how you could be fascinated and creeped out at the same time.

"Somehow, he realized he had a stool pigeon, and I can tell you what was found of that chap wasn't pretty. Set a neatly effective example for anyone who might decide to betray him. The Feds could never find anyone else willing to turn. At any rate, he escaped."

"To here?"

"That's where the story gets murky," James explained. "There was an auto crash. A fire. Pretty horrific. Your Feds weren't able to connect the accident with their boy until a few days after it happened. The body was so badly burned they couldn't get prints, but it looked about the right size, what was left. And they made an i.d. from partial dental records."

"Partial?" Jessica repeated skeptically. "I mean, if he had a rep for being such a mastermind, didn't anybody think he might have faked his death? Couldn't he have faked the dental records, substituted someone else's for his own? Brrrr! It gives me the willies to think about whose body must have been in that car."

James pointed out, "Your FBI had its doubts, kept their eyes open for him to rear his head, but nothing. The trail went completely cold. So, with some very real espionage to deal with, our friend finally went on the back burner."

"Except he's not there any longer. So, what put this charmer on the front of the range?"

"Good question. Early this June, a demolition crew was working a bombed-out office building in Berlin. When they were pulling up the remains of a floor, they discovered a cache of partially destroyed records on spying activities in the U.S. I imagine you can guess whose records they found."

"Three guesses and the first two don't count," Jessica wise-cracked. "Go on. Did the records say your pal was hiding out here on Long Island Sound?"

"Not exactly. Apparently, the papers confirmed that this chap, identified as Georg Zottigstrauch, was under orders to lie low until he was needed. Seems he was sent to Canada, first, then down to the Midwest, a place called Quintinsville, in 1942. In fact, the records that could still be deciphered were dated as late as 1945, when things were going pretty sour for the boys in Berlin. The last orders that could be made out from the damaged documents were for him to sit tight in our town for some time after the war was over. He'd be activated again when the time was right for the Reich to rise again."

Jessica wouldn't have been in the least surprised if her hair were standing on end. Finally, she managed, "But we won. They gave up. I thought all this Reich-will-rise malarkey was only in the movies."

James frowned, considering how best to put something dreadfully unnerving. Finally, he answered, "All I can say is that for some people, it's never over. But if we can track them down, neutralize them, we can prevent them from doing any damage, here, Europe, wherever. Don't push the panic button yet, love. The biggest reason I took this job from Dick Streeter was to put a stop to this danger."

"Oh, Mr. Streeter is the wonder boy behind this bright idea," Jessica surmised, not sure how that made her feel about the guy. She'd worked for him, herself, that time in San Francisco. There was a lot she liked about Mr. Streeter, but there was more she didn't like about him putting James back in harness. Still, he *had* been instrumental in bringing James back to her.

James only resumed when the ambivalent hostility to Dick Streeter had passed from her expression: "Dick knew I was considering this teaching position in the same place where those documents indicated our boy was hiding. That made me the lucky lad whose presence wouldn't look suspicious. No one would have any reason to suspect me of some quiet investigating."

"Investigating? Why does anyone need to investigate? The Feds were going to arrest this guy a few years ago, so they must know what he looks like. Why don't they just trot in and do their own dirty work?" Jessica questioned, impatient at yet another unfair burden dropped on James.

"Because they don't know what Zottigstrauch looks like *now*, Jessica. The *Abwehr* report contained the intel that he'd had plastic surgery, but no photos of him survived. There's a general description, height might not change, but weight and hair color . . ."

"So, it's your job to sniff this rat out," Jessica concluded, not happy that James did, indeed, appear to be the best man for the job.

"I'm afraid so. You know firsthand that the FBI borrowed me from SOE and the OSS to help expose quislings in this country."

"Yes, yes," Jessica agreed reluctantly. "I also know how dangerous the work has been for you. I do realize the importance of stopping this Zoggystruck."

"Zottigstrauch."

"Yes, sure, whatever. But listen to me, James; I also see that you've been through too much already. I see the nightmares, the nights without sleep that the war has left you."

"Jessica," James began slowly, "I can't put the past behind me until it *is* done. This man keeps the danger alive. This is a job that *I* have to do. And there isn't someone else who has the kind of 'in' to this community that I have. Drop a stranger in here without a cover story as legit as mine and my man will spook. That cannot be allowed to happen."

Jessica sighed but admitted, "All right. You're right. I hate it, but you're right. However, mister, and get this through your noggin, I'm not going anywhere. I'm the kind of gal who sticks."

"I don't want you anywhere around this bastard," James insisted. "I haven't told you everything. The *Abwehr* file has a full background, some of it typical: Oxbridge education; mastery of several languages, with perfect accents; being sent to North America; marrying a Canadian girl to fit in . . ."

"The last part sounds a little like you," Jess bantered.

"Except for the part about his wife and child mysteriously disappearing when she started asking questions about him right before he fled. Considerably later, they found one of the bodies. It wasn't pleasant," James stated levelly.

"Oh," Jess made a little *moue* with her mouth. "That does sound coldblooded."

"Now you understand why I want you away from here," James earnestly said.

Jessica looked off into the fireplace, thinking. She felt James's eyes on her. Finally, she came to a decision and turned back to him to ask, "Does your suspect know who *you* are?"

James paused, not sure where Jess was going. He replied, at last, "I don't see why he should. I have a legitimate reason for being here, and I've been meticulous about not drawing inordinate attention to myself or asking too many leading questions."

Jessica nodded, concluding, "So, you don't want attention drawn to you, correct?"

James nodded warily, sensing a trap looming, but where he wasn't certain.

"So, my friend," she began, "do you really think that if I suddenly pack my bags and take a powder, no one—especially a wary Nazi infiltrator—is going to say, 'Hmm, what's with those two?'"

"I think people might say I sent you back because I was concerned that you were rattled by the murder . . ."

"Except there are more than a few people around here who know me too well. So, when their tongues start wagging, your Nazi pal is going to take a suspicious look at you. Anyway, you seem to be forgetting that we're only a few hours from New York. If this guy can run rings around a bunch of secret service agencies, he's going to be able to figure out how to catch a train or drive a car into the city. Wouldn't you feel better if I were right where you could keep an eye on me?"

"What about your sister in California?"

"My leaving would still look suspicious. And do you *really* want me in Liz's vicinity when you're trying to keep all this on the q.t., even across the continent?"

James scowled, recognizing Jessica's logic but not liking it.

Jess pressed her point, "Besides, if I bail on teaching with Terry now, both he and Nigel will be pretty sore. I can see them making a really big deal. The kind that will draw too much attention to us."

Even as her words rolled out, Jessica caught James starting at the names of their colleagues. Or maybe it had only been one of the names. She said slowly, "James, I want to talk about the elephant in the room. You never told me if you had a particular suspect in mind."

"No," James began slowly. "I didn't want to alarm you. I thought if I could persuade you to leave, you wouldn't be as involved and there'd be less chance of your letting slip anything." He paused, perhaps hoping that might be enough to hold Jessica. The look in her eyes told him otherwise. He added, "After a bit of discreet nosing around, I've narrowed it down to two possibilities."

"And the winners are?"

"These two chaps," he replied, "have the right profile to fit Zottigstrauch's history, even their educational backgrounds are similar." James paused, looked Jessica square in the eye, and asked, "Jessica, won't you trust me on this one? Leave it alone."

"It's too late for that," she informed James quietly. "I'm already in this up to my, well, maybe not my neck, but definitely my shoulders. I've helped you before. I can do it again."

James fiercely insisted, "You were in danger those times. I don't want to do that to you again."

"Okay, okay, cool down," she placated her husband. "By 'help' I don't mean fisticuffs with fivers. More in line with creating a smokescreen by standing around looking beautiful and acting charming. You've already convinced me this guy is bad news from way back. So I would like to know whose way I should stay out of."

"Well, you shouldn't have much trouble with one of my suspects. It's the chap you saw chatting up your friend Terry the day we arrived. He goes by the name of Nicholas Spenser. Your description of him set me thinking. So, after a little quiet research, I discovered the time he arrived here dovetailed with my quarry's 'relocation.' His physical description generally matches. He keeps a low profile around town. Fits again. The time I chatted him up in his store, he actually used a couple of phrases typical of the area in Canada where Zottigstrauch was working."

"*You* chatted with him? *That's* keeping a low profile?" Jess burst out.

"Nothing suspicious about a fellow having a bit of a look about a shop, trying to find a birthday present for his wife," James answered.

"Oh? What'd you get me?"

"Wait six months and find out. Anyway, I didn't find out any more by talking to him than what I've told you. I couldn't chance prying too much just then."

"And I saw Terry talking to him," Jessica brooded. "I just can't believe that Terry would be mixed up with a bunch of Nazis."

James shrugged, adding, "He could just be a customer, or . . ."

"Or?"

"He could be under compulsion. It comes back to Jessamyn Crane."

"You think *she* was in league with your fifth columnist?" Jess questioned, incredulous.

With a shake of his head, James explained, "No, I think she got in the way. Remember I told you about the chap who tried to put the finger on our subject? His body was discovered by chance when the county drained a small lake, chained down to a cement block. The *Abwehr* file revealed that was how Zottigstrauch's wife would be found. Apparently, this was our friend's preferred method for disposing of unwanted corpses."

Jessica was so horrified, it took a moment before she could say, "What a monster. But you can't believe Terry was involved in her death. Look at his reaction. He was in shock, really in shock. Oh my goodness, is Terry in danger if he is involved with this Zaftig . . . , whatever, guy?"

"Maybe not," James quickly tried to calm Jess. "There's another suspect in my sights, and he's the one who has me worried about you."

Possibilities circled like hungry ospreys in Jessica's brain. James had shown a funny reaction when she'd mentioned two colleagues earlier, and since he seemed to see Terry as at worst only a minion, that left . . . .

"Nigel?!" she exclaimed. "No, you can't possibly mean *him*, James."

Her husband nodded, his expression revealing how little he enjoyed confirming her conjecture.

"But . . . Oh, dear, he did come here in 1943, after your man took a powder from Quintinsville. Still, Nigel Cross has a history at St. Barnabas. People can verify he lived and taught there. And aren't there records not only of his taking a degree from Cambridge but of his serving *against* the Germans during the first war? Doesn't that blow your suspicions sky high," Jessica pressed eagerly.

"It might, except for the fact that the *Abwehr* has a history of placing 'sleeper' agents whom they had recruited even right after the last war. More to the point, Jessica, they also have a history of stealing identities from chaps either taken prisoner and executed or not reported killed in action, especially if there were no families to question the identity of their plant. Nigel was a POW during the Great War," James patiently explained.

"But what about the family Nigel left St. Barnabas to help out for two years before he came here—a sick brother, wasn't it?" Jessica argued.

"A brother whose sickness conveniently ended in death. No loose end to check. Or the brother might have been a fellow traveler. No, I'm afraid that Nigel is still very much on my radar. Remember, Nigel started teaching at St. Barnabas in 1927 and left in 1940 to nurse that sick brother in Québec. He was hired as Chair here in 1943. The dates don't have to be an exact match to Zottigstrauch's, just allow for a reasonable overlap. And before you raise the question, Quintinsville is within traveling distance from St. Barnabas. A fellow could go back and forth, pretending to be off on business trips from one end or doing research or visiting family on the other." Seeing her distraught expression, James added, "I know you like Nigel, but you have to admit that he's a strong candidate."

"I guess you think that his knowing about Jessamyn at the wreck, his tie clip, that could all link him to her . . . disappearance," Jessica posited, miserably. "Whatever their relationship, if she got in his way, threatened his secret, he could have, um, taken care of her and lost his tie clip in the struggle."

"That's why I'm just as glad that you didn't let Nigel know everything you saw in the hulk, or that you have that tie clip."

"But, James," Jess tried one last time to keep hope alive, "you haven't definitely settled on Nigel, have you? There's still a chance it's the other guy? What exactly do you know about *his* history before he showed up here?"

James allowed, "Not much. There's some evidence of him living in New York and Pennsylvania prior to Margaret Point. He emigrated from

England in the late 'twenties, with a decent university education and also served in the first war."

"Ah, ha!" Jessica insisted. "So, he also could be an *Abwehr* plant! I'm telling you right now that I vote for him being your guy. Spencer looked like a predator when I saw him."

James smiled wanly, before responding, "I wish this investigation could be based on a referendum. Unfortunately, it's got to be based on facts."

"But Nigel *could* be innocent," Jessica pressed.

"Could be, but that's a prodigious 'could,' my friend. Now you know why I don't like the idea of your staying here, especially since you're spending quite a bit of time rubbing shoulders with one of my prime suspects."

"I'm sorry," Jessica replied, not at all sorry, "but that's precisely a reason why I need to stay. Just as I said before, my leaving would look suspicious. Except if I leave now, out of the blue, I won't just raise suspicions; I'll seriously tick off Nigel. He's counting on me to pinch-hit for Terry. Is it really sensible for me to make him sore in any way, to prompt him to give either of us more than a second thought? And even if this antique dealer is your man, news is still bound to get back to him that something's funny about the Crawfords. Nope. You need me to stay here and make you look as innocent as an Andy Hardy movie."

James didn't have a counterargument, and he didn't look happy about it.

Jessica figured this was exactly the time to let her husband in on some information that had been burning a hole in her head all afternoon: "There's something else you ought to know. Brother, does it make more sense after everything you've told me—I'm just not exactly sure what kind of sense it makes."

"Yes?" James questioned, attentively.

"James, I don't think Phil's exactly in on anything, I'm not even sure how much he knows, but, by gosh, I think he is wise to *something*, something that scares him."

"Go on."

"You don't sound too surprised," Jess noted.

"Novack spends a lot of time traveling the area, staying in the shadows. I would be surprised if he *did* miss much. Go on."

"Okay, well, today, not long after Rose dropped me off, Phil Novack paid a visit. While I was feeding Blackie, he told me he'd heard about us discovering Jessamyn Crane, and he was concerned. I don't doubt that he was, but sometimes I had the distinct feeling he was testing me to see how much I knew about her death. Then it slipped out that he knew something he couldn't tell. He blamed Terry for her death, but I had the impression Novack didn't see Terry as *directly* responsible. All the time I assumed he was talking about some kind of gangsters being guilty, but after hearing what you've just told me . . .Well, I'm beginning to think that Terry somehow got her in Dutch with your quarry, whether it's Spenser or Nigel. When I urged Phil to tell the sheriff what he knew, he was *not* happy; said he'd deny everything and make me look like a hysterical female unless I kept my trap shut and my nose out of the whole mess."

"I couldn't agree with him more on the last point," James concluded. However, at Jessica's narrowed eyes, he added, "He might, indeed, know something or have seen something. Yes, I do think you may be on to something. How deep he's into this, I can't say as yet."

"I can't believe that a man who suffered so much from the Germans in the war would ally himself with your fiver. If anything, wouldn't he want to even the score with them?" Jessica pointed out, not wanting to believe the worst of her sometime friend.

"He is a troubled man," James cautioned Jess. "Who knows what persuasions someone like Zottigstrauch might use on him. Who knows if he's in this by virtue of his own free will. Anyway, I can't claim that he's mixed up with Zottigstrauch without more evidence. I still need to make sure that you tread carefully with Novack. I think he trusts you, but it's a trust that you can't afford to cultivate."

"Even if it would help you?"

"You've done enough for me in that department," James returned abruptly. "I'll find a way to get at the truth on my own. It's my job, not yours."

"Lots of luck. The only confidant he seems to have is Blackie, and I've never heard of a talking horse."

"Of course, of course," James concurred, preoccupied. Then his eyes were on Jessica, and he insisted intently, "All kidding aside, Jessica, I think you'd be smart to stay away from Phil Novack–and Blackie, too.

Novack's going to be a magnet for trouble sooner or later if he knows anything at all. Zottigstrauch isn't about to stand for anyone gumming up his plans once he's aware they're in danger, and I don't want you anywhere around when he decides to take care of loose ends."

"Don't worry about that," Jessica assured, a little sadly. "Phil was way ahead of you. He wished me a not-so-fond farewell and warned me not to butt in where I didn't belong."

James smiled a little, relieved, and briefly observed, "Good man. I hope I can wrap this up before it's too late for him. I wish I could talk to him, but I'm afraid that would be tipping my hand."

"So Zottigstrauch *doesn't* know that you're on his trail? You're sure?"

She was not all that reassured when James could only say, "He shouldn't."

Jess didn't push the point. It wouldn't pay to. Instead, she asked, "All right, then, James. What do we do now?"

"I continue digging. *You* sit tight, and that includes keeping mum about not just what I've told you but, I'm afraid, anything you think might have a bearing on Jessamyn Crane's murder, should the police question you. I can't afford to have that constable looking too closely at Nigel and spooking him if he is Zottigstrauch. I'll need to keep Terry off the radar, too. If he is involved, I don't think Zottigstrauch will trust him not to break. *I* wouldn't after today's display. At best, my quarry might fly; at worst, he might first find it necessary to muzzle your chum, permanently. I'm no fan of Clarke's by a long chalk, but I wouldn't wish him in Zottigstrauch's bad books."

"But James, if you think Terry might crack, couldn't you get enough dirt from him to nail our Mr. Z? Or couldn't you just bring Nigel and Spenser in for questioning? Wouldn't that solve all your problems?"

"I wish it were that simple. I'm afraid I haven't been clear enough. First of all, Zottigstrauch isn't a man who would crack that easily. But, as I said before, this assignment is more complicated than just running him in. My job is to find out what he's up to now: how far he's gotten with his plans and who else is involved. I've been tasked to follow the chain to the final link, so no one else can pick up where he left off. I have to tread very carefully."

"I'll say," Jessica agreed somberly. Disturbed by the prospect of

James coming into contact with this Zottigstrauch, she continued, "It sounds as if you might have to worm your way into his confidence."

"Or that of someone who's afraid of him and looking for an out," James considered.

"Won't you have to reveal yourself for that, to prove that you *could* give him a safe out?"

"Yeah, that's a bit of a sticking point, isn't it? That's a part of the plan I'm still working on."

"Are you thinking that Terry might be your ticket in?" Jess wondered, full of misgivings.

Apparently James shared her doubts, for he answered, "He's too weak. Even if I could win him over, I've no doubt he'd sell me out to save his skin if things got hot. I more than suspect that Jessamyn Crane was murdered to put the fear of God into him, as much as to silence her." James then turned the topic, "But that's assuming Terry Clarke is tied in with Zottigstrauch. I'd look a right fool if I tried to turn Clarke, and he had no idea what I was getting at—not to mention the fact that I'd have no assurance that he wouldn't let slip something in front of the wrong party. After all, he has connections to both my suspects: Nigel being the chair and Spenser being so chummy with his wife. I certainly couldn't have him detained until the case was settled without raising too many questions, not that I'd want to do that to an innocent chap, even someone as obnoxious as Clarke."

"Well, I'm not exactly Terry's Number One Fan," Jessica added, "but considering how much he's suffering over Jessamyn's death, I wouldn't want more added to his burden. Even if he is a two-faced cheater."

James tilted his head reflectively and questioned Jess, "Do you think, if he is involved with Zottigstrauch, what happened to Jessamyn might put him in mind for a little revenge?"

"Terry? No. In my experience, he's a lot of sound and fury signifying nothing. I'm sure he's upset now, but I don't think he'd have the intestinal fortitude to go up against a big leaguer like your Zottigstrauch. Remember, this is the same guy who used his family connections to sit out the war in D.C. And Terry might have loved Jessamyn enough to grieve her death but not enough to buck his wife for a divorce."

"Hmm," James considered. "Well, then, it looks as if I need to continue doing some quiet digging to find a way in. One thing bothers me, though, and maybe it's a good sign. I'm not sure."

"What's that?" Jess was almost greedy for some ray of hope in this dark business.

"The body's breaking free, coming loose like that. Zottigstrauch was smart enough to cover it, so the fish wouldn't get at it, so it could decompose undetected. Then why wasn't he smart enough to secure it better so she wouldn't surface at all?"

"Mmm," Jess nodded, till some cogitation made her question, "Say, you said they found that stool pigeon's body when they drained a pond, right?"

"Close. A small lake."

"And that was his 'preferred' disposal method, right?"

"That's what the recovered documents recorded, yes. What are you getting at, Jessica?"

"This—Long Island Sound is part of a big, rough ocean, not a quiet little pond or lake. He didn't take into account what tides and a Nor'easter could do. Maybe, your mastermind isn't the über-genius he used to be. If he makes one mistake, gets sloppy or overconfident, he may make some more."

James turned over Jessica's conclusion, finally conceding, "Yes, I suppose you could be right. It makes sense. Even so, I wouldn't for one minute underestimate him. And you'd better not, either my love."

"Don't worry! You've convinced me to watch my step, but calmly, nonchalantly. And who knows, maybe Miss Innocence may overhear something that only makes sense if you know what to listen for."

James shot Jessica a sharp look and warned, "I'm serious, Jessica. Don't go playing nosey Parker. This Zottigstrauch is a devil. One slip on your part, and Bob's your uncle, you'll be wearing concrete spectator pumps. Tell you what. I'll make you a deal. You keep your nose clean, and I won't push you anymore to leave campus. Agreed?"

"Okay," Jess promised. "I don't intend to stick my neck out. I'm perfectly happy not to get killed so I can live to collect one of Roosevelt's greatest gifts to the nation, social security. But if you do need someone to bounce ideas off, I'm your girl. If I happen to hear something–Don't give me that look. I swear, no eavesdropping–I'll tell you. Is that okay with *you*?"

"Fair enough," James agreed, adding. "I do value your opinion." Leaning forward to tap Jessica's forehead, he finished. "There's some valuable grey matter behind your pretty face. I just want to keep you safe."

"I know," Jess replied, taking his hand, holding it for a moment, then releasing him to say, "So, is that it? Anything else?"

"What more do you want?"

"You have me there."

"Well," James began. "Have we kissed and made friends? Am I forgiven for not being entirely on the level with you all this time?"

Jessica leaned forward and kissed James before saying, "James, you know I love you. Of course you'll be forgiven." Then she pointed a finger at him and warned, "If you *ever* keep me in the dark like this again . . ."

James's hand closed around that threatening digit and he responded, "Everything on the square. I promise."

They literally kissed and made friends then.

But James was still far from at ease. He knew too well of what his quarry was capable. Damn, but he wished he'd had some way of turning down this assignment—but who else was in the right position to neutralize the dangers that Georg Zottigstrauch was brewing? Would that he could at least have kept Jessica far away from all this mess. Yet he knew that her instincts, her intelligence, her support were resources he could ill afford to do without.

Chapter Seventeen

Monday, July 22

From the ocean, a breeze swirled around Cameron House, brushing against Jessica through the open, mullioned window in James's small office. Absently she played with the collar of her blouse, splashed with tropical flowers, complimentary to the white skirt of her suit. Her jacket hung from the back of the chair behind James's desk. The clanging buoys and moaning ships' horns couldn't make this growing twilight anymore melancholy, though melancholy seemed too mild a description.

They'd come from a "town meeting" Wanda Angelovic had called for the campus community to address the tragic discovery on the beach yesterday. Cool, crisp, and in control, President Angelovic had assured them that there was no danger, the sheriff was hot on the case, and security patrols had been increased. She'd struck just the right note of sympathy for the loss of Jessamyn Crane by asking everyone to remember and honor her, while urging anyone with any insight into the young woman's fate to contact the police. The meeting had ended with a sense that the situation was well in hand, with only lingering trepidation. Except for Jessica and James, who had the misfortune to know better. Correction, there were probably certain parties at the meeting who were not so much in the know as just plain guilty.

"Ah, Jessica, I was looking for your husband. I didn't expect to find you here, but excellent."

The tired voice behind her made Jess stiffen, though she tried to hide it. She turned as casually as she could and observed, "Nigel, that weary tone doesn't go with a word like 'excellent.' It's a better fit for 'At least *something*'s gone right today.'"

Nigel Cross barely smiled. A man so drained, so exhausted hardly appeared gifted at nefarious plotting. What that tie clip might imply about Nigel's feelings for Jessamyn Crane melted the fear that had frozen Jess's heart.

"Nigel, are you all right? It's not tactful of me to say it, but you look dreadful. Please sit down."

"No, no," he rubbed his eyes with one hand, the other, Jess just now noticed, gripped a briefcase. He continued, "I haven't time. But I do need to talk to you, about Terry. I need to know if you can take over for an entire week."

"Me? Why?" Then Jess skipped from surprised to leery, "What does his nibs think about that?"

"Terry actually asked that you do it," Nigel replied simply.

"Are you serious? Terry? I know we've been getting along better lately, but *me* take over his pet project? I'd have expected he'd rather have his nails torn out one by one, while being forced to watch a Bowery Boys movie," Jessica returned in disbelief.

"Yes, well, it took me a bit by surprise as well," Nigel agreed, wearily squeezing the bridge of his nose between his thumb and forefinger. He must have been trying to forestall a whale of a migraine. Now, he looked at Jess and explained, "It seems that our stellar scholar is far too devastated by this recent unfortunate discovery."

"He did take it very hard, the poor girl's death," Jess allowed, trying not to rub salt in Nigel's wounds.

"Yes," Cross agreed, his tone inarguably sarcastic, as his gaze drifted away from Jess, "such a close family friend."

Her surprised expression at his unmasked scorn prompted Nigel, when he turned back, to make an apology that wasn't quite an apology, "That was not terribly politic. Well, rumors to the contrary, ice water does not flow through my veins." His eyes moved back to the window behind Jessica when he reflected, "It was a terrible thing done to her. A woman like Jessamyn deserved far better; she deserved far better than Terry Clarke. A smart, lovely person, but so many bad choices."

Jess's heart went out to Nigel. *No way was this a Nazi murderer who could ruthlessly liquidate Jessamyn, let alone his own wife and child.* Then again, she'd not always been 100% at identifying Nazi monsters.

"Nigel, I'm so sorry," she began. "You must have known her, quite well. I wish there was something I could say . . ."

"It's all neither here nor there," Nigel cut off Jess, a curtain descending between them. "The question is, will you take over for Terry, just for this week? With summer classes canceled for tomorrow's memorial, you're only needed for a few days. Will you do it?"

Jessica needed to re-orient herself to Nigel's all-business mien, but she gamely answered, "I can try. No need for the kids to take a loss. I have to admit that I really love working with them. I wish the opportunity had come up under happier circumstances."

Ignoring Jessica's last observation, Nigel opened his briefcase and, as he pulled out a binder, explained, "These are Terry's class notes. I'm not going to tell you to follow them blindly, but I'm sure you know better than to think Terry would give you *carte blanche*."

"Got it," Jess agreed, accepting the binder.

"Fine," Nigel nodded. "That's one worry off my mind."

Jessica smiled, a little sadly, then added, "Oh, wait, didn't you want to see James? He's at the secretary's desk. In fact, I'm surprised you didn't see him when you came in."

"No, no. I came up the spiral staircase, so I wouldn't have seen him there. I just saw his light on and thought I'd ask him to speak to you, but it seems we're all set now." Nigel paused, and, when he spoke, he seemed sincere, "Thank you, Jessica. I really appreciate this. I'll remember it."

Before she could say anything, Nigel was gone.

Jess frowned to herself. *That man could not be not the devil James had described. Or could he? A master agent wouldn't find acting sincere much of a stretch.*

She did not look forward to sharing this meeting with James.

Friday, July 26

Late afternoon and the setting summer sun was turning everything a mellow copper. The weather had finally shifted so that a powerful breeze rushed off the ocean, stirring everything with a refreshing cool, including the two figures sitting just beyond the rising sand dunes. You wouldn't see them from the strand unless you really looked, but they could enjoy the sweep of beach, straight, then curved, heading toward the campus to their right. The beach also extended to the left but was hidden by a mass of chunky boulders rising thirty feet for about another quarter of a mile.

Jessica Minton sat up, laughing into the wind that thrust her long, dark, curling hair away from her face and rippled her silky blouse like a lemony flag. The uneventfulness of the past few days, along with the enjoyment of teaching, had gradually softened last Sunday's horrors. There had been one close call, after class, when Alicia Wraxton had approached her expressing way too much sympathy for Terry's suffering and an equally disturbing animosity toward Carolina. It took some careful persuasion to make Alicia realize she would ultimately foment scandal for her idealized Terry, not to mention strife at the school, on top of putting herself on a hot spot. The latter points were Jess's main concern. Though pretty sure she'd gotten through to Alicia, Jessica decided a confab with Rose was in order to ensure the kiddo had cooled down.

After letting Jess know she'd done a good job defusing the "Alicia crisis," James had been careful not to dwell on his larger concerns about Zottigstrauch. To some extent, she sensed that coming completely clean with her was a huge load off his mind. So here she was, tousled by the salty wind, luxuriating in the sunset's now amber light, watching the sky turn blue to aqua to turquoise while flocked with clouds pinked and oranged underneath by the setting sun.

James had made her laugh, genuinely laugh this gorgeous evening, this moment of dusky summer repose. Stretched comfortably on his back on the blanket they shared, he'd recounted undergraduate misadventures to drive off almost all her lingering worries—though a few might linger in the cove beyond the rocks. Joseph's Cove, where the derelict had held Jessamyn's, Terry's, Nigel's and even Phil's secrets. How many tragedies had been washed out to sea but not out of existence by the storm? This wasn't the first moment tonight the location for their picnic seemed odd to her.

"Here now, none of that look," James chided. "I didn't take my wife on a late afternoon picnic to have the blue devils nipping after her. Give us that beautiful smile again."

Jessica leaned down, her face close to James, and questioned, "Okay, all joking aside, why here? We have a huge stretch of beach, and you park the car we borrowed from Rose and David around the corner from where the hulk used to be, the place Nigel Cross told me to steer clear of. What gives?"

James quirked his mouth and answered, "Perhaps, I was curious if Phil Novack was leveling with us about what happened to the wreck. I wanted to check out for myself how much was gone. And a chap and his lovely wife having a romantic picnic make a nice cover . . ."

"Oh, that's what was really on your mind?" Jessica sat up, arms akimbo with mock indignation. "How flattering. All this romance is just a lot of banana oil to throw people off the track."

"I wouldn't say it's banana oil entirely," corrected James, sitting up and taking Jessica in his arms. "No one said we couldn't mix business with pleasure."

He kissed away her protest, temporarily, until Jess held him back to question, "What happened to all that concern about sending me away so I wouldn't be involved? I smell a rat here somewhere. What's the catch?"

"The catch is," James explained patiently, though a little impatient to continue the romance, "you and I won't go any further than the top of those rocks. I keep an eye on you, get the layout of what's in the cove, and don't appear to be doing anything but having a romantic outing with my lovely wife."

"That's the second time you've called me your 'lovely wife' in ten minutes." Jessica's tone and expression were skeptical, but her arms were around James's neck. "Maybe you're also thinking if you butter me up, then throw me the bone of letting me tag along tonight, I'll be more amenable to your shutting me out of the rest of the investigation?"

"Quite the foxy one, aren't you?" James observed with a twinkle. Then with a genuineness that touched her, he added, "Seriously, Jessica, I know you want to help me. I know you're no weak sister, but I'm not going to do anything that will put you in harm's way. This is a bad business, and you've risked yourself enough for me in the past. The best way you can help is not distracting me by making me worry about you. All right, then?"

Jessica nodded. She leaned in to give James the kind of kiss that took both their minds off their troubles. She was highly successful. So successful that it took her a few moments to realize it wasn't her heart, but hoof beats she heard pounding. Jess pulled back to stare down the beach to their right, below them. James was right with her, questioning, "Who?"

"I'm not sure, but it's a guy and he's really pulling out all the stops," she answered, continuing to watch before bursting out, though in a whisper, "Why it's Terry. What's the bee in his bonnet?"

The last word had barely escaped Jess when James pulled her down on the blanket beside him, his expression telling her it wasn't for romance. He waited a fraction of a second, then slowly raised his head, just enough to see without being seen.

"Your friend Terry certainly seems to be riding hell-bent for leather," James finally observed, wheels turning in his head.

"'Hell bent for leather'?" Jess echoed curiously, still flat down. "Since when does a Milton-Northern, Oxbridge-educated boy talk like Randolph Scott?"

Without turning, James offered a quizzical, "Randolph who? Never mind. He's slowing down. Wait, I think he's sighted something beyond the rocks, maybe inside the cove. Our boy is *not* running away from anyone. No, he's meeting someone in the cove. Rather odd, isn't it, to meet someone all the way out here?"

Jessica frowned. *Had Terry come up with a new girlfriend already? Good gosh, had Alicia suffered a backslide? No, no. Whatever Terry's problems, he wouldn't prey on students, and he certainly had been too genuinely devastated by Jessamyn Crane's death to pick up a substitute* this *fast.* Then James's sharp whisper startled away Jess's thoughts.

"Good Lord, it's your friend Novack!"

Jess raised herself level with James to see for herself, his hand keeping her down enough to hide her from sight. There was Phil Novack on Blackie, the horse's neck bowed with pride as they splashed through the surf, coming from beyond the rocks.

"Well, what do you know about that?" she breathed as the two riders met. Their horses circled; Terry's chestnut was blowing hard, its flanks and neck flecked with foam.

"Not exactly two chaps you'd expect to find so matey," James observed, then added, "Though I can't say their body language looks all that chummy."

"I'll say," Jessica agreed. "Phil never had anything good to say about Terry, and Terry was more than a little hostile when we met in the cove that time. But then, they acted as if they didn't know each other very well."

"Does seem a bit rum that two chaps with a history like that would be up to secret meetings," James reflected.

"Look," Jess pointed out. "They're riding together around the rocks into the cove." She turned to James and added, "A nice place to chat unobserved, isn't it? Of course Phil wanted to keep me out of there. Oh, my goodness, what does this say about Jessamyn Crane? They killed her because she was in with them? Nigel *is* the one?"

"Don't jump to conclusions," James cautioned. "We need more facts. We don't know for certain all this does connect to Zottigstrauch. But it's odd enough to merit investigation. If I could just hear what they were up to." James looked at the rocks rising high around the cove and speculated, "Maybe from the top of that rise. I could hide behind some outcroppings at the top. The wind's blowing toward me. I might be able to catch enough of their words."

Jessica followed James's gaze, then turned back to him, disagreeing, "No, I've a much better idea. There's a cleft in the rocks that leads into the cove, nigh onto impossible to find from this side. But with its outcropping, you could hide and probably better hear voices from the cove."

"Right," said James, getting up. "Tell me how to get there."

"No," Jess shook her head, also on her feet. "It's a bit complicated to explain or to get through if you haven't done it before. But I can take you. Let's go."

"Absolutely not. I'm not going to chance your being seen . . ."

"James," Jessica reasoned, "I know how to place us in the cleft so we can't be seen. You don't even know how to navigate the passage. You need me. Anyway, if they see you but not me, my goose is still cooked. They know they can get to you through me."

James started to argue; but, even as he did, he calculated the sense in Jessica's words and relented, "All right, but keep low and out of sight."

"Deal," Jess agreed. Pointing to their blanket, she said, "Leave this here. Follow me—and snap it up."

Despite the massive pile of stone muffling their approach from Terry and Phil, Jess still explained softly, "Follow me closely. It's a bit tricky, avoiding being seen. The cleft's big enough for a horse to get through. That's how Terry, Phil, and I left the cove last time. But there are a couple of tight turns with outcroppings that can hide us—with this fading light, and if they're standing at an angle that blocks their line of vision, we're probably good."

"That's a lot of 'ifs,'" James remarked, equally softly.

"I'd rather have a handful of 'ifs' than a boxcar full of 'nos,'" Jessica countered.

"That was a pearl of wisdom worthy of your sister."

"Yes, well, next time you want profundity, take Bertrand Russell along on one of your romantic picnics *cum* stakeouts."

"No thanks," James replied. "Somehow, I doubt he's nearly as a good a kisser as you, though I could be wrong."

Jess smiled, then put a finger to her lips. She led James up to, then along, the mass of jutting, slick grey rocks and showed him the passage cut by eons of violent geology. The sand seemed to almost pulse a faded white along a passage appearing to lead directly into a wall of stone, but actually angling sharply to the right.

Jess only hesitated a moment, refusing to let the enormity of what she was risking daunt her. She plunged into the gloom between the rock walls, with James right behind her. Thank God the sand muffled their footfalls. Too bad the Almighty hadn't taken care of the chunks of rock thrusting up here and there. The straightaway curved slightly to the left, so they could just make out some of the beach around a large outcropping directly before the cleft opened narrowly onto the beach. No one was in sight, but the sounds of a tense confrontation drifted into the passage.

That's when one of those small rocks protruding through the sand, hard to discern in the twilight, nearly sent Jessica flying and blowing their secret presence sky high. Or would have, had not James grabbed and steadied her. Jess suppressed a gargantuan sigh of relief that, along with her stomach, had tried to heave through her mouth. Good thing circumstances demanded silence. The last thing she needed right now was James making smart remarks about her alleged "expertise" navigating the passage. Well, the second to last thing. The last thing would have been Terry or Phil demanding, "What the hell are you doing here?"

James's arm around her, Jessica picked out a few words: "We don't get paid . . ." (Terry) "Big time . . . professor . . . worry . . . paid pretty well" (Phil). She and James crept close to the last outcropping concealing them and stopped, as the disjointed sounds gradually coalesced into discernable sentences. Still, the cold wash of the ocean prevented the words from being crystal clear.

"I'm a professor not a movie star–and you've no idea what I need for myself, to restore my family standing. To win back that life. It's none of your business, anyway. Just do as you're told or there will be consequences." The anger in Terry's voice carried above the ocean.

Phil's was unruffled: "Consequences, huh? Like what happened to your girlfriend?"

Jess felt James tighten his grip on her shoulder at what those words might imply for her safety.

"You leave Jessamyn Crane out of this, Novack," Terry commanded. "What happened to her had nothing to do with our arrangement. She didn't know about this, not everything. It's just as the sheriff was theorizing; she must have had a secret life in New York that even I didn't know about. Just as she didn't know about . . . this."

"You really believe that, Clarke? Come off it, buddy. Face facts. She met you here. She knew this place. One way or another, she overheard what we were planning–or maybe you came here to make some secret arrangements with your mastermind buddy . . ."

Jess looked up at James, but his features, shadowed by the twilight, gave away nothing. Uneasily, she returned her attention to the men arguing on the beach. Phil spoke now.

"She could have been tucked away in the hulk when you and he didn't know it–or maybe you *thought* he didn't know she was there. I'll bet she was trying to talk you out of this, save your skin; but your boy found out and took care of her, permanently. I only know what you tell me about this guy; and, like you said before, he doesn't want 'complications.' What I can't figure out is why you're still tied up with this creep after what he did to her. Or maybe you're too afraid to face . . ."

"Damn you, Novack! You're not going to make me feel responsible for what happened to Jessamyn!"

They could hear a scuffle. Instinctively, Jess moved closer to James. She'd have given her eye teeth to peer around the outcropping yet not be seen.

Silence.

Questioningly, Jessica glanced up at James. He only shrugged.

Maybe the boys had kayoed each other.

Finally, Novack's voice apologized, "Sorry, Clarke. I can't have a guy take a poke at me and let him get away with it."

Jess strained to hear more. *What had Terry replied?* The wind seemed to whip their words away and out to sea. Darn! Why wouldn't Dame Nature cooperate? Then, Phil's words were clearer.

"Okay, you're right. I was out of line. Maybe I just want out. I never signed on for murder. Maybe I'm taking it out on you 'cause I think I'm just as trapped as you are, and I don't want to admit it. We've gotten ourselves into a bad bargain, brother."

"Just get it through your head, Novack: there is no out with this man. We're in straight down the line. You don't cross this guy." There was a pause, as if Terry struggled with something brutally painful: "Even Carolina's jumpy as a cat around him, and she used to think that she had him wrapped around her finger. She's only just realized that he played her from the start. Anyway, it'll all be over soon. I'll have my money, you'll have yours, and in two weeks he and his 'package' will be on their way to . . . well, the less you know the better."

Phil Novack's question hooked her curiosity, "*You* know where he's going?"

Terry parried. "*You* don't need to know."

"No, I don't want to, either. Remember, you're the one who said your pal doesn't like 'complications,' and it looks to me that a guy who wants to make a clean getaway might consider it a little 'complicated' to leave around anyone who might be able to point out where he'd 'gotten away to'–if you catch my drift."

"Your concern is touching, Novack. Never mind what I do or don't know. Just follow instructions and stay away from Jessica Minton."

Jess looked sharply to James, and his features were not impassive on hearing her name. But he stayed composed and signaled her to sit tight and listen before jumping to any panicky conclusions.

Phil's response was impatient, "All right, all right, if it keeps her off your pal's radar. But then why have *you* been getting so palsy with her."

"It makes perfect sense, and you know it," Terry snapped. "Our benefactor doesn't trust any new faces, so he wants me to keep an eye on her. And he extrapolated I could keep tabs on her husband through her. I had her all clear, our boss saw no threat, until you started buddying around with her, putting our business . . ." And off went his words with the damned wind, only returning on, "It's your fault the boss gave her a second look. Maybe if you like her so much, you might consider what that means for her."

That little nugget had Jessica's knees going all watery. What did Zottigstrauch think Phil had told her? She could feel the tension in James. This was almost his worst nightmare: her, not him, in Georg Zottigstrauch's sights. But things were getting hot and heavy out there. She'd better muffle her anxiety and pay attention.

"Me, Clarke? Don't put this off on me. I'm not like you. I've already told her she shouldn't be bothering me and Blackie," Phil partially lied.

"That's no good. She's such a damned do-gooder, she'll probably go contact the VA to get you into a shrink or something."

"Yeah, well, I also said if she didn't want to make enemies for that husband of hers, she shouldn't be so chummy with a guy a lot of people around your school see as a Section-Eight."

"I'll give you credit, Novack. That just might do the trick. She's pretty crazy about the guy."

"Sure, why not? He's not bad looking, in a shaggy, high-brow way. And he's pretty smart, but not pretentious."

A glance at James's smile prompted Jess to give him a gentle but firm elbow to the ribs. She couldn't have him going all smug and lovely on her.

"You sound as if you were sweet on him yourself," Terry crabbed. "Just let us worry about him. Chew on that for a while—but do it in your cabin, alone, till I give you the word."

The talking had ended; and, shortly after, Jessica and James heard hoof beats as someone rode off toward campus. Blackie made a long, friendly whinny, giving Jess a few unnerving minutes for fear it had been directed to her. But then there was the splashing of Phil riding the horse into the surf.

Jessica offered James a querying look, but he signaled her to wait as he listened. Finally, he peered carefully around the bulge of rock obscuring them from the beach, gradually stepping clear of it for a full view of the cove. James signaled her to follow. and the two walked cautiously to the opening of the cleft.

The cove stretched empty before them, foot and hoof prints the only traces of that terrible secret interview. The wind and surf would erase those soon enough. The cove, itself, seemed somehow vulnerable with the wreck washed back into its salt-sea grave. Only a few broken ribs of dark wood, impaled in the ocean-swamped sands further out, hinted the presence of the hulk and its secrets.

"I see Novack didn't lie about the wreck," James observed.

Jessica turned to her husband with an incredulous, "That old ship is all you've got to comment on?"

"Oh no. I've got plenty to say, but more to think about," he answered, still watching the water beyond. "More than I care to think about, especially where you're concerned."

"Yes, I know," Jess said grimly. "When those two let their hair down, they mean business! *Do* they suspect you, James? I know I want to stay off their radar–but please don't say 'I told you so.'"

James looked back at Jess and only observed, "It's getting damned cold and damp here. What say we put off mulling the possibilities until we get back to the car?"

Jess smiled wanly, appreciating James's tactful response, and agreed, "Brother, you've got yourself a deal."

Approaching the rocks, Jess noted that James was assiduous about brushing over their prints on the beach. Was she relieved that he had masked their presence or disturbed that he felt he had to? Passage through the cleft was no more comforting. The deepened twilight made their journey darker and danker, about as pleasant as a bunion in tight shoes.

But they made it through and returned silently to their blanket; collected and stowed their things in the "boot," as James called it; and slid into the car. All this time, Jess had the distinct feeling that behind his taut expression James was running all the train times from here to the city for her deportation.

Behind the wheel, James turned the key in the ignition, but before he shifted into gear, he turned to Jess for a quick, "This is why I wanted to send you away."

Jess couldn't speak, so jumbled and unnerving were her thoughts. James had the car on the road and moving before he continued, "But I can't send you away just now, for precisely the reasons you enumerated. You're right, damn it. If Georg Zottigstrauch and his crew have their eyes on you, I can't afford to raise their suspicions by packing you off where I can't keep *my* eye on you."

Jessica remained silent, thinking over James's statement. Was she trapped in the eye of a storm, not knowing when the hurricane wall would sweep over her? Might her husband also be in the gun sights of this vicious agent? The asphalt rushed toward them, but she didn't see it any more than the sandy expanse dotted with scrub or the ocean aside the road. At last, Jess spoke: "You never really answered me, James. Is this Georg Zottigstrauch on to you? Terry seemed to think he's suspicious of strangers in general, but does he keep Terry in the dark about a lot?"

"Good questions," James mused, though far from amused. "I wish I had the answers. I've been thinking, though, and it doesn't make sense to me that Zottigstrauch would recognize me as someone with a mission to track him down. He's been in sleeper mode for some time, and I think if my handsome face had been on file for his perusal from the *Abwehr*, I'd certainly have been nicked long ago in France. I don't think I've done anything since I've been here that would ring any alarm bells if I hadn't been a questionable proposition to begin with."

"I wonder," Jess considered. "Could Terry have put the finger on you?"

"Terry? Why?" James was puzzled and definitely interested.

"Think about this," Jess began, working out a theory that had been percolating in her brain since they'd left the cove. "Terry told us he was with the OWI, propaganda. I gathered from some things he said in front of me that he was privy to some classified information."

"I wouldn't expect the FBI and the OSS, or Army Intelligence, to be handing out portraits to the propaganda office—not exactly keeping the service secret, is it, love?" James countered.

"No," Jess emphatically shook her head. "That's not where I was going. Maybe Terry didn't get his classified info from being in the propaganda office. Maybe he was actually in Army Intelligence. We both know he wouldn't be the first guy not to be on the level about what he did in the war."

James let out a thoughtful whistle. "There's an interesting and disturbing possibility. Do you think he might have been working both sides even during the war?"

"I don't know. Well, maybe not. It seemed like, from what we heard on the beach, that Carolina brought Zottigstrauch to Terry, and since you said our master spy has been in sleeper mode while Terry was in the service, it sort of rules out that possibility," Jessica decided. "But your pal sounds like a real operator, trapping Terry and Carolina by playing on their desperation to restore their families with a pile of cash. I hate to think that Terry would sell his soul by getting involved with a Nazi. But *did* he know exactly what he was getting into until he was trapped? Who knows what kind of pressure Carolina put on Terry to follow her lead. He may have cheated on her, but she still seems to wear the pants in that marriage."

Jess noticed James take a quick glance at the slacks she was wearing and smile. Yet when he spoke, he didn't waste any time with wise cracks, "Whatever the case, I need to fill in Dick Streeter on what we learned tonight. I've already asked him to run a more stringent check on Terry Clarke since Crane's murder came out. Now, I think I need a face-to-face with Streeter, the sooner the better. Looks like I'll be catching a train for the city tomorrow morning. Maybe you'd better join me."

At first, the thought of hopping a train for the city, maybe catching up with Lois and Iris, gave Jess a happy thrill. At first. But a little thought prompted her to point out, "No, bad idea. I made plans to go riding with Rose tomorrow afternoon. We've been talking about this in front of a lot of people, including Terry and Nigel. We can't take a chance my doing anything unexpected will provoke the slightest questions."

"I don't like leaving you alone," James countered, eyes still on the road.

"Well, I'm not thrilled to be alone, but, hey, I have Dusty to protect me."

With a sharp look, James warned, "Jessica, I'm not kidding around here. This is serious business . . ."

"I know, I know," Jess assured her husband. "I'm sorry. I thought a little humor might lighten the mood–apparently it was about as light as Sidney Greenstreet. Sorry. Don't worry. Please. I intend to play things safe, and how!"

James was quiet. Whether she'd placated him or not, Jess wasn't sure. Then a hopeful thought struck, prompting her to break the tense silence, "You know, we both might still be very much in the clear. Wouldn't your Nazi pal have blown town if he really thought someone was on to him? Why would he hang around if he thought someone might nab him?"

James didn't speak for a moment, finally admitting, "I wish I could agree with you. Unfortunately, I have an answer for you. Remember, your chum Terry said that Zottigstrauch was planning to ship out somewhere with a package shortly. That tells me he *has* to wait. Perhaps his way of skipping out isn't arranged or has been set for a date he can't change. You could be right, but I won't bet on it. What I wouldn't give to know what's in this package and where he intends to take it."

"Secret documents, maybe?" Jess conjectured. "Treasury plates? Cash? It has to be something you could hide at Phil Novack's. I guess that rules out plutonium."

James smiled grimly in response, but was thinking out loud, "Yes, Novak's cabin. It seems to me it's west of here. Not terribly far from the cove. It looks as if I'm going to have to get in there for a good look around–and soon. Yes, I definitely have to get into the city and see Streeter, make sure I can do my job and still work all the legal angles. Won't do for Zottigstrauch to slip through our fingers on a technicality."

"You have to search Phil's place," Jess said slowly. "If you find something, James, what will happen to Phil?"

James glanced at her, his features hard to read in the evening gloom, but there was sympathy in his voice, though his words conveyed a harsh truth, "He's in this, Jessica. He's helping a traitor. Murder's even involved. If I find something in the cabin, I can't conveniently forget where it turned up."

"I know," Jess allowed, frustrated, "but you heard what they said tonight. Phil didn't know what he was getting into. You could tell as well as I that he wouldn't have been a part of this if he'd known. Terry certainly made crystal clear to Phil what would happen to him if he didn't go along. He's being forced now . . ."

"It's not in my hands, Jessica," James quietly informed her. "All I can do is try to find out what he's holding for Zottigstrauch—if I can do it in time. Doing a search is a tricky business."

"Well, whatever turns up, I think that you should keep in mind that Phil Novack lied to Terry to protect me. Remember, Phil warned me off Terry and the murder. He hinted to me there was something deeper going on involving the Clarkes, but he didn't tell Terry that."

"He might not have wanted Terry to know he'd shot his mouth off to you. He could very well have just been trying to save his own neck, Jessica," James pointed out, though not enjoying disabusing Jess of her perception of Phil Novack.

Jessica was silent. She still believed in Phil, but her husband was convincing.

James went on, "Look, Jessica, when I make my report, I'll include your views as well. Dick Streeter thinks you have a good head on your shoulders. He'd want to hear what you thought. But that's all I can promise."

"I guess I can't ask for more," Jess conceded. "Thanks, James, thanks for listening to me."

"All part of the service, Madame."

But neither of them could muster much of a smile or end the silence that stretched between them for several minutes. It was Jess who finally spoke: "I have to ask. What we heard tonight, did it bring you any closer to deciding who Zottigstrauch really is? Spenser or Cross?"

James shook his head, answering, "Can't say Terry gave away anything useful in that direction. I guess I'm with Moses when the lights went out."

"In the dark," Jessica finished for him, knowing his old aphorism.

James allowed himself a quick smile, then he was back to business: "I wish that I could bring Clarke and his wife in for questioning, but that would be enough to spook my Nazi friend. He's egotistical enough to think he could outfox one agent, but too smart to stick around if his whole network was in danger of betraying him, 'package' or no."

"Maybe you could just stake out Phil's place until Nicholas or Nigel shows up," Jess suggested.

"When do I start? For how long? What is Novack going to hand over? To *whom* is he going to hand 'it' over? The odds are Zottigstrauch would be cautious enough to send Terry or Carolina for a pickup. If they were seized, would he stick around for them to out him, even if it knocked his plans into a cocked hat? No, I have to get in there and see if I can find out what Zottigstrauch is hiding with Novack."

"That won't be easy," Jess sighed. "It's not as if you have all the time in the world to wait for Phil to step out. And that cabin is not exactly something you can sneak up on. You can see for miles around from it."

James frowned, "How do you know so much about the layout?"

"Oh," Jess was a tad embarrassed to admit, "Rose and I went riding the other day. And, well, I told her I was curious about where Phil Novack lived. I had her show me. But I'd seen him riding off in a different direction, so I knew he wouldn't get mad at me for not keeping my distance. Anyway, nobody's the wiser, unless you're suspicious about Rose and Flicka. So it's just as well I did, because now I can tell you something about the outside layout."

"You don't have to."

"Oh?"

"Never mind that tone," James returned, though not harshly. "It's my job to scout this area. It's your job not to give me a headache worrying about you."

"Hey, buddy, just keep in mind that I got you into the rock cleft so you could hear that that crew is all under this Zottigstrauch's thumb. I didn't exactly put us behind the eight ball then, did I? You could at least hand me a 'nice job, kid'."

"Nice job, kid," James allowed. "And, no, you didn't exactly make a dog's dinner of things. In fact, there is something in particular you can do that will be an enormous help to me."

"Yes?" Jess wished her eagerness weren't tainted by nerves.

"When you go back to work with Terry, I want you to help me out by acting as if you haven't the foggiest notion of spies or murder or conspiracies—any of this. That may keep you off their radar. Can you act natural with Terry, knowing all you do?"

"If I have to, yes. In fact, it'll be a pleasure to pull the wool over Terry's eyes now that I know all his 'bury the hatchet' business was just a lot of soft soap. I must have been a grade-A sap to be taken in," Jessica shook her head. She thought and added, "So, do you think all his rending of hair over Jessamyn Crane was just an act, too?"

"Genuine or not," James commented, "it doesn't seem to have deterred him from his pact with Zottigstrauch. Though to be fair, Terry has good reason to be afraid, very afraid, about stepping out of line. Your friend Terry is in fathoms over his head. He made his pact with the devil; and, though that's his own fault, it's still a terrible place to be."

"Then I'm glad I think I dissuaded Alicia Wraxton from getting tangled up with Terry. I'm not sure I talked her out of her crush, but I'm pretty sure she's not going to act on it," Jessica decided, grabbing one straw of hope.

"What is it with adolescent, immature women and this Clarke chap, anyway?" James "innocently" pondered. "Why are they such easy meat for him?"

"Why do I feel vaguely insulted over that observation?" Jess returned with a hint of menace.

"Not at'all," James pleasantly disagreed. "Your taste in men has decidedly matured since you were a mere schoolgirl."

"Oh, and what am I now, Grandma Moses?"

"If I tell you you're a woman of charm, wit, discernment, and compassion, will I be allowed to sleep in the house tonight?"

"You forgot great beauty."

"That goes without saying, love."

"No, it doesn't."

James reached over and brushed Jessica's shoulder to say, "Joan Bennett, Hedy Lamarr, and Vivien Leigh rolled into one."

Jess gave her husband a playfully triumphant smile, then slid closer to him, putting her head on his shoulder. They had this moment for themselves, at least.

Chapter Eighteen

Saturday, July 27

Saturday morning was a gorgeous day as Jessica saw James off at the train station. The salty ocean breeze played with Jessica's hair and fluttered her navy and white-polka-dot silk shirtwaist dress. They walked quietly to the train, James natty in a summer suit of taupe, their fingers linked, lingering the connection before he had to go. James was downright troubled about leaving her behind, and Jess wasn't crazy about seeing him go. But she knew she couldn't let him worry, so she kept it light, not too light, though. He needed to know that she was taking this whole megillah seriously.

Now, at the train, Jess smiled up at her husband, in his arms, and played into his cover story for this trip, "Don't work too hard at the library. I don't want you coming home sneezing from digging through all those musty volumes, like the last time."

"Don't worry. This work is nothing to sneeze at."

Jess smiled slightly but only said, "And remember to get yourself some lunch this time."

James nodded, kissed her again, and his eyes said, "Take no chances." Then he was on the train, even as the whistle, then the conductor, commanded, "All aboard!"

Jess craned her neck, searching to glimpse James through a window as the train chugged with gradually increasing speed out of the station and on to New York. Her heart sank as she realized that she couldn't pick him out.

So, here she had twenty minutes to kill, er, pass, until she could grab a bus back to campus. Maybe she could head over to the inn for a cup of tea or coffee and something sweet to nibble. Worrying about getting James to the train on time had left no time for breakfast. Her duty done, Jess was absolutely ravenous. She moved swiftly into the coolness of the station; the floors, black-and-white tiled, clicked under her heels as she passed the white-washed walls and red trim. No one to notice her but a black-suited station master leaning over the ticket counter, talking to some lady

Still, on reaching the open doorway to the street, Jess paused. A glance across the street, up to the right. Yep. There was the antique shop, just as closed as it had been when she and James had gotten off the bus earlier. *Wait. Did the blinds on a second-floor window sway, as if someone had been peeking through?*

So what! Jess forced herself to conclude. *I'm just an average gal, strolling out of the station on a pleasant Saturday morning.* At least that's how she'd look once she stopped gawking. Jess pushed herself out of the station to cross the street—after a quick check for traffic. New York City survival habits never died.

Walking up Main Street towards the inn, Jess fleetingly allowed herself a little relief to be traveling in the opposite direction to Nicholas Spenser's shop. Better yet, this stroll was actually a nice tonic, what with the bright sun, lovely breeze, and pleasant passersby and shopkeepers. Lingering before the milliner's was particularly therapeutic, though window shopping was all she could afford here. Still, no reason she couldn't enjoy *looking* at an absolutely yummy white straw cap, with a slightly upturned brim sheltering a slick black feather lashed from left to right. Mmm, the hat *was* yummy, but the price would probably give her indigestion.

"Woo, aren't those hats dreamy! I love that green satin toque!"

The voice drew Jessica's eyes away from the hats to the two girls' faces reflected in the window. Delighted, Jess turned and greeted, "Hi, Alicia, Lauren. What are you doing here so early?"

"Us?" Alicia answered cheerily. "We're working at City Hall, earning extra money by helping organize and update all the old property documents. They're mostly places with delinquent taxes or that were abandoned."

"You wouldn't believe all the little fishing shacks on the beaches and small islands," Lauren rolled her eyes.

"On top of classes and your assistantships? Don't you girls have any free time?" Jessica smiled.

"We do now, for about half an hour," Alicia grinned. "We got into town early."

"So, we have time to show you something special," Lauren added gleefully.

Before Jess could say more, each girl had taken her by an arm, turned her around, and hurried her down the street, away from the inn. Lauren continued, "We couldn't believe it when we saw it, could we Alicia?"

"What?" Jessica puzzled, smiling but also unsettled by their direction.

"You'll see," Alicia teased.

Lauren, not as good at keeping a secret, hinted, "You were telling us about it the other day. This really matches your description."

"Of what?" Jessica pretended to wrack her brain, "Lady Macbeth's dagger? Hamlet's sword?"

"Nope," Lauren laughed. "You're ice cold."

"Put a lid on it, Lauren," Alicia warned. "You'll give it away."

They were, indeed, approaching the antique shop, making Jessica want passionately to dig the heels of her navy pumps three feet deep into the concrete. Maybe that wouldn't be *quite* in keeping with her promise to keep her profile low. Anyway, the place was closed. She'd seen the sign with its big block letters only minutes ago. What harm could it do only to look in the window?

"I won't give it away!" Lauren argued. "We're almost there. She'll see it sitting in the window."

"Oh, just pipe down, *will* you, Lauren?" Alicia groused.

Fine, Jessica decided, *"it" will be sitting in the window of a closed shop. I can "ooh" and "ah" "it"–then take a powder, nonchalantly, of course, before a possible Georg Zottigstrauch got wind I'd ever been there.*

Only the sign at the shop had been flipped to "OPEN," and Lauren was lamenting, "Oh no! It's not in the window. Somebody bought it!"

"Don't be ridic," Alicia insisted. "The proprietor probably switched the merchandise on the display. C'mon, Miss Minton, we'll find it for you. Let's go inside."

"Oh, ah, really, girls, that's not necessary. I still don't even know what we're looking for," Jess tried to insist calmly.

"Don't be silly, Miss Minton. We're going to see you get a shot at this . . . thing," Lauren persisted, "especially since we heard Carolina Brent Clarke say she was interested in buying it. She's not going to snap it up under your nose if we can help it."

Jessica protested, "If it were under my nose, I'd know what 'it' is. Won't you at least tell me . . ." They had pulled her inside. ". . . what we're looking for?"

Jessica started as the chimes atop the door announced them. However, nothing happened in response—not even Peter Lorre popping up from behind the counter on her right to regard them furtively. That left Jess barely relieved enough to take in her surroundings.

"Did you just shudder, Miss Minton?" Lauren asked. "I guess it is a little damp in here."

"Yes, it is," Jess agreed, taking in the smell of old wood and fabrics, to which ocean-side air had not exactly been kind. Still, the bookcases, tables, chairs, shelves, desks, china, and tapestries were arranged tastefully. Not cluttered. Apparently, someone had effectively planned displaying the merchandise. He could have dusted a little more, though.

"Achoo!" Lauren's sneeze punctuated Jess's conclusion.

"God bless you," Jess said kindly. "Do you need a handkerchief?"

Lauren shook her head and fished one of her own from a pocket.

Jessica glanced around the one-room, albeit a large room, shop, saying, "So, where is the whatsit? And what *is* the whatsit that I impressed so powerfully on you girls?"

The sooner they found "it," the sooner they could get the heck out of here!

"Not 'whatsit,' 'what not,'" Lauren giggled. "Remember you told us you wished you could find a whatnot table for your cottage? We heard Carolina Brent Clarke saying she saw one here, in the window, that she liked. It sounded exactly like what you were looking for, and we didn't want her to get something you wanted."

"Oh well, looks as if she beat us to the punch," Jess said, she hoped not too quickly, "I don't see a whatnot table anywhere. That's okay. She saw it first. She's entitled to it. Let's go . . ."

"No," Alicia shook her head. "We overheard her talking yesterday afternoon. I don't think she'd have time. It's only 9:30 in the morning now."

"I don't see the table anywhere, Alicia–or anything else that pulls my heart strings," Jessica replied. Lauren sneezed into her handkerchief, or rather released a volley of sneezes into it, so Jess added, "Maybe we'd better go before Lauren sneezes herself right through the plate glass window."

"No, I'm sure it's here somewhere," Alicia resisted. "I really want to see you get that table. It's exactly what you're looking for, honest. Maybe it's in that backroom, through that door behind the counter. If we can talk to the proprietor . . ."

"No! I mean, why bother the man? I don't even know if I could afford . . ."

But Lauren was already tapping the bell next to the register.

Damn! Jessica's heart sank. If Georg Zottigstrauch didn't kill her, James probably would. Why did this have to happen to her? For once, Jess found herself hoping Nigel was James's quarry–or at least that the store's proprietor wouldn't hear the bell.

As minutes stretched on without any response, relief began to creep through Jess. So she said, "I guess he's not available. We'll just come back another time." *Boy, what a whopper!* "How about joining me at the inn for a snack?"

"We can't. We don't have time now," Alicia absently responded. Turning to her friend, she ordered, "Lauren, hit it again."

Lauren's hand was just over the bell, when Nicholas Spenser appeared in the doorway behind the counter and assessed the three of them.

Jess still remembered that face from his meeting with Terry the day she'd arrived. Close up, he was impressive: tall, wiry in an expensively tailored grey suit set off by his red silk tie. *No wonder he never dusts if he dresses like that.* His face was lean and his eyes black and piercing. His head was shaved, shiny and finely shaped–a man who saw he was losing his hair and responded by sacrificing whatever remained to display a beautifully contoured skull.

Was this guy a shrewd Nazi sleeper agent or a shrewd businessman sizing up customers? Darned if I can tell only by looking.

A glance at Lauren and Alicia, he dismissed them as mere kids. His eyes were on Jessica; he addressed her: "May I help you, Madame?"

Hmm, no menacing Erich von Stroheim German accent, but a pleasant, professional crisp roll of syllables. Not English, definitely, but something not quite American, either. He continued, "Have you been able to find what you want?"

The "been" was pronounced with a long "e." *Of course, Canadian. Well, that was his story, whether a cover or the truth. Yes, Nigel, Nicholas, and Georg all had the Great White North in common.*

He regarded her with mild expectation, making Jessica realize she'd better stop woolgathering. *Here goes*, she thought, forcing herself not to shake.

"Yes, well, my students brought me in. They told me that you had a whatnot table that I might be interested in. Apparently, it was on display in your window."

"Ah, yes," understanding, then regret: "Unfortunately, that was purchased yesterday, and shipped early this morning to a woman who is a teacher at the girls' college. I imagine that is where you're from, as well?"

"Yes," Jess affirmed, giving him her most winning smile, "I'm working with another professor at Margaret Point this summer."

"Oh, a new teacher, then? I don't think I've seen you about the town. I often see faculty from the school here, at the inn or on the street, taking the train into the city. Mrs. Brent Clarke, the woman who purchased the table, frequently comes here. A woman of most discriminating taste."

Jess thanked God that the girls both seemed too intimidated by Spenser's resolutely ignoring them to air their views on Carolina. She smiled charmingly and agreed, "She is an artist. You'd expect as much, wouldn't you?"

"Do you know Mrs. Brent Clarke well?" Spenser inquired pleasantly. "Did she recommend my establishment to you?"

"No, I'm afraid I barely know the lady," Jess smiled, her cheeks beginning to ache from the effort. "We're in different departments. I'm in English."

"Ah, so you must know her husband, Professor Terence Clarke? Also an individual of taste. He has been here to purchase some lovely jewelry for his wife. He's a gentleman who does not settle for second rate."

Was this celebration of Terry's champagne taste a ploy to establish a cover for his and Carolina's association with Spenser or a sales pitch to entice her to spend big bucks on his "exclusive" wares? Jessica only continued smiling and nodded.

Then Lauren worked up the nerve to interject, "Miss Minton is married to a professor at the college."

"Indeed," Spenser still only addressed Jessica. "But 'Miss'? I'm afraid I don't understand."

"My married name is Crawford; however, I use Minton professionally. I'm also an actress on stage and radio."

His mien actually left her a little self-conscious about being part of the "disreputable" profession of radio acting. Nazi or not, she didn't like this guy.

Spenser inquired, "Ah, an actress teaching at the college? What do you teach? Drama?"

"Shakespeare," Jess supplied smoothly, happy to slap him with a little cultural caché. "I've quite a bit of experience 'on the boards.' I'm assisting Professor Clarke with his class—and I'm also working on my masters' degree."

Maybe she shouldn't have laid it on quite so thick. She didn't want this guy to think he'd burned her. Spenser only smiled and drew on a little *Antony and Cleopatra* to pronounce, "Ah, you are a woman of many parts, of 'infinite variety.'"

"Yes, you might say that, but I don't think my 'salad days' are behind me yet," Jessica matched Spenser's Enobarbus and raised him a Cleopatra.

"Of course not, Miss . . . or Mrs.?"

"Jessica Minton is fine."

"Miss Minton, then. Of course not." Bringing his hands together, Spenser continued, "Well, then. I'm so sorry that the piece you wanted has been sold. However, perhaps you could find something else that would serve you. What type of abode do you wish to furnish?"

"I live in one of the faculty cottages. I don't know if you're familiar with them. I'm not sure how similar mine is to the Clarkes' place," Jessica explained, trying to figure out how she could avoid blowing her cover without blowing her bank account.

"It's Jessamyn Crane's cottage," Alicia offered, refusing to be ignored.

Spenser's features darkened and he said, "Ah, there's a terrible tragedy. When I read about her murder in the papers, I asked myself: why would anyone want to harm such a lovely lady? From what I knew of her, the sheriff's theory about her connections to a criminal element in New York sounded incredible. Still, one never does know what secrets people hide, does one?"

Jessica resisted the urge to blurt, "*you* should know" or even "the Shadow does." Instead, she asked, with what she hoped seemed like natural curiosity, "You knew her, then?"

Spenser offered the hint of a shrug before answering, "A tad. You see, after she came in with Mrs. Clarke, she liked my shop well enough to have me sell some of her work on consignment. She actually was rather popular. Visitors from the city loved her art. It even led to some gallery showings. In fact, your Nigel Cross became something of a collector."

"I've always thought Professor Cross's taste would be insightful," Jess answered neutrally. "Jessamyn Crane must have been quite a talented woman. Do you have anything by her here?"

Spenser seemed to calculate briefly before replying, "No, I'm sorry to say. Her creations moved quite fast. So, now that she's gone, you'll excuse my pragmatism, I'm a bit in the lurch when I get requests for more of her work." He hesitated before continuing, "The young lady said earlier that you're living in her cottage. There wouldn't be any pieces left there that I might broker, if you don't mind my asking?"

That was an odd question for a Nazi sleeper, unless of course said sleeper believed Jessamyn had somehow hidden incriminating evidence about him and his conspiracy in one of her works. Some symbol or code in a painting?

"Do forgive me, Miss Minton. I've been terribly crass. Sometimes the businessman in me overrides all else. I don't want you to think I'm a tasteless ghoul."

Jess wondered if a *tasteful* ghoul would be acceptable, but she kept that thought to herself. She was just glad Spenser had misread her hesitation as something far less sinister than it was. Or was he playing it cool?

He continued before she could say anything, "It's not merely the money. I don't want you to think that. Miss Crane was a splendid artist. It seems a shame that if any more of her work existed, it wouldn't see the light of day, that her audience would be denied."

"Of course," Jessica pleasantly lied through her teeth, for once not feeling guilty about it. "I completely understand what you mean. No one who loves art wants to see beauty smothered in the dust and cobwebs of obscurity. Beauty is truth and truth is beauty, so we must put the truth out there."

He smiled, but Jess couldn't help reflecting, *My, what big teeth you have, Grandpa.*

Spenser's response, however, didn't imply he wanted to take a bite out of her: "Exactly. So glad that we see eye to eye. Now, you must tell me, did she leave any works in the cottage?"

Jess immediately thought of that odd sculpture that even C'thulhu would find repulsive. She also thought that it would be a toasty day in the Aleutians before she gave this character an excuse to pay her a call.

"Honestly, I don't think there was much of hers left behind, beyond some basic furniture." For once she could say something to this chap that might not become fraught with dangerous implications. "As far as I know, her belongings were packed up. Whether they were all stored somewhere on campus or shipped back to her family, I couldn't tell you."

"Ah, but would you be able to recognize her work if you had it, Miss Minton?" Spenser had turned the tables so swiftly, Jess almost felt breathless. "I could, and I would, be happy to come to your cottage to help you discover any hidden treasures she might have secreted."

"Wow! That sounds so neat!" It was Lauren. "Like a treasure hunt in your own home."

The withering glance that the slender, hawk-faced man deigned to briefly drop on Lauren decidedly quenched her ebullience. Even the usually indomitable Alicia seemed to shrink into herself. All Jessica could think was, Nazi or snob, this character was just plain mean. Whatever the case, he was *not* getting within ten feet of her place.

With good grace, but clearly brooking no argument, Jessica informed the man, "That won't be at all necessary, Mr. ah, Spenser, isn't it? If you found something, which I doubt would happen, I just couldn't in good conscience make money off that poor woman's death. It just seems wrong."

He bowed his head, then looked Jess square in the eye to reply, "Of course, I understand perfectly. However, should you come across any pieces and decide that you do want your find evaluated and brokered, I would be happy to provide the guidance you would sorely need."

This guy never gives up! Jess couldn't decide if the hard, dark eyes belying his gracious demeanor were those of a manipulative traitor or a manipulative businessman. Either way, she didn't want to encourage his snooping around her home. She was darned glad he didn't know about her lovable little Crane monstrosity!

"That's so kind of you," Jess returned pleasantly, drawing on her actress's skills to cloak her true thoughts. "However, with people on campus to help me like the Clarkes and Nigel Cross, as you pointed out, there's absolutely no need to trouble you. I insist."

He smiled thinly, and Jess pretended not to notice just how slender that smile was when he warned, "You might consider that Mr. Cross or the Clarkes might have their own interests at heart rather than yours."

Then Alicia interrupted, "Omigosh! Look at the time. Lauren, we've got to go."

"Me, too," Jessica added. "So nice to meet you, Mr. Spenser. What a shame we couldn't do business."

"Ah, but we already have, indirectly," he said knowingly.

"Excuse me?" Jessica blinked, disturbed that this man had connected with her without her even knowing.

"Your husband, some time ago, came in here and had a lovely long chat with me. He bought you a birthday present." Spenser's tone was easy, affable, but just a little too knowing. "Didn't you know?"

"My birthday's not till January," Jessica countered, a bit off balance. *Where was he going with this tidbit?* She couldn't help querying, "You remember him? How long ago was that?"

"I'm very good with faces," he answered pleasantly. "I never forget one. However, I shan't tell you what he bought you. I wouldn't want to spoil the surprise. You do like surprises, don't you, Miss Minton?"

"Depends on the surprise."

"A wise answer," he nodded. "A wise and circumspect answer."

Jessica gave Spenser a quick, uncertain smile, and was turning to follow the girls to the door, when he startled her by pressing something into her hand, explaining, "My card, Miss Minton, should you change your mind. I think we could do a profitable business."

Jess nodded, again quickly, still unsure how to read Nicholas Spenser. Was he trying to lure her into a business deal that would bypass Nigel or the Clarkes? Could he be offering her and James a bribe to keep their noses out of his nasty Nazi business? She automatically slipped the card into her pocket, but insisted, "I really don't think so. I'm afraid I have to go. Nice to meet you." Only superb control kept her from choking on *those* last words. Then, *thank God*, she was outside with the girls.

The two girls linked their arms through Jessica's and started her up the street. It was a few moments before Lauren faked a shudder and broke the silence with, "Brrr! Did you get a load of that guy? Boris Karloff has nothing on him!"

"I'll say!" Alicia agreed. "What a ghoul, a grave robber. Wanting to pick through Jessamyn Crane's things to make a fast buck."

"You don't think he wants to preserve her art?" Jess asked with mock innocence.

Alicia rolled her eyes. "Oh sure. More like he wants to preserve his bank account."

Lauren added her two cents, "And did you hear that banana oil he put out about Professor Cross. He didn't think I caught it, but I did. I definitely think, Miss Minton, if you find anything of Miss Crane's you should talk to Professor Cross, first. I'd trust him way more than that guy back in the antique place."

Jessica noted that Lauren did *not* include the Clarkes in her defense. *Good call, kid.* Then Jess pursued the track of some curious, new information: "I didn't know Professor Cross was such an expert on *avant-garde* art."

"Oh, you'd be surprised," Lauren chirped. "He seems really sardonic and aloof, but one day in the campus gallery, I was looking at a painting I couldn't understand. He happened to come over to admire it—and ended up explaining it to me. Now, I really like that kind of art. Sometimes, when I run into him on campus, we talk about it. Isn't that neat?"

What an unexpected, even appealing, side to Nigel! Unless he were Zottigstrauch using Lauren to make himself look like a good guy. And what about his collecting Jessamyn's art? The appreciation of an unrequited love or a ploy to use her work to disguise the package Terry and Phil had discussed? Maybe even using the role of unrequited lover as a screen for his true identity?

"Miss Minton, did you hear what I said?"

Alicia had spoken,

"I'm sorry, Alicia," Jess apologized. "I was distracted. It's a lot of work taking over for Professor Clarke. I've got bloody tragedy on the brain."

Lauren giggled, "Alicia was comparing that antique guy with Sailor."

"How so? I don't see the connection. I don't think Mr. Novack is that bad."

The girls looked at each other, surprised, then back at Jess, and she realized she'd slipped even before Alicia asked, "Novack? You know his actual name?"

"Well, why not?" Jessica brazened it out, but in easy tones. "Everybody has a name. I chatted with him when he rode by. Nothing important. About his horse. Isn't that a beautiful animal?"

"It's kind of funny, a sailor having a horse," Lauren pointed out.

"Maybe it's a sea horse," Alicia punned.

"Ha, ha," escaped Lauren. "No, it just makes you wonder, what a sailor is doing with a horse."

"Actually," Jess informed the girl, "It's no big secret. He wasn't in the Navy; he was in the Coast Guard. You know that they have mounted coastal patrols. You must have seen them since you've been here, especially around Joseph's Cove. He might have done that before he went to sea. Maybe that's how he knows how to ride."

Jess was more than pleased when both girls nodded and Lauren went so far as to say, "And, I'll take Sailor, Mr. Novack, over that dealer any day. At least he doesn't pick over the dead. Ick!"

Jessica added, "And Mr. Novack did serve his country. Anyway, it's getting late. Maybe you'd better hightail it to City Hall before they send out a search party!"

"Okay, Miss Minton," Alicia good-naturedly agreed. "Sorry about the table—and that guy in the store. Will we see you on Monday? I know you told us that Professor Clarke will be back then, but you didn't say if you'd be, too."

Jess hesitated. She'd only been asked to fill in for the past week, and Terry hadn't said anything specific to her about the upcoming one. She probably ought to call him to find out what the story was, but the thought of talking to him after what she'd overheard in the cove pierced her like an ice pick. Still, she had promised James that she could carry off interacting with Terry, Carolina, and Nigel as if nothing had happened.

"I don't know yet, girls," Jessica answered honestly. "If I don't hear from Professor Clarke today, I'll have to give him a buzz and find out. But I do have to thank you for last week. I had a ball teaching!"

"Same here," Lauren grinned.

"Yeah," Alicia added. "Well, we've got to split. Bye."

Jessica watched the girls hurry up the street. Once they were out of earshot, she closed her eyes and uttered the granddaddy of all sighs! *What a fine mess!* James would absolutely blow his stack when she told him she'd been in the antique shop, chatting away with one of his suspects. Yet, how could she have extricated herself from the situation without making the kind of scene they were trying to avoid?

She started up Main Street, wrapped in thought. Maybe she had handled everything just fine, after all. Being in the store could certainly have been the behavior of any normal, unsuspecting woman dragged in by a couple of teenagers searching for a bargain. If she'd seemed at all prickly, her behavior could likely be chalked up to resisting Spenser's sales pitches. The only thing was that now Nicholas Spenser knew her face, her voice, *her*. She was no longer just a name he might hear in passing.

And what about his closing comments? Again, how did Jessamyn Crane's art play into all this? Jessica's thoughts turned to the one piece by Crane in her cottage. What a relief Spenser didn't know she had it. But *was* it really important? Georg Zottigstrauch's "package" was with Phil Novack. Could there be some connection?

Then again, maybe Nicholas Spenser was just a guy trying to make a buck—which shifted suspicion right onto Nigel Cross's square shoulders. Whatever the truth, Jess wished she'd gone straight home today. The whole morning screamed for a "do-over." Did she ever dread explaining all this tonight when James returned. Maybe she'd better substitute her breakfast pot of coffee with a case of scotch.

Chapter Nineteen

Saturday evening

The standing lamp created a sanctuary of soft yellow light around Jessica Minton, trying to write a letter to her sister. While Dusty snuggled up alongside on the couch, Jessica glanced over her shoulder, out into the night beyond the sliders. Madame Moonlight had transformed everything into a dreamy, blue-grey landscape. Normally, Jess would have delighted in this illumination, with the murmuring wash of waves and the delicate touch of a cool, summer night breeze. But, normally, James would have been here, and here wouldn't have been smack in the middle of murder and espionage.

Back to the letter! So, what have you written so far?

"Dear."

Hmm, she couldn't even get to Liz's name. That was writer's block all right, a block of steel-reinforced concrete. Lord knows it wasn't that she had nothing to tell Liz; it was just that she had nothing she could chance putting on paper and sending out the door. Wouldn't a call, hearing her sister's voice, being able to ask for advice, have been grand? Except a call to the West Coast would cost "a pretty arm and a penny," as Liz would say—and Jessica knew better than to risk her terrible tale being overheard by any of the operators between her and her sister. Besides, she had no right to drag Liz into this mess after all her sister had been through the past three years.

Jess chewed the end of her pen, then stopped and looked at the cat comfortable next to her, front paws demurely tucked against her chest.

"Say, Dusty, what's your considered opinion on what I should write?"

Dusty ignored her. *Probably dreaming of mouse fricassee.*

So, Jess was back to staring at the pad of stationary on her lap, blank but for the truncated salutation. After next weekend, she could write Liz about the college garden reception, as well as presenting the trophy at Rockingham Park the following day. More importantly, she could tell Liz what a hit the two ensembles that her sister had designed for her had been. Jess hadn't the slightest problem playing the mannequin when she was on the receiving end of free couture.

What a dope! She'd been so wrapped up in trying to square away her own troubles, it hadn't occurred to her just to ask Elizabeth about all the fun she was having in California. Soaking up the sun? Meeting movie stars? Never mind being a good little businesswoman. The ink seemed to flow now. Finally, Jessica rested her pen and examined what she'd written. A train horn mourned through the moonlit evening. Would James be on that train, at last? She looked at her watch. Ten o'clock. Fortunately, trains from the city ran up until one o'clock. But would James be on one? David Nyquist had taken a call from him while she and Rose were riding this afternoon. All he'd said was that his research was taking longer than expected. He'd still be home tonight, but it would be very late, so not to wait up. He'd grab the bus home or a taxi if the bus wasn't still running.

That left her sitting with a half-finished letter, Dusty, and maybe a resistant mouse of two. Being alone, with all she knew seething beneath the surface of Margaret Point, was the main reason she was still in blouse, slacks, and shoes–an ensemble more conducive to making a getaway than slippers and a nightie.

"How would I do, Dusty, trying to outrun Zottigstrauch and his minions in a pair of feathered mules?–I mean, I'm in the mules."

Dusty merely rolled over on her back, then stretched her front and hind legs downward in an impressive show of musculature.

"I feel so much safer now. Especially if you ever wake up."

Jess's head sank back against the couch; her eyes closing as she thought: *What is keeping James? Did Streeter have some new or additional information? Were they planning to drop a net on the whole crew right now? What I wouldn't give for it all to be over. Not to have to bite my tongue in front of Rose. For there to be one less care burdening James.*

Where would it all end? What would happen to Terry, Carolina, Phil? Even Blackie? She still didn't believe that Phil was as willing as the rest. *And what about Terry? He'd seemed so devastated by Jessamyn's death.* Between that reaction and his conversation on the beach with Phil, she couldn't believe that he'd been involved in her murder. *Yet Terry was still deeply involved in the whole espionage plot.* Of course, finding out that he'd gotten chummy with her under Zottigstrauch's orders made Jessica feel considerably less charitable toward him. Still, his reaction to Jessamyn Crane's death revived more than a trace of pity in Jessica.

And who is Georg Zottigstrauch? Nigel Cross or Nicholas Spenser? Recollection of this morning's encounter with the latter twitched through Jessica. Maybe she *was* relieved to have missed James's call this afternoon, dreading to tell him she'd stood face to face with one of his suspects. Nevertheless, she might not have given anything away. In fact, he might not even be James's quarry–which pointed a finger directly at Nigel Cross. Jessica groaned and rubbed the heels of her hands into her brow with frustration.

"Dusty," Jess confided, "this whole mess stinks to high heaven."

Dusty cracked open her eyes and reached one fore paw out to graze Jessica's arm comfortingly, before retracting it slowly to her chest.

"That was the most energy-efficient display of compassion I've ever seen," Jess smiled tiredly, scratching her pal's neck.

Jessica leaned back against the top of the couch. Moonlight, swashing tide, buoys clanking, a soft and salty breeze drifting through the window, together, were positively soporific. It had been the kind of day that really took it out of a girl. Then there was no more gauzy moonlight for Jessica; her eyes had drifted shut. It wasn't long before she and her furry companion were both gently snoring.

Dull hoof beats gradually drew closer. Jess was back racing Rose across the meadow, approaching the cool woods. Domino's powerful muscles moved smoothly beneath her. Rose, her brown hair streaming behind and glinting chestnut in the sun, laughed as her mount Flicka edged ahead.

The sudden, sharp clatter of hooves on stone jolted Jessica awake. Turning abruptly to the sliders behind her, she was confronted with a tall black nightmare whinnying at her in the moonlight.

"Gach!" Jessica leaped up and away from the couch. Dusty had disappeared under it.

A disgusted equine snort pulled Jessica almost completely awake. She swayed, while her mind cleared enough to grasp that no nightmare, but a flesh and blood horse confronted her.

"Blackie!" burst out of Jess, even as she started across the room. "Where's Phil?"

As soon as Jess had the sliders more fully open, Blackie was head-butting and nuzzling her. But her survey of the patio revealed that Novack was nowhere in sight. Then Jessica's eyes caught the horse's saddle: a slipped girth left it angled against his barrel.

"You guys have an accident, Blackie?" Jess asked aloud, holding the horse's bridle, facing him again. He towered over her, a formidable animal who snorted then pawed the flagstones impatiently. Another head butt reassured her that Blackie held her in good standing. *I guess all those apple snacks made an impression.*

But what about Phil Novack? Did the slipped saddle say it all? The equipment failure must have knocked him out of the saddle, and force of habit (or the lure of carrots) had brought Blackie on here. Phil had said that Jessamyn had treated the horse to snacks, too. Blackie snorted again and shook his head, his mane shivering in a silky dark wave. Rubbing his nose, Jess looked him in the eye and asked, "How come you didn't wait for him to get back in the saddle?"

Blackie shook his head again, whickered, then pulled a surprised Jessica back toward the balustrade. He pawed the flagstones with an echoing clatter. Jess bit her lip, awake enough now to put two and two together. Blackie wouldn't dump Phil and just leave him; she'd seen enough of the two's byplay to know better.

"Is he hurt, Blackie? We need to go find Phil and help him? What am I saying, questioning a horse? I must be nuts." Blackie gave her an affronted snort, and Jessica admitted, "Okay, okay. If I have conferences with my cat, it's not such a big step to larger mammals."

Jess leaned over the rail and peered down the beach, back towards where Novack lived. The moonlight still shone soft blue overall, clear enough to allow her to see an injured Phil Novack. *Nothing.*

She started to pull back, to go inside and call . . . call whom? The Coast Guard? Security? But then she'd have to wait for someone to get here, and she couldn't even begin to tell them where to look. Just somewhere between here and Novack's. Worse, what if this "accident" had something to do with Zottigstrauch? Would she be calling attention to something that she was supposed to keep under wraps?

The night breeze was pushing strands of hair across her face; Jess impatiently shoved them away. There was one thing she could do that was fast and discreet: ride out to find Phil, herself. Maybe she could put him on the horse and get him to a place where he'd be safe or get care. Even if she couldn't move him, she'd at least know where he was and could ride Blackie for help. That was quicker than waiting to get someone on the line, explain the situation, and then wait some more for them to get to her—and only *then* go look for Phil. Still, James wouldn't want her riding out alone on the beach. To tell the truth, she wasn't crazy about the thought, either, knowing who could be lurking in the shadows. But Blackie was pawing anxiously because Phil was out there, somewhere, in bad shape.

Tying Blackie's reins to the balustrade, Jess said, "I'll be right back."

Once in the house, Jess wrote up three notes for James, explaining what must have happened to Phil and that she was going to backtrack Blackie's earlier prints through the sand. Swiftly, she tacked each note up in different places he was bound to see. After her experience with Terry, she knew better than to put anything on the front door. By the time she'd tacked up the last note, Jess was already running James's reaction through her imagination, and almost lost her nerve. Was she nuts? What if this was a setup? No, Phil wouldn't set her up. She'd stake everything on that, especially after he'd tried to protect her. The bottom line was that she couldn't leave a man down, maybe with a concussion or an injured spine. If Phil could have gotten up, he'd have been on Blackie. And this horse wouldn't just run out on him.

Jess made sure that Dusty was hiding safely under the couch and was almost across the room when the simple solution hit her that she could try calling Phil Novack to let him know she had his horse. Maybe he had told her to stay away from him, but he'd certainly cut her some slack if she were only trying to let him know that Blackie was safe with her. Except the plan didn't work out so simply. Sure, she was able to find Phil's number in the directory, but no one answered. No matter how long she let the phone ring. Something was very wrong.

Jessica was across the room and through the sliders, slipping on a lightweight dark jacket. Blackie looked over and snorted at her approach. As Jess reached the stallion, his dark eyes steadily on her, she breathed, "Bro-other, I never realized what a big one you are. Sixteen is a lot of hands—and I do believe you are more."

Blackie bobbed his head, then gazed down the beach. He wanted to get going. Jess recalled how much she'd wanted to ride this horse, but looking the prospect in the teeth, so to speak, she hesitated. She'd ridden for years, but even Domino wasn't as big and temperamental as this former racer. *Be careful what you wish for.*

"Okay, Blackie, take it easy while I fix this saddle," Jessica cautioned the big horse, with a pat to his neck.

Quickly, but calmly, she moved the saddle back into position and tightened the girth. Other than a snort, Blackie didn't seem to object. So, Jess gave him a "Good boy," rechecked the girth to make sure it was truly snug, then moved to mount—but halted. She was 5'4" and Blackie's sixteen hands, plus, made the stirrup hard to reach with no one around to give her a leg up.

"You couldn't have dragged along a mounting block, could you, pal?" Jess queried. Then she smiled and turned Blackie so he was next to the balustrade, her improvised mounting block.

Settling into the saddle and taking the reins, Jessica quipped, "Good Grief, a girl could get a nosebleed up here."

Blackie's response to the unfamiliar weight was to toss his head and skitter on the flagstones. Jessica was having none of that. She managed to straighten out Blackie's head and divert his skitter into a circle that ended with him facing the gap in the balustrade.

"Okay, Blackie, it's off to the races, only let's keep it down to post-parade speed for now."

Clapping her heels to Blackie's flanks, Jessica had the horse moving carefully down the path to the beach. He was spirited, but also smart, too smart to risk his slender legs on the fairly steep grade. Leaning to the side once they hit the beach, Jess was able to sight Blackie's earlier trail, discerning where galloping hooves had churned up the sand, then skidded to a stop to ascend the grade. Aloud, Jess decided, "Phil's going to be really happy about my stuffing you with apples and carrots now."

This was the point at which Jess should have shifted into high gear. Instead, she looked back up at the cottage. No one. James wasn't going to ride in on Silver and save her from making the rescue all by herself. Nope, it looked as if Tonto was on her own tonight.

"Okay, son," Jessica clapped her heels to Blackie, "let's go."

They moved out at a rapid trot. Blackie pulled determinedly at Jessica's arms, impatient to travel faster, but she was just as determined not to go too fast to read the trail. Even with moonlight, she needed to keep a sharp lookout for hoof prints, maybe even for the injured Phil.

The breeze that drove her hair off to the side was also playing with the sea grass on the ridge above her. Out of the corner of her eye, Jess perceived its eerie waving fingers, almost as if someone were pacing alongside them, rustling the plants. She forced her attention back to the prints in the sand, then on ahead where the beach curved around a rocky neck. The rocks glinted black and shiny above them now. You could hide in there, maybe even get off a good shot. She automatically slowed the big horse beneath her; he tossed his head and pranced impatiently. No one moved up there in the moonlight. The only sounds were buoys worried by the ocean's restlessness. Maybe Blackie was right to pull on her arms, strain to go faster. Every second could count for Phil.

Jess let the horse have more rein, and they trotted rapidly around the rocky bend. Immediately, Jess's heart was in her mouth as two figures came into view, about a quarter of a mile down the beach. A glance at the tracks in the sand encouraged her, for they seemed to lead smack dab towards the two.

"Looks like we're in luck, Blackie. That could be someone helping Phil!" Jessica cheered, and she set the horse at a rapid clip toward the forms. She glanced off to her left, where a ridge of marsh grass had been succeeded by dark rock cliffs. There would be a road beyond, out of sight, so the rescuer down there might have a car.

Blackie's movement was fluid and powerful, so much so that he had almost gotten away from Jess before she could rein him in. A jockey she was not. Still, she was a good rider and managed to slow him down, but not before enjoying a surge of exhilaration at his power. Unfortunately, the thrill died quickly when she came close enough to recognize that the two people on the beach were only a young man and his girl enjoying moonlight on the Sound.

Disappointed, Jessica ignored the couple's slightly inebriated greeting and kept Blackie on his old trail. A ways past the two, things really went south. It was getting darker, obscuring the tracks. Jess pulled Blackie up and he bobbed his head with annoyance.

"Sorry, fella," she said, looking up into the sky where gauzy black clouds were enveloping the moon. It wouldn't go pitch black on her but reading the tracks would be a darned sight harder. And Joseph's Cove was coming up. She didn't want to navigate that if she couldn't see very well. Was that the way she wanted to take, anyway? If she couldn't read the trail, it wouldn't matter, would it? Her eyes went back up to the cloud-dimmed moon, and she sighed. If she couldn't get moving soon, she'd have wasted the time she'd thought she'd saved by not waiting for the authorities. Jess shot a heavenward glance for: *You know I could use a little help here, God. I'm just trying to get a friend out of a jam—do unto others and all that jazz?*

Was she nuts or were the clouds breaking up, drifting? *Yes!* The clouds glowed from inky to smoky grey, then the moon broke free, scattering shreds of darkness. They swiftly splashed through the low tide at Joseph's Cove, and, thank heavens again, the trail lay ahead, leading down the beach, around another curve of rocks. This looked familiar, so Jess knew she was close. Saluting heavenward, she declared, "Now that's what I call service."

Jess sent the impatient Blackie into a canter. Yes, they were very close to Novack's digs. Did that make her more or less relieved? If he was hurt back at the old homestead, it wouldn't have made sense for Blackie to run to her. Horses stayed where they felt safest, most at home. If her place was safer, what might she be riding into at Novack's cabin?

Or maybe she was letting her imagination run wild. Maybe Phil Novack was sitting in his house with an injured leg or something, phoning around for help, even calling her to see if she had Blackie. Then why *had* Blackie run to her instead of back to his stall? Why hadn't Phil answered when she'd phoned?

They rounded the curve and Jessica pulled up the stallion. No more time for questions: Phil Novack's cottage was about a quarter of a mile away on the grass-tufted sandy rise that now framed the beach. *Hmm, lights are on. Someone must be home. Someone you want to see or someone you'd better avoid? And if Phil's home, why hadn't he answered the phone? Maybe, a guy could get indoors and turn on a light, but did that mean he wouldn't pass out afterward? If it was Phil who put on those lights. So, go on or go back?*

Unexpectedly, Blackie settled the question by sending out a series of clarions that could have awakened the dead in China. No sneaking away *or* forward now. Oddly enough, there was no response. No one burst with excitement or relief from the house. Neither did the lights wink out to hide anyone lurking nefariously within. The scenario of Phil injured and unconscious in the house came back to haunt Jess. All things considered, it seemed the most likely explanation and the least possible one to ignore.

The barn didn't come into sight until Jess crested the rise aboard Blackie. There it was, directly ahead, a small affair, only big enough for one or two stalls and storage of tack and feed. It stood a ways back, its door snuggly closed. Jessica pulled up Blackie to take in the whole compound: the barn directly ahead, with a little paddock and feed and water troughs; a small cottage, almost a shack, to her right, much closer. Only one floor, a wood-shingle roof, and weathered clapboards. The roof extended over a wood-planked porch at the front. Light shone through the window looking onto the porch and through the open front door. *Open?*

Jessica scanned the flat area around her: *nothing, no one.* No sounds but the tide. Not even insects. *Still as a graveyard in the moonlight. Lousy metaphor, that.* She started to call Phil's name but stopped. If he was silent because he was unconscious what was the use? That's the reason she kept her trap shut, she told herself. Jessica's eyes returned to the door opening into the cottage. A quick glance at the barn again. Back to the cottage. No, if she were injured she'd aim for the house to collapse in. Besides, the barn was shut up.

"Okay, son," Jess said more quietly than she'd expected, "let's check things out."

She urged Blackie over to the house at a walk. Her hesitation was only minuscule before she slipped out of the saddle, and bobbled, thinking, *Whew! It's a longer way down than I thought.*

Jess tied Blackie's reins to one of the porch supports, then instructed him, "Don't you go anywhere."

Blackie nuzzled her in moral support before Jessica turned and strode to the doorway. Leaning on the doorframe, she surveyed the one-room digs Phil Novack called home, hoping to find him within.

Chapter Twenty

Saturday evening

No one. An overhead light, shielded by a tin cone, illuminated the room harshly. To Jessica's right, below the wide window, light also shown from a lamp on a wooden desk that had seen better days. A candlestick phone sat on that desk, too. Against the wall on the left, was an old pot-bellied stove, a rocking chair before it and a box of kindling to one side. Directly across from the doorway was a bed, while to the far left a kitchen area was set off from the main room by a counter. A cast-iron frying pan and sundry dishes and utensils were drying in a strainer next to the sink behind the counter, another window over the sink. The ice box and stove were to the right of the sink, beyond them a cupboard or a wardrobe.

On the far wall of the cabin, an open door revealed part of a claw-footed tub. *At least Phil had indoor plumbing.* The floors of the cabin had once been snugly planked, but weathering had warped them. Rugs were scattered about to keep out drafts. Phil hadn't been so lucky with the sand tracked or blown in.

Yep, every light in the place was on, but no one was home. Something was really off here. Jess cast a glance back at Blackie, who seemed at ease. That reassured her, a little. *So, what now, with no Phil Novack in sight and his house looking like something left behind by the lost colonists of Roanoke Island?* She hadn't found an injured Phil between here and her place, so he probably wasn't hurt, at least by being thrown. With no sign of a struggle in here, Jessica didn't think he'd been carried off by Zottigstrauch's crew.

Maybe he'd left a note behind, somewhere.

Jess stepped into the room, automatically closing the door behind her and calling, "Phil? Mr. Novack? Are you here? Are you hurt?"

Nothing. Funny, somehow calling out made her feel less of an intruder. Jessica found herself next to the desk, strewn with papers and opened envelopes. Her hand went forward, but she stopped. *Snooping into a guy's mail was intrusive, but definitely. Wasn't it also a federal offense?* Anyway, she'd probably just mess up clues that James would need to look into. She'd certainly reveal that someone had been poking around Novack's stuff. *Yet wasn't this a prime opportunity to look for that special "package" Phil was holding for Zottigstrauch? A package you wouldn't recognize if you fell over it. Maybe Phil was even now handing his secret whatsit over to that Nazi rat. Leaving his door open, his lights blazing, and his horse running wild while he did it?*

None of this added up. Maybe she should stop looking for deep, dark secrets and concentrate on the most down-to-earth explanation: Phil had gone off in search of Blackie after the horse had somehow gotten away. As much as she thought she knew what went on between Phil and the horse, she could have been dead wrong. Blackie could have been spooked by a passing car on that lonely road and taken off. Maybe the smart move would be to leave Phil a note that she had his horse.

Her decision made, Jess grabbed a pen off the desk, scanning for a piece of blank paper. *Nothing.* She'd have to write on the back of one of these envelopes, which gave her the perfect excuse to check them and see . . . they were just a bunch of bills and something from the V.A. *Darn! Well, wouldn't you know it, this pen wouldn't write. Damp sea air. Perfect excuse to open one of the drawers and look for another.* But Jessica didn't. Someone knowing she'd only left a note here was one thing, but evidence of her poking through this desk suggested she'd been sticking her nose where it didn't belong.

Jess scowled, glancing up at the wall above the desk, for the first time noticing the pictures tacked there. A few of shipmates, Phil with a guy resembling him holding the head of a horse in the winner's circle at Rockingham Park. The horse wasn't Blackie, though. Phil was a lot younger, and a lot happier. The picture had been taken eleven years ago, long before his brother had died, before a world war had shot a ship out from under him, before he'd gotten mixed up with this prize bunch. Phil had caught more than his share of tough breaks. *What was he catching right now?*

Jessica paced across the room, thinking hard. *What to do? Too bad one of those pictures hadn't been signed, "Thanks for being a swell henchman, Your Pal, Georg Zottigstrauch."*

She was standing next to the counter now, tapping her fingers. *Stay or go? If Phil had been hurt in a riding accident, she'd have found him. Who knew when he'd be back, or if he'd be back alone? Then again, could he be in the barn? No, that made no sense. He'd hardly have shooed off Blackie then locked himself in there. But someone could have driven off the horse and taken care of Phil in the barn.*

Blackie was snorting and pawing outside. He even let out a nervous whinny. *Phil? No! Blackie wouldn't have sounded so rattled, so defensive. Good grief! Maybe whoever approached was no friend at all! And here I am in a big open room with no back door!*

Blackie was really antsy now, but at this angle, Jessica couldn't see why through the window over the desk. Could she duck into the bathroom? No time. *The counter, only the counter!* Scowling at the hand dealt her, Jess dashed behind the counter, barely pausing to grab the cast-iron skillet. *A girl never knows when denting a Nazi noggin might become imperative.* Crouching behind the counter, she gnawed her lip and prayed that the Gene Krupa drum solo her heart was pounding out couldn't be heard by anyone but herself. What she wouldn't have given to tuck herself neatly into the cabinets under the counter, but no reducing plan could do that trick.

What was she going to do?! This invader only had to round the corner and she'd be sunk. Why hadn't she sat tight at home and waited for James? Why did she have to be such a fourteen-karat, do-gooding sap? That was when Jess noticed that Blackie had settled down. Had Georgie boy slipped him a lump of sugar with a Mickey Finn? Shouldn't the unnamed visitor have reached the door by now? What was he waiting for? Something was fishy. Jess gripped her frying pan tighter, almost wishing it were all over.

"Jessica, you know I can see you right through this window."

Jess half-whirled/half-jumped up–to face James regarding her, amused, through the window over the sink.

Sliding to the floor, she leaned back against the counter and started to glare at her husband. No, what was the use? How could she complain when she was face to face with James, not a murderous fifth columnist? And, frankly, that James was not reading her the riot act was more than enough cause to tamp down her temper.

Jess looked her husband in the eye and said, "You could have called out and come through the front door, like a normal guy would have done."

"And go past that fire-breathing dragon in a horse costume? I think not."

"You still could have called out to me. I would have called off the big, bad pony for you," Jess returned, putting down her defensive cooking utensil but still not getting up.

Here, James sobered a bit and explained, "The horse was acting all nerved up, the door was shut, neither you nor Novack was anywhere to be seen. It seemed to me the wisest move would be to survey the interior to see what was what before I waltzed in." He paused before adding, "You could have used some of your four-footed friend's horse sense about coming here alone."

Jessica looked away. She hated to admit he was right. Finally, she turned back and questioned warily, "You're not going to give me what for?"

"Do I need to?"

Jess insisted, "How could I chance leaving Phil Novack hurt? I genuinely believe Blackie came to me for a reason. How could I abandon the guy if there was a chance I could find him fast?"

James surprised her by allowing, "I know. I'd never leave a man down if I could save him. But you've got to be better about making the call."

"Okay," Jess nodded. "I read you loud and clear. But I still don't know where Phil is or if he's all right." She got up and crossed to James at the window, finishing, "I can't figure out what to do now."

"I have one suggestion. Call off that vicious nightmare out there, and we can have this conversation together, inside. I'm not looking forward to trying to squeeze through *this* aperture."

"I think I can manage that," Jess promised lightly. "And, James, I'm really glad you're here."

He crooked a smile at her and said, "Right, now meet me by the door."

Jessica dashed to the door and came outside as James rounded the corner. When he stepped onto the uneven planks of the porch, Blackie accosted him with a threatening snort, accompanied by the evilest of eyes. James hesitated, giving Jessica a querying look. She winked at him, then went to Blackie, saying, "Take it easy, big guy. Everything's good. He's on our side."

James cautioned, "Be careful," as Jess reached the horse and rubbed his muzzle then stroked his neck.

She soothed, "That's it, fella. That's it, boy, good boy. No sense getting those pointed Arabian ears in an uproar over another pal." Seeing Blackie calmer, if not exactly tranquil, Jess said to James, "The coast is clear. He's as gentle as a lamb."

"A 1,500-pound lamb with sharp teeth and hooves," James remarked coolly, coming along the porch.

Jess glowed a little. For despite his trepidation James was clearly impressed with, even proud of, her ability to calm the horse.

When James got to the doorway, he made a swift survey of the room before questioning, "You're sure it's clear?"

"There aren't many places for a guy Phil's size to hide."

"What about the wardrobe? And the bathroom door is only partly open."

"Oh, well . . ."

"That's all right. You sit tight here with the horse. Keep him between you and any open areas. Better untie him in case you need to get away fast."

"I will not leave you . . ."

"I don't want to waste time arguing, Jessica." James was not angry, but he was decisive. "You owe me that much peace of mind after what I went through hot-footing it here."

"Yes, all right," Jess relented, not without qualms, undoing Blackie's reins.

When she looked back, James had slipped into the house. She held her breath, silently cursing that she couldn't follow his movements. What if someone were hiding in the bathroom—and armed? What about the wardrobe? Who might lurk there? Terry? Carolina? Phil? Zottigstrauch? Doubt tied a knot in her innards. Blackie's anxious snort made Jessica look up sharply.

James was in the doorway, unhurt and alone. She smiled as he beckoned with one hand, though her smile tightened on noticing that the other hand returned his SOE Colt .32 to his shoulder holster. She hadn't seen that ugly weapon in some time. That "peacekeeper" brought home to her the seriousness of their situation. But she forced herself to tie up Blackie, giving him a pat before she dashed into the house. On turning around, Jess found James giving the outside a quick check before closing the door to focus his attention back on her. When he did, he had her in his arms and said, "Don't make me worry like that about you."

After a moment, Jess stepped back within James's hold, beginning sheepishly, "You're taking this much better than I expected."

"Don't look a gift horse in the mouth, love," James wearily cautioned. He brushed back a few dark strands of Jessica's hair before adding, "You were fortunate not to have been there when I found your note—Dusty is still burrowed under the couch."

"Wise guy, if I had been there, you wouldn't have needed to read the note."

"Right," James allowed skeptically. "Now, I've got to get down to cases."

"Oh, my heavens, yes! What have I been thinking? We've got to find Phil. I told you I hadn't checked the barn. Is that your next step?"

James hesitated, and Jessica was immensely disturbed to recognize his *really*-bad-news expression.

"James, give it to me straight."

"All right, Jessica. Since we don't have all night, I don't have time to put it gently. I've been in the barn . . ."

"And you found Phil there?! They killed him, that's it, isn't it?" Jess turned away, her stomach aching.

James turned her back to him and clarified, "I didn't find him . . ."

"Yes?"

James quashed that hopeful little syllable: "I didn't have to. The barn is clean but the sand outside the barn was . . ."

"Disturbed? There was blood?" Jess crushed back tears, but her voice gave her away.

James frowned at the distress he was causing her; nevertheless, he continued calmly, "Jessica, I want, I *have*, to level with you; but I need to know you can take it."

"I can," Jess asserted, tipping up her chin.

"All right, then. No sign of a row, exactly. The sand was smoothed over, as if someone had covered up signs of a struggle."

"But the cover-up, itself, is a giveaway," Jess concluded quietly.

"Precisely. Whoever was here was sharp, but not quite sharp enough. They covered their tracks but brushed the sand all the way out to the road. I found the tracks for two cars and marks of a man's and a woman's footprints."

"How many people do you think were here?"

"Hard to say, Love. Definitely two, whether they came in separate cars or together while someone waited in the second car, I can't say."

"And I wonder who *that* couple could be," Jess added. Then she questioned, "But why *assume* Phil has been killed?"

"My guess is that he became more of a liability than a useful tool, especially after we heard him, Friday, threatening to upset their little applecart. Georg Zottigstrauch plays for keeps."

"But Terry and Carolina, as much as I don't like them, I can't believe they'd commit murder for him."

"They might not have had a choice, Jessica. However, we can't stand here discussing it. I don't know how much time we have." James pulled out and put on a pair of gloves as he continued, "I've got to give this place a damned thorough combing." He patted the breast pocket of his jacket and said, "Can't waste the opportunity to use this warrant after Dick Streeter went to so much trouble to get it for me. He wants all his "Is" dotted and his "Ts" crossed, so there's no chance of anything I find getting tossed out on a technicality. Now, do me a favor. I need to concentrate 100% on my job. So, take a seat in that rocking chair and keep an ear open in case our hypervigilant pal Bucephalus gives us a whinny if he tumbles to anything rum."

"You think they might come back?" Jess nervously questioned.

"I don't know," James answered, flipping through, then holding up to the light, envelopes on the desk, careful not to frame himself in the window. "I suspect not. They have to dispose of Phil and clean themselves up. However, I'm not about to take a chance on our getting trapped here."

"What about the package, James? Did they take it? Did they leave it here?"

"I can't say for certain," James admitted, still concentrating on examining everything on the desktop, then putting it back exactly as it had been. "My guess is they wouldn't leave it here unattended. But just in case, I intend to scour this place. You never know what might turn up: some bit of insurance Novack kept in case they tried to double-cross him; some clue that could help tip the scales when put with other intel I've dug up."

"That insurance policy doesn't seem to have done Phil much good," Jess bitterly observed. A painful realization hitting her, she blurted, "James, is all this my fault? Did he turn into a liability because he was trying to cover for me?"

James paused and gave Jessica a penetrating look before cautioning her, "Phil Novack bought himself a one-way ticket the minute he threw in with Zottigstrauch. Right now, Jessica, you've got to let me get on with this, so we can leave here while you still look like small beer to Zottisstrauch."

Jessica nodded. She really couldn't expect James to indulge her with a bout of hand-holding over Phil. To distract herself, she looked to the door separating them from Blackie and concentrated on listening to him. But he was quiet–a relief, sort of.

Jess turned back to James, who had just finished with the top of the desk and now tried the middle draw. Definitely locked. She expected a *sotto voce* "damn." Instead, James pulled a ring of universal keys from his inside jacket pocket. It didn't take many tries to find one that did the trick: the central drawer was now open.

"I'm going to have to try a lot harder to hide your Christmas presents," Jess observed.

James allowed himself the luxury of a brief smile at her, then was back to business. Jess leaned forward to concentrate on James's deftly sifting through the drawer's contents. He paused, his hands on something she couldn't discern. A "Hmph" escaped him. Jess had all she could do not to demand, "What? What? What?!" as her husband flipped through some papers, his back now to her. Finally, he whistled low and said to himself, "This is interesting, very interesting."

That tipped the limit on Jessica's self-control: "For Pete's sake, James, what did you find?"

He turned back to her, smiling, to reply, "Tell me what you make of this, Jessica. Here's a bankbook with regular entries of $500 every month since the beginning of April this year. Seem a bit peculiar to you? A damned sight more than the standard disability check, wouldn't you say?"

"And how! But what does it mean, exactly? Pay-offs from Herr Zottigstrauch?"

"Could very well be."

"That's wonderful, James. This is the kind of evidence you're looking for," Jessica encouraged hopefully.

The smile faded from James's face as he further considered the significance of what he'd found. He frowned and said, "Evidence, yes, of what we already pretty much knew, that Phil Novack *could* have been in the pay of Georg Zottigstrauch, but no indication of who Zottigstrauch really is. It's not as if we have a canceled check signed by Nigel or Spenser. And it's not as if we could bring in Novack now to sweat the truth out of him." Then, seeing the pain in Jessica's eyes at his allusion to Phil Novack's fate, James added quickly, "Sorry about that, Jessica . . ."

"Never mind," she interrupted. "We can't undo the past, but maybe we can get some justice in the future. Keep going. What's in the drawer on the right?"

James gave her a quick, quiet smile and pulled open the unlocked drawer. Another "This is interesting." He removed a cardboard accordion folder. Standing it on the desk, James sifted through the contents, remarking, "Commission; discharge papers; income tax records; letters from his brother, name of Val," a pause to scan the three short letters, then, "Hmph, one includes a bill of sale for one 'Black Guardian,' a Thoroughbred racehorse, for one dollar from Vladimir Novack." Looking at Jessica, he finished tiredly, "Well, now you know the horse's real name. Only a dollar, eh? Not much of a champion, I'd say."

"Quite the wise guy, aren't you?" Jessica returned, trying to raise their spirits.

He looked curiously at the typed bill of sale and wondered, "Why not just give him the horse, for free?"

"Oh, I think that's for tax purposes," Jess explained. "I know Iris's sister Pansy did the same thing so Iris wouldn't have to pay a gift tax. Yes, that's it, a gift tax. But, say, I'm curious, are the rest of Blackie's papers in there, from the Jockey Club?"

James raised an eyebrow and questioned, "You think I have time to look?"

Jess surrendered, "Okay, okay. Don't go out of your way, but if you *happen* to see . . . or maybe, after you're done, *I* could take a gander . . ."

If James had worn glasses, he would have been staring over them at Jess.

"Or maybe not," she relented.

James tapped the top of the desk, surveyed the room, and stated, "Right, back to work, then."

Jessica returned her attention to Blackie, beg pardon, Black Guardian. Only an occasional snort of the bored rather than alarmed variety from him. Jess was beginning to sympathize with him, till she noticed that James had lined up the bank statements and a few other documents to photograph with a mini-camera.

"Say, mister," Jess cracked, "so far, I've seen you pull out a gun, gloves, a ring of keys, and a camera. You don't happen to have a corned beef sandwich somewhere in that jacket, do you?"

Without missing a beat while photographing, James replied, "It's what all the undercover agents are wearing this year. And I like to come prepared when my wife plunges headlong where she shouldn't."

Undaunted by the last remark, Jessica returned, "I'm glad you had time to pull it all together and rescue me. What? Are you photographing, the letters, too?"

"You never know whom they're really from. There might be an embedded code. I'll get my hands on some other signatures of Novack's brother to verify if they're actually from him. I'm not a cryptologist or graphologist, but Streeter has some boys who can do the trick."

"You're not going to run back to the city tonight with these, are you?" Jessica pressed, concerned. "I know you wouldn't want to trust the mail, but you look beat."

"Don't worry about that," James assured her, finishing up and now reorganizing the materials so they would appear undisturbed. "Dick gave me two 'assistants' today to help me keep an eye on things here." James paused as if forcing himself not to say too much, then continued, "Apparently, I'm not moving fast enough for the chaps upstairs. They think I need some help to grease the wheels a bit. Fine, then. One of my little helpers can slide back into the city with this film."

"Maybe it's a compliment," Jess tried to encourage. "How many guys get their own henchmen?"

"I wouldn't exactly call them my 'henchman,'" James ironically corrected her. "I think Dick assigned them to ensure I didn't make a dog's dinner of this assignment. They'd wanted at least Zottigstrauch's real identity by now. They weren't particularly happy about Crane's murder making such a splash."

Indignant, Jess was on her feet, barely keeping down her voice, "We've only been here a few weeks. If this guy's such a mastermind, and he's had all these years to cover his tracks, how do they expect you to just waltz in and tag him? Really! And Jessamyn Crane's murder, that happened before we even arrived! Would I ever love to give Dick Streeter a piece of my mind!"

James put out a placating hand and tried to calm her: "I appreciate the sympathy, Jessica, but don't take it out on Dick. He's got to answer to desk jockeys above him. And we have to get this chap before he can get away to start something new. No excuse, no matter how good, lets anyone off the hook if Georg Zottigstrauch can take up where the Third Reich left off. Cheer up, love, at least they assigned me a car for the duration."

"A car? Why a car?"

James had crossed to the bed to continue his search before answering, "I had to motor my two chums up here some way. So now we have one fellow in town to keep an eye on Spenser and another working on campus to help me keep tabs on Cross."

James set to work on the bed, testing for lumps, for texture differences in the mattress, the pillows, looking under the bed, at the springs and underside of the mattress–then he was done, his hands empty, his expression tight. Nothing.

"Do you think the package is still here?" Jess questioned. "Maybe Phil hid it from them, or they hid it until they could come back for it."

"That would be lovely, wouldn't it," James acknowledged, surveying the room.

"Well," Jess worried, "if Zottigstrauch took it away, aren't you afraid he'll do a fade before you can catch him?"

"Fortunately, if you remember," James answered as he moved his search to the kitchen, "we overheard Terry say the package and Zottigstrauch couldn't leave town for another two weeks. Since they didn't know we were in on their chat . . ."

"We have no reason to doubt that time frame," Jessica finished.

"That still doesn't leave me a great deal of time," James added before crouching down behind the counter.

Jessica sighed, turned away to listen for Blackie–all was peaceful–then looked back to James. So frustrating, just waiting, but she wasn't about to interfere with his search. Still, he was something to watch: no cushion unplumped, no loose board untested for a secret cache, no cupboard or drawer unchecked for a phony back. The bathroom also was subjected to unfailing scrutiny–with everything precisely restored. *Definitely, no more hiding Christmas presents in the apartment.*

James was leaning against the counter, out of sight through the windows. His sour expression told Jess everything, but she couldn't help asking, "Nothing?"

James looked at her sharply, arms folded in annoyance, then answered flatly, "Not a damned thing–aside from all those curious deposits."

Jess crossed to him. Her hands on James's arms, she tried to encourage, "That's still something. It proves, well suggests, that there was some funny business going on here . . ."

"But what and with whom? Certainly, it seems Novack was up to something he shouldn't have been, but it looks to me as if Zottigstrauch's turned him into a dead-end . . ."

Jessica winced and dropped her hands at those words.

"Sorry, Jessica. I didn't intend to be so blunt. Novack's gone and, as it is, we can't directly link Zottigstrauch to the deposits. It's so damned frustrating, to have my suspicions confirmed but not with enough evidence to nick Georg Zottigstrauch. Perhaps in the letters . . ." He changed gears and decided, "Well, there's nothing to do for it now. The sooner we're out of here the better. I left the car about a mile down the road, around the bend, so I could approach as unobtrusively as possible. It'll get us home fairly quickly."

"Probably," Jess agreed, adding with a straight face. "Except you're going to have a heck of a time getting Blackie into the back seat."

James frowned at her. "The horse? No, you have to leave him here. When someone finally comes looking for Novack, they should find the horse here, so no one knows you were involved."

"What?" Jessica burst out. "Leave Blackie? Alone? Who knows how long before someone finds him. He could starve or dehydrate. He might even wander into the road and get hit by a car. No dice! I found him; he's my responsibility."

"He's not a stray kitten," James reasoned.

"No, he's three-quarters of a ton of horseflesh who needs to be watered and fed and sheltered," Jessica returned.

"And you propose to do all that without making anyone suspicious about how you got the horse of man who has mysteriously disappeared? Especially the people who made him disappear?" James questioned skeptically.

"As a matter of fact, while you were making like a bloodhound in here, I gave the matter some thought. I've come up with a pretty convincing yarn that doesn't meander too far from the truth."

James signaled her to go on, but cautioned, "Make it snappy. We can't stick around here all night."

"I'll singe your ears with my alacrity. Just try to keep up. The horse came to our cottage; he knows me and my apples. Nothing fishy there. I called to let Phil know I had his horse, got no answer, so I rode Blackie back and found the place empty. I returned home with the horse (couldn't leave him all alone and uncared for!), then called the police when I got back. You got here so quickly, our stay here doesn't blow the timeline I created."

James mulled it over and concluded, "That actually works."

"Sure," Jessica went on, "Better yet, no one need know that you were here. I'm not going to say anything about that. And you made pretty darned sure *you* left no evidence of poking around. Even if I've left a few fingerprints, that doesn't contradict my story."

"Except for the skillet."

"Okay, I'll wipe it off; then let's get out of here. This place gives me the willies."

Blackie suddenly unnerved James and Jess with a shrill whistle. James had his gun out, pushing Jessica back from harm's way, as he approached the front window. Blackie was snorting, but calmer.

Did he recognize the intruder? Jess wondered. She whispered, "What is it?"

James peered carefully, then with a somber expression, beckoned Jessica to approach cautiously. As she came closer, he said quietly, "Take a look. If I'm not mistaken, it's a dead ringer for your friend Terry."

Puzzled, Jess hesitated. Nevertheless, she came to the window, and James backed away to let her takes a look. At first, all Jessica saw was Blackie sidled away from the barn, almost parallel to the porch.

"I don't see any . . ."

"Take a look by the barn. Toward the ground."

"The ground . . . ?" Jessica's words trailed off as she caught sight of the large-cat-sized creature, black with a broad swath of white down his back, ambling along the side of the barn.

She turned back to her husband and said, "A skunk, huh? Terry's dead ringer? Cute. So cute I ought to crown you for scaring ten years off my life. Where is that skillet, anyway?"

Chapter Twenty-One

An hour or so later, although it seemed more like days, Jessica found herself barely able to keep her eyes open as their car carried her and James back to their cottage from the stables. Jess watched her husband, a man intent on the road. Thank God, James was alert–though she wasn't quite sure how after his long day. Looking out the side window, she saw the buildings were dark. Not much chance of anyone noticing, let alone stopping, them. *Thank heavens for small favors*. The only lights were the twinkling of ships out to sea, the stars and moon, and the Chapman Lighthouse.

Waking up more now, Jess's curiosity about what exactly had happened in New York today got the better of her. There'd been no time to talk, what with her riding Blackie back while James was in the car, bedding down the horse, and having to put up a good front for a stable hand. Next, she'd put in a call to the sheriff, who made clear he couldn't do anything until after the requisite waiting period. Knowing she couldn't reveal that Phil Novack wasn't coming back, Jess had accepted, and that had been that.

Now she had James to herself and could finally question, "So, what did the great man say about what we overheard in the cove?"

"I was wondering when you'd get around to asking," James replied. "He didn't exactly hand out bouquets."

"Meaning?"

"Meaning, as I said before, I'm not moving fast enough, especially since we only have two weeks. Apparently, I used to be able to deliver the goods with an alacrity far more conducive to their timetable."

Jessica uttered an emphatically unladylike snort, giving her the slight pleasure of seeing James quirk the faintest of smiles. Nevertheless, she fumed, "*He* gave you this assignment; *he* should know how difficult it is to pin something definite on such a sharp cookie. How can Dick not realize that you have to step lightly; or you'll spook this guy before you can nail down what his plans are, or who's on the other end of his chain?"

James answered, "Sure, Dick understands that, but he needs results. Excuses, even justifiable ones, don't cut any ice if I fail."

They pulled up before their cottage, and Jessica, grabbing at straws, suggested, "Are you sure you couldn't get Carolina and Terry to turn on Zottigstrauch if you offered them some kind of immunity? I don't think they feel any loyalty to him, just fear."

James faced her to reply, "I agree that loyalty has nothing to do with their bond to him. First, it was for money, and I've no doubt now they're running scared. Zottigstrauch probably had Jessamyn Crane liquidated, then forced them to kill Phil Novack and dispose of the body to pound home what happens to double-crossers. Killing Phil had the added 'virtue' of entangling them in a capital crime."

"That's dreadful," Jess shuddered. She rested her head on her hand, her arm propped against her seat, and added, "So our discovery that Terry and Carolina are definitely working for Zottigstrauch, that there's some sort of package in play, does that mean anything?"

"It gives us grounds for a wiretap on their line and for searching their cottage, as well as Phil's," James replied.

"Why not just tap the lines or do a search of the two guys you suspect?"

James shook his head, "Dick and I discussed this. Zottigstrauch's too damned smart to give himself away over an open line, as well as to recognize if his line's tapped. The same goes double for knowing if someone's been tampering with his home sweet home. Terry and his lovely wife—not so perceptive. And they're ripe to panic and make an incriminating call. Theirs is the line I got the warrant for."

"Warrant? But with the threat to our country and all, Dick Streeter waited for one?"

"He found a judge. We didn't wait long," James knowingly answered. "Besides, you Yanks have a little document called the Constitution that says we really ought to. Myself, I think it's a document with some rather nifty ideas that oughtn't be trampled, lest we all end up becoming like Herr Zottigstrauch and his crowd. Dick claims he just wants to be sure no one wriggles free on a technicality, but I rather suspect he's flashing that cynicism to mask a streak of fair play and justice."

"Okay, that's actually reassuring. I've spent enough time with Shakespeare to understand about how absolute power corrupts," Jessica agreed. "But now are you going to have to pull off another search? Isn't Nigel going to get suspicious if you start canceling classes to do some spying–let alone if you get caught?"

"Ah," began James, with an irony Jess wasn't quite sure how to read, "that's part of why Dick's little helpers are here. It's felt that I might be more efficient in the background, spinning my web. The chaps upstairs see me as more useful stepping back and just observing, fielding the information for my friends to act on. I'm to take a less active role from now on."

"Will you get in Dutch for giving Phil Novack's cabin a once over?"

James shrugged, answering, "They can't argue with opportunity. And what's done cannot be undone."

He still didn't sound exactly pleased at his new position.

"Well, that takes some of the burden off you," Jessica posited tentatively.

"Yeah. Though I sometimes think that they might feel the old boy isn't quite up to snuff, needs to be put out to pasture."

Jessica paused before querying carefully, "Would that be so bad?"

James gave her a sharp look, but smiled wanly and said, "I think it would make you very happy. Can't say as I blame you." He thought a moment, before adding, "Can't say *I'm* entirely convinced it would be a bad idea, at that." He shifted gears and asked, "But what about you, love? Take my mind off big troubles and tell me about your high drama deciding between a scone and a muffin with your tea at the inn"

"Um . . . ye-es," Jessica temporized, "about that . . ."

James recognized that tone. He gave Jessica an uneasy, "Go on."

Jess's mouth twisted with reluctance, but she forced herself to push on: "We-ell, things didn't go quite as I'd planned. But it was *not* my fault. I tried to get out of it, and it would have looked downright suspicious if I'd *wrested* myself free. You know how inexorable teenagers can be."

"Jessica, cut to the chase. Suspense is *not* something I can enjoy right now."

Jess plunged forward: "Alicia and Lauren dragged me into you-know-who's antique shop to look at a table. I tried to get out of it, but short of kayoing both of them and making a run for it, I couldn't. Hold on to your hat: I met Nicholas Spenser."

James sank back against his door; his left hand fiercely rubbed his brow. When he finally dropped the hand, his look was so piercing, Jess wanted to kick herself for giving him one more fardel to bear. She held her breath, waiting for James to blow.

Instead, he seemed to reach some conclusion and calmly questioned, "What did he learn from you?"

That seemed to come out of left field, but she'd take it. James was back on the job, no time for temper—and she had no time for guilt.

"Not much, I think. The kids said that I taught at the school. I didn't add any more than that I was also an actress. He vaguely remembered you buying a present for me. To be truthful, he didn't seem interested in probing much. He was more interested in impressing me with what good taste Carolina Brent Clarke had for shopping with him. He wasn't at all concerned about hiding his connection with the Clarkes. Still, there was something oddly interesting about that."

James cocked an eyebrow and queried, "How so?"

"He apparently brokered Jessamyn Crane's artwork. Sold a lot in the city—and to Nigel Cross. The interesting part was that he was looking for more of her stuff. The girls mentioned we have Jessamyn Crane's cottage, and he wanted to come out to see if we had anything of hers. He was really insistent."

"What did you say?"

"I invited him over for a highball. What do you *think* I said?"

"Jessica," James said firmly.

"Sorry. I thought a little healthy sarcasm might lighten the mood. Bad call. Of course, I discouraged him. I wasn't rude, but I said if I ever found anything of hers, I wouldn't feel right selling it. I thought I'd better not tell him about that weird little piece on the console."

"How did he take it?" James's tone betrayed no more than deep thought.

"Not badly. But he did give me his card, just in case."

"Mmm," James considered. "Still have the card?"

"Yes. It's on the kitchen table. Why? Are you going to check it for prints, or *does* Streeter have Zottigstrauch's prints?" She read James's expression and said, "Of course not. That would be too easy. So why do you want the card? You don't intend to invite *him* into our home!"

James thought out loud, "It might be useful if I can make him play the fly to my spider. I'll have to mull this over."

"Wouldn't that give you away?" Jess countered. "Your superiors wouldn't like it, given their recent orders, would they?"

"As for the chaps upstairs, they wouldn't argue with success if they found out after the fact," James replied. "The rub is that contacting him is a move that would have to be delicately played–and I don't like the thought of him being near you. What was your impression of Spenser?"

Jessica had to orient herself to the turn in the subject; but quickly found her way, answering, "I didn't particularly like him. He snubbed the girls and seemed way too pushy for my taste. I also wasn't crazy about how snooty he was about his clientele. But that doesn't make him a Nazi– just obnoxious. Anyway, would he want to stress how chummy he was with Carolina and Terry if they were his minions? And yet, the way he talked about Nigel's strong interest in Jessamyn Crane's work, I felt, I don't know, as if he was trying to suggest there was a funny link there."

James nodded, "At any rate, it also strikes me that he did too neat a job of both emphasizing a connection between Nigel and Jessamyn and explaining away his own connection to her and the Clarkes–all in one brief encounter."

"James," Jessica wondered, "while we're on the topic of his fascination with Jessamyn Crane's work, I was thinking that maybe something she created is the package Phil was supposed to be holding. If Carolina and Terry have it now, or it's hidden somewhere on campus, maybe campus is where you, or your assistants, need to be looking."

"Except why call attention to it by asking to come to our home? Phil Novack was supposed to have the package, but he never left us anything."

"Well," Jessica reasoned. "If Spenser claims he wants Jessamyn's artwork to broker in New York, he has an excuse for looking around. But here's the really clever part: if he covers himself by looking in places he knows the special piece isn't, then he distracts people from where it really is."

James suggested, "And Zottigstrauch has the psychic powers to know that today two teenagers would drag you into his shop for a look about?"

"Oh, right, that is a little too coincidental, isn't it? Gee, I don't know what to think anymore," Jess despaired.

"Cheers, love, it's not your job to do my thinking for me. Let it go for the night. I'll have to."

Jessica smiled weakly and nodded.

Tired as he was, James was still the gentleman. Leaving the car, he circled around to let Jess out. Putting his arms around her, he said, "Things will look fresher in the morning."

Coming to the gate, James had enough spirit to open it with a wave of his hand and say, "Shall we, Mrs. Crawford, before 'Dawn walks in russet mantle clad'?"

Jess gave her husband a skeptical look, pointing out as they moved up the path holding hands, "*Hamlet*, of all the plays you have to quote *Hamlet*–right before the ghost shows up to warn of 'murder most foul.'"

"'There needs no ghost come from the grave to tell us that,'" James noted.

"You're suddenly getting almost chipper," Jess observed, as they walked along. "Not that I'm kicking, but after all that doom and gloom about what a threat your pal is, why the change in tune?"

They reached the porch and James stopped to explain, "Let's just say I'm beginning to see where Zottigstrauch may not be quite so invincible. Whether it's Spenser or Cross, neither of them has shown any real indication he knows how much of a threat I am. And whichever one is my quarry is under pressure because the master plan is getting complicated by attention-grabbing murders. So, I'm in a position to probe them without their knowing it, if I do it right. I'll just let them think I'm an innocent sap they can pump for information about Phil's disappearance or any pieces we have by Jessamyn Crane. Of course, the more oblivious I look, the more likely their egos will cause them to slip." James thought a minute and added, "And I think your showing up in Spenser's shop might have been for the best, all things considered. Made you look innocent, unaware."

"Dopey?"

"I'm not getting trapped by that one," James wisely responded. "If you can outfox me, I won't stand much of a chance against Zottigstrauch."

"There's an insult in there somewhere," Jess noted with mock skepticism, "but it's too late for me to be able to figure it out." Then she added archly, "Although all this web-spinning you're doing doesn't sound to *me* as if you've lost your touch!"

James smiled, unlocked the front door, and paused before turning back to Jessica to say, "Still, it would make me a lot happier if you found an excuse to visit Liz in California."

"Well, that fills me with confidence," Jessica returned. She added, "I told you before, I'm the kind of gal what sticks. Anyway, we both know, my taking off would raise red flags. So, no. You're stuck with me."

Yet Jessica didn't feel quite as confident as she sounded, especially when she noted how James did a quick check before letting her into the cottage, just in case.

Chapter Twenty-Two

July 30, Tuesday morning

Six-thirty A.M. was a glorious time for a ride. The sun was bright, but a breeze off the ocean tamed its power to burn. Seabird acrobats loosed their voices with playful exuberance and even the clang of buoys seemed less a warning than a greeting to the salt-scented winds.

That was Jessica Minton's take as she strode alongside the stone wall between campus and the beach. She could have chosen a more direct route to the stables, but the seaside rejuvenated her wearied heart and mind, feeding into her anticipation of the first pleasure ride on Blackie, aka Black Guardian. Moving past Cameron House, Jess had to admit that part of her light mood was due to no longer working with Terry Clarke. She and James had decided that the sooner she gracefully bowed out of her involvement with him and his class, the better. She'd called Terry to explain she'd come in Monday and Tuesday. However, from then on she'd be tied up preparing for the fall return of her radio program. Surprisingly, Terry had acted perfectly at ease for a man mixed up in murder only the night before. Jess almost wondered if he were innocent of Phil's disappearance. Then again, Terry had more than a little acting talent.

Monday, before class, that talent seemed to fail him—and Jessica's own abilities had been put to the test trying to play it like the proverbial cucumber. Initially, Terry had seemed merely curious when he'd tried to extract from her information beyond what she'd already told campus

283

security and the sheriff. Yet Jess had detected in his eyes, and in his difficulty letting the subject drop, definite disquietude. It had been some relief when Terry finally changed the subject to a play he claimed to have seen with Carolina in the city that weekend. Neat trick, tossing in an alibi. Fortunately, he seemed to have no idea Jessica knew better. Maybe he was just happy with not having to keep up a front for her. She'd like to think he wanted her out of the whole mess for old time's sake.

Anyway, the two stable buildings were now directly before her, the one on the right full of horses. The other would be empty until the autumn semester, when needed for returning members of the equestrienne team's or their competitors' mounts. The smell of hay; horse; and, yes, even horse scat brought her comfort and security. Jessica Minton Crawford might have enjoyed prancing around 21 in heels, slinky gown, and hair elegantly coiffed; right now, however, she luxuriated in a plain blouse, jodhpurs, and riding boots, with her long hair efficiently compacted into a French roll. As she entered the barn, a man in his forties came away from the first stall, his eyes dark and merry, his face lined by hours in the sun and years getting out of bed at the crack of dawn.

"Morning, Miz Crawford. Guess you're here to take your new pal for a spin. I tell you; he's aching to get out."

"Is he, Stan?" Jessica enthused. "Great! Sorry I'm late this morning. You already fed him, right? I had an emergency in the kitchen—flaming flapjacks."

"How did Mr. Crawford take that?"

"Oh, I just convinced him that char-broiled is the latest in pancakes."

"I'll bet," he snorted. "So, you want me to tack up Blackie for you?"

"I can do that," Jess insisted brightly.

Stan kidded, "C'mon—you gotta let me do something. Since you brought him here, you've been feeding and watering him, walking him, grooming him. You're gonna put me out of a job."

"I let you muck out the stall," Jessica playfully countered.

Stan gave her a skeptical look and replied, "Yeah, thanks. Real generous of you."

Jessica grinned then proposed, "How about we make saddling up the big guy a joint effort?"

"Sounds good to me, Miz Crawford."

"Okay, but first let me visit with my buddy. I brought him something."

"Big surprise."

The two made their way down past the rows of stalls on either side of the barn. Of course, there was an occasional pause to rub the nose or scratch an ear of a friendly equine. Blackie was in the last stall on the right. Scenting their approach, he whickered a greeting.

"The big fella really likes you," Stan approved.

Reaching into her jacket, Jessica unwrapped some carrot sticks from wax paper and said, "Likes me, huh? Wonder if it has anything to do with these."

She wouldn't let the big horse scarf up the carrots all at once, holding out a few in one hand and enjoying the feel of the soft mouth lipping her palm, then the strong teeth brushing it.

"Yeah, this guy sure likes you," Stan went on. "An' he's real definite about who he don't like."

"Whom doesn't he like?" Jess inquired, scratching Blackie's chin now that the carrots were gone. "Not you, Stan."

"Nagh, me and him get on just fine—but some of the other professors . . ."

Jessica tried not to let the jolt of curiosity show. Only glancing back briefly at Stan, still rubbing Blackie's nose, she ventured, "You don't say?"

"Sure, those two Clarkes were by here yesterday afternoon. They sometimes ride, too, you know. Always manage to bring up how much better things was back in horse country, where they usta 'ride to the hounds.' Mrs. Clarke is always making a big deal about her family breeding hunters in Snowfree Springs, a place called Selbywood."

"So, you think the big guy doesn't like snobs?" Jess joked, having worked her way up to scratching Blackie's ears.

"Who knows?" Stan shrugged. "All I can say is that the minute he got wind of them, he pinned back his ears and started snorting. Then these two, not so smart about horses as they think, still came right up to the front of the stall to get a good look at the 'mystery horse,' they called him. Blackie was having none of that. Didn't like being gawked at. He almost charged through the door. I had to chase those two away before he hurt himself."

Jess smiled, thinking that Stan had clearly been more worried about the horse than the people, but, in this case, she couldn't blame him. Blackie was right on the beam in terms of judging character! Knowing discretion was probably the best policy, she tactfully observed, "Well, he's practically a lamb now."

"Just remember when you get in the saddle that this is no lamb—and he's aching to get out. Restless guy. Full of p and v."

"He *was* a racehorse, though apparently, he kept company with the cheap runners."

"You don't say? Hey, he's got the right lines. Nice conformation, but you can see where the right front tendon was fired from bowing."

"Really? I never noticed," Jess was genuinely surprised.

"Yeah, well, I used to be a groom on the racing circuit around here: 'Gansett, Suffolk, Rockingham. I saw a lot of gimpy platers in my day"

"I never knew that." Jess was intrigued. Should she ask if he had known Phil's brother, Val? But that would be admitting Phil had talked quite a bit to her, something Georg Zottigstrauch would not like, should it get back to him. Jess didn't think for a moment Stan was in league with that crew, but she knew he liked to gossip. She only asked, "So tell me about it. I love hearing stories from the backstretch."

Stan brushed a hand over the dome of his forehead to his receded dark hair and said, "That was ten years ago."

"Before this guy's time."

"Oh, yeah. This horse isn't even ten years old. I looked at his teeth the other day, just out of curiosity. He's only about six or seven, I'd say. I'm way more of an old-timer than him."

"So, when you were on the circuit, you must have seen some big names like Discovery or Equipoise or Seabiscuit," Jess eagerly suggested.

"Oh, yeah. Never made a dime on any of the big names, though. In fact, I lost more money playing Seabiscuit at the Rock. 'Course that was when he was a two-year-old, before Tom Smith got ahold of him and made a champ outta him. But never mind. You get this horse out and put a little exercise in him, or he'll be kicking down the barn soon."

It didn't take long for them to gather the tack and have Blackie ready to go. They led the well-muscled animal out into the courtyard, his coat gleaming jet in the sun.

Stan remarked, "See, this guy's a true black. No red or brown when the sun hits him. An' look at those hind quarters—plenty of acceleration. I bet this baby could really move. Only a claimer, huh? Must have had some bad habits that messed him up."

Jess, on the big horse's left, reached under his neck to pat the other side, saying, "He's a perfect gentleman with me."

"Hey, maybe that's it. Politeness and good manners make a nice saddle horse, but they don't win races. A champion needs grit and fire, bottom they call it," Stan reasoned.

"Like Equipoise biting his competitors," Jess added with a twinkling eye.

"Don't knock the Chocolate Soldier," Stan grinned. Then he asked, "You ready for a leg up?"

Jess nodded and Stan had her on board in a jiffy. Blackie snorted and danced excitedly beneath her.

"Don't let him get away from you," Stan warned as Jess turned Blackie's impatient dancing into a controlled circle. "Yeah, that's good. Take him out nice and slow. Walk him out. Where you riding him?"

"I thought I'd take him down to the beach," Jess answered, easing into sync with the horse's movement. His mouth was sensitive to handling, his body powerful beneath the strong grip of her legs. She finished, "Not many people there at this hour, and the sand will be easy on his feet."

"Yeah, good idea—but he's a big horse and he's got spirit. Make sure he knows who's boss. Give him a gallop—he needs it—but don't let him get away from you. You sure you know how to stand in the irons to slow him down?"

Jessica nodded. "I'm a little rusty, but remember I told you that I had a friend, an exercise rider, who taught me at a little training track in Massachusetts?"

"Well, okay, don't forget, even if he's no Stymie, he's still a racehorse, and you're no Eddie Arcaro."

"I got you," Jess agreed, suppressing just the slightest urge to say, "What in Sam Hill have I gotten myself into?!"

Jessica clapped Blackie lightly with her heels, pointing him to where the stable yard opened into the roadway. He took off at a trot, betraying his determination to break into something faster. Jessica, however, was equally determined not to let him do an imitation of Whirlaway across campus. She was more than a little relieved when Blackie opted to let her guide him at a restrained pace down a path that led through an open gate to the beach.

Of course, even the gentlemanly Blackie was not above giving a little buck or an impatient prance on their way, but Jess had been riding for enough years to hold her own with him—just. And she was getting used to the rhythm of his gait. It was an adventure, staying with this fellow, but the thrill of achieving it shot her through. Blackie snorted; his neck bowed under restraint as she kept him down to a trot to let him warm up. Then Jess gradually let the reins out a little more to ease him into a canter than a gallop.

Ocean wind and the slip stream of Blackie's growing speed whipped her face, dancing free strands of her hair and fluttering her blouse. Blackie gradually stretched out his powerful neck and they took off as his hindquarters propelled them forward. Jessica pushed herself to keep in rhythm with her flying mount. She ought to have been afraid when the scenery shot, no blurred, past. She was, a little. But the horse was joying in his freedom to move, to fly across the sands, while Jessica was caught up in that exhilaration as she and the stallion seemed as one. *How could anyone call this racer on the sharp wind of the north anything as pedestrian as "Blackie"?*

Would that James could see them, even race with them. "Not bloody likely," she could hear him declare.

"That's all right, son. It's you and me," Jessica called to her cohort in splitting the breeze. The horse cocked an ear back at her and responded by nearly pulling Jessica's arms out of her sockets as he poured out a burst of speed.

That brought Jess back to reality. What was she thinking, letting a horse who'd bowed a tendon run full out like this? She was already trying to pull the stallion in before completing the thought. Blackie was not interested, even when she repeatedly threw the command "Whoa!" into the pot. This was the moment when Jessica Minton could have panicked. But she didn't. That was a luxury she couldn't afford, not for her sake nor for Blackie's.

Jess's arms were absolutely murdering her. She had Blackie's head bowed, which slowed him a bit, but not enough. Time to launch that standing in the irons schtick. Determinedly, Jess forced herself up, fighting for balance, then joying as her body locked into a familiar stance. And Blackie, independent but well trained, gradually responded, downshifting into a lope, a trot, a walk, and finally allowing himself to be brought to a stop.

Jessica's initial relief as she relaxed into the saddle slid into alarm. Had she put the horse's leg under a strain? Would she be able to cool him down so he wouldn't overheat? Well, he wasn't blowing like an exhausted racer. Just shaking his head and snorting, a little winded but not blown out. Jess reached down to stroke his shoulder and neck, happy to discover they weren't foamy with sweat, though not completely dry. She sat up and shook her head, at last leaning forward to whisper in Blackie's ear, "If this doesn't take the cake! That's how fast a plater runs? Bro-o-other!"

Blackie snorted again and pawed. He was tired of standing around.

"Okay, okay. I get the message, Mr. Big. But we're going to return at a much more sedate pace. That was some half-mile you gave me. It's time for the two of us to take it easy."

Blackie extended his neck and shook his head, mane quivering in a shiny black wave.

"*No* back talk, mister."

Blackie responded like a gentleman when Jess clapped her heels to his barrel. Even at a less jet-propelled pace, it was a thrill to guide this powerful animal. Passing her cottage, Jessica glanced up. No James. Just as well. He'd probably have had apoplexy if he'd seen the two of them sailing by earlier.

When Jessica later rode into the stable yard, Stan was on break with a new guy, both on a bale of hay, taking intermittent slugs from their bottles of Moxie.

"Hey, you're back!" Stan called, pushing off the bale, leaving behind his bottle. "How'd it go? I see you brought him in nice and peaceable."

"And all in one piece, both of us," Jess grinned, pausing to nod to the other stable hand. The young man nodded back and returned to the barn. *Hmm, was he one of James's assistants?*

"So, the big fella behaved himself?" Stan asked, giving the horse an affable slap on the neck. "You handled him all right?"

"Yes and no," Jess admitted from her seat above Stan. "Let's say we came to an accommodation—after he tried to give me a half-mile in 48."

Stan stepped back and asked, "He ran away from you?" Before Jess could answer, Stan had looked the horse over and run his hands over his leg. Stan nodded and approved, "Eh, he's not blowin' or nothin.' Didn't even work up a lather. Leg isn't hot. That's good."

"I slowed him down gradually," Jessica explained. "I even managed not to go flying when I stood up in the irons. Then I made him walk back. Not exactly his idea of a good time, but being a gentleman, as I said before, he humored me. I did right?"

Stan replied, "Almost like hot walking him. He looks good. So, let's get you out of the saddle and get the tack off him. I'll give him a rub down . . ."

"*We* can do that," Jessica corrected pleasantly, slipping from the saddle on the side opposite Stan. She managed to hide bobbling a little when she hit the ground. *It was like being in skyscraper country up there. How did those jockeys do it?*

"Sure, sure," Stan was agreeing as he started them toward the barn, leading the dark horse.

"I feel better knowing you think I did okay cooling him down, coming in. And you ought to know."

"Yeah, I started at the track as a hot walker, before I was a groom," Stan affirmed. "That was a dull job: walk the pony so many paces, let him drink from a bucket of warm water, walk him some more, drink, walk, drink, walk for 15 or 30 minutes. I had one ornery character who'd take a slurp, knock the bucket over, then, if you weren't paying attention, he'd try to let you have it in the seat of your pants with his big choppers."

"Ouch!" grimaced Jess. "I'm glad our Black Guardian has much more class!"

"Oh, that reminds me, your talking about my time at the track," Stan began as they entered the stable. "I was going to tell you something funny about this horse, but I forgot when you got me going about the horses I'd seen."

"Nothing to worry about?" Jess asked, her face puckering.

"Naaah. Just odd. I'll show you when we take off his bridle."

They had Blackie in the stall and Jess held his bridle while Stan uncinched the horse and hung the saddle over the side of the stall.

"Gee, Stan, you've got me on pins and needles," Jess teased, peeking around the stallion's head. Then looking her equine buddy in the eye she kidded, "Don't tell me you're harboring shameful secrets."

The minute those words escaped her, Jess inwardly cringed. Blackie might well harbor the secret of what had happened to Phil. Worse, her thrilling ride had come at the cost of Phil Novack's life. She felt like a worm.

Jessica didn't have a chance to let guilt eat any deeper, however, for Stan was at Blackie's head saying, "He's got a tattoo."

"A what? A tattoo? What horse has a tattoo? Was he in the Marines or something?" A quick survey of the horse and Jess finished, "I don't see any tattoos."

"It's not where you can see it. I found it when I was checking his teeth. It's in his mouth, the inside of his upper lip. See."

While Jess still held Black Guardian's bridle, Stan pulled up the horse's upper lip, and there, on the inside, was tattooed the letter V followed by four numbers.

"Well, I'll be," Jess muttered as Stan released Blackie's lip before the horse decided to take retaliatory action.

"What do you make of that?" Stan asked.

"I don't know. I've never seen anything like it, not that I spend a lot of time in horse's mouths," Jess answered, puzzled. Stan slipped a halter onto Blackie and removed the bridle. All the while Jess reflected, until something shifted to the front of her brain. She corrected herself, "No, wait, I think I have read about this being done to Standardbreds."

"But he ain't no trotter or pacer," Stan pointed out.

"Not the way he *runs*," Jess concurred. "Let me think some more, though. You know, I believe I read something about tattooing in Chitzenega, that island nation in the Caribbean. Down there, horse racing is bigger than baseball up here. I think they tattoo their horses like that, for identification."

"Could be this guy's an immigrant," Stan nodded, patting the stallion's neck. "You have his papers?"

"No, just his real name on a bill of sale. The police said we ought to keep that document if we were going to take responsibility for him. What about I write to the Jockey Club, give them his name and the number? Maybe they could tell me about him."

"Good idea. Let me know how it turns out. Why don't you write to the Jockey Club of Chitzenega, too? Do you have to know Spanish?"

"I don't think so. The country's pretty cosmopolitan. Anyway, if I have any trouble, I can always ask Judy Ricardo or her husband to help me. They love horses, too."

"Yeah, that's right. And when they came by the other day, your friend here was as well-mannered as any gent."

Jess resisted commenting on the horse's ability to read character, only saying, "Sure, writing both jockey clubs is a swell idea. Maybe I'll even do it when I get home this morning. But for now, let's give this fella his rub down. I'll tell you, I can't wait to put these shoulders under a hot shower. They're killing me from trying to hold him down."

"George Woolf you ain't! You couldn't hold back a driving horse till the last minute like he used to, God rest him."

"I'm more like Virginia Woolf," Jess quipped.

"Who?"

"Let's just say she could swing a mean metaphor rather than a whip."

"Iceman wasn't big on the whip. You're thinking of Arcaro."

"Must be," Jessica agreed, massaging the big black horse's forehead before she went for a cloth to rub him down.

Around four o'clock found Jessica Minton sitting back reading a *Turf and Sport Digest*. Showered and changed into a robin's egg blue silky, short-sleeved blouse and light-weight chocolate-brown slacks, she relaxed into one of the wicker chairs on her front porch. To her left, between her and a second chair, was a little table where she'd stacked a year's supply of *Bloodhorse*. Jess paused from reading and surveyed the front garden. In the afternoon sunshine, the blues and lavenders and purples of the delphinium deliciously complemented the vivid pinks and soft yellows of the hollyhocks. The iridescent darting, hovering, and soaring green, blue, and red dragonflies left her feeling as if she were in a fairyland out of Maxfield Parrish. Unfortunately, she remembered that her garden was just as susceptible to demonic serpents as that nifty little piece of real estate that was the first address of Adam and Eve. Jess wasn't at all given to the willies at the sight of real snakes, but the metaphorical, human variety . . . ?

Jessica forced her attention back to her racing magazine. What she really wanted was that article on ringers and lip tattoos, but the afternoon's perusal of her journals had left her frustrated, realizing she'd left that issue back in New York. A call to Lois requesting her friend post the right magazine to her *tout suite* had taken care of the problem. Sort of. Who enjoyed waiting? And speaking of waiting, how long before she had an answer to the letters she'd sent to the American and the Chitzenegan Jockey Clubs?

A dark car came up the road from the direction of the school. As it glided to a stop by the gate, Jessica recognized Dick Streeter's little "donation." Her spirit was willing to trip gaily down the garden path to greet her husband. However, her flesh, after battling three-quarters-of-a-ton of Thoroughbred, was just too darn tired to do more than happily call, "Hi there, handsome!"

James had just shut off the ignition and was reaching for his briefcase on the seat beside him when he heard her. Jess couldn't quite see his smile, but she could hear it in his voice when he slid across the seat and leaned out the window to answer, "You look comfortable and cool there."

Jess called back, "Comfortable, yes. Cool? In July?"

James pushed open the door and got out, closing the door behind him. He came up the path, wearing the expression of a guy tired from a long day but at ease because he was home.

"So," her husband began, walking up the steps, "how was your ride? Today was the big day."

Jess settled back in her chair to enthuse, "Out of this world! He's some horse! It took all my strength . . ." James's eyes went concerned, so she soft-pedaled, "but he cooperated. You don't have to worry about me. He's a dream. But I'm still a little stiff. Otherwise, I would have met you at the gate."

James rested against the porch rail, then put his briefcase down, teasing, "I wondered why you didn't prance down to the car with my pipe and slippers."

Jess leaned forward, one arm across her knee, the other akimbo and returned, "You don't smoke a pipe–but maybe I could hire you an Irish Setter for the slippers."

"Would Dusty allow that?"

"Good thing you know who the real boss around here is," Jess gibed, sinking back in her chair. "Anyway, what about you? How'd things go for you today?"

For a fraction of a second, James's eyes shadowed and Jess thought, *Shoot! He thinks I'm asking about his case.*

But the shadow disappeared, and James answered, "Good, good. The students are bright. They love the material. Good discussions." He stopped to think, then looked straight at Jessica and said, "Alicia Wraxton, she's infatuated with your friend Terry, isn't she?"

Jess started at that assessment. At last, she said, "What clued you in?"

James tilted his head and shrugged, "A few things. She quotes him too much–and I overheard her giving another girl hell for making some sarcastic comment about his 'friendship' with Jessamyn Crane. It was an understated, witty kind of hell, but the gist was infernal, nonetheless. What do you think?"

Jessica twisted her mouth, finally saying, "I got wind of that situation from her a little while ago. I tried to discourage her without telling her any of the really horrid details. I was hoping it had worked. What you heard, are you worried?"

"I don't know," James answered, folding his arms in front of him, thinking. "I'm concerned about innocent bystanders getting dragged in."

"Oh, I don't think Terry would ever take her up on it. For one thing, he may have an ego, but he wouldn't do anything as blatantly risky as getting mixed up with an underage student. Besides, don't you think he'd be way too jittery to draw attention to himself, for fear of angering Zottigstrauch? He knows what happened to Phil and Jessamyn."

"That's what I'm concerned about, that Zottigstrauch might see Alicia as needing to be eliminated if she poked her nose into his circle," James replied darkly.

Jess raised her eyebrows, but reasoned, "Maybe, James, but he can't keep bumping people off without raising some suspicions. Besides, I don't think Terry would cotton to hurting a kid, especially after what happened to Jessamyn. Phil was a big boy; that was another matter. Even if he were afraid of what Zottigstrauch could do to him, do you really believe that Terry could be forced to hurt an innocent kid?"

"I've seen good people do terrible things when enough pressure was put on them," James answered tiredly. "I'd feel much better if that girl could be steered away from anyone connected to Zottigstrauch. Do you think you could divert her without giving anything away?"

"You think that *I*, an *adult*, can persuade a teenager not to do something stupid that she really wants to do," Jessica responded skeptically.

James's expression plainly told her that this was not a topic he found amusing. So Jessica placated, "Okay, okay. Let me think. I've already talked my way out of Terry's class, so that nixes any chance of my keeping an eye on her there." (James frowned at that complication.) "The best I can promise is to get Rose to help me keep her occupied outside of class. That might work, actually. It's indirect enough that Terry won't notice what we're up to. And don't worry about Rose. This is something we can work on without bringing in Zottigstrauch. After all, Rose wouldn't want to see Alicia do something stupid. She has two girls, so she knows from stupid kid behavior."

James thought over her words, nodded, and concluded, "Right, then, not too bad. The mission just cannot bear any more complications."

"Fine," Jessica pronounced. "Now here's a problem that you can solve for *me* in a snap. My shoulders are killing me. Sit down over here and give them a massage, will you?"

James shook his head, amused. The doubts were still there, if in abeyance, but at least he had no doubts about how to knead his wife's shoulders. So, he grabbed onto an island of distraction in these choppy waters of deadly uncertainties and moved the empty chair to behind his wife and sat down. Jessica swanned her neck, arched her back, and pulled her shoulders back into her husband's hands, almost purring, "Mmmmm."

"So, mistress mine," James began, allowing himself a quiet smile, "what else were you up to today? How is that pony of yours?"

"Oh, swell," she answered dreamily, starting to turn as she explained. "Stan, the groom noticed something really interesting. He has a tattoo."

"Stan?" James queried drolly, shifting Jessica back into position.

"No, you dope. The horse. Black Guardian has a tattoo."

"A tattoo? What's it say, 'mater'? I'm sorry, more likely 'ma mere/mare.'"

Jess turned just enough to give James the fisheye and chide, "*That* was dreadful."

James grinned back, repositioned Jess to continue his massaging, then went on, "So what's the story on the tattoo?"

"The story is—Mmm hmm, that does feel good! I've no doubt why I married you—ow! Okay, I'll get back on track. The story is that Blackie has a serial number tattooed on the inside of his upper lip."

"That does sound odd. Who would, *why* would, anyone do that?"

James paused his kneading, intrigued.

"Hey, keep going!"

"Oh, sorry. Right."

"Mmm, yes! Okay, well my theory is that it's an identification number. They do it to harness racers here and to Chitzenegan racehorses, by law, to keep owners and trainers from running ringers . . ."

"Ringers?"

"Yep. You run a slow horse a few times; he loses, driving up the odds. Then you substitute a fast horse disguised as the slow one, run him under the slow one's name, bet a bundle, and collect a bigger one when he wins. With the tattoo, though, i.d. numbers are different for each horse. So, no matter that it's not hard to either find a horse's double or do a little touch-up job to get the same look, the numbers still distinguish them. Chitzenega's been doing it for years. I was reading an article, earlier this year, or maybe from last year, about proposing to do it here. After a big scandal over a 'ring' of 'ringers' this year, the Jockey Club is looking into going that route in the States.

"So, I figured with Black Guardian's name and that tattoo, the Jockey Club, either here or in Chitzenega, could give me the lowdown on him. I sent off two letters today. Hey don't stop now!"

Jessica twisted to her husband, but he wasn't looking at her, just frowning and thinking. Finally, he faced her and levelly said, "Jessica, I wish you hadn't done that, written them."

Genuinely flummoxed, Jess took a moment to respond, "I don't read you, James. What's the harm?"

"What have I been saying about not calling attention to us? To my case?"

"I'm not," she disagreed. "Just to the horse. I don't think *he's* a fiver. Remember, Chitzenega was one of our 'Good Neighbors' in the southern hemisphere during the war."

"It's not a laughing matter, Jessica," James warned, dead serious.

His tone got to Jess, and she now spoke seriously: "I'm sorry. I didn't mean to be flip. But how would Georg or his gang know what I'm doing? The jockey clubs will get back to me, not them. Anyway, if the horse mattered to them at all, they certainly wouldn't have let him gallop off when they, um, took care of Phil."

"True but think: directing attention to that horse directs attention to them. He was owned by one of their circle. I don't want there to be any reason Zottigstrauch gives you a second look."

James was on his feet, taking his briefcase, even as Jess got up behind him. She questioned, "So, I shouldn't ask about Phil's brother and the horse when we go to Rockingham on Saturday? That's where Phil told me Val sent him from."

Turning to Jess, James rubbed the bridge of his nose, saying, "At this point, I'd say probably no. Right now, I think I'll go upstairs and catch a cat nap. A chap always thinks better after he'd had a rest."

Jessica compressed her lips, terribly regretting she'd made heavier a burden she'd wanted to alleviate. She offered in weak recompense, "Aren't you hungry? I could fry up some hot dogs. We have plenty of potato salad left over from yesterday. Even just a cup of tea?"

James wanly smiled, touched her face, then said, "Maybe later. Right now, I could really use forty winks. It's been a long day. You go ahead and eat, though. You could use the sustenance, after fighting that wild horse and all. Just work a little harder at keeping that profile lower."

The kiss he gave her was quick. Then before disappearing into the house, James paused and said, "That is a bit queer about the horse."

Damn! She hadn't really expected her letters to complicate James's assignment. Jess gathered up her racing journals and started in for her lonely repast. Well, not entirely lonely. Dusty was always on the prowl for table scraps.

Chapter Twenty-Three

August 1, Thursday afternoon

In a two-piece, short-sleeved linen dress of taupe and white chevron stripes, Jessica Minton reclined on her living room couch, Dusty snuggled against her. Opposite, on the other couch, sat Rose Nyquist, legs tucked under her, in forest-green summer slacks, complimented by a rose blouse. While the *Afternoon Symphony Program* on the radio provided delightful background music, a pot of tea and two half-emptied cups reposed on the coffee table between them. Rose had just finished recounting her misadventures at the beach this morning with her girls, including Kat's excited mistaking a patch of seaweed for jellyfish, Tess's shark sighting turning out to be Watson from Chemistry in a really pointy bathing cap, and David's ending up as a Jim Dandy imitation of a lobster after he'd fallen asleep in the sun.

"Sounds as if you kids encountered everything but the Loch Ness Monster," Jess chuckled.

Rose leaned forward to nab another cookie and asserted with a twinkle, "If Nessie could get a taste of these homemade shortbread cookies, he'd probably slither up from the deep and flop down on your doorstep." A nibble on her dessert and a sip of her tea inspired Rose to finish, "Ah, heavenly."

In spite of yesterday's concerns, Rose's enjoyment made Jessica's eyes sparkle. She good-naturedly replied, "Well, I guess I'd appreciate even a sea monster's seal of approval, but I can't say I'd like what all his slithering and flopping would do to my garden."

Rose chuckled, adding, "Jess, if ending your association with Terry gives you more time to perfect your culinary skills, I'm all for it. When do we get the strawberry and white chocolate scones?"

"Whoa, sister," Jess laughed. "I knew suspending sugar rationing would have a rebound effect, but we may end up bounding up two more dress sizes."

"Never mind," Rose assured Jess. "We'll work it all off riding. Hey, maybe we can get the fellas to take us dancing? Judy Ricardo told me about this swell ballroom in the Saul Hotel in New London. She and her husband love to go there."

"I doubt I could ever keep up to those two. Remember when we saw them do the tango at the Autumn Harvest Dance? I just about ate my heart out!" Jess didn't add that after too many bad parachute landings, her husband did not have the knees for heavy-duty light-fantastic tripping.

"Well, there's still hiking and swimming and riding. In fact, we can invite Lauren and Alicia. That's a natural way to keep Alicia from thinking too much about Terry Clarke." Here Rose paused, putting down her tea to add, "Speaking of whom, I can't believe I almost forgot to tell you. I have some interesting news."

"About Terry?" Jess questioned, mightily tamping down her uneasiness. She hoped that Rose hadn't gotten a scoop by poking her nose into Zottigstrauch's dark business. Yet anything Jess could get on Terry might be useful to James.

"Sure, about Terry. It seems that our chum might be bidding us adieu by the fall. There's a rumor going around that he's being courted by the University of San Juan in Chitzenega."

"Chitzenega?" Jessica couldn't help blurting. "That's out of the blue, isn't it? Why would he go so far away?"

So far away from questions about Jessamyn Crane? Phil Novack? Mysterious packages? *From* Georg Zottigstrauch or *with* him? Whatever the case, both men would certainly appreciate that despite its WWII Good Neighbor Policy, Chitzenega was notorious for resisting U.S. extraditions. Then another thought struck Jess.

"Rose, how does Carolina feel about picking up and shuffling off to San Juan? Won't it affect her career? Does she really strike you as the 'whither thou goest' type?"

"More like the Witch of Endor," Rose remarked. "Anyway, Jess, it was probably Carolina's idea in the first place. To be honest, I'm not even sure how true the rumor is. It could be Terry trying to pressure Nigel into caving to some demand. It certainly would make life sweeter for all concerned if the two of them did move on to greener pastures. At this point, I don't think Nigel would miss Terry, no matter how much of a headache replacing him would be."

Unless Nigel planned on heading that way himself. 'Twere safer not to encourage Rose to consider too closely relations between Nigel and Terry. So, Jess simply concurred, "Mmm."

Seeing Jess decline to pursue the topic, Rose changed the subject: "You still haven't shown me that sweet little number that Liz whipped up for you to wear at tomorrow's reception. Lucky girl, having a fashion-designer sister."

"It has its advantages," Jessica smiled, happy the conversation had moved to safer ground.

"I can't believe that both our guys have to go out of town that day," Rose shook her head. "David to help his kid brother with legal problems and James to see the dentist. He remembered that appointment at the last minute, didn't he?"

"Sure did," Jess confirmed, a bit more emphatically than she'd intended. Fortunately, Rose was more interested in snagging another cookie. That left Jess a moment to wonder if James's appointment was really with a *Dr.* Dick Streeter. James had resumed being a bit cagey about exactly what he was up to, to keep her from worrying about him and, likely, to save her from having any beans to spill inadvertently. He was only successful on the second count.

"Never mind, Rose," Jess added, crushing down her own concern with a light tone. "We girls will just have to go stag—more canapés for us!"

"Too bad," Rose mused. "James is going to miss a good chance to schmooze with the powers that be. It's a big wing-ding. They've even invited prominent citizens and merchants from town."

"James hates to schmooze. Whenever he's had to, he'd come home and grump at me all night," Jessica revealed, amused.

"I can buy that," Rose nodded. "I don't like to schmooze, either. To be frank, I just go for the food. Sometimes, Nigel and I do stand on the sidelines and crack wise to each other about the really pompous types—all very hush-hush."

"Fair enough," Jess approved with a playfully decisive nod. "Anyway, back to the fun part of the whole deal. What are you wearing?"

"What am *I* wearing? Never mind that. You're the one with the couturier outfit. You still haven't really told me anything about the little number your sister cooked up. Describe it."

"I can do better than that," Jess responded, popping to her feet—and provoking a glare from the cat she'd disturbed. "It's hanging in my closet upstairs. How about I show you?"

"Great!" Rose piped up, on her feet. "Lead on, Sacajawea."

"Gee, Rose, I think you're the first person I've known who could pronounce that name."

"Why not? Aren't I a mistress of American letters?" Rose pronounced expansively, adding, "Just don't ask me to spell it."

"Fair enough," Jess agreed. "But sit down and enjoy the tea and treats. No sense in our both clomping upstairs."

"Jessica Minton Crawford," Rose sniffed. "I am as graceful as a swan. I do not clomp—leastwise when I'm wearing loafers."

"I'll keep that in mind. Now sit back and keep Dusty company. She had an exhausting day playing with a crumpled cellophane cigarette wrapper, which we all know *couldn't* belong to James Crawford, who *definitely* no longer smokes."

"Uh, huh," Rose returned. "I'm staying out of that one, pal. You just trot upstairs and get that dress."

Jess winked at her friend and was off up the stairs. When she reached her bedroom doorway, Dusty shot past her inside.

Entering, Jess found the grey tabby already on the bed, watching to see where her human went next—which was to the walk-in closet next to the door. Jess pulled the dangling chain on the closet light, picking out the garment bags holding the two outfits her sister had sent, then unzipping them to see which encased the dress she wanted. But, had she imagined it, or was she hearing the front door, now voices, downstairs? One male? Oh, James had probably taken a break from preparing his classes and wandered out of his den to visit with Rose. Except—the tones had grown agitated.

Quickly, Jessica exited the closet, garment bag in hand. Dusty was standing at attention, her tiger-striped tail abruptly tacking back and forth. *Rose and James wouldn't have some kind of beef going.* Now it was quiet.

There was a light step on the stairs, and Rose was suddenly in the doorway, urging softly but no less urgently, "Jessica, you've got to get downstairs, *pronto.*"

Disturbed, Jessica questioned, "Rose, what's wrong? It's not James . . . ?"

"James nothing–it's Carolina Brent Clarke and that guy from the antique store. I forget his name . . ."

"Nicholas Spenser," Jessica supplied, fighting to keep disquiet from her voice.

"Right, that's it. Wait, why do you look so shaky?"

"Me, no, nothing, never mind," Jess insisted, fighting against the realization of one of her worst fears. She had the presence of mind to distract Rose with questions that she, herself, actually needed answered, "What are they doing here? Does James know?"

"I don't know about James," Rose responded. "I just know that when I answered the front door, they, well Carolina, barged right in. That Spenser guy was kind of in tow. Anyway, she was going on about showing him some piece of Jessamyn's that she *knew* was here. I tried to slow them down, but you know her. Short of clobberin' her, there was no way to stop her. She won't listen to me, but it is *your* house. You've got to get down there and put a bit in her teeth or she'd turn everything upside down."

"Say no more," Jess replied, dropping the garment bag on the bed. Maybe she'd been nervous before but now she was mad. "C'mon, let's nix this invasion right now." Jessica was almost out of the room, when she turned back to Dusty and warned, "And as for you, Mistress Furry Face, no turning my dress into your latest daybed."

Jess didn't tell Rose that as angry as she was at this rude invasion, she was also wrapped in a white-hot sheet of fear at the possibly Georg Zottigstrauch was in her house. At least James hadn't been drawn out of his study and into the fray.

However, all Jess's determination was daunted when she rounded the corner of the stairs and froze, almost causing Rose to bump into her.

Carolina and Nicholas Spenser were at the radio console next to the fireplace, handling the odd little sculpture with the compartment hiding Nigel Cross's clip. What if they discovered she had the clip? That would open up a can of too many worms to enumerate. Might they even take the clip and use it against her and James somehow?

But they didn't even seem to notice her, so intently were the two examining the piece, their backs to her. Or maybe they thought noticing her, in her own home, was beneath them. Just as Phil and Jessamyn had been beneath their concern? That thought got to Jess. She demanded, "What in Sam Hill do you two think you're doing with my sculpture? Put that down this minute!"

Unfortunately, Jessica's challenge broke into Carolina and Spenser's examination so abruptly that the woman fumbled her black-gloved grip; and, if not for the dexterous reflexes of Nicholas Spenser, the piece might have smashed on the hearth stone. He tucked it smoothly under his arm, against his chest, and smiled the smile of innocence to say, "Mrs. Crawford, you startled us. I'm sure that wasn't your intention. Mrs. Brent Clarke was just showing me this piece of Jessamyn Crane's—one of her rare sculptures. So, you see you do have a piece by her, after all. You didn't even know it."

"Of course, she has one, Nicholas, dear. I told you there would be at least one or two pieces here. I have all Jessamyn's records in my department," Carolina beamed through emerald eyes, beneath the dip of her black, straw-lacquer picture hat. Then, one hand on her alligator shoulder bag, Carolina turned to Jess and Rose, her curvaceous form highlighted by the fit of her turquoise linen two-piece dress. The red-haired woman switched on the charm to chide affably, "Goodness, girl, you could have scared a cat out of nine lives. Is that any way to treat your guests?"

Jess felt the subtle pressure of Rose's grip on her bare arm and bit back any comment on Carolina's resemblance to a cat or its ways, let alone to another household pet, usually of the female canine variety. More frustrating, though, was not knowing if the two had discovered or removed the clip. Nevertheless, Jess disciplined herself to point out calmly, "Guests are usually invited and don't paw their hostess's belongings, Carolina."

Nicholas Spenser went suddenly confused, looking at Carolina, saying with discomfort, "Carolina, you told me there was no problem coming here, that Mrs. Crawford wouldn't mind . . ."

"Of course, there's no problem," Carolina insisted smoothly, imparting Jessica a barely detectable icy glance. "I can't imagine Jessica would want to suppress art . . ."

"I'm not talking about suppressing art," Jessica set things straight. "I'm talking about someone marching into my home, uninvited, and taking my property." She extended a hand and continued, "Which I would like back, if you don't mind, Mr. Spenser."

Maybe going on the offensive was taking a risk, but *wouldn't* any normal person in her shoes be offended? Wouldn't it look odd, if she didn't give them at least *some* what-for?

Nicholas Spenser surprised Jess by turning a questioning look on Carolina, asking *her* for direction. When Carolina just tightened her Max-Factored lips, he started to hand over the ugly little sculpture, apologizing, "Of course, Mrs. Craw . . ."

Carolina deftly intercepted, taking the piece into her own hands and smiling, if not triumphantly, then pretty darn close to it, yet insisting sweetly, "You'll do no such thing, Mr. Spenser. This is not hers. It either belongs to the estate of Jessamyn Crane or the college."

"Not at all," Jess countered, swiftly taking advantage of Carolina's focus on Spenser to snatch the sculpture out of the other woman's hands. "You see, I purchased several items outright, including this little beauty." As Carolina started to argue, Jess pleasantly inquired, "Would either of you like to see the receipt?"

Carolina opened her mouth, white teeth gleaming against creamy crimson lipstick, then shut it in defeat. Nicholas Spenser eyed Carolina with dissatisfaction before stating coldly, "Mrs. Clarke, I'm highly disappointed in you. This is not the situation you led me to expect."

Carolina gave the ladylike equivalent of a snort and walked away, toward the couches. Rose also walked off a little ways, but only to hide a guffaw at the Dragon Lady's comeuppance.

Jessica, however, was in no laughing mood. It killed her to have the statue in her hand but not be free to check on the tie clip. To top it all off, she was on edge trying to figure out what the game was. This

Spenser character might merely be an officious antiques dealer. He certainly wasn't acting like a Nazi mastermind. Of course, if he were a mastermind, he wouldn't be much of one if he acted like one. Still, if he were Georg Zottigstrauch, this was a pretty darned nervy move, but a good way to check how much she or James might know, to get a feel for them as opponents. And she couldn't believe that Carolina had so much free time on her hands, what with acting glamorous minion to said mastermind, that she could go traipsing around trying to score a cut on an art broker's deal. So, that let Nigel Cross off the hook, she smiled to herself.

Or did it? Maybe Nigel was using the two of them to divert suspicion from himself. If he wanted the tie clip connecting him to secret meetings in Joseph's Cove, or to know if she had it, or even this sculpture itself, wouldn't it be clever to send Spencer with Carolina to decoy suspicion away from himself? Still, how would Nigel know she had his clip? Why would it matter that she did? Or was he just trying to play it safe, never really trusting that she hadn't run across something incriminating at the derelict? Whatever the case, she had to play this game just right—and it wouldn't hurt to keep James out of the picture right now, whether Georg Zottigstrauch was testing them by proxy or in person.

"Mrs. Crawford?"

Oops! Spenser was talking to her and here she was woolgathering. Sure, she was playing it real cagey.

"Mrs. Crawford, do accept my apologies," Spenser offered, seeing he had her attention. "You've been upset by our intrusion. I assure you that I would never have been so bold had I not been led to believe that my presence was acceptable."

What a gracious, sincere sort he appeared. He almost had her. Jess clutched the statue a tad tighter and was disturbed to see Nicholas Spenser silently note her reaction. Unless she cooled down, she'd practically assure her two guests that she had something to hide.

"It's all right," Jessica allowed. A hard glance at Carolina. "Clearly, you were ill-advised. I guess everyone is jumpy with all these murders . . ."

"Murders?" Carolina repeated curiously. "Aside from my friend, who else was murdered?"

Jessica inwardly groaned at that royal gaffe. What had she been thinking? She had presence of mind enough to conclude that honesty, sort of, might be her best save.

"What do you think happened to Phil Novack, Sailor?" Jess began. "He's been gone how long with no trace? Everyone saw how much he loved that horse. It's clear that he wouldn't leave him behind unless there was some funny business."

"Sounds like foul play to *me*," Rose agreed, sidling over to her friend.

"Logical," Nicholas Spenser agreed. "Unpleasant but logical. Or one might even suspect that Novack had had a hand in Miss Crane's demise and couldn't take the pressure of her discovery. Perhaps he was a suicide."

Jessica noted that Carolina was strangely silent on all this off-hand speculation about her "dear friend's" death. Then again, if your "friend" were more intimate with your husband than with you, you might not be too heartbroken at her demise. Who was to say that you, yourself, hadn't taken a hand in it?

Rose ended the pause with, "To tell the truth, I don't think Sailor was the killer type. Furthermore, I'm getting fed up with people treating veterans as if having battle fatigue is the same as being crazy."

"Certainly, you are correct," Nicholas Spenser assured Rose, quickly, embarrassed.

"If anyone in this room should know about Sailor, it's Jessica," purred Carolina. "Isn't that right, dear? People have seen the two of you chatting away, thick as thieves. And that horse made a bee line for your door, I hear. What do you think happened to him, Sailor, I mean, Jessica? Being so chummy with him, you must have picked up on his being involved in some kind of funny business. Just think, this is your golden opportunity to set the world straight, clear his name."

Jess thought, *Jeesh, does she think I just fell off a turnip truck? Nice try with the flattery and even playing on my loyalty, but I'm not buying.* Jess only said, "Sorry to let you down, Carolina. I only talked with him a few times, and I'm nobody's mother confessor. We just talked about horses. No deep, dark secrets, not even Blackie's. As for the horse running to me in a crisis, well, he does like his carrot and apple treats. Although I will admit that horses are supposed to be good judges of character."

The reply was bright and easy, but Jess knew from the glint in Carolina's eyes that she was remembering her unceremonious recent retreat from the big horse. Jess had a momentary twinge that she might have overplayed her hand but decided her dig looked perfectly natural considering Carolina's behavior since barging in.

Nicholas Spenser spoke now, seeming to confirm Jessica's assessment: "Ah, well, it's not our place to speculate. I'm only interested in Jessamyn Crane's art. If nothing is available, then that's that—although I'm sure I can broker a nice price for you, Mrs. Crawford, should you change your mind."

Jessica shook her head.

"You're sure?" Nicholas took one last stab, his tone pleasant enough.

"Yes. I like it," she answered simply.

Spenser nodded, and Jess wished she could read his eyes. Disappointment? Displeasure? Anger? No, they were opaque to her. He only stated, "That said, Mrs. Crawford, please accept my apologies, again, for this misunderstanding. This is not how I do business." He sent Carolina a piercing look that Jess (and everyone in the room) had no trouble reading. Carolina tightened those full coral lips and turned away, but she'd clearly gotten the message. Spenser finished, "If you ever change your mind, you have my card. You can contact me *directly*, Mrs. Crawford. Other than that, all I can say is, again, I do apologize."

They were heading for the door, making Jessica so happy she could almost sing—not just to get rid of the two but to have a chance to sneak a peek at the statue's compartment and check on the tie clip. Distracting Rose shouldn't be that hard. Spenser's hand had the door open, he stepped back to allow Carolina to precede him. That's when . . ..

"Hello, guests here?"

The study door had opened, and Jessica started as James sauntered in.

What the heck? Mr. James Crawford, what do you have in mind?

However, Jess had no time to puzzle further over what her husband had up his sleeve. Carolina and Nicholas Spenser turned their attention directly to him, eyes speculative. Carolina took the lead with: "Oh, hello, James. I wondered why we hadn't seen you. We came to convince your wife to part with the interesting sculpture she's holding. We'd give her a good price, but she just can't be persuaded."

James glanced at the piece and remarked, "*That*? It's a bit on the homely side, isn't it? I don't understand her attraction to it."

Hmm, Jess pondered. *I guess if these two are that interested in the statue, my smart guy husband doesn't want to antagonize them or for us to look too attached to that thing–but I did almost have them out the door, and did he forget that Nigel's clip is in there?*

Rose stepped in with, "Jessica *likes* homely things. Oh, nothing personal, James."

"Thank you, Rose–I think," he returned. He turned back to Spenser and said, "You may not remember me, but I was in your shop before. Bought someone a birthday present, which I think we can all keep confidential until January."

Jess relaxed a notch as James made nice with their guests, reinforcing his initial appearance to Spenser as nothing more than an innocent husband with nothing more on his mind than finding the perfect present for his wife.

It seemed to have worked, for Nicholas Spenser replied. "Yes, quite. You'll be happy to know I haven't given away the identity of the gift to your charming wife, Mr. Crawford. And I do so regret we had a little misunderstanding about this piece by Jessamyn Crane."

"That sculpture?" James asked, nodding at the piece. "I thought she was a painter. Isn't it Carolina who creates plastic art?"

"That's what makes this work so special, James," Carolina fairly beamed. "Jessamyn rarely did sculpture, and Nicholas knows that a rarity like this will command quite a sum. You or I couldn't get the best price for it, but Nicholas has exactly the right expertise and connections. If you put yourself in his hands, you and your wife might win a lovely little nest egg."

"Why, Carolina," Rose innocently observed, "It's so nice of you to help them with no chance of remuneration for yourself. Or, Mr. Spenser, is there some kind of 'finder's fee' that might make its way into Carolina's snappy little alligator bag?"

"Certainly, I would be grateful to Mrs. Brent Clarke. Nevertheless, I really don't see any need to discuss financial details if there is not going to be any sale. Is there, Mrs. Crawford?"

Spenser and Carolina had played their parts exactly like two people hoping to make a killing on a piece of art. Or maybe Spenser wasn't playing. Again, it occurred to Jessica that Nigel could be using him as a stalking horse, with Carolina carrying out the hunt from here. Despite these battling conjectures, Jess merely shook her head and replied, "I like my homely little number."

"You do mean the statue?" James queried.

Jessica nodded, smiling, but her mind still raced. With one suspect right here, she wished James would use his wiles to subtly grill the guy or at least trip him up. Still, it wouldn't be very safe for her and Rose if he got his enemies to tip their hands in front of them.

Spenser wrapped up the visit with, "Come along, Carolina. Let's leave these good people alone. There's that sherry you promised me."

James good-naturedly saw the two to the door. *Ah, great,* Jess thought as Rose followed James in seeing the two off. *Now I can peek inside the statue's compartment before Rose turns around and sees me.* Holding the little statue down, she anxiously pulled open the compartment. It stuck a little and her heart plummeted when she couldn't see the clip in the partially opened drawer.

"Say, what're you doing there?"

Rose's affable query startled Jess into fumbling the statue, nearly dropping it, saving it, but still spilling the tie clip onto the floor. Right at the feet of her friend, who had just descended to join her. Well, at least Carolina and Nicholas Spenser hadn't snatched it, and maybe Rose wouldn't notice . . ..

"What's this?" Rose bent and retrieved the clip. "N.B.C. Say, I've seen this thing before. It's Nigel's. He lost it last spring. He mentioned to me that he was looking for it everywhere . . . Wait, Jess, what are *you* doing with Nigel's clip? Why did you have it in the compartment as if you were . . . You were! You were hiding his clip. What the hey?!"

Sinking onto the couch behind her, all Jess could manage was the less-than-articulate, "I, I, I . . ."

How could she outright lie to her friend? But how much could she admit to her? Jess didn't know for certain that this clip connected Nigel to Jessamyn's murder or James's case. But she couldn't be certain it didn't, either. Her glance went past Rose to James for help. He didn't roll his eyes, but she could see it took a gargantuan effort not to.

"Jess?" Rose persisted, not accusing, exactly, but definitely confused.

The Lone Ranger did ride in after all, with a mustache and a British accent.

"Rose," came James's voice as he joined them, standing beside her, "we thought it might be Nigel's, but we weren't sure." In answer to the question Rose was starting to form, James went on, "We didn't turn it over to him or ask him about it because we found it under circumstances we thought best-kept mum, to save Nigel embarrassment."

"Oh," said Rose, raising her head knowingly, "You must have found it here. You guys figured out there had been something between him and Jessamyn, and you didn't want to put him on the spot."

Jessica shot James a glance, then questioned, "There *was* something between the two of them? But what about Terry? I thought she was *his* girl? You mean to say she was two-timing a two-timer?"

"No, no," Rose waved her hands as if trying to erase part of what she'd said. "I'm not exactly sure what the story was. I think something started with Nigel but never went very far. Then Terry entered the picture, and she changed her mind about Nigel. Unfortunately for Nigel, he didn't about her."

"Didn't you once suggest they barely knew each other," Jess pointed out, puzzled.

"Sorry, kid. It seemed the right thing at the time. You didn't really need to know, so . . ."

"It was none of my business," Jess concluded.

"That's about the size of it," Rose agreed. She paused before adding, "but if this little item showed up here in April, that was long after Terry became her choice. That's funny."

"Is it?" James countered casually. "Could Nigel have been here without something funny being afoot?"

"Well, she did have one or two small faculty get-togethers. Come to think of it, I might have seen Nigel here then," recalled Rose, bouncing the clip in her palm. "You don't think I need to mention this to the police investigating the murder?"

"Do you want to?" James responded, playing on Rose's reluctance to put Nigel on the spot. "*Does* that clip actually indicate something significant about what happened to Crane?"

"No," Rose responded decisively. She gave the clip in her hand a sour look, then put it down solidly on the coffee table.

Jess managed not to heave a sigh of relief. Still, she hesitated to pick up the clip and put it back where she'd hidden it. She couldn't put her finger on why, exactly.

Rose was sitting down, speaking her thoughts aloud, "Real bad luck, wasn't it, those two pawing the place where you'd hidden the clip?" She looked uneasily from Jessica to James and questioned, "Holy mackerel, do you think they saw it when Jess and I were upstairs? Is that the real reason Carolina was so interested in that piece of junk?"

"What makes you even think that Carolina was interested?" James questioned.

Rose shrugged, "I, I don't know, exactly. Well, I do know that you can't trust anything she does. Maybe she'd like to blackmail Nigel; it doesn't have to connect with the murder. He's a proud guy. He wouldn't want his weakness for Jessamyn exposed, especially to have anyone make insinuations there was more going on than there was. She might use that to leverage some favorable deal for her husband. Or maybe she'd just like a little extra lettuce. I don't know. There's just something funny about this little visit today. Don't you think so, Jess?"

With tremendous effort Jessica managed to remain fairly circumspect, only saying, "Eleanor Roosevelt she's not. I never liked that woman. Carolina, not Eleanor. Every time I've seen her, she's tried to pick a fight with me. Maybe this was just one more attempt to get my goat."

Rose allowed, "I guess you're right. She always seems to be calculating new ways to put herself ahead or tear someone else down. She couldn't care less about whom she crushes."

"Sounds as if she must lead her husband a merry chase. Poor chap couldn't be the king of his own castle with her around," James surmised.

Jess wasn't exactly sure where James was going. Perhaps trying to see if Rose knew anything valuable, without giving away anything that might put her in Dutch?

Rose snorted, "Terry? She leads that boy around by the nose. She led him out here, then down to Washington D.C. during the war, then back up here again. You can bet your bottom dollar it's her idea to head for Chitzenega and start anew in the tropics."

"Chitzenega, eh?" James inquired, sitting on the arm of Rose's couch. "Where did you hear this? Good Lord, what does Nigel say?"

Rose explained, "As I told Jess earlier, it floated to me down the grapevine. Now that I think of it, I might have heard it from our secretary, Tricia. How she found out . . . hey, is there anything secretaries don't know?"

"They usually know more than any of us," James concurred dryly, "even the Chair—speaking of whom, what does Nigel say about all this?"

Rose gave James a knowing look and answered, "It's not the sort of thing I want to discuss with him. You never know where a rumor is going to lead you or when it could send someone on the warpath after you, whether it's true or not! I don't know; maybe I shouldn't even have said anything today."

"I think you can trust Jessica and me not to blab anything confidential," James smiled. Jess wished she didn't know how much more those words meant than Rose realized. Her husband continued, "But you're smart to keep your own counsel." He paused to lean forward and snag himself a cookie before continuing, "Don't get caught in the crossfire of an academic power play. I've learned the wisdom of that on both sides of the Atlantic. As for Nigel, I'll wager that he not only already knows; but that if you did say anything, he might see you as a bit of a nosey Parker. Sharp as he is, if the pressure's on, he might not be able to distinguish the bearer of bad news from the bad news. Say the wrong thing at the wrong time and, next you know, you've got yourself in the thick of a nice mess."

Rose sighed and apologized, "Gee, James, I really thought this position would be a swell place for you to relax, to do what you love. Instead, we've got more scandal, intrigue, and murder than *The Whistler*, *Suspense*, and Jessica's program combined!"

"At least you don't have Horlas," Jessica comforted her friend.

"Or zuvembies," James added.

"That makes me feel better, sort of," Rose sighed. "Okay, it's getting late, kids. I'd better go home so I can get some of my writing done before the girls come back from town. Those matinees don't buy you unlimited time."

Jess and James both walked Rose to the door. Pausing there, Rose told her friends, "Thanks for an entertaining afternoon."

"That's one way to look at it," Jessica dryly concluded.

James smiled before saying, "Say hello to David and the two glamour queens of Margaret Point for us."

"Will do," Rose grinned at James. She turned to her girlfriend to say, "I'll call for you about 2:00 tomorrow. Alreet?"

"You're on the beam, man," Jess jived back.

"Wouldn't it be 'on the beam, kitten'?" James joined in with a straight face.

"Cats, kittens; we're all hep here," Rose kidded. "Especially that slick chick who just pounced on your jumped-up couch."

Dusty blinked approvingly at Rose before she left.

Jessica closed the door carefully behind her friend, taking time to think about how she could approach James. Finally, she turned and, opting for humor, put to her husband, "Well, how 'bout that mess?"

"How about it," he returned. "But let's skip the jive and switch to English. I feel as if I'm trapped in a Cab Calloway song."

"Fine," Jess agreed. "What do you think that visit from Carolina and Spenser was all about?"

James considered for a moment, then looked down at the set-up on the coffee table and pointed out, "A chap thinks better with a little something on his stomach. I see some cookies, but any more tea?"

"Tea and cookies?" Jess folded her arms skeptically. "I suppose when you were in occupied France, you and the *maquis* never plotted to outfox the Nazis unless you had your tea and cookies, first."

"Darling, that was France—we waited for the wine, cheese, and bread." He ignored the fisheye Jess gave him, continuing, "So, I'll just nip into the kitchen for a cup and be back in a jiffy. Then you and I can have a pow-wow."

Jessica started to protest, but James was already on his way. She couldn't be mad, though. If James wasn't brooding, even had a sense of humor about things, that certainly was a good sign. Jess went to the couch and sat next to Dusty, scratching her friend's neck while reflecting. Maybe James was planning to pull a rabbit out of his hat even now in the kitchen. She knew him well enough to realize that the brief retreat was his way of taking time to think. He was not one to toss off half-baked ideas, so it behooved her to be patient until he could present her with a fully baked one. Too bad the waiting killed her.

313

James returned, a cup but no saucer in hand. She motioned him to give her his cup so she could pour. He didn't speak, yet; he didn't sit, either. His restlessness told Jess he had a lot to get across but was working to get it all just right.

After taking his cup, James nodded thanks, and, as he fixed the tea to his liking, finally began, "If that was Georg Zottigstrauch, it was a bit of a bold move, coming right into our house."

"So, you think Nicholas Spenser, not Nigel, is the one you're after?" Jess posited, unable to escape a shudder that he *had* been on her home turf.

"Unless Nigel sent Carolina in to check up on us. He could have been using Spenser as cover, even a distraction."

Jessica didn't like to admit that she'd had a similar thought, but she voiced her larger concern, "Should we be afraid? I mean, they were in our *house*. They see how we live. They were handling that plug-ugly thing. Wait, do you think *it's* the package? No, that can't be right. I've had it since we came here; it wasn't with Phil. It couldn't be in two places at the same time. I just can't figure this, James. Why were they snooping around that thing if it's *not* important? Why were they *here*?"

"To check us out," James responded quietly. Jessica could see he was watching her to see if she could take the implications of such suspicions about the two of them.

So, she tamped down the anxiety threatening to crumple her from within and questioned, "They're wise to you? They know that you are after Zottigstrauch, is that what you're trying to tell me?"

"That's one possibility," James answered carefully. "I won't deny that, but it might not be quite that bad."

"What do you mean?" Jessica asked, hopefully, at first, then more skeptically, "What other reason could they have for checking us out?"

James had taken a sip of his tea while she spoke. He gave her a twisted smile, then answered, "I suspect the main reason there's any curiosity about us is not that Zottigstrauch is certain about us but because we stumbled across two of their murders. If you look at the circumstances, as unexpected as our ending up in that position is, there's nothing to indicate we were *trying* to uncover them. We didn't go looking for a dead woman on the beach; we didn't follow Phil around. You were just bringing back his horse. I suspect they only want to make sure that we haven't inadvertently stumbled across any information that could incriminate them."

Jessica leaned back into the couch, rubbing the back of Dusty's head, letting James's words sink in. Finally, she conjectured, "So, you're saying that we have nothing to worry about?"

James smiled wanly and corrected her, "I'm not about to go that far."

"Oh, *such* a relief."

James put down his cup and sat next to Jess. Putting an arm around her, he squeezed her shoulder before saying, "Look, love, you didn't give anything away. You were a bit cross with two people barging into your home and pawing your things. Perfectly natural. They'd probably have wondered if you had something to hide if you hadn't shown a bit of temper under those circumstances. You did all right."

Jessica nodded, smiling slightly. James's last statement prompted her to ask, "So, I suppose that you didn't try to trip them up when you had the chance because you wanted them to underestimate you, to think you were just an oblivious, obtuse loving husband with nothing to hide?"

James crooked the corner of his mouth and answered, "Yes, that's about it, although I think I would have gone for 'harmless' and 'innocent' rather than 'oblivious.'"

"Don't forget 'obtuse,'" Jess added, feeling a little, but not much, better.

James let that ride and continued, "I don't mind telling you that it was a trial not to try to draw out Spenser or Carolina. But I wasn't about to chance arousing his suspicion, especially with you and Rose there. No, my best bet is to let him think he's in the clear, so he gets cocky, cockier than this little visit. He may be clever but sometimes ego will out."

"Again, that sounds as if you think Nicholas Spenser is your man," Jessica conjectured. "I mean, he was the guy you saw today."

"I also saw Carolina, and, as I said earlier, she could be using Spenser as a distraction and reporting back to Nigel. I'm sorry, Jess, I still can't rule out Nigel."

"But if Nigel is Zottigstrauch, that means he killed Jessamyn or had her killed," Jessica argued. "Rose seemed to think he was in love with her. Would he do that? Although, I suppose if he murdered his wife and child . . ."

"The scenario would make a handy smokescreen for his actual personality, too," James pointed out.

Looking down, all Jess could say was, "What a God-awful mess!"

James drew her closer, putting her head on his shoulder, putting his head on hers, before saying, "I could bloody well kill Dick Streeter for dragging us into this. It wasn't supposed to be like this. It wasn't supposed to involve you."

Jess rubbed James's arm and said, "It's not me. It's you. The war should be over for you. Other guys are allowed to try to forget, to move on, but not you. They never let you go. I just don't know what I can do to help you, to . . . I don't know, to give you a better life."

"You do plenty," he said gruffly into her hair, gruffer with himself than anyone. "I'm just not done yet. That's all there is to it. But this should be the last one. I promise. I'll find a way to make it the last one. It's just that it's a big one."

"I know, I know," Jess replied, falling silent, thinking, resolving, at last saying, "Only about a week now. That's all."

"Eh?"

"About a week now," Jess repeated, moving to face James. "Last week Terry said the package would move out in two weeks. That leaves you one week to break the case, to positively identify Georg Zottigstrauch and find out what he's up to."

James smiled wanly and agreed, "Right you are. And Dick's been holding my feet to the fire. So, I don't think it would hurt, at all, to bring him that ugly little work of art so his boys can go over it when I go into the city tomorrow."

"To see your dentist."

"Exactly. And you might want to skip that college affair and go into town as well. Pop in on Lois. Get together with Iris."

"Stay off Zottigstrauch's radar, not be alone here?" Jess added to his list of activities.

James's expression could have given Robert Mitchum a run for his money in the wryness department before he said, "I don't expect anyone is wise to you, Jessica. Nevertheless, I don't like leaving you alone, only to be on the safe side."

"Well, you've really nothing to worry about in terms of me being alone tomorrow," Jess assured her husband. "Rose is coming to get me; we'll be at the reception all day, surrounded by tons of other people–academics, administrators, some students, Rotarians . . ."

"Rotarians?"

"You know, local business folk. Chamber of Commerce types."

"Like Nicholas Spenser?"

"Maybe. But, as I said, Rose and I will be together. I could even see if she'll stay with me until you get back, or I could stay with her. Good enough?"

James's skeptical expression was not the answer she was looking for, so Jessica pressed, "You have to do what you have to do, and I have to do what I have to do. My solemn duty is to drink tea, eat cucumber sandwiches, and look gorgeous–and if I *should* happen to overhear anything interesting . . ."

James interrupted, quietly but with an intensity that knocked the friskiness right out of Jessica, "Don't draw *any* excess attention to yourself, particularly from Nigel, Terry, Carolina, or Nicholas Spenser. And I'm going to be back by 5:00, I promise you. On your end, promise me not to take any chances, Jessica."

"Don't worry!" Jess assured James, anxious to quell his worry. "I promise the only attention I'll draw will be to Elizabeth's knock-out creation. Satisfied?"

James regarded her thoughtfully, saying at last, "No. I'll only be satisfied when we've put this whole rotten case behind us."

"Me, too," Jessica agreed. Attempting to lighten the mood, she mused, "Hmm, I especially hope it isn't Nigel, for your sake."

"My sake?" James raised an eyebrow.

"Yup. I don't imagine he'd be in much of a mood to hire someone who broke his cover, destroyed his nefarious plot to rule the world, and then turned him over to the FBI."

"Most likely not," James remarked. "Though I can't imagine he'd be overly pleased if he were an innocent man who discovered I had been investigating him with the same goals in mind. And by the bye, I'd rather you didn't talk up our going to Rockingham Park. It would be better if no one got it into his head we could check up on Phil's background–just to be on the safe side."

Jess patted James's hand and got up, saying, "You got it, Ace. So, let's see. This tea must be colder than a sneer from George Sanders. How about I make you a fresh pot?"

James nodded, even smiled a bit, but Jess could see his eyes were weighted with care. He probably wanted something a lot stronger than Darjeeling. It was up to her, then, to do the stiff-upper-lip bit and hide from him the fear shredding away at her attempts to cheer him.

Chapter Twenty-Four

August 2, Friday

Jessica Minton sat at her vanity between the bedroom's dormer windows, a satiny, dressing gown over her frock while she put on her make-up. A bit of mascara on her lashes, a touch of pancake on her cheeks, a dash of deep pink to her lips. Then, on went the coil of gold necklace, followed by the clasp of matching earrings. Now, she surveyed her handiwork.

Not bad! No one would suspect all the worries and fears that had been nipping maliciously at her. Thank goodness she'd had the opportunity to take Blackie out for a couple of rides over the past week; so, she and the horse had blown off some steam together.

But James had no such outlet, had he? Jess brushed her hair for the 100th time, maybe a bit more vigorously than she ought, working off frustration at feeling so useless to the guy she loved. Useless? Even a liability?

A glance at her watch, and Jess muttered to no one in particular, well perhaps to Dusty on the bed, "I have got to quit crabbing and finish getting dressed. Rose'll be here any minute, and I still haven't fed you, Dusty."

One feline eye peeked through the slit of nictating membrane at the word "fed."

Determined not to let doubts conquer her, Jessica sprang up, undoing her robe to reveal a gorgeous white silk dress, fitted in the bodice, with a graceful A-line skirt that swirled as she moved and flatteringly shaped itself to her when she stood still. The square neckline revealed its wearer's collarbones without dipping too low. What Jess thought really gave it elegant flair was a pattern on the bodice of abstract shapes, almost like an archangel by Picasso, in unexpectedly complementary soft liquid blue, green, and pink, bordered by silver. *A girl couldn't feel too low in a dress like this!* Jess had to hand it to Liz for designing a frock that could take the edge off trying to catch Nazis without getting eighty-sixed.

"Okay, Dusty," Jess promised. "Let's go get you some chow." Dusty flipped over on her stomach, then was on her feet. Jess laughed, "I knew that would get you up!"

A few minutes later, Jessica was spooning cat food into Dusty's dish, already feeling much more like herself. She was going to have a great afternoon with her pal Rose Nyquist. All she had to do was drink tea, make small talk, chuckle at Rose's *sotto voce* commentary on some of the more pompous sorts, and look beautiful–for Liz's sake. Fortunately, whatever shortages were still in place, Wanda Angelovic always managed to ensure that her campus ate well. *Uh oh, I better not eat too well. Liz will kill me if I burst these seams!*

The knock on the front door brought Jess back to reality.

"Okay, Dusty, that's Rose. I'm off. Don't exhaust yourself figuring out where to sleep," Jess called, rushing from the kitchen to get the door. Dusty barely cocked an ear, intent on doing justice to her lunch.

Jessica opened the front door on her friend Rose with, "Right on time! And don't you look snazzy!"

Indeed, Rose Nyquist did cut a snazzy figure in a cap-sleeved white dress with red and light blue chevrons over the bust and a matching blue belt. Her light brown hair was brushed gently off her face with glittery combs and ensconced in a red snood.

"What really brings it all together are those spiffy red tennis shoes," Jessica winked. "C'mon in."

Rose agreed, "Oh sure. They're not quite as nifty as those lavender mules of yours, but they'll do."

"Wise guy! Let me just kick off these things and step into *my* tennis shoes. I have a bag to carry my sandals, like you. Why don't we consolidate them, then change in James's office and stash everything there? I like walking, but not up that road in sling backs."

"Say," Rose requested, "would you mind putting my camera in there, too?"

"Camera?" Jess echoed as Rose took out her brownie. "What are you? Jimmy Olsen?"

"Something like that. Nigel wants me to take some shots of people from our department at the tea. I guess he thought we could get more notice, and maybe better funding, if we were more prominent in the brochures or alumni newsletters."

"Really?" Jess queried, checking to make sure she'd put all the necessaries in her clutch. "I'd never have taken Nigel for a publicity hound. Are things so bad that you need to drum up interest that way?"

"I wouldn't say bad, Jess, but every little bit helps. It always pays to keep a high profile if you're competing for funding. Anyway, I enjoy it. Nigel knows I'm pretty handy with a camera."

Jessica grinned, "Maybe he's hoping you'll get a shot that someone might pay to hush up."

"Really? Like a trustee with his finger up his nose?"

"Sure," Jess laughed, feeling how delicious it was to be able to kid about Nigel Cross's intentions. And then the two friends were off.

The afternoon for bringing alumni, local community leaders, faculty, and students together had been set up on the terrace, as well as part of the adjacent lawn behind Cameron House. The view looking out into the sparkling-blue Long Island Sound was downright artistic between the skimming pleasure craft and dashing wisps of clouds. Tables along the chateau-like building were set up with silver tea urns, elegant china, lovely silver, and three-tiered servers wherein resided sweets and savories. Guests circulated about the terrace. Even the students who were allowed to attend had dolled themselves up a bit, while men who might have preferred comestibles a bit more red-blooded made small talk or connections. Tables, some with umbrellas in the school's colors, were set up on either side of the balustrade bordering the terrace.

At one of those tables, *sans* umbrella, Jessica and Rose had retired after an hour of schmoozing. Jess had just extracted sunglasses from her purse to comfortably regard the parade of higher education and business before her.

As Jessica put on her sunglasses, Rose teased, "Oh, now you want to go incognito?"

"Ha!" Jess returned. "No, I'm just trying to keep from going blind in this glare. And squinting does create crow's feet, you know."

"Oh, what are you worried about?" Rose chuckled. "You work in radio!"

Jess tipped down her glasses to fix her friend with a baleful look, then turned her eyes back to the show of folk before her, musing, "They do say that this television is the coming thing."

"Television?" Rose scoffed. "Who can afford it? Besides, I think movies and radio have the entertainment front all sown up. People don't change that fast."

"Mmm," Jess replied, taking a sip of tea. "Isn't that what the monks said about the printing press?"

"Monks are more Medieval, the printing press is more Renaissance, oh Shakespeare scholar," Rose kidded. She switched subjects with, "So, what do you think of this shindig? Not bad, huh? They went all out: three kinds of tea, real clotted cream, and four types of scones. How about those curried chicken-and-raisin tea sandwiches? Yum!"

"I'll say! And best of all . . ."

"No salmon and sardine sandwiches!" both chums asserted in unison.

"Seriously, though, Rose," Jess shifted the topic, "I really enjoyed meeting some of your alums. How about that woman, class of '29, who's now mayor of a small New Hampshire town? She was quite a pistol."

"Oh, you only like her 'cause she's a fan of your program," Rose teased.

"It doesn't hurt that she has good taste," Jessica returned. "Actually, though, what really gave me a kick was her comment that the best guidance she got for navigating the minefields of politics was reading *Richard III*."

"I've always maintained that taking the literature course is the best training for life," Rose asserted airily. "Although I think American lit might be a better guide."

Jessica shrugged, "I have to admit that after reading *Wieland*, I'm glad that Edgar Bergen uses his powers for good instead of evil."

"You girls don't mind if I join you? I'm all talked out and my feet are killing me. I've just got to take a break."

It was Wanda Angelovic.

"No, not at all," Rose assured her. "Please join us."

"By all means, take a break," Jess added.

The tall, dark-haired woman placed her cup and saucer on the table before slipping into a chair at Jess and Rose's table. Wanda let escape a powerful sigh before whispering to her companions, "It's the nth degree of tacky, but would you lose all respect for me if I slipped off my shoes?"

Jessica smiled and said, "Take a peek under the table skirt at our tootsies and feel free to join us. No one can see."

"We won't tell if you won't," Rose assured the exhausted and footsore college president.

"I'll tell you; sometimes being 'fearless leader' is the living end." Then she perked up and asked, "Anyway, Rose, how are the girls?"

"Just fine. The little dears are at home now. Tess thinks she's babysitting, as the eldest, but I had Alicia Wraxton stop by to keep an eye on things, disguised as a hep older friend. The girls are having a whale of a time this summer, swimming, hiking, riding, drawing, fighting with each other. Fortunately, Alicia is a darned good referee."

Wanda good-naturedly agreed, "I know exactly what you're talking about. I had three sisters, and we could have used a ref, ourselves. If we'd had one, I might not have gotten this little scar here on my cheek. Remind me to give you the whole story sometime. Maybe I'll wait till after your girls are grown up, though. There are some things mothers are definitely glad their children don't tell them. But, anyway, are you two having a nice time? Met some people you enjoyed? Tea and refreshments up to snuff?"

"Wanda, relax," Rose assured her. "As long as you're with us, you're off duty."

"You really think I can be?" Wanda asked, skepticism spicing her humor.

"Maybe not," Jessica added, "but take it from me, everything today is downright divine. Look at all those folks mixing and mingling. You're giving all these people, from trustees to faculty to students to alums, a lovely time, a wonderful impression of the school and what you're trying to accomplish here."

"I have to do something after what's happened, lately," Wanda sighed. "Trustees and parents are nervous about the safety of the girls and the reputation of the college. Locals are starting to see us as a place where people disappear or get murdered, maybe both. I just hope this little fête will focus people back on all the good we've been trying to do. I can't have people thinking of Margaret Point as the place where dead bodies wash up if that's going to compromise our ability to fund these young women's educations."

"No, of course not," Jess agreed, but her voice was a little shaky. She hadn't expected it, but Wanda's reference to Jessamyn Crane's corpse slammed home the unnerving memory of finding it on the beach.

Wanda immediately read Jess's expression and apologized, "Oh, I am sorry, Jessica. What a blockhead I am to forget your experience–and I believe I heard that you had become friendly with Sailor, Phil Novack. You must feel bad about his disappearance, too. How insensitive of me."

"It's all right," Jessica quickly assured Wanda, glad her sunglasses hid that condolences over Phil actually made her feel guiltier over her likely responsibility for his fate. She added, "We don't know for sure that he's, well, not still with us."

Wanda Angelovic consoled, "No, we don't. You can keep hoping. He could come back–and it is so kind of you to take care of that horse of his. A beautiful animal."

Jess smiled and agreed, "He certainly is. He's such a pleasure to ride! And he's a friendly sort, too. Do you ride, President Angelovic?"

"It's Wanda when the three of us are sitting out of the glare of school politics. But to answer your question, Jessica, no, not even on a pony as a kid. I'm a full-blooded city girl, and, to be quite frank, any animal bigger than an Irish Setter makes me nervous. The only horsepower I want to tangle with is under the hood of my Chrysler."

"That sounds like James and horses," Rose piped up.

"Really?" Wanda queried. "Your husband has a phobia?"

"I might not go quite that far. Let's just say he's not exactly in line to be the next Eddie Arcaro," Jessica replied.

"Too tall," Rose interjected.

"That, too," Jessica concurred. "He had a scare as a kid that left him cold on the equine species. Fortunately, he's not scared for me when it comes to horses. In fact, he even gets a kick out of my interest in racing."

"Nothing illegal, mind you," Rose playfully added.

"Somehow I doubt Jessica had any plans to set up a betting parlor on campus," Wanda smiled. "I don't think she'd be apt to do anything to jinx her husband's good standing here."

Jessica gave Rose a glance, then carefully repeated, "'Good standing' you say? I'm more than happy that James is well-regarded. I know I'm biased, but I happen to think he's tops."

"You're not the only one. Nigel Cross has said some nice things to me about him, especially how he's given up his time to work with Nigel."

Jess wondered if that help was a sign of James's altruism or just his keeping tabs on a suspect. That question passed quickly, for she wanted to hear the rest of what Wanda Angelovic was saying: "I've been impressed, myself, with his teaching. Sometimes I wander around to do some thinking—and I occasionally stop outside an open door to enjoy hearing what goes on in the classroom. I like what I heard outside his. He knows how to challenge our young women to think, but he always does it with respect. That's the way to develop minds that can reason for themselves, test themselves and others. God knows we need that, where we've been since Hitler and Tojo called the shots—and where *we* might be going in this country if we're not careful with the red-baiting and all." The preoccupied woman seemed to catch herself. She brightened to continue, "But what I really wanted to say was that James is doing a fine job. Of course, I can't make any promises right now, but we do feel we've been fortunate to have him this summer. I'm just sorry that he's not here today."

"Dentist appointment," Jessica explained.

"Hmm," Wanda responded as her eye was caught by Porlock motioning her to join him with an alum, a professor, and a Rotarian (each known as the dullest of his ilk). "At the moment, I think he might have the better deal. I'm afraid duty calls. It's been a swell break, ladies. Thanks!"

Wanda had swiftly slipped back into her pumps, bounced to her feet, and was all ready to march back into professional harness. However, before she left, she put a hand on Rose's shoulder and pointed out, "Rose, I hope you noticed that I heeded your advice and nixed the salmon and sardine sandwiches."

There was hardly a beat's hesitation before all three women uttered, "Blech!"

As soon as Wanda Angelovic had disappeared, Rose put a hand over Jessica's and chuckled, "Did you get that? They like James!"

"I know, I know, Rose. Do you think this means they're really interested in offering him a permanent place?"

"You know there's all kinds of political and financial whatsits to deal with, and nobody can promise anything, yet. Still, things look good for our boy. And if Terry and his nightmare of a wife hit the road, it could be the perfect setup," Rose crowed, but not loudly.

Rose's reference to the Clarkes prompted Jess to a quick but searching survey before she commented, "Speaking of whom, I haven't seen hide nor hair of the Bickersons today, have you?"

Rose glanced around before answering, "No, not at all." Looking at her chum, she asked, "You aren't kicking, are you?"

"Relieved is more like it," Jessica answered candidly. "After that little visit Thursday afternoon, I was nervous that they might ruin the possibility of a perfectly lovely afternoon."

"Instead, not only weren't they around, but you had a nifty chat with Wanda."

"So, where do you think they are?" Jess asked, still looking around.

"I don't know," Rose shrugged, pausing as she lifted her teacup. "Funny, this is just the kind of shindig they adore. A sterling opportunity for them to show off in front of people who don't know them better. But, you know what? Who cares! You're having a grand day; don't let them jinx it for you. Enjoy."

"I'm entitled?" Jessica queried, reflecting on how much more she had to deal with than Rose realized.

"You bet! In fact, we both are. Say, this tea is getting cold. Let's freshen it up–but leave your sunglasses on the table. If someone thinks it's unoccupied, we might lose it."

"Ah, so I have to give up my incognito status," Jess lamented with a grin, slipping into her shoes, sliding the straps over her heels. "Why don't you leave the camera, too."

"What, and miss all the great opportunities to take candids?"

Strolling across the terrace with her chum, luxuriating in the August warmth as much as the praise bestowed on her husband, Jessica dared to feel good. Maybe it was being well-fed, maybe it was the pleasure of Rose's company, maybe it was that she didn't have to put on a mask for Terry and company. Whatever the case, this afternoon Jessica Minton felt free. Darned if she wasn't going to enjoy it as long as she could. For all she knew, Terry and Carolina were missing because James and Dick Streeter had broken the case wide open and carted the whole kit and kaboodle off to jail. Well, maybe that was a little too much to hope for.

Chapter Twenty-Five

A few hours later, the August sun was cooling down. Some distance from the party, Jessica Minton reclined on the lawn, leaning on one arm, the other resting on her hip. One of the pup-tent-sized napkins served to protect Liz's white silk number from grass stains. Facing an armed Georg Zottigstrauch would be less terrifying than facing her sister peeved over the desecration of one of her sartorial creations. Almost. Jess gazed out into the silvery blue ocean, broken by leisurely cresting waves. Raising her head skyward, she was surprised by a Great Blue Heron sailing over the waters, head and neck proudly tucked into a graceful "S"–probably heading for a "self-serve" fish dinner in one of the nearby marshes.

Jess's smile grew as she reflected that it had turned out to be a wonderful afternoon! Rose was such a grand friend, dependable, and a heck of a lot of fun. Earlier, Rose had set her up for a "test shot" in the garden next to Cameron House, posing her and insisting that James was a dope to miss her in this dress. When Jess had suggested a pose with a little oomph, rather than a sedate standing shot, Rose had cracked that they didn't want the parents or trustees to get the idea they were running a training school for the Bur-Le-Q. It was swell to have a pal to be silly with.

That friend was now wrapping up some shots with faculty and students. Lauren, a late arrival at the tea, was one of Rose's subjects and her assistant as well. Seeing herself as more hindrance than help, Jessica had strode away to work off some of the sweets and savories she'd tucked into over the afternoon. Now, she was just relaxing, out of everybody's way, smiling into the Long Island Sound and thanking the Lord Almighty for such a wonderful day. Good food, good people, gorgeous weather. What more could she ask for? Oh yeah, no Nazi fiver and Company to worry about. Well, at least she knew for certain the "Company" weren't around, perhaps the fiver, as well. Maybe she was getting a day off for good behavior. If so, she was going to hold on tight to it. She wished James had had the same blessing.

Funny, even encountering Nigel Cross today had put her mind at ease rather than on red alert. His kidding with Rose about her photographic mission; his tip of the hand that he was pleased with James; his dry irony over some of the more obnoxious types at the tea; his genuine, to her mind, relief at the Clarkes' absence; and his praise of Lauren's work–all hardly seemed the ways of a Nazi. She fought against the poison of admitting that that might be the point. No, she wanted to trust her instincts about Nigel Cross. Rose saw him as a right guy. Didn't her opinion matter? Hadn't James seemed to lean somewhat more towards Nicholas Spenser being his quarry after yesterday's visit? The man certainly had a history of being tied in with not only the Clarkes but Jessamyn Crane. Still, the question nagged her, would a super brain like this Zottigstrauch boldly show up on James's doorstop? Would he be so sloppy? Or *was* he being sloppy? He hadn't said a single thing to let you pin anything on him, not really–but he had gotten the opportunity to check out James and her in their own home. So, was he suspicious of James? The thought haunted her, despite James's neat performance as an unsuspecting chap.

"Shoot!" Jessica softly muttered, pulling up a blade of grass. What had happened to the carefree ambiance of her afternoon? Curses on Georg Zottigstrauch for rearing his ugly head again! Well, she would not let him get her down. It *was* possible that he and the Clarkes had even escaped already, except what comfort was that? He would get away scot-free, not just with murder but to carry out his plot, whatever it was. Besides, it had been clear from Terry's clandestine conversation with Phil that Zottigstrauch wasn't planning to leave for at least a week.

So intent was Jessica on her thoughts that she didn't perceive she was no longer alone, until an unexpected companion plunked down on the grass beside her and "ominously" observed, "There be deep, dark thoughts brewing behind that troubled visage."

Jessica started, recognizing the voice of Terry Clarke.

He put out a steadying hand and cautioned, "Whoa, girl! You look like a sentinel confronting the ghost of Hamlet's father."

It briefly struck Jessica that of all the ghosts in Shakespeare, Terry had cast himself as one of the most noble and wronged, the bit about being shut up for a harrowing stint in Purgatory aside. But she was smart enough not to give away her thoughts.

"Geesh, Terry," she shook her head. "Did you have to sneak up on me? You took ten years off my life!"

"That would make you . . ."

"Old enough to know better," she finished. "Say, isn't it a little late to be joining the party?"

"Oh, Carolina and I were held up coming in on the train. No, don't worry. She didn't come with me."

"I didn't say I was worried," Jessica corrected Terry. Had she failed to mask her relief at Carolina's absence, or was Terry just referring to the general opinion of his wife?

Surprisingly, Terry's response put Jess somewhat at ease: "No, you didn't say anything. You didn't even 'look' anything. Being married to a Brit must have improved your stiff-upper-lip capacity. No, I take that back. You always were a lady."

"Thanks," Jess replied with a skeptical furrow of her brow. She wished Terry would go away, let her have back her respite from all the deadly game playing. But Terry went on.

"I guess she made something of a spectacle of herself yesterday. That's how she is when she gets a bee in her bonnet, especially about art. She's just a steamroller when it comes to enlarging her collection or promoting a discovery that redounds to her credit. I hope you won't hold a grudge."

That was Terry all over. No "I'm sorry my wife might have hurt your feelings"; only "Don't hold her *faux pas* against me." Jessica, however, was well past being offended by Terry's social misdemeanors, and she didn't want to make a big deal over the incident. No way would she give Terry reason to run to his boss reporting she or James had been rattled.

"No harm, no foul, Terry," Jess replied matter-of-factly. "If anyone deserves an apology, it's that poor Mr. Spenser. *He* must have been *so* embarrassed by Carolina's dragging him in and putting him on the spot. Poor old fellow."

That ought to lay a nice layer of salve on any Nazi mastermind's suspicions of her or James.

"Oh, 'old' Spenser? Well, he's not that old. Anyway, he must be used to Carolina by now. She's been dragging him all over the state and then some, trying to get him to promote her artistic finds. He does all right for himself, though. Makes a tidy profit on his sales. No, I wouldn't feel too sorry for him."

The last sentence had an edge that left Jess wondering. Terry, despite his earlier causal tone, had let slip he did *not* like Nicholas Spenser. Because as Georg Zottigstrauch he had kept the proud Terry under his thumb? Worse, he had taken away Jessamyn Crane. Hmm, maybe in this mood, Terry would get careless, let slip something useful to James. She'd grab anything to make James's life a little easier.

"Yes," Terry went on. "She definitely leads him around, but he's made a nice pile of ducats off Jessamyn's work. He can really make a bundle trading off a dead artist."

So, that was a perfectly non-Nazi-related explanation for Terry's bitterness, as well as Spenser's relations with Carolina and Jessamyn. Yet Jessica wasn't convinced of the antiques dealer's innocence. If she could find the deft phrasing, work up the nerve, to press this topic a little further . . ..

"So, Jessica, where's your beloved spouse? I see you came stag today, like me."

"Not exactly stag, Terry," Jess corrected him. "Rose and I came together. David was busy, so she had Alicia stay with the girls . . ."

"Oh ho! That's right! I have a bone to pick with your chum, my colleague, over that little maneuver. I wanted Alicia at the tea today. She's one of my shining stars. I wanted to show her off, impress the alumni and trustees with what I've done . . ."

"What *you've* done?" Jessica raised her eyebrows. "You weren't her only teacher, Terry. And I think the *student* ought to get a little credit for her own success."

She saw Terry's dander start to rise, but he surprised her by suddenly laughing, "I suppose you're right! You always could prick my ego when it started to expand too much. Deflating it via slow leak with your needling always was a neat trick. You saved my bacon more than once back in the old days by preventing my pride from antagonizing the wrong people. "

"Has it exploded recently?" Jessica ventured, not sure where the conversation was leading.

"Let's just say I may have shot off my mouth more than I should have— and Carolina's not the kind of helpmate to encourage circumspection in a fellow."

Now it was Terry's turn to study the ocean, then shift his gaze to his own blade of grass, twirling it between his thumb and forefinger. The sun glinted out the reddish lights in his dark brown hair, and Jessica had no idea what to make of his confessional mood. Part of her wanted to get up and run away from Terry's letting down his guard. She'd been here before with him. Yet she still felt some compassion for the person she'd known long ago, even though she didn't know how far she could trust the man he was now. And there was the chance Terry might tell her something to help put the bracelets on Georg Zottigstrauch. Even so, Jessica still didn't feel quite right about taking advantage of Terry's vulnerable state.

Terry was continuing, "There was a time, not very long ago, I thought things would get better, were getting better. I should have known it would all fall apart. I should have known there was no escape."

Terry fastened those blue-crystal eyes on her, and Jess abruptly turned her head away. She was terrified those eyes could burn down the walls she'd erected to disguise her knowledge and to protect James.

"I imagine you're thinking I shouldn't be telling you all this," Terry said. "I'm just not in a position where I have anyone to turn to anymore, with Jessamyn gone."

Jessica intently studied an ant threading his way through the grass jungle. Lucky devil, being part of a group-mind and not torn by loyalty to a husband, a country, and pity for a weak person reaching out. Was Terry looking to her for advice on how to get away from Zottigstrauch or was this a ploy to get her to reveal what she knew?

"You're not saying anything," Terry sighed. "Okay, I know when I've overstepped my bounds. I guess I have no right, after all this time, to expect so much from you. It's just that I remember your big heart, and I thought for old time's sake . . ."

332

That was a mighty tug on the old heart strings, and Jessica couldn't help looking back at Terry to say feelingly, "I don't know exactly what you want from me, Terry."

For a moment, his eyes lit with happiness. Was it with hope she could help him or pleasure that he'd gotten a nibble on his hook? That scared her, for Jessica realized she was in way over her head.

"Hey! Professor Clarke! Miss Minton!" Lauren Fleet interrupted, bounding up behind them. "Professor Nyquist wants to see you right away! She wants you in some pictures."

Saved by the bell or, in this case, the bobby-soxer! Jess thought, relieved.

Terry let slip a furious look that, when he faced Lauren, had swiftly morphed into playfulness. With mock seriousness, he told her, "Far be it from us to keep the eminent Rose Nyquist waiting in her valiant quest to immortalize in Kodachrome the erudite of Margaret Point."

"Or we could just let her take our pictures," Jessica deadpanned. Yet, despite her show of humor, Jess felt decidedly unnerved by Terry's quick change. What were his true feelings and what was his mask? Which had she been responding to a moment ago?

Lauren laughed, and Terry helped Jessica to her feet. She somehow managed not to shudder away from this man she did not really know. After an expansive sweep of his hand and a behest to Lauren to "Lead on," he guided Jess with a hand on her elbow.

How galant! But Jess wasn't buying, even as Terry kept up the playful banter with Lauren. Still, it wouldn't do to jerk free, no matter that his touch gave her the willies. What should she think about their little conversation? Had she blown a chance to help Terry escape Zottigstrauch (and help James in the process)? Or had she narrowly avoided being played for a sucker? Well, the answers were on hold for now. She could only comfort herself with the thought that even if she hadn't pried a soul from Satan's grip, Mr. Scratch hadn't pried anything out of her, even by proxy.

It was a little while later, and Rose had staged a few "candids," creating a light enough mood to brush back, if not away, the misgivings haunting Jess. At the moment, Jessica had stepped out of the way to watch her friend line up Terry, Lauren, an alum, and a trustee for a shot.

Terry certainly didn't seem to be holding any hint of a dark side now, turning on the charm for both the trustee and the alum. He was definitely making them feel proud to have him on their team, at their little academic club, except they didn't know he'd been scheming to jump ship for a better opportunity. But that hadn't seemed to work out for him, until he'd apparently gotten a call from Chitzenega's University of San Juan, a respected school that just happened to be in a country with extradition policy extremely unhelpful to the good old USA. Georg Zottigstrauch's destination as well?

Jess lifted her teacup for a sip but was interrupted by a man drolly chiding, "That must be your fifth or sixth this afternoon. Pretty soon we'll have to cut you off."

Jess turned to face Nigel Cross, looking dapper in a blue and white seersucker suit and pulling off wearing a bow tie without looking goofy. She volleyed back, "Don't worry. I'm not driving."

"What about managing on those stilts?" He nodded down at her high heels.

Jess smiled and explained, "No problem. Rose and I both brought a change of shoes. We'll be cruising out of here in sneakers."

"Wise decision. I knew you were resourceful. Just like that husband of yours. I can always depend on him to come up with an insight most people miss. I never know what he's going to pick up on next. That must be why his scholarship is so original. I shouldn't be saying this, but . . ."

Nigel was cut off by another man, whose voice came from behind Jessica: "Mrs. Crawford, I'm so glad to have found you. I really need to speak to you."

Jess barely managed not to blanch on recognizing Nicholas Spenser's voice. She turned to see him cool and collected in a snappy, grey summer suit and charcoal tie. Just lovely: she was literally caught between the two candidates for the dubious honor of being Georg Zottigstrauch.

"I'm sorry, Mrs. Crawford. I didn't mean to startle you," Spenser said, nodding a greeting to Nigel.

Jess made a major effort not to betray her dis-ease, carefully putting down her cup and saucer. No sense rattling them in her hands. She smoothly replied, "That's all right, Mr. Spenser. I didn't expect you. Do you know Professor Cross?"

She couldn't see Nigel's expression. However, looking at Spenser, she could see *his* eyes narrow and harden, ever so slightly. Yet Spenser's tone was still cordial when he answered, "Of course I do. You must have forgotten that I mentioned he was one of the collectors of Jessamyn Crane's work."

Jess couldn't help stealing a glance at Nigel. He looked bored, except there was the slightest tightening of his jaw.

Nicholas Spenser went on, "I wanted to apologize again for yesterday afternoon. I never would have come in like that had I known we were intruding. It's just that Mrs. Brent Clarke led me to believe that you wouldn't mind, that you'd be happy to sell that piece. You know how overwhelming her enthusiasm is when it comes to promoting art."

"Yes," Nigel agreed with the merest trace of sarcasm, "Carolina is nothing if not 'enthusiastic'—about art."

Spenser took the barest of moments to give Nigel a queer look, then turned back to Jessica and said, "I hope you won't hold that afternoon against me."

"Oh, not at all," Jessica assured him, putting on her most charming smile and praying to God those stony black eyes couldn't penetrate through to the jumble of fear, anger, and anxiety within her.

"And if you do change your mind . . ." He offered her his card, again.

Jess slowly took it, realizing she already had one but not wanting to prolong the encounter longer than necessary.

Spenser had been speaking while she was thinking: ". . . because I could get you a nice price. There's an interested buyer in Chitzenega . . ."

Chitzenega, again?!

"Dr. Cross," Nicholas Spenser continued, "perhaps you might be interested in selling some of your paintings?"

That question sent Jessica's eyes to Nigel. He only replied smoothly, "I don't think so."

"Ah yes, sentimental value of a colleague's work?"

"Something like that."

"Do take my card, anyway, should you change your mind."

Nigel did not take the card. Instead, he stated, with the slightest hint of the corrosive in his suave tone, "That would be a waste of your card, wouldn't it?"

Spenser displayed a nervous tic of a smile, leaving Jessica to wonder if even Georg Zottigstrauch were that good a player. Then he turned to her and said, "Good afternoon, Mrs. Crawford. I'm afraid I must get back to my shop." A quick nod at Nigel and he was gone.

"That was rather interesting," Nigel observed, watching Spenser disappear into the crowd. He looked back at Jessica and surprised her with, "I never knew you had a sculpture by Jessamyn . . . Crane."

"Yes, well, I never knew you'd be interested," Jess answered simply. True as far as it went. She wished Nigel didn't seem so concerned with the same item that had drawn Nicholas Spenser's attention.

"Ah," was all he said at first, looking thoughtful. Jess had an urge to offer him the piece created by the woman for whom he'd cared, but instinct checked her generous impulse. Anyway, how had Nigel known the item was a sculpture and not in Jessamyn's usual medium? If only she had the nerve, and skill, to elicit something from Nigel that could clear him.

"Something bothering you, Jessica? You seemed to have fallen down the rabbit hole just now. Did that fellow Spenser upset you? Officious type. A bit of a ghoul, profiteering off Jessamyn's death."

Jess wanted to put a reassuring hand on Nigel's arm. No, that wouldn't do. The man had way too much pride and reserve to deal happily with her knowing his secret romantic sorrow. Unless he were Georg Zottistrauch creating a sand screen of emotion for the fact that he were her actual killer.

Jess pushed both possibilities aside and remarked, "His buyer in Chitzenega couldn't have much taste if he wanted to buy that ugly little number. I've seen Jessamyn Crane's paintings; Rose took me to one of her campus gallery showings. Believe me; this thing is not in that league. It's downright creepy."

"You don't say?" How much interest lurked behind those words? "And yet you don't want to part with it for a tidy profit?"

Jessica thought fast, then gave Nigel a casual shrug and explained, "Let's say I was hardly in the mood to give something to two terribly obnoxious people. Sometimes saying no to someone pushing you around is a bigger profit than any amount of money."

That was certainly no lie!

336

Before Nigel could comment, Rose, Terry, and Lauren joined them and took over the conversation. Rose announced, "That's it, Nigel, I'm off the clock. Margaret Bourke-White, I am not! Any tea left?"

"I could use something with a bit more kick," Terry asserted with a twinkle.

"A fine comment to make in front of the tender ears of a student," Nigel dryly "reprimanded."

Terry corrected, "I'm looking for *coffee*. A much more manly drink, right, Lauren?"

"Sure, sure, Professor Clarke," Lauren piped in, a bit nervously, excited to be allowed into conversation with the upper echelons but not at all certain where the humor ended and danger began.

Rose came to her rescue: "I think Lauren should go out for photographer on the school paper. She did a bang-up job setting up some shots and even took some nice ones, herself. There's a grand one of the President and several students."

Terry, however, wasn't quite ready to give up the floor and launched into, "Say, Jess, there's someone I'd like you to meet. He's around here somewhere. You'll get a real kick out of this. Too bad your husband isn't here. He would, too. Oh, there he is." A wave to another group of people not far off, and Terry called, "Sam, Sam, come over here. You've got to tell this lovely lady the same yarn you were telling me before."

A boyish man broke from his companions and approached them. A thatch of light brown hair, glinting golden in the sunlight; warm brown eyes that sparkled jovially; and a smooth face bearing a cheery expression gave the impression of one far too young to be a college teacher, but also made you want to get to know him better. Terry welcomed the newcomer affably, so much so that Jess almost couldn't believe how miserable he had seemed not long before.

"Sure, Sam Steinwall here is new to Biology. A great guy," Terry went on, introducing him to everyone, but saving Jessica for last. "And this is the woman I told you that you had to talk to, Jessica Minton. You've got to tell her what you told me earlier. I know she'll get a kick out of it."

Jess smiled, thinking, *Oh, he must be a fan of the radio program, or maybe he saw me on the stage. No wonder he looks a little shy.* She said cordially, "So, Professor Steinwall, what's your story?"

"It's the funniest thing, Ma'am. I was a gunner on a bomber, and in '44 I was shot down over France. The *maquis* rescued me and smuggled me back through the lines. Darned if one of the guys in the group wasn't a dead ringer for a Joe I've seen around campus. When I told Terry my story and described the fella, he told me that I was talking about your husband."

Jessica felt her warm smile vanish in the flame of horror sweeping through her. She recovered herself swiftly, whether swiftly enough, she wasn't sure, forcing that smile back on her face.

"Yep, well, this guy was a dead ringer," Sam went on, turning to Nigel now, "Down to the longish hair and mustache."

Rose casually interjected, "I don't know, I imagine all those Resistance guys must have been pretty shaggy. Living off the land, in the woods and caves and whatnot. I can't imagine bringing along a barber would have been a high priority."

Jess found her balance enough to joke, "Of course, I can just hear the commander saying, 'Eh, Pierre, scratch the medic and the munitions guy and bring along *le coiffeur*. We have to look good for the raid tonight.' You can't properly blow up a fuel dump with a shaggy head and a five o'clock shadow."

"Sure, I guess you're right. I think this fella was French, anyway. He spoke to the others like a native–didn't actually talk to me. But he sure could have been your husband's twin," Sam concluded.

"James speaks French pretty well, doesn't he, Jessica?" Terry recalled.

"Sure, but he also sat out the war with health issues. I told you that, Terry," she corrected, keeping her tone as light as she could. "Want to write England and check it out with his draft registry?"

Was that last remark too much?

Rose rode to the rescue with a wise crack, "Maybe he projected himself across the Atlantic like something out of Flash Gordon?"

"Maybe Jessica's husband has a secret life," Nigel conjectured, his expression amused.

Jess could no longer discern how innocent Nigel's amusement was, her intuition blocked by shock and anxiety. Nevertheless, she had enough presence of mind to mask how rattled she was and joked, "If he does, I hope it's bringing in a hefty second paycheck."

Rose, ever the friend, led Sam onto a new topic, asking him all the usual questions for a new kid on the block: how did he like his department, the students? Did he have a family here? How were they getting along? *Thank God the small talk drew the group into far less treacherous ground.* Ignored at last, Jessica withdrew ever so quietly from the conversation, if not the group. She mounted a vaguely cordial smile on her features, but her mind kept going in circles. Was Sam Steinwall's revelation enough to wipe out James's entire mission? Dared she hope she'd covered for her husband? Thank God Nicholas Spenser wasn't here! Did that matter? Both Nigel and Terry were.

If she could just sneak away and warn James. How, though? She'd have to go through the campus operator whether she called from Cameron House or home. And whom would she call? She glanced at her watch: after 4:00. Calling James was a moot point, anyway; he'd be en route now. It wasn't as if he had a portable Ameche with him. How about the two contacts he'd brought back with him? How *about* them? For security's sake, she didn't know who they were. Damn, James had tried so hard to keep her out of harm's way that she was helpless to return the favor.

What on earth had made Terry tip his hand, anyway? Wouldn't it have been easier to neutralize James if he didn't know his enemies were wise to him? Weren't they afraid that letting on to James would force his hand? Could Georg Zottigstrauch be such a cool cucumber that he was willing to gamble that James still wouldn't act for fear of spooking the Nazi away from following through with his plot? Was Zottigstrauch so good that he knew he could outplay James, pull off his caper before he and his plan could be identified?

Jess quickly surveyed the people surrounding her, afraid her ruminations might raise suspicion. No, they all seem unconcerned with her, except Lauren, who was giving her a peculiar look. Jess firmed up her smile for the girl, and Lauren turned away–a little too quickly. What was that about? Before Jess could think further, Nigel was talking about having to attend to some mail in his office, Terry was explaining he had to head for his own office because he owed Carolina a call, Lauren was deciding to visit Alicia at Rose's, and the little group had drifted apart. Jess found herself standing alone with Rose.

"Well . . ." said Rose as the two stared at each other.

That one word told Jessica that Rose was giving her the opportunity to explain why Sam Steinwall's strange anecdote had distressed her, but only if she chose to. Jessica would have given a million dollars to level with her friend, but the truth wasn't hers to tell. She would have ponied up another million for some solid advice on how to warn James.

"Well," Jessica repeated, trying to smile. "So ends our day. Who would have thought sitting and drinking tea would be so exhausting."

Rose thought for a fraction of a second, but followed her friend's lead, responding, "It's putting on the charm for several hours that has us beat."

Jess could see that Rose was observing her closely. It took great effort, and not a little guilt, to disguise her concerns with a weary but relaxed, "Yes, I guess you could say that. So, since it's getting late, maybe we should head out. I wouldn't be surprised if James is back." Was there a quiver of her true fears in those last words? "How about I pop up to his office for my bag with our sneakers? You go get together all your camera stuff, and I'll meet you in the Great Hall."

Rose was still watching her, thinking, but all she said was, "Okay. If that's what you want. See you in the Great Hall. Just, don't rush. Take it easy, Jess."

The friendship and sympathy in those last words ate at Jessica's heart. Would that she could accept the help her friend subtly offered. But that was out of the question as things stood. Jess gave Rose a quick smile and promised, "I'll be back in a jiffy."

Jess was off across the terrace and into the building, the speed of her strides drawing all her concentration, saving her from dark broodings about what Zottigstrauch's next move would be and how helpless she was to protect or even warn James at this moment. She found herself at the foot of the staircase that swept up to the landing of the second floor. Exhausted, she stopped and leaned against the carved post on the left side of the stairs.

Jessica's head bowed. Good Lord, what could she do? What would come next? She wanted to get home, to see if James were back, to fill him in on all that had happened, but she was so beat right now. Would Zottigstrauch risk directly striking at James when he was so close to getting away? True, he had acted boldly, having Terry engineer Sam Steinwall's revelation, a move that would alert James that his identity was no secret to the Nazi. Yet it was a shrewd act at the same time: without James's knowing exactly who was the war criminal, Zottigstrauch's indirect exposure of her husband unnervingly intimated James's vulnerability to a cagier opponent. On the other hand, she wasn't entirely certain that Zottigstrauch's cat-and-mousing (apologies to Dusty) didn't suggest the kind of ego that might not fear the exposure of striking out. Damn! If only James were here to do damage control. If only she had some means to warn him about what he was walking into.

Jessica started at voices coming up behind her. She straightened up, quickly glancing back. Good, no one she knew. *Something* was going right—at least not going horribly. Well, she couldn't keep Rose waiting forever. A glance up the broad staircase, a quick recollection of the English Department's layout, and Jessica decided that was not the way to go to James's office. Nigel and Terry could be still up there. If she went through the main doorway, she'd run right into one or both of them. No, better to sneak up the spiral staircase, pop in and out of James's office, then back again. The sooner she finished her task, the sooner she could get home to await James, or warn him if he were already there. If she weren't already too late.

Her high heels clicked across the tile floor, sounding like that gal in the Val Lewton film, stalked through stone tunnels in Central Park by a night-prowling panther woman. The marble steps that curved up to the next floor didn't promise to be any quieter under those high heels. Swiftly, Jessica pulled off her sandals and went up the steps, cold beneath her feet. Surrounded by smooth granite walls, she felt as if she were ascending the inner spiral of a Nautilus shell.

Jessica had just silently padded around the final curl of the hidden staircase when the sound of furiously shuffled papers caught her attention through the open doorway. Automatically, she slowed, not sure why exactly, until the certitude dawned on her that someone was in James's office, while James should still be *en route*. Carefully, she peeked around the corner to see that the intruder had not quite closed the office door. Now the sound of someone yanking out a desk drawer escaped through the doorway, but the perpetrator appeared only as a tall form, probably a man, shadowed through the opaque glass on the door. Then the form moved toward the door; and Jessica, with a quick glance behind her, backed speedily, noiselessly, around the obscuring curve of the staircase.

Who the devil was snooping?! Certainly not James. Jess's heart seemed to snag on a beat at the sound of the office door opening wider onto the corridor above her, beyond the curve of the stair. Silence. The silence of someone watching, checking. Then the door closed. *Had the intruder gone back inside or left? No sound of footsteps. He must have gone back to his snooping.*

Momentarily, fury surged through Jessica. *How dare anyone invade James's office?!* She would be perfectly within her rights to charge up the stairs and give the intruder a piece of her mind—except, justified or not, that confrontation would expose a desperate, maybe deadly, man. Whether it was Terry or the great man himself, James's warnings had sufficiently sunk in for Jess to know that forcing Zottigstrauch's hand was not smart. *What should I do? Creep back down the stairs like a surreptitious cat? Then how to explain to Rose not having the sneakers? Damn!* She was stuck here until she could tell that the snooper had actually gone.

As if in answer to her silent gripe, Jess heard the door open again. *Thank God the janitors weren't very good at oiling hinges around here!* Unfortunately, this situation was *not* the one Jess wanted, for, after a hesitation, footsteps revealed the intruder coming down the corridor in *her* direction! A wave of adrenalin swept Jessica, wobbling her knees. She grabbed the rail on the wall to steady herself, then started to turn for a dash down the stairs. Except Jess now heard the footsteps halt—so did she. *He must be listening.* The world seemed to freeze into a small still point. His footsteps resumed, but away from her.

Jessica sank against the wall, determined not to go down. After a few minutes, she pulled herself together. Straightening, Jess forced herself back up the way she'd come. She only hesitated a second before pushing herself into the corridor.

No one. To her right, the office doors ahead of her were closed. She forced herself to peek around the corner to her left at the foyer and Tricia's desk in the reception area beyond. Still no one. Who knew what lurked in the offices, in the classrooms on the other side of the corridor's wall opposite James's office. Her feelings oddly mixed, Jess pushed herself to make the relatively short walk to her husband's office. Thank God, she found herself alone, yet frustration taunted that she hadn't been able to get a clear look at the phantom prowler.

As she took James's key from her pocket, hand shaking, Jessica tried to run down the suspects with access to a key. There was Tricia, the secretary, but she wasn't a man and Jessica had no reason to believe that she was under Zottigstrauch's control. However, Tricia had an extra set of keys in her desk, and Jess didn't know if she always kept them locked up. Nigel, as chair, might have a key to Tricia's desk. But Nigel hadn't seemed unsettled by Sam Steinwall's revelation about James. No, he'd just made that little remark about James having a double life. Too obvious a remark for an incognito Nazi, or did its very obviousness make it an extremely clever misdirection?

Jess unlocked the office door and shoved it open. She blinked in surprise. Everything looked normal. If she hadn't heard the angry search, herself, she'd never have believed someone had been rooting around in here, searching for . . . what? Jess stepped into the center of the office, thinking, *A guy would have to be good to tear through here and not leave a detectable trace.* James was that good. Apparently, so was this guy. Did that mean it hadn't been Terry, or had Terry been trained by a master? Terry and Nigel had both mentioned they'd be in the building. Did that rule out Nicholas Spenser? After all, she had no idea where he'd gone once he'd melted away from her and Nigel. But Nigel had said he'd be in the building now.

She went over to the desk. Nope, nothing seemed out of place here, either. Well, she knew James certainly wouldn't leave something worth finding here, any more than at their cottage. Such a pitiful consolation. Despite knowing that she couldn't afford to waste time, Jess sank into the chair behind the desk. Her head in her hands, she came darned close to having a good cry.

"Jess? For Heaven's sake, what's wrong?"

Startled, Jessica looked up to see Rose standing in the doorway, worried. Caught unawares, Jess couldn't mask her feelings.

Rose took one look at her friend, then swiftly turned and checked up and down the corridor. Facing Jessica again, she put a silencing finger over her lips, closed the door behind her, pulled up a chair at the desk, and sat down. Rose began, "Now, look, Jessica. You know I'm not one to butt in where I don't belong, but you've got something tearing away at you big time. If you don't talk to me, you're going to explode. Come clean, kid: what kind of a jam are you in?"

Jess sat back, putting her hands forcefully down on the desk in frustration. What she wouldn't give to be free to level with her friend, but what right did she have?

Rose read the struggle in Jess's eyes and said, "All right. I think I can make it easier for you. You're not betraying a secret if *I* tell *you* what it is. James didn't sit out the war with a heart problem. He *was* the guy whom Sam Steinwall saw in France. And it's pretty clear to me, if he's on the q.t. and you're a wreck about it getting out, that he's still on the job–a job that concerns people right here at Margaret Point, probably even Jessamyn Crane's murder and Sailor's disappearance."

Jess started to answer, she tried, but she couldn't come up with the right words. What *were* the right words? She didn't think she could flim-flam Rose into dropping her unnervingly accurate extrapolations–partly because she was almost running on empty when it came to being clever, mostly because she just didn't want to lie to Rose. Maybe if Rose knew a little more, she'd understand how vital it was to keep things quiet. At least, at this point, she wouldn't be giving James away to her friend.

"So, I really tipped my hand this afternoon?" Jessica began slowly. "Did *everyone* see?"

"Well," Rose cocked her head, recollecting, "You made a nice save. You were quiet for a bit, but then people could also have seen you as only tired."

"Rose, *you* picked up on me," Jess pointed out, dissatisfied.

"I'm one of your best friends. *I* know you. I can see when you've been sucker-punched. Besides, there are other things I've seen in James and you that tie in."

"Really? I don't understand. We never say . . ."

"It's not what you say. It's the looks, the hesitations, the extra alertness, and–all sorts of little things. You're forgetting, David came back to me out of combat in North Africa with a million-dollar shoulder wound. People forget; it's not just the physical wounds that haunt a guy. I've seen those ghosts in James—and you, sometimes, that walking on eggshells. I've done it, too. Still do. But most people don't get it unless they've been there. I doubt Terry gets it, with his cushy tour of duty in D.C. Nigel, probably. It's been thirty years since he was at war, but who knows how long the healing takes."

Jessica leaned back in her chair. Rose's comments about Terry and Nigel comforted her in more ways than her friend realized. So, even if they had been looking, maybe they didn't know her well enough to accurately read her. Nevertheless, she had a more immediate concern. What should she say to Rose right now? Maybe it wouldn't be wise to tell Rose everything, but clearly any denial would not wash with her friend. It might even make her more suspicious. She had to tread carefully.

Jessica began, "Rose, I really think you should talk to James. We both should, together. James needs to know what you've figured out, what you think anyone else might figure out. I don't feel right giving away anymore without his say-so. He knows what will SNAFU his plans better than I do. But, truth be told, yes, James didn't sit out the war in some ivy halls.

"Now, I've got a question for you, Rose, especially since I saw someone I couldn't identify searching this office. Don't worry; he didn't see me. I'm positive. How much damage do you think Sam Steinwall's story did?"

"With Terry, Nigel, and Lauren? You don't suspect one of them of being up to no good? We can certainly eliminate Lauren. That leaves . . . Nigel and Terry? That can't be—except they both did have connections to the murder victim. Oh!" Rose suddenly realized something new. "Terry and Nigel were here before I came in. You were *alone* with both of them."

"But I'm all right, Rose," Jessica assured her friend. "We're both sitting here nice and cozy."

"Cozy is hardly the word I'd use," Rose countered.

"I can't exactly argue with tha . . ."

Rose cut in, "Wait, this *is* peculiar, Jess. When I went by Terry's office, I could hear him arguing on the phone with someone. But this is even screwier. When I was in the foyer, Nigel came rushing out of the corridor leading to his office, you know, not the one outside this office.

He had his briefcase under his arm, and he looked white as a sheet. He was so hot under the collar that he almost knocked me down and, even then, barely noticed me. I just thought he'd found something annoying from one of the more Neanderthal trustees in his office. Are you telling me he found something in here, in *this* office? Oh, Jess, you can't be saying that he's under investigation by James. I can't believe it!"

Jessica hesitated. Things certainly didn't look good for Nigel Cross. Had he found something in James's office that spooked him? Yet would a "super spy" be so easily spooked? At last, Jess said to her friend, "Rose, I don't know what to believe. I certainly don't know what to tell you, except that you and James need to speak. I know he will want to keep you out of harm's way, but I do think if you tell him how everything looks from the outside it might help him do damage control, even plan his next moves. However, I don't dare say anymore. I'd better let him do the talking."

"I'm your friend. I want to help."

"And I'm your friend. A friend who has no intention of putting you in harm's way if she can help it. So, all I can say is, tell Alicia she's on overtime. You're coming home with me to wait for James. I don't think it will be too long. He promised to be back about 5:00."

At first, Rose seemed undecided, but she said, "Okay, okay, but just one more thing."

"Yeah?" came Jessica's wary response.

"No more tea. I've had too many gallons for one day."

Jessica managed a wan smile, noting, "That'll certainly be a first for us, no tea. I hope Dusty can stand the shock."

Chapter Twenty-Six

Jessica wasn't sure whether she was relieved or unsettled to see James's car parked out front as she and Rose approached the cottage. Jess turned to Rose, and the jittery look her pal returned revealed they were perfectly in sync. *Lovely.*

They got close enough to see James unlocking the door, his back to them. Normally, Jessica would have fairly bounded up the path. All she could manage now was to walk faster. Ever on the alert, James turned sharply to face them. From the way he stood, he'd clearly had a long day– and now she and Rose were going to stretch it out like a winter night in the Arctic. Still, weary as James's features were, Jess perceived his eyes light up to see her.

"Ah, two of the loveliest ladies of Margaret Point," he smiled, coming down the steps, then the path, to meet them. "How did the President's affair go? Everyone sufficiently stuffed and charmed by our gracious leader . . . ?"

He stopped, reading their faces and not being at all at ease with that text.

Jessica glanced at Rose, who gave her a nod to proceed as they reached the gate. Tapping anxiously on the post, Jessica responded, "Let's just say it was interesting."

"*Interesting,*" James observed slowly. "Is that another word for 'disastrous'?"

"We'd better talk inside," Jessica nodded toward the house.

James made a swift, almost imperceptible, glance at Rose, and Jessica revealed, "It's too late to leave Rose out of this conversation."

James's features darkened considerably, so that Rose burst out, "James, don't get sore at Jessica. *She* didn't give anything away."

"But we do need to talk *inside*," Jessica insisted.

James quickly appraised them before nodding abruptly. Swinging open the gate, he said, "After you, ladies."

They reached the door, which James shoved open, after a quick glance around letting Rose go first. One hand on Jessica's arm, he stopped her and asked, "Am I going to need a whiskey for this?"

"A double."

"Maybe I'd better hold off, then. It sounds as if I'll need my wits about me."

The three were sitting with Rose and Jess facing James across the coffee table. He was quiet, thinking, hooded eyes giving nothing away. Finally, James spoke, "All right. Let me have it."

Jessica took a deep breath and, after momentarily floundering, gave it her best shot: "You know that saying 'I have some good news and some bad news'? Unfortunately, we just have bad news and worse news. The bad news is that Rose figured out that you were in Special Operations Executive."

"Don't blame her, James," Rose insisted before he could say anything. "Jess didn't spill the beans. I figured it out, and there was no way she could plausibly deny it."

James raised a brow, then nearly floored both women by smiling, just a little, and saying kindly, "It's not an ideal situation, but it's not the end of the world, you're finding out, Rose. I know that you've a good head on your shoulders. You're not about to shoot your mouth off. Anyway, what's in the past is over and done with."

Rose nervously elaborated, "I also told her I thought it's not all in the past, that you're on a case *now*."

James surprised Jessica by smiling easily at Rose to say, "Rose, how could you think that? The war's been over for a year . . ."

"Maybe this is where I should tell you about the worse news," Jessica cut him off in a controlled voice. "Rose put two and two together when a new prof swore you were a dead ringer for someone working with the Resistance in France. He said it in front of several people."

"Yup, a 'dead ringer'," Rose affirmed, alarmed to see the color drain from James's face.

348

Jessica pressed on, hating that her words seemed to slice into James, "He had originally told Terry, and Terry made him repeat it in front of us—and Nigel."

"Nigel," repeated James slowly. "And Terry." His face really was white now. He leaned forward, arms on his knees, eyes contemplating his steepled fingers. He said nothing, nothing at all.

Good God! Jess punished herself. *How could I have brought such trouble onto James? How in heaven's name can I make it right?*

"How did Terry and Nigel react?"

James's words were calm, but so unexpected that both women started. He proffered a quick, "Sorry, ladies, but you need to think carefully and answer my question."

"One of them searched your office," Jessica answered intently.

James, deeply worried, questioned, "He didn't see you, did he, Jessica? You knew better than to confront him?"

"Oh, yes, yes," Jess reassured James, eager to tell him something had gone right. "I heard him when I came up the spiral staircase. I did see a form through the glass window, but I was careful to keep hidden. I wish I *could* have seen his identity. No, don't worry. I'm a firm believer in the maxim asserting the superiority of live chickens over deceased ducks."

"Good girl," James nodded his approval. "I can't have anything happen to you." For the briefest of moments he smiled, then it was back to business: "So, you've no idea who was in my office, other than it was a man?"

"Someone tall," Jess added helplessly.

"That narrows it down to 90% of the men on campus," Rose glumly noted.

James's attention was now on Jessica's friend: "Rose, were you with Jessica then? Or did you see someone or something significant about that time?"

Jess nudged Rose, who answered, "I'll say! Right before I found Jess, Nigel Cross came tearing past me down the main stairs. If I ever saw a guy sore about something, he was it! But, James, you don't think Nigel is . . . You're not after him?"

James would only answer Rose with another question, "And Terry Clarke, where was he all this time?"

"Well, as I told Jessica, I heard him in his office, having some kind of dust-up on the phone. I assumed it was Carolina, since he'd said he had to call her about something. He didn't say what, though."

James leaned forward to tell them, "Listen, both of you, this is important. I want you to tell me exactly how both Terry and Nigel reacted when they heard the story about me with the Resistance."

Rose answered, "Terry treated it as if it were some kind of a joke on Jessica."

James turned to his wife and asked quietly, "And how did you react, Jessica?"

Jess closed her eyes, briefly, and accused herself, "Like I'd been sucker-punched. I'm sorry, James. It just came so out of the blue."

James sighed, but put a hand over Jessica's and said, "Don't beat yourself up. This isn't your job."

Rose leaped in, "Now wait a minute, you two. It wasn't that bad. Jess, you didn't gasp and faint or anything. *I* noticed because I know you. Honestly, kid, you might have felt sucker-punched, but you didn't really look it. I don't think."

"But how would she have seemed to someone who was trying to get a reaction out of her? Someone who wanted the story confirmed?" James questioned Rose.

She reluctantly admitted, "I can't say for certain, James. *I* don't think she *clearly* gave herself away."

James's bitter smile showed he found only lukewarm comfort in Rose's assurance. He pressed on, "And Nigel's immediate reaction?"

Jessica took that one: "He made what seemed like an off-hand comment about you having a 'secret life' I didn't know about."

"Nigel does love his irony," James remarked, sinking back on the couch. Jess could see him trying to decide whether that irony applied to his actual secret life. Trying to be helpful, she pointed out, "What makes me wonder is why did he go from coolly sardonic to tearing through your office, then rushing out in a fury?"

Rose looked from one to the other, finally saying, "Okay, wait a minute here. Are you two saying that you're suspicious of Nigel or Terry? Why? What's their connection to your case? What *is* your case? What the dickens is going on around here?"

Jessica looked to James, knowing he should field this one.

"James, Jessica, I want some answers. You have to let me protect my family. How dangerous is the situation? Good Lord, is there a connection to Jessamyn Crane's murder and Sailor's disappearance? You guys need to level with me."

James leaned forward again and took Rose's hands calmingly in his to ask, "Rose, you trust me, don't you?"

"I'd trust you better if I knew where all this was going."

James nodded and concluded, "Right. That's probably better than I should expect under the circumstances. So, listen to me. I'm sorry for the deception–and don't be angry with Jessica, either. For my safety, for *your* safety, she kept things on the q.t."

"Okay, I can accept that," Rose said carefully. "I just can't accept any threats to my family."

"I don't see any threats to your family if you play things the way I tell you. What we've talked about, what I'm about to tell you, as much as I *can* tell you, cannot leave this room. Not even to David."

"I don't like to keep secrets from him . . ."

"Even in his best interest? Even if doing so helps me to catch a fifth columnist who won't accept that the war's over and seems to have plans to start the next one?"

James didn't browbeat Rose, his tone and words reasonable and genuine. That struck home with her, for, after thinking it over, she said, "That's why you're here, to nab this guy?"

James smiled crookedly and explained, "Actually, I came here to teach nineteenth-century British literature. My handlers found out that this chap was in the area, in disguise. So, do the maths and figure out whom they chose to identify him."

"And you think it's Nigel or Terry?" Rose concluded in disbelief. "Honestly, James, can you believe it of either of them? Terry's way too busy showing off to have time to plot world domination. As for Nigel, well, he's always been a stand-up, if sardonic, guy. And I honestly believed he cared about Jessamyn"

"Those sound like effective covers, don't you think, Rose?" James quietly pointed out.

Rose wasn't sure how to answer, so she just asked, "What do you want me to do?"

"Absolutely nothing."

"Huh?"

"That's the way to keep yourself in the clear. Steer away from those two as much as you can, but don't do anything to draw attention. I can tell you that one way or another, this mess will be done within about a week."

Jess barely managed to quell a shudder at the thought of for *whom* things might be "done with." To avoid alarming Rose, she suppressed her worries over James.

"So, you don't think I should take the family and leave town?" Rose slowly questioned. "Until after the storm breaks?"

"Only if it's normal for you to decamp right now," James answered. "As I said, don't draw attention to yourself, for your sake and Jessica's, as well for the sake of my mission."

"Point taken," Rose agreed. "It's just that I can't believe the guy you're after could be either Terry or Nigel." Then she added, "Although if I had a choice, I'd pick Terry. Nigel would be off the hook, and we'd all be rid of Terry and his ego."

A glance at his watch and James decided, "It's about time we took you back, Rose. What say Jessica and I run you home in my new chariot?"

His words were light, a smile played on his lips, but Jess could read her husband's crushing concern at this latest turn.

"Good idea," Rose concurred, getting up. "However, after all those gallons of tea, I need a visit to the powder room. So, if you'll excuse me . . ."

After Rose had disappeared up the stairs, Jessica turned to her husband and said earnestly, "James, I'm so sorry. I didn't want things to work out this way . . ."

He raised a quieting hand, then slipped over next to her on the couch to say, "Don't punish yourself. I should be apologizing. I don't know who deserves a poke in the nose more for getting you into this fix, me or Dick Streeter."

"I vote for Dick," Jess said decidedly.

James nodded agreement and Jess rested her head on his shoulder. After a moment, she looked up and wondered, "I don't get it, James. Why throw in your face that he knows who you are? I mean, I do get the ego aspect–looking for us to squirm. Still, if Zottistrauch admits he knows that you know, isn't that just daring you to drop a net on him?"

"I've been giving that a great deal of thought, too," James answered. "and, yes, it's definitely an act of ego. But it's actually a clever one. He plays his hand to take me down a peg, showing me he knows who I am even if I'm not sure who he is. But he's still playing me. He's figured out that I want more than him, that I'm after his plans, his allies. Otherwise, I would have hauled in the whole kit and kaboodle of suspects. No, he knows we have to separate the wheat from the chaff to get what we really want—and he's rubbing my nose in the fact that I still can't positively identify him yet. I believe he sees aggravation as an effective way to keep me from thinking straight, especially if he drags you into the mix."

"So, do you think it's Nigel?" Jessica asked. "He was there, at the reception. He and Terry could have set their little trap after Terry got the story from Sam Steinwall."

"Was Nigel the only one of our suspects taking tea today?" James queried.

"Oh, no, not at all. Nicholas Spenser came late—and apologized about yesterday, again. He wasn't in the group when Terry had Sam tell his story, but that doesn't mean Terry couldn't have told him earlier. He might even have been with Terry when Sam first blabbed. So, that lets Nigel off the hook . . . Well, no, not if Nigel were the one searching your office. Oh, darn, James! I'm going in circles. I mean if Nigel isn't Zottigstrauch, why *would* he be searching your office?"

"A good question," James concluded, tiredly. "A good question for which I have no answer, at present."

They were silent, both lost in uneasy thoughts. Still, though they were neither able to offer the other a comforting solution, they felt some comfort in the other. Finally, Jessica said, "Under the circumstances, perhaps I should bow out of the presentation at Rockingham Park tomorrow."

"A last-minute cancellation?" mused James. "Is that what a woman with nothing to fear, nothing to hide, would do?"

Jess shifted to face James and asked, "So, you do think we should go?"

James nodded and replied, "Actually, Jessica, I've been doing some thinking over the week, about Novack, his brother, and this horse. Something I can't quite put my finger on doesn't sit right with me about the whole business. I can't imagine they would have let the horse get away if he *were* valuable to them, so he's probably not the *actual* key. But it could be that if we had a casual chat with some people who knew Novack and his brother, it might clue us in on how Phil got involved with this bunch. That might get us a lead on our chum's identity. It's a long shot . . ."

"Then a racetrack is the ideal place to play it," Jessica finished with a mischievous smile.

James returned her a smile and squeezed Jess's shoulder, saying, "You never can tell. And if we motor to New Hampshire as if we hadn't a care in the world after my friend's grand play, perhaps he's the one who'll be pushed off-kilter—with my assistants on hand take note."

Jess leaned her head, again, on James's shoulder; his cheek rested on her hair. This felt so darned good that she almost couldn't feel the chill of those dark shadows James was trying to keep from haunting her.

Chapter Twenty-Seven

Saturday, August 3

The recently painted clubhouse and connected buildings gleamed white beneath soft green roofs that peaked and curved like tent pavilions. Jess was smiling, not just because she knew her sister's creation had turned a few heads: black, thin-crepe redingote over a surplice neck, empire waist dress of paisley in soft blues, pinks, and greens. The matching turban's swag hung down behind almost as long as her hair. A glow of hope had been restored even more effectively by her day at Rockingham Park. If anyone had told her yesterday that today would turn out so grand, she'd have said, "Go tell it to the Marines!" But she was, indeed, having a swell time up in the President's box, with the big man himself, "Uncle" Lou Smith. The godfather of thoroughbred racing in New Hampshire, Smith was the driving force who'd brought the track back to life by getting pari-mutuel wagering legal in the state; who'd founded the New Hampshire Breeders Association; and who'd pulled together the big bucks to rebuild and reclaim "The Rock" from human marathoners, mechanical motorbikes, and total disrepair. He'd made the track a showplace that not only packed in the pony players, often via special B & M trains from Boston, but drew respected owners like Greentree stable, Arthur Vanderbilt, the Whitneys, Bing Crosby, and William Kilmer.

Jess had gotten quite a kick out of hearing from Smith how much he and his wife enjoyed her program as well as from his plans for improving racing conditions for everyone from horses to his favorite folk, the bettors. She'd especially been impressed with his plans for the Horse Retirement Fund. One percent of every purse at Rockingham was donated to support buying up old racehorses and letting them finish their days on a farm. He'd brightened on that point, and the two had enjoyed a great confab about owing these hayburners more than retirement in a bottle of Elmer's Glue or a can of Kennel Ration. She really liked this guy: the pillowy cheeks, the affable style—as well as the sharp eyes behind his glasses that revealed a man always figuring how to stay on top and ahead of the game. Lord help you if you thought you could get in his way. At least, he seemed to be using the power of his smarts and grit for good rather than "evil." Too bad they couldn't enlist him against Zottigstrauch!

She'd felt unsettled only briefly. James had casually brought up during the conversation about pensioning racehorses that *they* had an old thoroughbred, one that had belonged to a fellow who'd trained at the Rock—Val Novack. Lou Smith had remembered Novack and his small operation traveling the New England circuit. Recalled he'd died suddenly last March or so of a heart attack. Had a brother in the service; no, that guy had been discharged after a run-in with a sub. Jess had nodded and smiled, letting James take the lead, knowing where all this was going. Still, she was too much of a Girl Scout to enjoy spinning a yarn. Maybe it wasn't just the Girl Scout jazz, though, because she had the distinct feeling that Smith could read her like a book. Unless she wanted to foul up James's plan, she'd better hang back and let him carry the ball. And he did, going on about the brother, Phil, living near them; that he'd not done well, with battle fatigue; and he could use some scuttlebutt about his late brother to buck him up—if any of Val Novack's old cronies were still around. Was there anyone with a good word or two for Phil Novack?

Lou Smith had nodded, thinking, and asked one of his assistants if Frankie Scutnik and Ceasare Lastalla, who were working the backside this meet, hadn't been with Novack at one time. Smith got a confirmation and promised that something could be arranged after the final race on the card. They'd meet Jessica and James at the saddling enclosure.

Jess had protested the guys would be busy with their charges, so she and James could go to their stables. Lou Smith had looked down at her black, open-toed sandals and queried, "In those shoes?"

That had brought a good laugh all around, though Jess still didn't feel right for not being entirely on the square. Nevertheless, when Lou Smith asked them the name of the old-timer that they were stabling, she'd perked up at getting some real news on her pal and said, "Black Guardian. He's a Chitzenegan racer."

Smith had mused how seldom they got Chitzenegan horses up at the Rock, though Bing Crosby had brought over some of his Argentinian stock. When she'd described Blackie, he'd shrugged, said maybe Novack had only run this horse down in Rhode Island or Massachusetts. Then, prompted by association, he'd told her about another black racehorse, Brass Monkey, who'd been running and winning when he was older than Lionel Barrymore. The conversation had soon turned to other exciting anecdotes, like when the hurricane of '38 blew Warren Yarberry off his horse and the announcer's booth off the grandstand!

With great racing, a lovely lunch, and engaging conversation, the day had nearly smoothed over yesterday's anxieties. Aside from his fishing expedition on Val Novack, James had encouraged her immersion in the excitement of the day, determined to spare her any more worry.

Now the field was being loaded into the starting gate for the main race on the card–the one where Jessica would present the winning trophy. Unlike in some races, there were no bad actors in this field, so the assistant starters got them into their stalls without incident. Jess had picked a handsome bay colt named Shiny Penny for his alert look and the steady improvement indicated on his form chart. There was that pause seeming to stretch into infinity while the starter, from his high platform at the gate, next to the rail, reviewed horses and riders to catch the supreme moment when all were poised and ready to break. The bell sounded, the gates flew open, horses burst from their stalls under yelling jockeys–and Babe Rubenstein's signature raspy voice declared with equal verve: "They're off!"

Jess's horse wasn't on the lead, though the race was only six furlongs, but she could see the colt in striking distance. The first quarter was surprisingly fast. When they moved to the half, Shiny Penny was in the thick with Elmo T and West Fleet. The three came flying around the turn into the stretch. Would this be a triple-dead heat to rival the 1944 Carter Handicap, where Jess had collected on Brownie? Now, Shiny Penny dug down and found some of that heart Jess had earlier glimpsed in his eyes.

Slowly the colt edged ahead. West Fleet cracked and began to fade. Elmo T still hung tough and tried to move up on the outside, only a neck behind. Where was that finish line?

Shiny Penny went to the well one more time, stretched out his bay neck, and kept it in front as they hit the wire. Thrilled, delighted, Jessica threw her hands in the air.

Smith shook his head at her jubilation. Starting them down to the winner's circle, he kidded, "I'd go broke if all my horse players were like you."

"It can't be because I win so much money," Jessica responded.

"No, it's because you don't *lose* enough!"

Awarding the cup to the owner was all a blur to Jess. It was a thrill to be today's celebrity, even if she wasn't handing out Belmont Park's Woodlawn Vase. The owners were as ecstatic as if they'd owned War Admiral. That made it all a treat! Jessica was even going to get a copy of the winner's circle photo. Wouldn't her agent get a kick out of that! Maybe a copy would make it to the wall of "stars" at the radio studio. She knew that her old pal Harry Shaftner would want a copy to hang behind the lunch counter in his drugstore. And then it was all over.

It had already been planned for her and James to enjoy the rest of the card from the stands. Lou Smith could go back to running the track full time. All the various interruptions during her visit, though handled quickly and expertly, told her that this man was never off the clock. He and his wife even lived in a nifty apartment atop the clubhouse!

After all the excitement, Jess was perfectly happy to forego her usual railbird status, take a seat in the grandstand, and surreptitiously slip off her shoes. Unfortunately, as the day's excitement dissipated, the disturbing questions lurking at the periphery of her consciousness forced themselves forward. What would they uncover about Phil and his brother from the two former stable hands? Perhaps, that both brothers were involved with Zottigstrauch? How Phil had gotten mixed up with the Nazi? How Blackie, a former plater, might fit into the picture? She could *not*, however, allow her jitters to show when they met Val Novack's two former workers.

The walking ring seemed almost ghostly with most of the patrons having trickled off and no more shiny, eager horses; snappy trainers; or jockeys in eye-catching silks. Still, the two men waiting for them weren't at all unfriendly. Both bore weathered faces from making the rounds of the New England/New York circuits for many years. Getting up at the crack of dawn and slaving away most of the day mucking out stalls, feeding and watering and grooming sore, temperamental, BIG animals wasn't exactly an Elizabeth Arden Beauty treatment.

Smith's assistant stayed only long enough to make the introductions, then Jess got the ball rolling, "We know how busy you fellas are, so we really appreciate your taking the time to see us."

The older of the two grinned broadly, "Yeah, Ceasare and me was really looking forward to mucking out a bunch of stalls and dodging a mess of cranky nags who like to put the bite on you, so to speak, when you don't feed them fast enough."

"Sounds like my husband," Jess cracked.

James feigned offense, offering, "In my defense, I have had all my shots."

"Oh, you're a Limey," the younger guy noted, hearing James's accent.

"Jeez, Ceasare," the older man dope-slapped his companion. "You don't call them that." He turned back to Jessica and James to say, "So, you'd like to get some dope on Val Novack, for his kid brother Phil."

"Something like that," James affirmed. "And don't worry about the 'Limey' reference–I took it in the spirit it was intended. At any rate, we do live near Phil's place, down in Connecticut. I don't know if you know what happened to him in the war . . ."

"A Kraut sub shot his boat out from under him," the older man supplied. "Yeah, Val said the guy was never quite the same after. Battle fatigue, huh?"

"Battle fatigue," James confirmed. "He can't stand to be around people much. My wife and I have been two of his only mates. He talks about his brother a lot. His death was something of a double-whammy, on top of the war and all that. We thought that if you had some stories we could bring back to him, about his brother and happier times, it might help him. Catch my drift?"

"Yeah, sure, I follow you," Frankie said. "Well, now let me see. I remember Phil used to work for his brother in the summers, then he joined up with the Coast Guard. I don't know how happy those times were when he worked for Val. See his brother had hoped the kid, heck he ain't no kid now, is he? So, anyway, Val had hoped his brother might come in with him someday. Phil really knew his way around a horse, 'specially the bad actors. But the track life wasn't for him. So he goes into the service to see something better—and then ends up all alone."

"I think he was just disappointed he couldn't be a jockey," Ceasare tossed in.

"I guess a guy 6'4" would have a little trouble making weight," Jessica observed, straight-faced.

"Yeah, too bad they don't race Clydesdales," Ceasare chuckled.

"Knock it off," the older man cut in on his friend. "They want to know about Val and Phil."

"Yeah, okay. Sorry," Ceasare relented, not the alpha of the pair.

Frankie went on, "Yeah, Val Novack was one hell of a trainer—beg pardon, lady. Heart of gold. Had a soft spot for a guy down on his luck—and a horse, too. He could patch up the sorriest, sorest old plater and make him, well, maybe not always win but at least bring home a piece of the purse. A big enough piece to keep Val's nags and his boys off the breadlines. It'd break his heart when he'd get some old horse going good and then someone would claim the horse out from under him."

"That brother of his near broke his heart, too," Ceasare added. "Always having trouble with money. Val always having to bail him out. I figured he enlisted to stay one step ahead of those guys he owed money."

"Ceasare, what's with you, badmouthing Phil in front of his friends," Frankie snapped. Turning back to Jessica and James, he said, "Anyway, sounds like he got himself straightened out in the service. Even got hisself a commission. He's not in any jam, now, right?"

Jessica smiled tightly and let James shake his head in answer. She didn't trust her voice, bitterly knowing that James's response was truthful insofar as Phil apparently was past all trouble now.

Frankie insisted, "Ceasare, you're forgettin' that not long before Val's bum ticker gave out on him, he said that Phil let him know he was in on a good deal that was going to square all his old debts and set him up fine. An' he wasn't about to blow his profits like he used to. He was going to stay on the beam from now on."

"That must have been a relief to Val," James agreed. "Did Val ever say what it was, this good deal? Maybe it's something we can talk about with him, keep him upbeat."

Both grooms thought for a bit, before Frankie shook his head. Ceasare let him speak for them both, "Nagh. Val wasn't exactly the talkative type, but it did give him peace of mind."

"Knowing Phil would give Blackie a home must have given Val peace of mind, too," Jess proposed.

The grooms looked at her quizzically. Frankie questioned, "Blackie? Who's Blackie?"

That brought both Jessica and James up short. They exchanged questioning glances, and Jess now took the lead, "Black Guardian." Two blank stares answered her. "This big black horse, a Chitzenegan bred that Val picked up in a claiming race but couldn't run." Still with the flummoxed expressions. "So he gave him, well sold him cheap, for a dollar, to Phil."

"Lady," Frankie finally said, "You got me there. Val had four or five horses up here in training the year he died, owned one of them, but none of them was black."

"He didn't even have a dark bay," Ceasare corroborated.

Jessica straightened, bewildered. She started to protest, give them the exact story Phil had given her, but James's quiet pressure on her arm silenced her.

James smoothly conjectured, "Maybe he kept the horse elsewhere and sent it on to Phil."

"Mister," Ceasare explained, "nobody stables a horse for the heck of it. These nags have to earn their keep. They're expensive. You've got to pay for stall space, feed, vet bills, help to take care of the horse. Nope, that's out of the question. Val Novack was a nice guy, but he was no Rockafella. I'm telling you, he and us and his horses all traveled together, and we never saw no black horse."

James conjectured, "Could he have bought the horse just for his brother, then cooked up the story about claiming a lame horse, so it would look to Phil as if he were doing Val a favor rather than accepting charity?"

"Yeah, that sounds like Val and Phil," Frankie nodded. Ceasare seconded the nod, even as Frankie elaborated, "Kid didn't want to be beholden, and Val knew how to get around that. Sure, that's probably the story."

The conversation moved on to old times, so that Jessica and James soon had a barrel full of anecdotes. It broke her heart to know that she'd never have the opportunity to recount them. She missed Phil, and, worse, she felt like a heel for using the dead guy to get at the truth behind Georg Zottigstrauch. The only salve she could put on her conscience was that this deception just might help get justice for Phil. Yet none of that conscience-salving did a bit of good at resolving her bewilderment over the fact that these two in-the-know fellows had completely blown sky-high Phil's back story on Black Guardian.

Somehow the conversation was back onto horses from Chitzenega, and Ceasare said, "Say, Frankie, remember last year there was a big gray horse here, running. He was a Chitzenegan bred."

"Yeah, his groom showed me that funny number tattoo on his upper lip," Frankie concurred. "What'll those South of the Border guys think of next? But, like you said, he wasn't black. He was a flea-bitten gray. That wasn't your horse. He was even worth big money. He took down a six-furlong stakes in 1:10 flat. Guy who owned him was from Chitzenega, too."

"What was his name?" James inquired.

Frankie and Ceasare shrugged, with the former saying, "Darned if we can remember. Picture was in the paper, though. Yeah, I remember; it was last summer. He rolled in with that big bag of bones and that old bag rolled over the whole field—paid a nice price, too. Then they rolled out for parts unknown. Maybe your black horse was part of their stable that didn't make the cut. Sometimes a big outfit will unload a cheap horse here or at 'Gansett or Suffolk or one of the smaller tracks down in New York. Val might have seen him on a run down there."

"Pictures that run in local papers, of stakes races, sometimes get picked up in *Turf and Sport Digest*," Jessica mused aloud. "I might be able to find that picture with a descriptive blurb of the horse and owner there."

"For Phil's benefit," James smoothly added. "He might be interested in his horse's former owner."

Jess smiled wanly in support. Pretending Phil was still alive was taking a toll on her. James gave her a quick study and seemed to decide that he'd gotten enough, that fishing for more information wasn't worth the wear and tear on her psyche. He wrapped things up, slipping both grooms a tip. Jess let him be the one to tell both men he'd give their regards to Phil.

Neither Jessica nor James had much to say once they'd been escorted out by Smith's assistant and thanked him and Lou Smith again for the day. Jess promised that tickets to her program would always be waiting for her hosts and their wives any time they were in New York. The Crawfords' walk back to their car in the late afternoon sun was a pretty silent affair. Both had a lot of thinking to do. Jess wished she could be certain James was serious with his explanation of Blackie's mysterious origins. Instinct told her something more was going on inside his head; however, she knew James well enough to realize he'd only open up when he was good and ready.

James unlocked and opened the door for her, giving her a tired but genuine smile. He still wasn't spilling anything, though, darn! So, Jessica sighed and carefully removed the turban and all its fastenings before getting into the car. She was darned tired of carrying the thing around on her head. Too bad it wasn't just as easy to disencumber herself of all her disturbing questions.

After closing the door on Jess, then sliding in on the driver's side, James asked, "So, what do you think?"

"I think," Jess began slowly, "That I'd like to know where in Sam Hill Blackie really came from."

James nodded, reflecting before asking, "Is that because you truly think the horse is relevant to the case or because you're wrapped up in him?"

Jessica thought deeply about her husband's question before answering, "I do care about the horse. Sure, I admit I'd love to know what his background is. Still, I have to tell you that there's something not quite on the level about him. I mean, your explanation makes sense, except a trainer and his crew follow the racing circuits together. Someone with plenty of money and a big stable can afford to take the horses back to the farm in the off-season. But Val Novack, he's small time. You heard those guys; he didn't have any money to spare. So when would he have the wherewithal to go looking for a charity horse somewhere his stable wasn't? Where would he get the cash to stable the horse separately? No, there's some kind of monkey business related to Chitzenega going on here. Maybe the owner of the grey horse paid Phil off with Black Guardian, as well as the cash the groom said put Phil on an even keel. Maybe Georg Zottigstrauch was passing himself off as a Chitzenegan sportsman—no, more likely he used the Chitzenegan as a go-between with Phil. What do you think?"

"Chitzenega did and does still have its fair share of Nazi sympathizers," James added. Then he asked, "Do you still have that racing magazine you mentioned? If we could trace the owner, we might catch a lead that can put us onto Zottigstrauch's plans. By the way, I forgot to tell you, I had my man in the stable copy your horse's tattoo. When I saw Dick . . ."

"At the dentists?" Jessica "innocently" queried.

"Certainly," James smiled faintly before continuing, "When I saw Dick, I gave him the number and all the attendant information—I must say he was impressed with your knowledge. At any rate, he's checking into it. So, we may get the information we need that way, though your magazine seems a much quicker prospect. Time isn't a commodity we can afford to waste, if Zottigstrauch is sticking to the schedule Clarke indicated."

"It's a quicker prospect if the mail is running on time," Jessica cautioned. "I didn't have the copy in Connecticut, but it should be one of the ones I asked Lois to mail me earlier in the week from New York." Jess thought again before speculating, "Chitzenega does seem to come up a lot in connection with Georg Zottigstrauch and his buddies. Remember Terry's new job prospect there?"

James looked away, over the steering wheel, before commenting, "I'm rather afraid that whatever Terry and his wife's intentions are, ultimately, Georg Zottigstauch will be going solo." He turned back to her and finished, "I think they're both in great danger."

Jessica responded, "It's hard for me to forgive Terry for outing you on this case, but I can't honestly say I want him killed. Slightly wounded, maybe . . ."

"Right, then," James decided, stepping on the brake and the clutch before turning the key in the ignition. "Let's get you back so that you can start your homework."

"Home," Jess sighed. "I guess we have one heck of a drive. I hate to think of you dozing off."

"That's all right, love," James assured her mischievously, "You'll doze and keep me awake when you start to snore."

"Oh, why you heel!" Jessica feigned indignation. "I'll have you know that as a respected, cultivated actress of the stage and the air waves, even my snoring is dulcet."

"As two sucking doves," James returned with a dollop of charm as he moved the car into the crush of traffic trying to exit the huge parking lot.

Jess sank back into her seat, wanting to relax, wanting to relish the oasis of humor. But questions of Phil and Blackie and Zottigstrauch's plans for Terry and his wife lurked in the shadows of her mind.

Chapter Twenty-Eight

Saturday/Sunday, August 3/4

Sitting at the kitchen table, flipping through her racing magazines, Jessica was comfy in a beige robe over her night gown–especially with that cup of tea beside her. James had retired to the study to read, carrying with him a glass of liquid fortification stronger than tea. From the chair on Jessica's left, Dusty rolled over, extending a paw in a luxurious stretch. Jess wished she could feel so relaxed as she flipped through the pages, pausing at a promising photo or title, then disappointedly pushing on. Her eyes beginning to burn at this late hour, Jessica was still far too restless to turn in. She'd also enjoyed a pretty solid snooze on the drive back. James had diplomatically remained mum on whether she had snored. Smiling a little, Jess picked up an early 1946 issue of *Turf and Sport Digest*. Turning to the table of contents, she thought, *Whoa! Somebody upstairs loves me right now!* Facing her was the title: "Chitzenega Inroads in the U.S.: Horses from the South Blitz the Northeast." Darned if the little picture to the right of the title didn't show a rangy grey horse in blinkers galloping home first. This article ought to say something about the grey horse's owner. If only it would turn out to be the right horse.

Jess eagerly started turning to the article, but something else from the index caught her eye: the head shot of a horse who could have doubled for Black Guardian, next to a different article: "Gone But Not Forgotten." *Hey, maybe the old boy had developed a following, as claimers sometimes did when they won often enough to save railbirds from turning into bridge jumpers. If this were actually Black Guardian. It wouldn't hurt to check. If it didn't pan out, there was still plenty of time for the other article.*

The first part of the article was about Dark Secret, a well-known handicap star who'd met a tragic but gallant end. *Oh, this article's probably about game racers, spanning claimers to stakes horses–an interesting slant these pieces sometimes took. The article might apply to Blackie. Still, a lot of horses look a lot alike, hence the problems with ringers.*

Jess flipped the page: the name of the pictured black horse almost jolted her out of the chair. She actually had to shake her head to clear it. Rapidly, Jessica scanned the photos of a horse who clearly seemed a double for her four-legged pal, including a picture of the 1945 Baxter Handicap dust up. *It couldn't be. No, it just couldn't be!* But there he was, moving just the way she now realized she'd seen him move under Phil, felt him move under her.

"Holy Mackerel!" was all Jess could finally manage. Did she feel amazed, stupid, terrified, enlightened, or . . . what?

How had she not seen this resemblance before? And yet, she knew the answer. You wouldn't connect the dots when your reality didn't tell you that the dots even existed.

James chose that moment to walk into the kitchen, partially emptied glass in hand. Tiredly, he smiled, "How goes the research? Say, you look as if you found something. The Chitzenegan connection?"

Looking at his glass, Jess warned, "Good, you're going to need that."

"After the past few days, I could use a whole bottle," James sighed, but he was intrigued by Jess's odd mix of excitement and trepidation. "Show me what you have, love."

"Just wait," Jessica answered, folding back the page and carefully covering the text so all James could see was a photo. She asked as calmly as she could, "Does this horse look familiar?"

James gave her a curious expression, then put his glass down to take a good look, saying, "You know I'm no expert on horses, Jessica. Let's see. Ah, that's . . . no . . . Yes?" He turned to her, perplexed, and asked, "Is that Blackie? I can see the way he arches his neck when he runs. Looks just like him." Suspicion growing, James noted, "Odd they'd have an article on a cheap horse in here, isn't it?"

"I'll show you something even odder," Jessica replied, letting her husband see the horse's name.

"Blue Warrior?" James puzzled. "Where have I heard that name before? Ah, right, you and Liz were talking about him the afternoon I told you I'd take this job. I remember . . . But you said he was dead?"

"Killed in a barn fire, along with his groom," Jessica answered. "Or maybe not. It wouldn't be so hard to substitute a similar horse. If he were badly burned, how would anyone see the difference?"

James cautioned, "Are you sure you're not letting all the recent intrigue get to you, Jessica? To me, lots of horses look alike. You even explained to me about ringers."

"That may be, James," Jessica countered, "but it makes sense that Blackie is Blue Warrior. There's his running style—and his personality. Blue Warrior was well known for having strong likes and dislikes about people, depending how they treated him. Isn't it an interesting coincidence that people started seeing Phil Novack with this horse a month or so after Blue Warrior allegedly died? It certainly explains why Phil's back story for getting the horse doesn't add up."

James picked up his glass, looked at it, then decided, "I could use a whole *case* of this now."

"Save some for me," Jess added before continuing, "And here's something else I never thought of before. Terry and Carolina are both from horse country in Virginia. Stan, the groom, once mentioned to me that Carolina said her family bred hunters at a farm called Selbywood in Snowfree Springs, Virginia. Damascus, Maryland is just a hop, skip, and not even a jump from the border."

"Damascus?"

"Where Blue Warrior had been retired—and supposedly met his demise. Those horse people know each other backwards and forwards. I'm willing to bet that Carolina was the inside man, as it were, who helped Georg Zottigstrauch plan and execute the horse-napping."

James sat down and gave Jessica a skeptical look before saying, "Georg Zottigstrauch? Took the horse? What would he want with a horse? Wait, are you thinking that the *horse* is his package?"

"Exactly!"

"A horse? Why a horse?" James was genuinely baffled.

"Take a gander at this article, James. It mentions that Blue Warrior's owner was offered $100,000 for him when he was racing. Look at Stymie and Armed. They're both winners of over $800, 000," Jessica pointed out.

"All right, but they're racing. You said Blue Warrior couldn't anymore because he was injured—and I hardly think that, even if he could, Georg Zottigstrauch would go parading around the country with a high-profile animal, no matter how much cash it brought in. So, where's the profit for him? Unless you think his plans are to undermine thoroughbred racing in America. Not exactly a red-alert issue."

Jessica shook her head, "James, a champion's purse money is one way to stay in business, but it's not the only one. You get more champion racehorses by breeding the one you have. Some people say breeding is really where the money is, 'cause when you've got a great stallion people practically throw dollars at you to bring you their mares. Look, here it says a guy from Argentina offered the owner $200,000 when Blue Warrior retired. If Zottigstrauch sold the horse, he could get himself a nice little war chest, now couldn't he?"

"Argentina? Not Chitzenega?" James questioned thoughtfully.

"I know," Jess scowled. "It would be so convenient if the Chitzenegan connection were listed right here."

"But sometimes a man might have someone front for him, if he didn't want anyone to know his identity," James considered. "Let me see the article. Dick might be able to check out the Argentinean if I give him the name. Ah, here it is. Right." He took a pen and notepad from his inside jacket pocket and wrote down the name, pausing to look up at Jess and say, "You're quite the unique resource, you know, Jessica."

She shrugged with mock modesty and said, "What's a wife's duty but to help her husband catch deadly Nazis by drawing on her extensive knowledge of horse racing?"

"Exactly what I've always said. Now, let me pick your brain some more. Any names of likely Chitzenegan horsemen in your magazine? Anything about the grey horse the stable men were telling us about?"

Jess showed her husband the other article she'd found. As he took notes, she mused, "There are a couple of things that still bother me?"

"Only two?" James didn't even look up.

Jess let the remark pass and continued, "I can't figure what's with the tattoo. Blue Warrior wasn't a Chitzenegan horse, and we don't tattoo Thoroughbreds in the States. So why does *he* have a tattoo?"

James pondered that one, then grinned to point out, "Your horse might if someone wanted to disguise an American horse as a Chitzenegan one. There must be at least one big black horse in Chitzenega, probably in the stable of Zottigstrauch's contact."

"Good heavens! That's so clever," Jessica agreed excitedly. "Think about it: turning a procedure to catch ringers into a method for sneaking one out of the country. I've got to hand it to Zottigstrauch."

"That's what I'm up against," James tiredly stated. "That's also why I'm going to tell Dick to focus on freighters heading out of New York, New Jersey, New Haven, maybe even Boston, for Chitzenega over the next two weeks, particularly if horses are registered in the cargo."

"That ought to keep Dick's guys busy," Jess decided. "But how can they cover all that shipping?"

"They can't," James admitted. "Not unless I narrow things down for them. I might be able to do that with some of these names to check on the manifests, including the Argentinean who wanted to buy the horse. It will work better all-around if we can get the goods on Zottigstrauch with the horse. Tying him to the theft of a horse where a man was likely murdered gives us strong leverage on him. With those circumstances, he'll be looking at the death penalty. But we have to know if it's Nigel or Nicholas Spenser if we're going to catch him with the horse."

Jessica warned. "He could hand Terry or Carolina the dirty work of taking the horse away."

James shook his head, "That horse, his package, means everything to him. He won't trust those two not to try and cut him out. He's a man who has to have control every step of the way. No, he'll be with that horse to make the exchange. He's not letting anything that precious to his plans get out of his sight."

"Well, that leads to my second question," Jessica said. "If the horse *is* so darned precious, why did they let him get away? Why let me keep him now?"

"I suspect," James began, "Blue Warrior ran off when they killed Phil Novack. They weren't exactly able to keep up with him, and they certainly couldn't take a car on the beach to catch him. But they acted on a good guess that you had him, checked it out, and let you hold him because, if you think about it, it's the perfect plan. We feed Blackie, protect him, keep him sound and healthy–all right under their noses. They have all the knowledge and none of the responsibility. And, of course, by leaving him to you, it looks as if the horse doesn't matter. When it's time to ship the horse out, they just plan out sneaking into the stable, loading him up in a van, and off they go–they think. My friend Zottigstrauch may have gotten wise to me, but I've been careful to hide that I have someone on the grounds who can watch the horse. Why should he suspect it, especially since he sees us as too thick to tumble to his shrewd plan? Which reminds me, first thing tomorrow I'll give my mate in the barn a heads up to keep a close eye on the horse. According to Terry's timetable, they won't be moving out the horse until next week. So, I needn't arose suspicion by grabbing a private chat with my contact tonight."

"Probably not," Jessica concurred, though she was ready to put an armed guard on Blackie immediately. But she deferred to the expert, only asking the practical, "Then, what should I do?"

"Stay out of the way of our suspects. Keep using your head, as you did when you didn't charge in on whoever was searching my office. The less I need to worry about you, the better I can do my job, and bring this whole damned thing to a close."

Jessica put her hand over James's, and he patted it with his free one. She tried not to think about the fact that he hadn't promised her that all would end well.

Late Sunday afternoon sunlight cascaded through the bedroom dormer windows. Sitting at her vanity, Jessica Minton put down her brush and tossed her dark hair over the shoulders of her white blouse splashed with tropical florals.

She turned to Dusty, who was placidly settled on the bed and inquired, "So, pal, do I come on like a gal with nothing more on her mind than looking good for dinner and a movie with her handsome husband?"

It had been James's idea, to go out tonight to give the impression of how little they had to worry about or hide. If an enemy seized the opportunity to slip into their home while they were out, he would find nothing, likely even confounding Zottigstrauch's suspicions. *Enough to cancel the implications of Sam Steinwall's story?*

The doorbell rang, startling Jessica as much as Dusty! Hearing James answer the door, Jess wondered who'd drop by late on a Sunday afternoon, unannounced.

The door downstairs closed. *Had the visitor gone? Was it safe? No gunshots or even sounds of struggling. Am I getting paranoid?* Dusty suddenly gave a "Brrp!"and jumped off the bed to run out of the room. Well, *if Dusty wasn't worried . . ..*

A minute later, Jess hit the bottom step of the stairs and paused. James stood by the closed front door reading something intently. Not liking the looks of things, Jessica called out, "James?"

He didn't turn right away; but, when James did, he wore the queerest expression. Jess crossed the room, asking, "What's wrong, James?"

Her husband looked down at the letter and gave his mouth a funny twist before handing it to Jessica with, "This was just delivered by special messenger. What do you make of it?"

Jess took the page from his hand. The letterhead made her blink with surprise. She puzzled, "Nigel? What does he mean by sending you a letter this time on a Sunday? Doesn't he know that Don Ameche invented the telephone?"

"Read on," James urged. "It gets even more interesting."

"Interesting, huh?" Jess commented as she confronted a formal request, or more accurately a polite command, that she and James attend Nigel forthwith in his office at Cameron House.

"What in Sam Hill?" Jess tossed off with a confused wave of her hand. "What's so important that it can't wait until tomorrow?" An inkling of the answer gnawed inside her. "And why *me*? I don't get this at *all*."

"We won't know for certain until we get there," James pointed out.

Jess's eyes flashed as she fumed, "Who does he think he is, bossing us around?"

"He is my superior," James answered. "Or he might also be the chap whom I'm trying to trap. Either way, I can't afford to ignore him."

"Is it safe to go?" Jessica questioned uneasily.

"Six o'clock, in broad daylight? The janitor will be cleaning the English Department, and I've seen Judy Ricardo regularly preparing for her class at this time. Egotist that Zottigstrauch is, he'd have to be bats in the head to try something with them around. Do you really think I'd bring you along if I thought there was any danger? No, this is either a test by my Nazi chum—or the department chair has something to say that I'd get myself into a fix by ignoring."

"Do you think he might be going to offer you the position?" Jessica suggested hopefully, not really believing all was for the best.

James shook his head, "Bless your optimism, love. I don't think good news often comes in the form of a peremptory summons, no matter how well-bred the phrasing. We'd better go and find out exactly what all this is about."

The sun streamed through the windows behind Tricia's desk in the reception area. Through them, you could see the ocean glinting invitingly far beyond. Of course, the desk was empty and the typewriter veiled under its black cover. Jessica and James passed that area quickly, even as Jess thought about Tricia's devilish smile, never non-plussed by the most frazzled of professors or the most anxious of students. Nevertheless, her thoughts swiftly reverted to James, who seemed quiet, imperturbable. Yet Jess knew he must be planning behind his wall of calm. She only wished she could do more to help than merely keep her promise to let him do most of the talking and follow his lead.

It took a few minutes to reach their destination in the warren of rooms and blind corridors making up this wing. Then, there they were: Nigel Cross's office, his name on the door and everything. That door was closed.

James turned to Jess and raised a brow "significantly," mocking the severity of the situation to put her at ease. She smiled weakly, appreciative, if not reassured.

James knocked.

"Come in."

The words were firm: not friendly, but not threatening, either. Before Jess could decide what Cross's tone portended, James opened the door and escorted her inside.

Nigel sat directly before them, a cold fireplace behind him. His desk was covered in precisely ordered stacks of folders. He didn't look up from his paperwork when he coolly instructed, "Sit down, please." One hand briefly indicated the two chairs before his desk.

Smoothing her skirt beneath her to sit, Jess considered that at least Nigel had said "please." Yet he hadn't looked at either of them. Further, though Nigel had never displayed the jauntiness of Mickey Rooney, she couldn't remember him ever addressing either James or her with quite that much of an Arctic edge.

James had taken the seat to her left, his hands casually folded in his lap. How did he pull off that cucumber routine, especially when Nigel continued to study his papers with an occasional jot of his pen? It occurred to Jessica that Nigel was keeping them dangling to shake them. The m.o. of a department chair or of a Nazi? Well, at some schools the difference probably wasn't so great. But Nigel had always seemed to like and respect her and James, to play square with them. Why the change? Would it make sense if he were Georg Zottigstrauch, and that "respect" and "friendliness" had been a front all along?

Boy, that steamed her! Maybe at one point, she would have been hurt, disappointed, but just too much had gone south lately. Still, blowing her top was not in their best interest, so she channeled all that anger into beating Nigel at his own game. She could play it just as cool, maybe even cooler.

"I imagine you're both wondering why I requested you come to me right now."

Nigel's unexpected words startled Jess, but not enough to knock her off her game. A shared glance with James, and she let him do the talking.

"As a matter of fact," James began calmly, "I *do* find it rather peculiar that you have this sudden need to see both Jessica and me. What is so desperate that you had to call us in on a Sunday evening? Is there some trouble you need our help in handling?"

Jess watched Nigel pause before smiling icily at the turn James had given the subject, establishing that *he* needed *them*. She silently gave her husband full marks.

"You help me," he repeated slowly. "Yes, yes." Nigel was reformulating his approach even as he spoke. "I think you can help me, though it might not be in the way you are expecting. You see, some rather unsettling information concerning you and your wife has come to my attention. I want you to help me understand how to deal with it."

Jessica's first thought was adamantly to deny the story Sam Steinwall had let slip. But she kept her cool. They needed to know exactly what this mysterious, damning information was.

"Jessica and I?" James leaned forward, convincingly bewildered, then, amused. "I can't imagine what anyone could find unsettling about us. Unless you have a problem with our spending the day at Rockingham Park yesterday. Don't tell me you're afraid we've created bad publicity for the college."

James gave Jess a quick glance of encouragement, and she took the hint to add, "Honestly, Nigel, I wasn't offering the girls lessons in bookmaking instead of Shakespeare when I substituted for Terry."

Nigel Cross looked from one of them to the other, doubt flickering in his eyes. Then he pulled two sheets of typed paper from a folder and glanced at the top one. His gaze shifted from Jess to James as he explained carefully, "I'm afraid this has nothing to do with anyone's interest in horses. This concerns a personal issue. An intrusion into my life, which, I must warn you, is not only offensive but illegal."

James sat back in his chair, folding his arms before him, and replied honestly, "Now, you have lost me. What are you talking about?"

Nigel studied James, studied him hard, before quietly, firmly replying, "I wanted to talk to both of you before I took action . . ."

"Took action?" escaped Jessica, whether colored by alarm or anger, she wasn't sure. James's hand briefly on her arm calmed her, somewhat.

Nigel faced Jessica and asserted, "Yes, took action." Now he turned on James and continued, steadily, "I'd been very pleased, impressed with your work. To be frank, I'd even drafted a report recommending the college hire you . . ."

"But," James supplied coolly.

Nigel eyed James narrowly before elaborating, "But I received this first disturbing letter on Friday afternoon. I found it in my office when I came here after the President's Tea." Here Nigel Cross seemed to stumble, but not for long, "It so alarmed me that I was driven to do something I shouldn't have–or perhaps I should have, after all. I found what the letter promised, and then I received a second, even more alarming, missive. That's why you're both here now."

At this point, Jessica couldn't keep quiet and demanded, "So what did those lying letters claim about James and me? If you're going to accuse us, we have a right to know exactly of what we're being accused."

"Yes," James supported her. "One can't defend oneself without knowing what the charge is. It's about time you stopped beating about the bush, Nigel. Of what are you accusing us?"

Nigel seemed pained to answer. He hesitated, again, but pushed himself to hand the first letter to James, instructing, "See for yourself."

Anxiety clumped in Jessica's throat as Nigel stretched forward to hand James a letter. When her husband shifted toward her to share it, Nigel began to protest, but James quelled that with, "If she shares the accusation, then she deserves to see the 'evidence' against her."

The writing almost knocked Jess off her chair. It was typed on a blank sheet of paper and warned Nigel that James and Jessica had convincing evidence of Nigel's involvement with Jessamyn Crane that could be used to tie him to her murder. Then the poison penster got even nastier, and more imaginative, claiming that the couple planned to use that information to blackmail Nigel into awarding James a cozy spot on the faculty. As proof of these claims, the writer promised that Nigel would find a photo of himself and Jessamyn Crane with what could be construed as a compromising message from him to her inscribed on the back. All he had to do was look in James's desk in his office. Jessica's part in the deal was finding the photo and other evidence in the wreck in Joseph's Cove. The letter was signed, "A Friend."

"Whose friend?" Jessica snorted.

James took a more practical tact and scoffed, "Nigel, can an intelligent man like you actually go for anything this preposterous? For God's Sake, I've read Victorian novels with less melodrama."

"Yes," Nigel Cross began in a controlled but pointed voice, "except that I did, indeed, find that photograph. I have it . . . well, never mind where I have it now. It's safe. Jessamyn's name and mine are safe, as far as the photo goes. Or did you make a copy?"

Nigel's words immediately led Jessica to accuse, "It was you I saw searching James's office Friday."

For a moment, Jess thought James might be displeased with her breaking that promise to keep a low profile, but something sparked in his eyes. He sat up and transfixed Nigel with the quiet, firm accusation, "It sounds to me that you, Nigel, have a bit of explaining to do—breaking into my office, poking amongst my belongings without permission."

"I did not break in. I had Tricia's keys," Nigel insisted stiffly. Then he seemed to get hold of himself. He leaned forward, eyes as threatening as an iceberg in "Rime of the Ancient Mariner," and charged, "You still haven't explained away the evidence supporting these charges against you."

"An explanation," James returned coolly. "You'd like an explanation? Then let's review the facts, shall we? You, yourself, said you were planning to give me a good report, recommend me. You'd indicated as much to me earlier, as we both know. So, Nigel, why would I jeopardize nearly a sure thing by threatening you in a way that would surely turn you against me?" Nigel began to argue, but James held up his index finger to quiet him before continuing, "Furthermore, what kind of a boob would 'hide' his evidence where it could be so easily found and removed? Not even locked up and apparently open to the view of a third party. You used to be a man of reason, Nigel. What's happened to you?"

Nigel had almost deflated. Then his eyes were on Jessica, almost making her shiver. She held strong, though, when he demanded, "You deny retrieving that photo?"

"I've never even seen a photo of you with Jessamyn Crane," Jessica retorted, unable to keep indignant fire out of her voice.

Nigel's eyes narrowed then fell to the other missive on his desk. Now they were back on Jess, steady, intent, probing. He pressed, "And this other letter, it mentions my tie clip. You deny finding that in the wreck and keeping it to use against me?"

That question knocked the wind out of Jessica—and Nigel saw. With a hard, knowing smile, he began to pounce with, "Ah . . ."

James cut him off, "Now just a minute, Cross."

"No," Jessica took over. It was time to do what her friend Bobby Ito called "Go for Broke." "I'll handle this. Now look, Nigel, I did find a tie clip with your initials at the wreck. That much is true, but the rest is all hog wash. Maybe I should have just given it back, but I didn't know how to do it without chancing you'd know where I found it. It would have been awkward for both of us if you knew that I thought you might have met Jessamyn there, for whatever reason. It also looked as if she could have been meeting someone else. I didn't want to open up that can of worms with you, either. I thought it would hurt *you*. I wanted to let the whole thing die."

That answer knocked Nigel off stride. His anger deflated like a punctured zeppelin, leaving the man staring down at the paper before him. He barely moved when James returned the other letter. There was an uncomfortably long silence. Jess stole a glance at her husband; his eyes signaled her to be patient, see where Nigel would go from here. Finally, Cross looked up at both of them, the pain in his eyes nearly breaking Jessica's heart. *Or was this virtuoso role-playing by a clever Nazi?*

Nigel spoke, slowly, fiercely, bridling but not suppressing his emotions, "You must understand. For a man like me . . . I'm always in control. But Jessamyn was something, someone like I've never known. I only went to the derelict once, to try to talk her out of the foolishness with Clarke. The clip never did fasten right. But to see her waste her life on . . . to lose her so cruelly, twice . . ."

Jessica started to reach out to comfort Nigel, remembering what she had gone through all those nights waiting for James to come back from France. Nigel sat up abruptly, forestalling her with a look. He turned to James and demanded piercingly, "Why would anyone want to frame you for blackmail? Why try to turn me against you? What would be the point?"

James leaned forward and pensively replied, "Good question, Nigel. It was likely typed by someone in the department. He or she used Tricia's typewriter. You'll recognize the crippled 'e' and the jumpy 'd.' Do I have any enemies here that I don't know of? You are the Chair. You know which cupboards are full up with skeletons. What do you think?"

Nigel sat and thought, a bit uncomfortably, under James's gaze. James was patient, waiting and watching the man across the desk. Jess, on the other hand, felt like the protagonist in the song "Forty Cups of Coffee." She would have killed to shout out, "Carolina Brent Clarke saw the clip at my home three days ago! *J'accuse!*" And who else had been right there with her but Nicholas Spenser? Or, again, had Nigel sent Carolina?

Now Cross was speaking, slowly, seeming to work through several possibilities, "I know there has been bad blood between Carolina and Jessica . . ."

Jessica wanted to protest, "Yes, but it's been her fault!" but James read her and shook his head. She cooled her jets.

Nigel went on, "I'm not putting the blame on you, Jessica. I'm just thinking about who has a motive. I never thought Carolina had it in for me, though, but perhaps she doesn't worry about whomever else she harms. As for her husband, I could see Terry resenting your success, Crawford, especially after he had setbacks of his own. Still, he may be leaving us for a position in Chitzenega, so I can't see the point. Yet, he knew about the wreck, and my feelings for Jessamyn. Terry would have had access to Jessamyn's possessions there–and elsewhere . . . Except . . ."

James cocked his head and repeated, "Except?"

"Well, on reflection, this attack on you suddenly happened after something highly curious. I'm just wondering about a connection. Jessica must have told you about how Friday afternoon, Terry brought over this new fellow who told us a rather interesting tale about meeting your doppelganger with the French Resistance during the war."

"I don't see the connection," James replied, putting on a convincing show of perplexity. "A case of mistaken identity and an attempt to destroy one man by blackmailing another. I'm afraid that spells *non sequitur* to me."

Nigel reflected, "Perhaps not. If you were in the SOE or connected with the OSS and you were working on a case now, someone might decide to throw a monkey wrench into your plans by tying you up trying to square yourself with me, or even by getting you arrested for blackmail."

James snorted, "Nigel, you can't be serious! First of all, the war is over. Second, I can assure you, much as I wanted to serve my country, medical reasons kept me sitting out the war. I can get a letter from my draft registry if you like."

It was a good save, Jessica decided, but her heart was still in her mouth.

Nigel gave James the once over, then said, "Of course. How melodramatic of me. I should never have gone to see *The Stranger* when I was in the city yesterday. It's just that a man likes to know what's going on around him."

James disagreed, "Sometimes I wonder if the less I know, the happier I'll be. A chap like me doesn't like to get in over his head."

"No," Nigel agreed, almost to himself. Then he took in both Jess and James to say, "That still leaves me in a quandary over these letters."

"Perhaps," began James, "the best thing to do is nothing at all."

Jess was not surprised to see Nigel look just as perplexed as she felt by James's suggestion. It was Nigel who spoke, "Now you're not being logical. Why would you let someone get away with slandering you like this? With attacking your wife and stirring up all this trouble?"

"And if our culprit thinks he has failed to stir up trouble?" proposed James. "If the goal was to set us against each other, and that doesn't happen, whoever is responsible will either give up or overplay his hand and reveal himself."

"If we play it that way, he might get off without suffering any retribution," Nigel countered, clearly displeased at that prospect.

"Not if he overplays his hand," James explained. "And if he just gives up, well, I don't need revenge if it's going to undermine the department. Didn't you say there was a good chance your main suspects will be leaving soon? Maybe this was their attempt at a nasty parting shot. Let's turn their fusillade into a fizzle."

Nigel considered; Jess held her breath. Finally, he said, "All right. For the good of the department." He put out his hand for James to shake and said, "No hard feelings, I hope. There's been such a strain around here this last year . . ."

"No hard feelings," James agreed, shaking Nigel's hand. As Nigel turned to Jessica to offer his apologies, she said, "At least it's all settled. They can't hurt you anymore with this."

Oddly enough, Nigel didn't exactly agree. He just acknowledged her with a distracted excuse for a smile.

And then Jessica and James were outside the office, crossing the classrooms, passing the reception area. Neither spoke. Neither trusted the walls not to hear, not to repeat. They only shared knowing, relieved glances. Yet James didn't seem all that relieved. It wasn't until they were in the front seat of the car, windows rolled up for privacy, that they felt safe to talk.

James faced Jessica and asked, "So, what did you make of *that*?"

She shook her head and answered, "Brother, that was something! But it does clear Nigel, doesn't it?"

"Does it?" James was skeptical.

Jess cocked her head in surprise and protested, "Why would he call attention to himself by dragging us in and making these bizarre accusations if he were a Nazi trying to keep a low profile? It's also not as if he would try to blackmail *himself*."

James countered, "Sometimes the best defense is a good offense. A bold move would be a shrewd maneuver to throw me off balance, evoke exactly the response you gave me just now."

"All right, all right, I get what you're driving at. But, well, to me, he seemed genuinely broken up over Jessamyn Crane. I know it could be part of a good act, but, James, my intuition tells me that Nigel was leveling with us."

James compressed his lips, mulling over Jessica's words, then he bobbed his head and agreed, "Yeah, I have the same gut feelings as you."

"Really?" Jess queried, hopeful that Nigel was off the hook, though still a little sore over his accusations.

James smiled sourly and warned, "Don't be so cheery. I'm not at all comfortable with my gastro-intestinal communications of late. They haven't been much help nailing down Zottigstrauch's identity, for that matter, Blackie's identity, or saving Phil Novack."

Jessica put a reassuring hand on James's arm and said gently, "You're only human."

James shook his head emphatically, his hand briefly over hers, then disagreed, "Nice try, love, but just giving it my best shot won't excuse failure. Too much is riding on me doing my job and doing it right, even if the demands are inhuman. Damn, but I feel as if I'm losing my touch. Maybe I've been at this game too long."

Jess glowered inside at Dick Streeter for pushing James too hard, too far, and for too long. But that anger, righteous as it might be, didn't help James. She owed it to her husband to snap him out of his funk. With mock seriousness, she commanded, "Don't make me slap some sense into you, James Crawford. Now quit your crabbin.' Let's ask ourselves the right questions and figure this thing out."

James blinked in surprise, then, a wicked smile spread beneath his mustache. He observed, "That was quite the belt round the head. But all right, miss, I'm over my hysterics. With what questions do you propose we start?"

Jess leaned against her seat to face James better and proposed, "How about asking ourselves what was the point of this whole rhubarb? If Nigel is Zottigstrauch, what would he gain by hauling us in and giving us that third degree? If, on the other hand, he isn't, what does the real Zottigstrauch hope to get out of Nigel putting us on the hot seat? And, let's face it, I doubt it's a coincidence things got hot almost immediately after Sam Steinwall tipped everyone to your war record."

"All right, then," James began. "Let's take the second possibility first. I think it's easier to address. Nigel was played off against me, a sound maneuver to tie me up trying to square myself with Cross, not just so I can keep my job but stay out of the can. I said as much to Nigel back in the office. What I didn't say was that the ploy of dragging you into the mess has the added effectiveness of distracting me with protecting you."

"Now you're cooking on all burners!" Jessica pronounced with an approving nod.

"I'd wait before I handed out the bouquets, love," James cautioned. "I may be cooking but I still don't have dinner on the plate, yet."

"What about the other possibility, James, the one my gut doesn't like. You never did finish explaining why that offense was the best defense."

"Look at it this way, dragging me in like this, again, hits me with trying to save my name and trying to protect you, both of us, from a criminal rap. And bringing up poor-mouth stories about Jessamyn, as well as making himself look as much a victim as us, is a lovely misdirection."

"True," Jessica had to admit.

James continued, "And wasn't it interesting that Nigel happened to bring up the rumor about me in the SOE? He suggested that I still might be involved. His making a connection between that and the blackmail wasn't impossible, but it was a bit odd, don't you think? All in all, our little office chat would have been a damned neat way to check out how his adversary handled a challenge, to probe for weak spots, and maybe even shake him up enough to put him off his game. All while acting the persecuted victim, eliciting our sympathy rather than our suspicion."

"But Nigel admitted to searching your office, James," Jessica carefully challenged. "Wouldn't that be a sloppy mistake for a guy who's supposed to be such a sharp operator?"

"He admitted it, Jessica, but *how* did he admit it? He portrayed himself as a victim manipulated by vicious types, who just happen to be people we already suspect. Do the maths, darling; Nigel's behavior hasn't cleared him. To be frank, the sheer boldness, the egotism, has Georg Zottigstrauch written all over it."

Jessica intently proposed, "So you think the other day, when Rose came upstairs to tell me Carolina and Spenser were at the cottage, our girl snuck a peek in the secret compartment of the sculpture and reported back to him that she'd found the tie clip, indicating I knew he'd been at the wreck? That I might figure out he was having secret meetings with Terry, not something romantic with Jessamyn?" Jess straightened as another possibility struck her, and she questioned, "Then why throw Carolina and Terry under the bus? Blame them for the poison pen letters? Remind us that they were heading for Chitzenega?"

"A test?" James mused. "Maybe he wants to see if I take the bait and have them picked up."

"Isn't he afraid they'll spill whatever they know to save their necks?"

"How much do you think he'd let them know?" James proposed. "I doubt it's much beyond that they're helping him get the horse to Chitzenega. I seriously doubt he'd trust them with the identity of his contact or what his plans with that character are, for just your reasons. Remember, getting that information is my main mission. Of course, we still can't let Nicholas Spenser entirely off the hook."

Jessica gave her head a bewildered shake and said, "You've really got me going in circles. He's still under suspicion with you? Well, at least that means I don't have to cross Nigel off my Christmas card list just yet."

"Not quite yet. Anyway, think about it. As I said before, this evening could have been planned as a distraction, and Nicholas was with Carolina when she had the opportunity to find the tie clip. He could easily have turned that discovery into an opportunity to do us mischief, ordering Carolina or Terry to send the letters once he knew you had something of Nigel's. I wouldn't put it past him to find a way to get into Jessamyn's things once he'd killed her and confiscate anything that might prove useful in pressuring anyone connected with her—hence the photo we saw."

Jess put her hand to her forehead and said, "No wonder you're getting grey hairs. This is all out of my league. I'm no help to you at all, am I?"

James smiled quietly and replied, "You're a help. You got me to calm down, organize my thoughts, and accept that I have to sit tight and not let this bastard rattle me. You helped me short-circuit that part of his plan."

"Really?" Jess brightened.

"Really. And the more I think about it, the more I see that our friend is getting rattled, himself. He should have played it cool after Sam Steinwall outed me. Instead, he stepped up his probing. It makes me think that his ego is finally starting to get in his way, that he's going to push his luck trying to make me step out of line. He can't help trying to prove he's the alpha dog. All of which is why I need to keep my temper and sit tight. In fact, I'm fortunate in that I have two extra pairs of eyes on the lookout that he doesn't know about. Just as important, Jessica, he doesn't know that we're on to the fact that the horse is his package. He thinks the horse is going to be easy to take, that no one is watching Blackie. He's going to find out he has another thing coming. So, my chaps and I will just have to keep our eyes open, wait, and see. Thanks, love, for helping me see that."

"Hey, it's in the spouse's job description," Jess shrugged nonchalantly, though she inwardly glowed at freeing James from his blue devils.

"Well, then, here's something else in the job description," James said as he slid across to Jessica and held her so close she almost lost her breath. The kiss that followed drove every thought from her head of Nazis and blackmail and murder.

Chapter Twenty-Nine

Sunday, August 4

The car pulled up before the Crawford cottage later that evening. Stars glinted overhead, while the porch light illuminated even into the garden. A half-moon tinted the rest blue-grey, casting long shadows around the side of the house. Jessica Minton turned to her husband. She appreciated his letting her doze. Her anxiety during the past days' troubles had caught up with her on the ride home.

"Back in the same day, my lady," James announced with a smile.

Jess sat up, yawning and stretching a bit, saying, "Sorry for drifting off on you."

"If one of us had to take a cat nap, better you than the chap behind the wheel," James kidded.

"Can't argue there!" Jess gave her shoulders a delicious backward shrug, then pronounced, more awake now, "How did we manage to salvage *anything* from an evening that started out so miserably?"

"Two Singapore Slings?" James suggested straight-faced.

"I noticed you put away a drop or two of Scotch with dinner, Mr. Crawford."

"Don't be jealous I can hold my liquor better than you. Professional training, you know. Anyway, sorry we got into the flicks late."

"It was an Abbot and Costello movie. It's not as if we missed a crucial clue for understanding an intricate plot," Jess smiled tiredly.

"Good enough," James responded. He hesitated, though, thinking before continuing, "A couple of things did niggle at me this evening."

"*Only* two? Okay, what's on your mind?"

"First of all, something Nigel Cross said, referred to, when he was trying to excuse himself for believing I was in the SOE. He made some vague remark about seeing 'the stranger' in New York. I'd like to know who that stranger is."

"Well, you can relax, pal," Jessica reassured. "*The Stranger* is a what not a who?"

"Eh?"

"*The Stranger* is a movie with Edward G. Robinson and Loretta Young. Oh, and of course, Orson Welles. It's playing at the Palace in town. Iris saw it a couple of weeks ago. Says it's pretty good. Edward G. Robinson plays a Fed on the trail of a Nazi hiding out as a professor on the campus of an elite prep school."

James offered a fake shudder and noted, "Lord, that cuts close to the bone. Let's avoid that one when we go to the flicks—although, do you think I might pick up some helpful tips?"

"Yeah, keep your eyes open for a guy who looks like Orson Welles, and, if you're alone in the gym, don't forget to duck."

"Ah, well now, you've completely spoiled the suspense for me, haven't you?"

"Actually, Orson gives himself away about fifteen minutes in," Jessica revealed. *Good, one of James's concerns put to rest.* Now if the next one could be as easy, she'd feel as if she'd earned her paycheck for being her spouse's best buddy. "So what's the other qualm, Mr. Crawford?"

"Yes. What grey hair?"

Jess knit her brows, having to recollect her smart remark several hours earlier about the effect of stress on her beloved's dark locks. She calmly fibbed, "None at all. Lighten up. Can't you tell when a girl's pulling your leg?"

"Some things a man just doesn't need to think about when he has bigger fish to fry, especially if that fish has swastikas on its fins."

With a bewildered expression, Jessica laughed, "James! Are *you* starting to channel Liz's screwy sayings now?"

James admitted, "Sorry, love, it's late and my brain has too many conundrums to work out."

"Well, I didn't marry you for your metaphors." She turned to open her door but froze. *Was that a movement, a shadowy something, someone, slipping around the side of the house near the kitchen?*

She gave a soft cry.

"Jessica? Everything all right?"

James's voice brought her back to reality. Straining to pierce the dark around the corner of the house, beyond the porch light and the half-moon's illumination, she answered carefully, "I'm not sure, James, but I think—I can't be definite—but it looked like some kind of movement, going around behind the house near the kitchen."

James said nothing at first. He leaned forward, peering around her, perusing the shadows, the terrain. He questioned softly, "What was it, exactly?"

Jess glanced at his lean face, so near hers, focused on nothing but the house. Feeling inadequate, she could only say, "I don't know. It looked like a shadow, a movement. It wasn't low to the ground like an animal. It might have been a person. I know it's late and I'm tired, but I really do believe I saw something."

James continued to look, then sat back and said, "I don't see anything now. But I want to check. You stay here."

"I don't like you going out there, James," Jessica worried.

He started to reassure her, but Jessica anticipated him: "Even if you do have a weapon. Can't we just drive on and come back when there's more light?"

"Some time around dawn?" James queried. "Not very practical."

"Who cares about practical? All I care about is staying safe, *both* of us, mister."

"I care, too," James reassured her calmly. "But if this is an opportunity to catch Zottigstrauch or one of his chums in the act or overhear some plans or just see what they're trying to pull here, I have to grab it."

Jessica didn't have an argument for that. She could only transmit her anxiety to James with a twist of her mouth.

"I know," he responded. "But it's all right. It's okay. I'm not going to take any foolish chances. Now listen to me and be sure to do what I say. I'm going to creep 'round the far side of the house. If you hear any gun shots or trouble, take the car and get Mitchell in Campus Security."

"I am not going to leave you," Jessica insisted furiously.

"What else are you going to do? Charge to my rescue and clock some bloke on the head with one of your spectator pumps? Unleash Dusty? Much less helpful than getting someone here who knows what he's doing. I'd send you after security right now if I didn't think acting jumpy with no solid reason would raise a red flag to our friends."

Jessica scowled. Sometimes she *really* hated it when James was right.

"Right, then. First thing, lock the doors. And I also need you to keep a sharp eye around you. If anyone suspicious appears, I want you to drive off for help. That sound will clue me in something's up."

James kissed Jess quickly, turning the dome light off before he exited the car (closing the door with surprising quiet), and was off into the night, circling carefully around the left side of the house. The moon's and the stars' light were not exactly James's allies. Yet, with luck, they might betray James's prey.

Jessica pressed her face against the passenger window. *Where was James now that the building hid him?* She prayed that he'd show up any minute and give her a hard time for being a nervous Nellie. This was one occasion she'd be delighted to be the victim of an overactive imagination—or one too many Singapore Slings.

Her eyes moved back to the kitchen side of the house. Nothing but blackness. Not reassuring. Then, wait, had she heard a voice? No repetition. No gun shots, either, though. That was good—unless a blade out of the dark shadows had found James.

That's when the front door opened, and there stood her husband, illuminated in the entrance. *How dangerous and inviting to a sniper. Wait a minute; he was inviting her, waving her to come in!*

Jessica rolled down her window and called, "James, is everything all right? The coast's clear?"

"The coast is clear," he answered. "Come in. Come in."

Jess hesitated. *Was this a trick? Could someone be using James as a lure? No, that was out of the question. He'd never betray me—or if he were forced, somehow, he'd give me a clever tip-off.*

Still not completely reassured, Jess called back, "Okay. Be right there."

She rolled up the window, got out of the car, and locked it. Clear coast or not, she hoofed it up the path, feeling increasingly better as she neared James and recognized the genuine pleasure in his eyes the closer she came.

Jess had just hit the porch's bottom step when James informed her, "We have an old chum of yours visiting."

She paused. James definitely didn't seem to be warning her off, yet there was something in his tone for "chum" that indicated this was no pal of his. But he extended a hand to draw her in, so Jessica automatically came up the stairs, into his reach, letting herself be guided into the now well-lighted room.

One step in, the door closed behind her, and Jessica abruptly halted. If this wasn't the living end! What was this man doing in her living room?!

On the couch facing her, a half-emptied hi-ball glass in hand, was a tall, lanky man on the low side of thirty. His hair was thick and reddish-brown. His face was longish, but the cheeks were baby-face material. The eyes were no baby's, however: brown and sardonically piercing. His dark suit, white shirt, and dark tie under a trench coat didn't *scream* "Fed," but the implication was clear. Nevertheless, the glint of his eyes and the twist of his smile suggested an unexpectedly subversive personality for a G-Man.

"Hooley, put a coaster under that glass before you leave a ring on my coffee table," Jessica Minton greeted him coolly. Even if this man had helped her clear her sister last year, he could still raise her hackles. And Hooley and James under the same roof? *Gadzooks!*

"I missed you, too, Jessica," he ironically tossed back, taking a drink, but putting a magazine under it when he set down his glass. Still, she knew he really had. Never mind that, what the dickens *was* he doing here? A possibility, crazy as it might seem, struck her. Jess turned to James with an incredulous, "You didn't call him in on your case, did you?"

"Good Lord, no!" James corrected her. "I'm just as surprised as you."

"And delighted?" Hooley queried. "Just as delighted?"

"You're a bright lad. I'll let you figure that one out for yourself," James returned. Then he added, "Now that Jessica is here, maybe we can all sit down, and you can fully explain yourself."

"Did Dick Streeter send him?" Jess was still questioning. Turning back to Jeff Hooley, she repeated, "Streeter sent you?"

Hooley shook his head and answered, "No one sent me but my ADA. I shot up here as soon as I got the word. Please, both of you sit down." His hand extended to the couch across from him. His deference was tinged with the sardonic.

"How graciousness, Hooley," James remarked, "especially since this is *our* home."

As he and Jessica sat down, James continued, "Now suppose you give us the straight story on why you were creeping about here."

Jessica settled with James on the couch. Their guest had started to answer James's less-than-cordial questions, when Dusty appeared from nowhere and leaped gracefully up next to Jess. As the cat regarded Jeff Hooley skeptically, he commented, "I see the gang's all here."

"You were saying about why you're here," James prompted.

Hooley nodded and proceeded, "Sure. Well, it looks as if your wife stumbled into, no, created, quite a mystery for my task force."

Jess exchanged a perplexed look with James, with her husband finally saying, "Never mind the double-talk, Hooley. What are you doing here?"

"Cut to the chase? Okay, you've got it. What's your wife doing with a real live, expensive horse that's supposed to be dead?"

Jessica insisted impatiently, "Back that up a bit. The only horse I have is . . ."

"Blue Warrior," Hooley completed, taking a letter from his inside jacket pocket.

Jess and James turned to each other, telegraphing that Hooley had confirmed their suspicions about the Thoroughbred. James took the lead with, "How the devil did you connect us with that horse?"

"Well, James, I'll tell you. After the last time I saw your wife and helped her close the books on the Wiesenthal ring, I was assigned to a task force set up to put the kibosh on the epidemic of ringers in horseracing across the country. I assume that being married to Miss Improver of the Breed over there, you know what a ringer is?"

"I've heard the term. Still, keeping an eye on a few bettors' investments seems rather small beer for you Feds," James remarked. "Is this even a federal case?"

"These ringers have cost millions of dollars, big bucks going into the piggy banks of organized crime—and the ponies are shipped across state lines, all over the country, *that* makes it FBI business, buddy."

James nodded acknowledgment, but Jessica pressed, "Okay, but what's that got to do with Blackie?"

"Blackie?" Jeff was genuinely puzzled.

"That's what our horse is called," James explained. "The one everyone seems to think is this Blue Warrior."

Hooley briefly thought that over before turning to Jessica to explain, "Our task force was working with several owners on a pilot program to prevent substituting horses, using a practice that has been working in England and Chitzenega for several years."

"The lip tattoo!" Jess finished, leaning eagerly forward. "No one was trying to pass him off as a Chitzengan horse, after all. Blue Warrior must have been tattooed as part of your plan, right?"

Jeff confirmed, "On the nose. Blue Warrior's owner had connections with someone in the Bureau and volunteered all his horses—the whole shebang. So, any horses that got claimed would move through the whole system. Same with any stock that was sold. We kept it on the q.t., the fact that we'd trained inspectors to follow these horses. That way, we could see whether it was a good way to track a horse before we went full scale, with the added benefit of keeping tabs on any wise guys who tried to pass off a ringer."

"So, the only people who knew what was going on . . ." Jess began.

"Were the owners involved in the pilot, certain members of the Jockey Club, and us," Hooley summed up. "A trainer or groom might see the tattoo, but no one was ever told what it was for or that we had records of which horse belonged to which letter and numbers." Another drink of scotch and, "So, imagine my amazement when the Jockey Club calls and rush mails me this letter from a gal in Connecticut asking about a horse with a tattoo that matches the most valuable subject of our experiment, a horse that happened to have been pronounced dead some months ago. I had all I could do to keep my director from having you picked up and hauled off in bracelets."

"Me?" Jessica snorted. "I didn't steal this horse—and what kind of an idiot would run such a successful scam, keep it under wraps for this long, then blow it by announcing she had the horse?"

"That's pretty much what I said," Hooley concurred. "And I added that I knew you, knew that you were too much of a Girl Scout to steal a horse or knowingly receive stolen property. I didn't mention it, but I figured your master spy of a husband here wouldn't let you pull off anything too larcenous."

"How fortunate we have such good friends in high places," James remarked.

"Yeah, well, I convinced my boss to let me handle it. I promised to hot foot it up here and get the straight dope from you on where the horse had come from—and of course return Blue Warrior to his owner."

Jessica's heart sank with Hooley's last words. Returning the horse to his rightful owner once she'd discovered his real identity had somehow dropped off her radar. Partly Blue Warrior's being caught in the spider web of James's work had pushed the thought from consideration. But she had to admit there was more going on with her. She had gotten used to thinking of Blackie (or should she say Blue?) as her responsibility. Didn't she have an obligation to Phil Novack's memory to keep the stallion safe with her? *Even though Phil had come by the horse illegally? But Blue Warrior had bonded with Phil.* Was it her duty to honor that bond, especially since she hadn't been able to save Phil? Still, the horse *wasn't* Phil's or hers. *And there was James's mission to consider. What a mess.*

Hooley couldn't have missed the turmoil in her features, but he misread it and demanded, "What's wrong? You still have the horse? He's all right, isn't he?"

James seemed to read her thoughts and took the pressure off Jess by answering, "The horse is fine. He's right here in the campus stables. But I'm afraid you can't have him just yet."

Hooley gave James a hard look, flaring, "*I* can't have him? What are you trying to hand me here, Crawford? It's not just Jeff Hooley you're messing with; it's the FBI. You can't monkey around with a federal investigation."

"Neither can you," James pointedly replied, leaning forward. "The horse is essential for me to complete *my* investigation."

Hooley sat back, repeating, suspiciously, "Your investigation? Wait a minute, just what the hell is going on here? And don't tell me you had the nerve to drag Jessica into this thing."

"James didn't drag me into anything," Jessica set Hooley straight. Maybe there was something swell about him being protective of her–but not at James's expense.

James's hand was briefly over hers, calming, then he was back to Jeff Hooley: "I'm only going to tell you this because the case is too important to let personal enmity get in the way. You're certainly not my closest mate by a long chalk, but you're sharp; you know your business. I can use your help because I'm up against a character who's no easy meat–and he's up to something that blows the worries of your task force to kingdom come–millions of dollars, organized crime, and all."

A slow, skeptical smile spread across Jeff Hooley's features before he finally replied, "You certainly know how to sweet talk a guy, Agent Crawford. This must be big time if you're out to make nice with me, or your version of making nice. So, let's talk turkey."

"Fine," James said abruptly. "Have you heard of Georg Zottigstrauch?"

Hooley sat up and took notice. He thought before answering, "Sure. One of the guys in the task force lost a partner to him. And he's always been one of the department's most wanted. A real bastar . . . Sorry, Jess."

"I've heard the word before," she wryly assured Hooley. "And considering what I've seen him do here, I couldn't agree with you more."

"Wait a minute. You're telling me that he's here and active?" Jeff Hooley turned to James. "That's your assignment? To nail him?"

"You're partially correct," James clarified. "Therein lies the rub. My task is to definitively identify him, but not just capture him. Apparently, he's up to something big. I'm only to bring him in when I've discovered what his plans are, who his contacts are."

"That all?" Hooley questioned skeptically, but for once in sympathy with James. "They don't expect much of you, do they? Well, that explains why you both asked me about Dick Streeter." To Jessica's quizzical expression, Hooley explained, "Outside, when your hubby came across me 'skulking.'"

Jess nodded. James, intent on Hooley, questioned, "Can I count on you?"

"Count on me to help put away that killer? What do you think, brother–but you'll have to square things with my ADA."

"Streeter should be able to manage it," James assured him. "He has the clout."

"Okay, okay, I'm in." Then Hooley was considering, saying finally, "But what I still don't get is how my horse fits into this whole deal."

Jess took over now, "What we've been able to put together is this: Blue Warrior is worth a lot of money as a stud. Not here, because he'd be so easy to recognize by people in the know, but disguised as a different horse in another country, where someone has the patience to wait until his offspring bring home the purses, which in turn will drive up his value as a breeding prospect. He's a perpetual cash generator. Since Chitzenega keeps coming up in connection with this case . . ."

"You think Zottigstrauch got the horse for someone in Chitzenega, and if you can nail Zottigstrauch you can trace his partner in a country that's not too chummy about extraditing garden variety, let alone war, criminals," Hooley finished.

"That's about the size of it," Jessica confirmed.

"O-kay," Hooley said, "But what the hell are *you* doing with Blue Warrior? Somehow, I doubt our boy Georg would just hand over the horse to the wife of a former SOE agent for safe keeping."

"Not everyone knows my background," James remarked. Jess noted he wasn't forthcoming about Sam Steinwall's blabbing.

"Yeah, okay," Hooley agreed. "I'd still like to know how Jessica ended up with a horse that everyone thought died in a fire but is actually some kind of a linchpin for a Nazi plot to raise the Fourth Reich. I mean, I've seen her get herself into some God-awful jams, but this one pretty much takes the cake."

"Hooley, listen for a sec," Jess commanded. "Zottigstrauch had the horse stashed with one of his subordinates. The guy, Phil Novack, was getting cold feet about being mixed up with this crowd, especially when murder entered the picture. We think your charming Herr Zottigstrauch had his flunkies kill Novack to prevent him from getting out of line . . ."

"Yeah, death does that . . ."

"*Anyway*, something went wrong: the horse got away and came to me. I took him in and that's how I ended up with Blackie, as he was called, aka Blue Warrior. James surmised no one interfered with me having the horse because my stabling him here keeps him safely under their noses till they need to ship him out."

"They?" Jeff repeated. "You mentioned 'flunkies.' How many people are we talking about? *Whom* are we talking about? Can you name names? More importantly, what's Zottigstrauch's aka in town? I'm going to go out on a limb and conjecture he didn't move into town introducing himself as a retired Nazi spy."

"That's where it gets complicated," James answered.

"It's not complicated already?" Hooley cracked.

"If you only knew," Jess sighed, scratching Dusty's neck.

Now she listened as James gave Hooley a complete rundown of their difficult situation, including the added pressure that they had at most a week before the horse would be moved out. At the end, Hooley let out a long, low whistle before concluding, "That's some pickle you've gotten yourselves into here. But it does make more sense in connection to my case. Good luck finding a tattoo on a horse that's been burnt to a crisp. And those two, the Clarkes, you say they're from horse country. Where exactly?"

Jessica took that one, "Terry's from an old family, long on ancestry but short on cash, in Norfolk, Virginia. Carolina's family used to breed and sell hunters, but their cash dried up, too. The really interesting part is that her family farm was pretty darned close to Damascus, Maryland. A place called . . ."

"Selbywood?" Jeff finished.

Taken aback, Jess questioned, "Yes, how on earth did you know?"

"I can add two and two. The groom killed in the barn fire along with the alleged Blue Warrior had worked there not long before. No one could run down any further leads on him. He'd seemed innocent enough–but I wonder if I dug deeper, would I find that Carolina Brent Clarke or her husband had visited her parents' homestead about that time."

"Terry did come back here in the summer or fall of '45, but I have no idea if he visited home last winter or spring to set things up," Jessica considered. "Or he could have been setting things up before he was discharged. He was stationed in D.C. during the war, and it's not very hard to get from D.C. to his wife's family in Virginia."

"And thence to the farm where Blue Warrior resided," Hooley finished. "Mmm, I'll make some calls and get more information on the case–and the movements of the Clarkes. Still, I've got to say I'm curious. What do you think would make those two, even that Novack guy, throw in with a creep like Zottigstrauch?"

James looked at Jessica, deferring to her better knowledge of Phil.

She decided to start with the less controversial subject: "Phil Novack, we heard from some grooms who'd worked for his brother, had gambling debts that suddenly disappeared. You don't have to be Einstein to figure out where the money came from. Still, from what I've seen of Phil, and what James and I secretly overheard once between him and Terry, I don't think he had any idea what he'd signed on for until it was too late. I'm convinced he was killed because he didn't want to be involved in murder or worse."

"Sounds like you knew this guy pretty well," Hooley observed.

"Not well enough to be any help to him. He liked to ride up and down the beach. He'd stop and we'd talk about the horse. But one time he did warn me he couldn't afford to be too chummy with me. That was the last time I talked to him. So, you know, Hooley, maybe what happened to him is my fault . . ."

"No," James said quietly, forcefully. "Novack made his own choices. That's all there is to it."

"You know, Crawford," Hooley began accusingly, "The more I hear, the more I think you've done a pretty lousy job of keeping Jessica out of this business. She's not one of us. She shouldn't even be here. I don't know what bugs me more, that I think you're losing your touch or that you've put her in jeopardy."

James fixed Hooley with a look that would have incinerated a man with less *sangfroid*, but it was Jessica who leaped in, "How dare you, Jeff Hooley?! James has been trying to get me out of town for some time now! It's been my decision to stay, I'll have you know. Anyway, do you really think my doing a fade to New York would put me beyond Zottigstrauch's reach? It might have tipped him for certain about James, though."

James looked Hooley straight in the eye to say, "I don't need to defend myself to you. What I was led to expect here and what I actually walked into is all beside the point now. Things are as they are. Are you going to help me set them right, or are you going to waste time trying to cast blame?"

That knocked Hooley down a peg or two, Jess noted. But she recognized that Hooley had struck a nerve, a bitter, guilty nerve in James.

"All right," replied Jeff, abruptly. Turning to Jessica, he said, "What about the other two, these Clarkes. Tell me about them. What are they in it for?"

Jessica nodded, then explained, "I do think they knew more than Phil when they got into this, but I also doubt they know everything. This guy sounds as if he plays things pretty close to the vest. I also don't figure them for blithely signing on for murder. Probably it all started out as a deal to make a lot of money and when things went sour, neither had the nerve to run out on him. I can see now Terry is afraid of this guy. It looks as if Zottigstrauch killed Terry's girlfriend."

"His wife must have liked that," Jeff commented.

"Unless she's thinking she'll be next if she doesn't play nice," Jess corrected.

"She's scared, too?"

Jess looked at James, and he took over, "Carolina Brent Clarke does seem to be hopping in line with as much alacrity as her husband."

"That's it?" Hooley finished.

"For those two, yes," James answered. "So, you're in?"

"Oh, sure, nabbing Georg Zottigstrauch and the next link in the chain? I'm in all right." Hooley agreed. He took a moment before adding, "But before I go any further in this, I need to verify that you really have Blue Warrior. Can you take me to the stables tonight?"

James shook his head emphatically, "With a torch, in the dark? Someone's liable to see us. And those horses get easily stirred up when someone comes in unexpectedly, especially with a light. Not bloody likely we'll be able to slip in, do our business, and slip out without being noticed. The last thing I need is to call attention to our knowing we have Zottigstrauch's bargaining chip. That's almost the only advantage I have right now. No, let me talk to my agent in the stables. He can set things up for us. And, much as I hate to keep dragging my wife into this, we need her there to soothe the horse. He's extremely picky about visitors."

Jessica quietly agreed. Knowing her part in this mission would take Blue from her life left her unable to say much more.

"Okay, then," Jeff decided. "You're on. So, tomorrow morning, first thing, I'll get my guys checking out the Clarkes. You can fill me in on more details. Too bad the left hand never knows what the right in our agency is doing. Someone might have actually known about our task force in your division and could have contacted us for our info on the Clarkes as soon as you were suspicious of them."

"So, that's it for the night?" Jess asked.

"Guess so," Hooley answered. Then he looked at James and said, "If you can give me a lift to my car, just off campus, I can drive back to my room at the inn."

"You left your car off campus?" Jess asked.

Jeff smiled quickly and explained, "I didn't want anyone to know I was paying you two a call until I knew exactly what was going on with the horse. Didn't want to spook anyone. Guess I didn't know the half of it."

"Not the foggiest," James agreed. He was on his feet and continued, "Right, then. I'll run you over to your car. If you want to make any calls in town, it *should* be fine. Just be careful what you say. You might want only to telephone from the next town, to be on the safe side. Be sure not to ring us up on campus; the operator might overhear and gossip." Turning to Jessica, he asked, "Coming along? Keep me company on the ride back?"

Part of her wanted to tell James all she wanted was to crawl under the covers with Dusty. But there was something in his mien that said he'd feel better if she weren't alone. And maybe he really needed her company right now.

"Only if I can call shotgun!" Jess declared, up on her feet.

"Fine," Hooley added. "I wanted to catch forty winks in the back, anyway."

But that's not exactly what happened. Instead, he and James made more plans for the coming days: Jeff making his calls, James joining him in town after classes, coordinating information, giving Hooley a lay of the land (including Spenser's antique shop), and possibilities for trapping Georg Zottigstrauch when he made his move on the horse.

Chapter Thirty

Friday, August 9

9:30 P.M. No moon tonight. Good news and bad for James Crawford as he cut across the greens between buildings, heading surreptitiously for the stables. A breeze, surprisingly cool for an August night, pressed steadily in from the northeast, making James turn up the collar of his dark windbreaker. Keeping as much in the shadows as possible, he was beginning to think more and more he'd lost his touch, or maybe Georg Zottigstrauch was just too sharp for him. Of course, all he needed was Jeff Hooley to ride to his rescue.

What he wouldn't give for a cigarette right now. Then again, bobbing along with a glowing red tip in the darkness wasn't exactly the smartest strategy. So, he'd left Jessica at the Nyquists, listening to the radio and playing cards. He'd told her before they'd gone out that he'd have to leave early to finish some grading, that David had promised him to provide her a lift home when she was ready. Jessica had given him something of a skeptical look, as had Dusty, but both had let it ride. Whether Jessica believed him or just didn't want to make waves in such critical times, James wasn't sure. Whatever the case, she'd be safe while he checked in with Ken, his man in the barns—even if an earlier rendezvous with Hooley had taken decidedly longer than expected. James gave the carrot in his pocket a little pat. He'd had to check in with his contact in the stables from time to time, and what better cover than to be there to feed my wife's horse carrots? Extraordinarily long carrots. It had required a bit of screwing his courage to the sticking place at first but, in spite of everything he'd felt about horses, Blue had grown on him—and it seemed the stallion was in the same state of heart. One time he'd gone there with Jess, and she'd kidded after he'd given Blue a calming rub on the cheek, "Judging by that pat and the way he's acting toward you, I think there's something more than a carroty cover going on between you two."

Anyway, he'd check in with Ken, then take a brief shift hidden in the barn, keeping an eye out for any felonious activity until Hooley returned. That should give him time to get home before Jessica. And, just like last night, he'd slip back here in the wee hours while Jess slept and return before she was up. Damn, he wished Zottigstrauch would make his move. It was murder, keeping these hours, trying to make sure Jess was safely out of the picture, and then trying to teach for three hours the next day. But the main event should be any day now. It had just better be sooner rather than later, before he and Hooley both collapsed.

Much as it pained James to admit, Hooley was turning out to be a bloody useful ally. James was taking part of Hooley's shift now because he'd just sent his "buddy" off to muster up some dandy little toys for keeping tabs on Blue Warrior and his would-be snatchers. He also had a funny feeling that Jessica had overheard part of their plans concerning some of their toys, careful as they'd been to keep her safely out of the loop. She hadn't said anything, though. Anyway, wouldn't they turn out to be fair-haired boys if they pulled this one off? And if they didn't? Ah, then let Hooley share the brickbats rather than bouquets with him.

James could make out the hands' quarters ahead, sitting before the two barns and blocking a clear view of them. Lamplight and music escaped the ground floor of the housing. James kept out of sight by circling toward the blind side of the building, which would carry him nearer the overflow barn behind the quarters, on the right. One thing, at least, he'd gotten right was to have the stallion moved there by instructing Ken to say that Blue wasn't getting along with one of the other horses. With the equestrienne team's horses gone for the summer, Blue had that building all to himself. Much easier, now, to keep their bait under surveillance. Hmph, why didn't he like to think of that animal as bait? He was only a horse. The only one he'd ever fed a carrot, like the one in his pocket now. And James actually didn't mind when the horse would give him the same kind of playful head butt he gave Jessica. Wouldn't that just take the cake: James Crawford getting matey with a horse!

The barns loomed vaguely in the darkness; James was moving quietly toward the stable hands' house. *Except . . ..*

Music and light still streamed out the two windows facing him about fifteen yards ahead. Something was missing, though. Why didn't he hear any voices, the clink of dishes or cutlery, sounds of movement? James paused, hidden in the shadow of a large maple. Why couldn't he see anyone moving past the windows? And why would four guys, not counting Ken in the barn, be up this late when they had to rise and shine at 4:30 A.M.? But if they *were* up, they'd be making noise, casting a shadow or two. Music wouldn't be playing into the silent evening.

James made a careful survey of the stretch of ground by the quarters, confirming that no one was on the watch for him. He noiselessly slipped up to the side of the building. Flattened against the wall, James moved carefully to the window, listening for any sign of life. *Nothing. This was bad. Very bad.*

He allowed himself a quick peek through the window and would have frozen had he less discipline. Instead, James leaned back against the wall, gathering his thoughts before he took a second, fuller look.

No, no one there to stop him, threaten him. No one hiding, plotting to pounce, but that fact was not in the least reassuring. Sure, all four hands were there, but James hadn't expected to see them all out cold. Two guys were sprawled over a table, cards and poker chips skewed every which way. One poor bloke was catching forty-winks on the floor. The last guy was the luckiest, collapsed in an armchair, white ceramic mug on the floor.

James hesitated. Check on them or the horse, first? He watched carefully. Yeah, they were breathing. Victims of one hell of a Mickey Finn. The toppled coffee mugs, the near-empty percolator on the stove clued him in to the method of delivery. So, what about Ken? Blue Warrior? That was when he heard a horse's whistle of distress.

Instinctively, he reached for his .32 and came up empty–he couldn't exactly have shown up, armed, at Rose and David's. His decision not to bring a weapon when Ken was on guard and Hooley was on the way now gnawed at him. But James didn't have time to waste agonizing over one more muck up. He was circling the stable hands' quarters swiftly, careful neither to be seen nor to trip over anything. At least there was one thing in his favor: the moonless night would hide him from anyone on the alert in the barn.

From the corner of the building obscuring him, James could see that the broad doorway to the barn was open to the night air. But that wasn't what riveted James Crawford's attention. It was the shifting, flickering silhouette crackling in the barn's loft. Of course! With the wind blowing away from him, he hadn't smelled the smoke before! *Zottigsstrauch wasn't very original after all, was he?*

Blue Warrior cried anxiously, driving James to dash across the courtyard, keeping off to the right and out of view. Obviously, Zottigstrauch wasn't about to leave his prize to roast. Someone must be in the stall with him, killing James's instinct to rush in and get Blue the hell out.

He paused at a horse trough by the entrance, soaking his handkerchief to cover his nose and mouth before slipping inside the barn and into the first stall, the crackling of a new fire overhead unnerving. Blue was stalled almost halfway down the barn on the left, on the near side of the opening to loft. From that loft, swirled the smoke.

Whose voice was that? Too soft to recognize. A whisper to soothe a spooked horse. A horse whose black bulk and the stall hid the speaker's identity. If that were Zottigstrauch or one of his creatures, odds were he would be armed.

A quick survey for a handy weapon. *Nothing within reach. Hooley wasn't due for some time. God only knew what had happened to Ken.* James was completely on his own—without his gun. Through all this, he was aware that the snapping and bumping overhead was intensifying.

The stallion was screaming and rearing. A female form backed out of the stall, blouse gleaming white over dark slacks. Too short for Carolina Brent Clarke, but just the right height for someone who should not have been here.

"Jessica!" James hissed through the wet handkerchief, racing forward, "What the bloody hell are you doing here?!"

She whirled, relief racing across her face, and answered, "Oh thank

God, James! Help me get Blue out! He's scared! Help me!" She finished by hacking out a long cough that unnerved the horse even more.

Bits of fiery debris were now dropping through the ceiling as James reached her. Swiftly, he pushed his wet handkerchief over Jessica's nose and mouth before moving toward the frightened horse, his own eyes now suffering smoke's sting. But Blue Warrior jerked the lead shank in Jessica's hands and backed deeper into the stall.

"Quick," Jessica commanded through her coughs. "Take off that windbreaker. Soak it in his water bucket. I'll cover his eyes with it. We can get him out if he can't see what's going on."

She spoke, definitively in charge, even as she labored against the increasing smoke. But the tension in her eyes told James how much terror she, like the horse, struggled against. The crackling, now, was more a vicious growling.

In the ever-increasing smoke, James whipped off his jacket and soaked it. Together, they blindfolded Blue, and James, though hacking, added to Jessica's soothing talk. The timbers between them and the exit were glowing, while they were tortured worse with the smoke. *Damn!* James knew fire from the blitz, which meant they had no time to kid around before the smoke knocked the three of them out cold and they all became roast toasties. But even blindfolded, Blue wouldn't budge.

Flames were flicking through the rafters now. They brushed flakes of fire from themselves, from Blue, before it could do harm. Then, above the fire's devouring, they heard the horses in the next barn beginning to whinny and whistle in distress. As if taking over as herd leader, Blue Warrior declared a challenge and suddenly almost dragged both Jessica and James down the length of the barn, away from the fire, and into the rear courtyard—even as their eyes stung with barely seeing for the smoke.

Jess and James both collapsed onto the ground, hacking out phlegm. Blue's head went down as he joined them. Before Jess could recover, James pushed himself up to a sitting position. *Where was Ken?* He couldn't leave a man down in the barn, but he couldn't leave their prize bait alone. Damn, he sure as hell wasn't going to leave Jessica alone, either. In the light from the house, he could see Jess's back heaving under her smoke-grimed blouse. His head started to spin again, but he shook it. He had to pull himself together.

James moved jaggedly toward his wife. *Thank God she hadn't passed out!* She still gripped the horse's lead in one hand, though coughs wracked her. Blue tried to nuzzle her, his terror of the fire distracted by this new concern. Then, as James drew nearer, the stallion's head went up and he snorted menacingly.

James stopped short. Except Blue was glaring *behind* him. Blue wasn't threatening *him*! That realization came too late. Even as James started to move evasively, something heavy caught him a glancing but powerful blow on the side of the head. That was all she wrote.

Chapter Thirty-One

When Jessica looked up from coughing, she was horrified to see James go down and out before her eyes. A swift glance upward revealed Terry Clarke looking down at his handiwork, his gun butt over its victim. From the corner of her eye, she saw Carolina Brent Clarke rushing around the side of the barn, her red hair floating, glowing in the light of the burning barn, against the black of her trousers and swing jacket.

It almost seemed to Jess that if she stayed silent, she could freeze them all in this moment. That was not to be. Terry's strained eyes fastened on her, even as Blue snorted and pawed. Jess only realized she was still holding the lead shank in almost a death grip when the stallion jerked her arm furiously.

The first words to escape her were, "What did you do to James? If you've harmed him . . ."

"Take it easy," Terry cut her off. "I just clipped him. He'll be all right, eventually."

"All right?" snapped Carolina as she reached her husband. "What do you mean 'all right'? Those weren't Zottigstrauch's orders. He'd love to get the woman alive, to calm the horse, but he wants Crawford out of the way permanently. How can you even dream about double-crossing him after what happened to the others, Terry?"

Carolina took out a gun.

Before Jessica could say or do anything to protect James, Terry shocked her by pushing his wife's gun-hand down firmly and ordering, "Take it easy. Crawford's not about to make any trouble for us. He's out cold. By the time he comes around, let alone can get on his feet, we'll be on our way to Chitzenega. Haven't you had your fill of killing?"

While Terry and Carolina were busy glaring at each other, Jess could have sworn she saw James stir in the eerie firelight. Or had she? He seemed so still now. She kept her mouth shut, quietly moving closer to the stallion on edge with the too-near fire and the too-threatening humans. If James hadn't been there, Jess thought she might have tried to swing onto Blue's back and make a dash for it—except she couldn't ride bareback, and the horse was just too big for her to leap up on. Somehow, she doubted either of the Clarkes would be willing to give her a leg up. They'd be too busy shooting her.

At least they were still arguing. That might keep them distracted long enough for James to recover and, what, pull a carrot on them?

"I don't have time to argue with you, Carolina!" Terry hissed.

"Maybe you would if you hadn't taken so long scuffling with that groom. You were supposed to have doped all of them in their quarters," Carolina retorted venomously.

Jessica quietly got to her feet, holding Blue. *How to escape without leaving a helpless James to these two wrangling sharks?* Unfortunately, Jess lost her battle to suppress her wracking coughing. So much for trying to sneak off.

Carolina leveled her gun on Jess without once relenting her vituperative attack of Terry: "All the others were knocked out. If you'd counted properly, you'd have noticed one was missing. *Then* you'd have had the horse out of the barn before I got the fire going. *Then* we wouldn't have had to lay low outside the barn while those two had a social call with the horse. If they hadn't gotten him out, he might have died with them. Zottigstrauch would have killed us and not cared how, as long as we suffered!"

"Who got us involved with that bastard in the first place?" Terry threw in his wife's face. "He played on your vanity, so you trusted him. Next thing I knew, we're under his thumb. And what *did* go on between the two of you to make you trust him so much?"

Jess nibbled her lip. *Would the Clarkes' mutual hatred keep them going long enough for help to arrive? Maybe James wouldn't recover in time, but someone might see the fire. Maybe Hooley would ride in for the rescue—if this cat fight (apologies to Dusty) went on long enough.*

"Going on between *us*?" Carolina fairly snarled. Even Blue froze at her tone. "That's rich, coming from you! What about you and my 'dear friend' Jessamyn Crane?"

Even in the firelight, Jess could see Terry's color drain, his features go fierce, wolfish. Instinctively, she moved closer to the safety of the big, black horse.

"Get the car and the van, Carolina," he finally said in a voice that Jess had never heard from him—and hoped she never would again. His hand raised the gun, so the barrel was pointing at his wife.

Carolina saw, raised her own gun, and for a minute Jess hoped for a shootout. Then the tall woman said sullenly, "All right, all right. But you take care of Crawford the way you're supposed to."

"Don't worry about that. I've cleaned up all the other messes."

Jess's instinct was to argue, to protect James, but reason warned she'd have better luck once Carolina was off the scene. Another long cough wracked her, but the other two ignored her.

Terry was telling his wife, "You pull the van up out front, and we'll bring the horse around. Otherwise, getting it back here, turned around, and back on the road will take too long. I'll take care of business here. "

Jessica bit her lip as Carolina gave her a cruelly satisfied look, then turned to her husband and warned, "See that you do."

Jess tensed as Terry watched his wife dash off to their left, circling the barn housing the horses. Those animals continued to whinny and shift nervously at their proximity to the burning building. *Why hadn't the alarm had gone off, unless neutralizing it had also been assigned to the Clarkes?* Those terrified horses added yet another boulder to the load of worries crushing Jessica. *First things, first, though!*

As soon as Carolina was out of sight, Jess went on the offensive: "Terry, James is down for the count. He can't hurt you if you just leave him. I know you're no killer at heart. Please, don't do this. You're better than this. He can't hurt you."

Terry turned to Jessica, his expression weary, and asked, "You know me, do you, Jessie? You really think I'm the same guy you used to know? A lot's happened since."

"So much that you'd kill a man in cold blood? A man who's no threat to you?" Jessica pressed earnestly, her voice as hoarse from emotion as from the smoke.

"Does it make you feel any better to know that *I* haven't killed anyone?" Terry questioned. "And I don't intend to start now. I told Caro I'd take care of him like the stable hand. She just doesn't know that means I only knocked them both out cold. I might not have been able to save Phil, or," here he almost choked up, "Jessamyn, or that groom back in Maryland, but at least I didn't take their lives, myself. I can wash away that much of the damned spot. What Carolina and Georg Zottigstrauch don't know won't hurt me. So, c'mon. I wish I could leave you here with your husband, but I'm not that brave."

Jessica hesitated, then went for broke: "Terry, why not break with Zottigstrauch right here, right now? Don't go with Carolina. Get on the phone in the other barn and call security. Turn yourself in. Maybe if you go state's evidence, you can make a deal . . ."

"I don't think so, Jessica," Terry shook his head. "Nice try. I'm in too deep. Besides, Carolina would just as soon shoot me as you and James, take her chances they could handle the horse without you. Sorry. No dice."

"So, you don't mind sacrificing me, just a little later? You know as soon as Zottigstrauch doesn't need me anymore, I'll be eighty-sixed. That's more blood on your hands."

Terry hesitated, but temporized, "I think I can protect you."

"Like you did Jessamyn Crane?"

As soon as she'd spoken that name, Jess saw she'd gone one step too far. And the horses in the barn were now squealing their fear. Blue let out a call in response.

Terry and Jess both turned to that barn. The fire hadn't spread there yet, but it would. Luckily, the breeze was blowing away, out to sea, but that wouldn't protect the horses forever.

"Follow me, bring the horse," Terry peremptorily ordered, heading for the barn full of horses.

"Terry? What are you doing?" Jessica puzzled, pulling Blue along with her, then taking a quick glance back at James.

"Where's that phone? Just inside the door?" Terry demanded.

Jessica riveted her attention back on her captor. Quickly, she answered, "Yes. Why? Oh, Terry, are you calling for help?"

Her hopes were not exactly assured when Terry answered, "Not the way you expect."

They were just inside the door, and Terry put down his gun to crank the box but not so far from his reach that he couldn't make use of it if Jess tried anything. A long, hard look told her as much when her eyes fell on the weapon. Once he connected with the operator, in a voice that was a dead-on imitation of Stan's, Terry coughed and hacked out, "Yeah, it's Stan at the stables. There's a fire in the barn, the one with only one horse. He's out but we need help with the other horses an' keeping things from spreading. Get here on the double. Gotta go. Get the fire trucks NOW! Step on it!"

Darn he was good! So much better than she'd ever remembered. Terry hung up and told Jess, "It isn't the horses' fault, and since we disconnected the alarms and conked out the hands, I kind of owe it to them. Now, come on. Carolina may come back any minute to check up on us. You don't want that, not if you want to save your James."

He moved her out of the barn then stopped them a few feet away, saying, "I'm going to check on your pal one more time, to make sure he's good and out. Just remember, I'll have my eye on you, so no false moves."

"Don't hurt him!" Jess pleaded as Terry moved swiftly over to the still form of James. Her coughing silenced further protests at the moment. Terry knelt, his back almost to her, but one eye peeled. He turned away for a few moments, and Jess seriously considered trying to make a break for it, until Terry looked over his shoulder and said, "Try anything, Jess, and I can make it bad for him. Don't make me regret cutting you even a little slack."

She frowned, dipped her head in acquiescence. Terry, now unafraid to turn his back on her, gave James's motionless form a once over. Then her captor was on his feet, dashing over to rush her and the horse around the corner of the barn. Still, Jessica managed one look at James. If Georg Zottigstrauch got his hooks into her, it would be her last. She had no illusions about his ultimate plans for her even if Terry did.

Where was Hooley? If he'd just show, Jess was sure he could get her and the horse out of this jam, either right here or by following them, especially if she had heard what she thought she had about the car he was bringing. At least James was in the clear, now.

Blue paced alongside them, surprisingly calm after all that had happened in the past quarter of an hour, not that he still didn't bob his head enough to make Jessica's arm ache. Terry was silent, grim, unsympathetic when she found herself coughing.

When they came around the barn, Carolina was standing by the driver's side of the car, its motor running, the ramp down to the attached horse van. Rushing to meet them, she fairly waved her gun and demanded, "What took you so long? We've got to get out of here!"

Blue balked and snorted at her.

"Calm down. We'll never get out of here if you rile the horse," Terry shot back.

"That's her job, isn't it? Keeping him tractable." Turning to Jessica, Carolina ordered. "Calm him down, load him up, or you'll be sorry."

Jessica glared back, but before she could counter, Terry took over: "Take it easy on her, Carolina. She saw me take care of her husband. She's sorry enough as it is. Though that's something I doubt you'd understand. Just wait in the back seat."

Carolina's eyes narrowed, but her concerns about time overruled her pride. She grumbled, "Just snap to it," and complied.

Terry nodded to Jessica, and she led Blue up the ramp, securing him by the lead shank and a second line. Giving the horse a pat, she softly promised, "Take it easy, boy, we'll find a way out somehow."

Jessica came out of the trailer, and Terry stopped her with a hand on her arm to warn softly, "I want you to play it as if James is dead. Don't overplay, but Carolina and Zottigstrauch need to believe that he's no longer a threat, understand? Now get in the front seat, and don't try anything. Carolina has her gun, and she doesn't like you."

"The feeling's mutual," Jess replied.

"Fine, just keep a lid on it. Now, I have to secure the van. Then I'll be driving. You get in the car, pronto."

Jess opened the front door, all the while thinking: *How do I play this as if they've really killed James? I've either got to seem completely devastated or filled with bitter hate.* She had paused as those thoughts rushed through her mind, looking back at the barn, then the van. Terry caught her, then scowled and impatiently signaled her to get in the car. Nervously, Jess turned away and slid inside, closing the door behind her. A glance in the rearview mirror showed Carolina's hate-filled eyes, icy-hard like emeralds.

"Just remember, dear, I have a gun," Carolina told her. "Any false moves and you'll get it. Got it?"

"Oh, I've got it," Jess returned, putting bitterness into her voice, but refusing to turn around. "I saw what your husband did to mine."

Yeah, bitter hate it was, flavored with sarcasm. That's what people would expect from her. That would be easier to deliver, the way she felt now.

"Did you?" Carolina almost gloated. "Good. And I'm not a tender-hearted fool like Terry. So, don't think for a moment I won't . . ."

"You won't what?" Jessica turned on Carolina, screwing her courage to the sticking place and playing her part to the hilt. "I know you need me. I know Georg Zottigstrauch wants, needs, me for his plan. You hurt me and he won't be happy at all. Really, if you think about it, he needs me more than he needs you or Terry once you deliver Blue Warrior. You better think twice before you hurt me. Just remember what happened to Phil Novack and the others. No matter how much you hate me, we both know that Zottigstrauch's wrath is a hell of a lot more horrible for you to deal with than your antipathy for me."

Jess turned away from Carolina, closing her eyes. She breathed a silent prayer that her aggressiveness, coupled with nailing Carolina's fear of her boss, had sounded the right note.

Carolina was silent before finally grousing, "Just be quiet and don't make me give you a flesh wound."

Now Terry was at the driver-side door, getting in, telling them, "All squared away. Let's get the hell out of here before someone shows up."

As if on cue, the sound of sirens startled all three.

"Good God, what are you waiting for?!" Carolina hissed.

Terry already had the car in gear and was pulling out into the central road, heading west, along the shore, away from the main entrance–and from the sirens.

"You were supposed to neutralize the alarms! How did they go off?" Carolina demanded.

"For Pete's sake, it's a dark night—who could miss a burning barn against a jet-black sky," Jessica automatically shot back.

"You're awfully defensive of the man who killed your husband," Carolina charged suspiciously.

Uh, oh! Come up with a good save and make it snappy, girl!

Jessica retorted bitterly, "Hardly, smart gal. I don't have to be Albert Einstein to figure out the next person you're going to blame is me. So, I thought I'd head you off at the pass before you decided to deliver on that flesh wound."

"What?!" Terry barked. "Carolina, you know Zottigstrauch would want her in one piece. And you, Miss Wise-Cracker, knock off lighting matches around Caro's short fuse. In fact, the two of you pipe down! I have to concentrate. It's dark and I'm dragging a horse trailer. I don't want to hear another peep out of *either* of you."

That suited Jessica just fine. She needed time to think, to make sure she played her part without antagonizing anyone into wounding her. At least James was back there, alive. Even the horses in the other barn stood a fighting chance now. But was there any help on its way to her? She had her suspicions, her hopes. Would that James could have given her the straight dope about what he and Hooley were up to. She suspected James had elected to keep her in the dark to make sure she didn't accidentally let something slip. She just hoped that when she'd put two and two together, she'd really come up with four.

The car moved with unnerving speed through the dark. Terry had taped the headlights to allow only slits of illumination, just as they used to do for the blackout during the war. It didn't make for calm riding. *What* could *make this a calm drive? Where were they going, anyway?* They had taken an unfamiliar route forking away from the shore. The urge to reassure herself by turning to look back for a sign that someone was following them was powerful—but she mastered it. Jess stared down at the hands she only now realized she'd clasped viselike in her lap.

How had she gotten herself into this mess? She'd known there was something off about James's leaving early and she'd had a bad feeling about Blue. Pleading a headache shortly after James left the Nyquists, she'd gotten David to run her home. Not finding James inside, she hadn't been able to resist the drive to check on Blue. Well, she hadn't been totally off. The Clarkes might have made sure the horse got out, but things might not have gone so well for James without her to inspire Terry.

At least James was in the clear. The odd thought that there'd still be someone around to take care of Dusty flitted through her mind. No! She'd be back to change that litter box, herself! She couldn't let her hopes slip away, though she hoped for better prospects than changing her cat's litter.

And now, weren't the criminal version of the Bickersons awfully quiet? In the faint glow of the dashboard light, Terry looked taut, determined, grim, and, yes, there was more than a flicker of fear in his eyes. *Was he afraid of what Georg Zottigstrauch would do once he was no longer useful? Was he thinking about a groom in Maryland, about Jessamyn? Yes, there was anger in his eyes, too.*

"I need a cigarette," Carolina's tense voice broke the silence. "Pass me a cigarette, Terry–and the lighter."

"I'm driving in the near dark, dragging a horse trailer, in case you forgot," Terry shot back tightly. "Don't distract me. Anyway, concentrate on keeping our guest covered. You can't keep the drop on her and puff away."

"She has been remarkably quiet," Carolina speculated. "You're right. We'd better keep a sharp eye on her. I wonder exactly what is going on in that devious little head of hers."

"I'm the prisoner of two criminals who plan to ship me off to Chitzenega as some Nazi nutcase's glorified groom–where I'll probably be bumped off once my usefulness is done. Pardon me if I'm not exactly a sparkling conversationalist. As I recall, Terry here did request that we both 'pipe down.' I like to honor the requests of people who could do me great harm," Jessica bit out.

"Knock it off," Terry silenced them, "both of you. Stop distracting me. It's damned dark out here, and we did a little too good a job of disguising the hideout."

Terry now turned them to the right, onto an obscure side road–a road just as bumpy as you'd expect of something seldom used.

"Hey, slow down," Jessica warned, thinking of Blue.

"Let *me* do the driving," Terry fired back. "The last thing I intend to do is take advice from my hostage."

"Well, you'd better think twice about that," Jessica countered. "If you know anything about transporting a horse, you understand how easy it is to knock one off his pins in a van. If Blue Warrior breaks a leg and has to be destroyed, you're going to wish you were back in the burning barn when Zottigstrauch gets through with you."

Terry didn't respond. Neither did Carolina. Still, he cut back on the lead-foot routine. Jess relaxed, slightly satisfied. She'd protected Blue and managed to slow them down just in case they were being tailed.

They turned to the right, and now she realized they were quite close to the shore, the scent of the sea and the wash of waves growing stronger. Brush and scrub obscured what in the light would have been a view of the ocean, but Jessica could sense they were running fairly close, perhaps along a cliff above the water.

Terry eased them to a stop, clearly remembering Jessica's warning about keeping Blue with all four hooves on the ground. Why stop here? It was just more brush. The question had barely entered Jessica's mind when Terry warned, "You stay put, Jessica. Carolina has you in her sights. Carolina, keep your eyes full on her. I don't trust her not to try something."

Carolina venomously advised Jess, "Don't doubt I won't shoot, either, dear."

Jess bit her tongue. Better her pride than her body should be wounded.

Terry was out of the car in a flash, pulling away brush camouflaging an old wooden gate. He swung the gate inward, then dashed back to drive them through, onto a road just as miserable as the one they'd left. He pulled the car to a stop once inside, going back to close and re-conceal the gate.

At this point, Jess couldn't help her curiosity and questioned, "Where the dickens are we? I can hear the ocean. What are we supposed to do? *Swim* to Chitzenega?"

"Never mind that," Carolina warned. "Just be quiet and you'll find out soon enough. What's keeping that man? Does he think we have all night? Oh, at last, you're back? What took you?"

"Patience, my pet," Terry answered as he slid behind the wheel and closed the door. "You don't want anyone stumbling onto the causeway at this point in the game, do you?"

Carolina gave Terry some snarky response, but Jess was too busy turning over the word "causeway" in her head to pay attention. *"Causeway"? We're heading onto an island? How far out? Far enough to receive a ship big enough to transport a horse? That meant Blue wouldn't be on any of the ships leaving the cities where the Feds were watching. We'll be on our merry way to Chitzenega via a ship that had already left port. Damn, that would be hard to track.* Once Blue Warrior was on the water, her slim hope of rescue would vanish!

The road gradually descended for about one hundred yards, the ocean washing relentlessly up against the causeway ahead. But the night was too dark to see much except the line of road running out about a quarter of a mile to, yes, it was an island. Scraggly pines ranging ahead on the island blocked any clear view of their destination.

The causeway was pretty darn narrow—too narrow for Jessica's taste. Only one car at a time could pass along it, above some angry rushing waters. Jess prayed that Terry was sufficiently familiar with this miserable excuse for a road that those slitted headlights gave him enough illumination to keep them out of the drink! They moved off the bridge and into the woods, dark branches scraping the top of the van. *Blue must just love this! Had he whistled defensively?*

A break in the woods appeared ahead, and Jess tensed. At last, she was going to discover whether Nigel or Nicholas Spenser was the Nazi murderer. She sank inside. This was a man, no a monster, whom she did not want to have to face. She especially didn't want to find out that the man she so dreaded was Nigel Cross.

They pulled into a clearing, before an old cabin not so different from Phil Novack's, though smaller. The cabin, standing between them and the ocean, looked to have a landing or dock built, no rebuilt, somewhat lower to its left. Carolina interrupted Jessica's thoughts with, "His car's not here. Where is he?"

"Take it easy," Terry ordered testily as he brought the car to a stop. "He's not about to miss *this* boat, literally or figuratively."

Jess relaxed ever so slightly that the inevitable was on hold. She studied the cabin directly ahead of them. It had been fixed up, a bit, but not as much as the dock. Of course, no one was planning to stick around. She turned to Terry as he switched off the ignition and asked, "What now?"

"What now?" he repeated, looking straight ahead at the worn planks of the porch. "Now we wait. Everybody out." A brief glance back at Carolina for: "You first, keep the drop on her while I give the horse a quick check."

Carolina nodded, hopping out, then jerking her head at Jess while ordering, "You heard Terry—out!"

Jessica was on the verge of smiling an acid comeback; however, Carolina's sour puss and her big, black pistol changed her mind. She didn't want to get the last word if it might *be* her last word. So, they were all pretty silent, Carolina and Jessica by the porch and Terry disappearing behind the trailer. The night was downright cold now, the wind rippling Jess's silky, smoke-smudged blouse and forcing her to brush away the dark hair driven across her face. Carolina started a little at that movement, then irritably grumbled at letting Jess unnerve her. The sudden sound of Blue snorting and stamping was followed by Terry's curses. Carolina muttered something about the damned horse belonging in a glue pot. It was bad news, indeed, when your captors were as unnerved as you, waiting for their boss to show.

Terry returned, saying, "Okay, the horse's fine. Ornery but fine. I'll be damned glad when we part company with him."

Jess's skeptical expression again warned Terry that parting wouldn't leave him very safe. He turned abruptly away and instructed, "Carolina, go back up the road and wait for Zottigstrauch. It'll go quicker if someone lets him in. You can ride back with him."

"Stay out in this cold night and wait? Why me?" she challenged.

"Because in your mood, I don't trust you not to shoot both Jessica *and* the horse. You've got a jacket on, so stop complaining. Besides, I need someone to warn me if we get any unexpected guests. Now knock off the arguing. I don't want to have to tell our fearless leader that you've been uncooperative."

Carolina glared, and Jessica wondered if she was about to get caught in the crossfire of a marital shoot-out. Bad news for Terry, too, since he didn't seem to have his gun out, while his wife all but had her finger pressing the trigger. Luckily, the flame-haired woman just scowled before heading up the road.

Terry turned to Jessica and said, "Okay, let's wait inside. You're freezing."

"If I'd known I was going to be kidnapped this late, I'd have brought a sweater," Jess remarked as they stepped onto the porch.

Terry nodded in the direction of the door, which he pushed open for Jessica, and instructed, "Stop right inside the door. I'll light a lantern, so you don't fall and break your neck, or try to make a break for it."

"Make a break for it?" Jess countered, stopping in the doorway. "Make a break to where? The Atlantic? I suppose you think I'm Esther Williams?"

"I think you'd better get in there and behave," Terry warned, but not exactly harshly.

Jessica stepped carefully into the darkness. She waited tensely while Terry followed, apparently finding a lamp behind her on a table near the door. When the glow came up, Jess got a gander at their surroundings in the one-room cabin. An out-of-commission fireplace faced them. There were a few chairs and tables, all clean enough but hardly the stuff of *Better Homes and Gardens*. Still, it would do for a brief hideout. The wall facing the sea had no windows at all, while the windows on the sides and the front, behind her, were all securely blocked with what looked like newly added outside shutters.

Terry guided her by the arm across the room and said, "Take that chair over at the fireplace. I know I don't have to tell you not to try anything funny."

"And leave these luxurious digs?" Jess cracked, moving to the end of the mantle over the hearth, trying to keep up her nerve.

"I knew you'd play it smart," Terry surmised. "Just take it easy and wait. Zottigstrauch will get here soon enough. He's not a guy to let things slide. This means too much to him."

"Does it, Terry?" Jess questioned, thinking desperately about how she might be able to reach him, not just for her own sake but because he had saved James. She owed him for that and their past. She questioned, "How much does this mean to *you*?"

"What's that supposed to mean?" Terry demanded.

"It means, Terry, this whole business isn't you," Jessica answered earnestly, the ghostly lamplight just reaching her and Terry from across the room. "I said it before; I can't believe you're willingly a part of this whole deal. You're no Nazi lover."

"Believe what you like," Terry responded, discouraged, "but I'm in up to my neck, and I can't get out. No one walks away from Georg Zottigstrauch. No, the three of us are stuck. Give up fighting it, Jessica."

"But how did this happen to you, Terry?" Jessica tried to understand, hoping to find a way to reach Terry and bring him back.

"How? Stupidity, pride, greed, pick one, pick them all. He's a sly dog, that Zottigstrauch. Came to me through Carolina. He'd sucked her in first. He has charm, that guy, real charm. Weaseled out of her exactly how desperate both of us were to make enough to restore our families, got her to bring me to this place called Bertrille's. It was a high-class clip joint. Four-star restaurant and nightclub fronting illegal gambling beyond a very special secret door."

"But gambling didn't win you the fortune you were banking on," Jess completed. "I still don't understand how a gambling debt mixes you up in treason and murder."

"When you're one-hundred grand on the hook to a guy named Rocky the Shark, you do what the guy who bails you out tells you," Terry explained bitterly. "Anyway, it didn't start out as treason and murder, merely a little horse snatching. And he really knew what he was doing when he went after Carolina. He knew about her family's proximity to Blue Warrior's farm. He made it all sound so easy: getting a groom whom Carolina knew hired in the stallion's barn, bribing him to scout out the layout then grab the horse. It seemed like a harmless way to work off the debt. Some rich guy loses his horse, but heck, he has insurance and plenty more horses. Nobody really gets hurt, including me by Rocky."

"Until the groom dies in the fire," Jessica pointed out. It seemed superfluous to ask about Blue's body double at the moment.

"Yeah," Terry agreed, his crystal-blue eyes shining bitterness. "He does things like that. He slips in one more little hook to keep you in his net—doesn't matter who suffers—cold-blooded bastard, isn't he? First, it's gambling debts, then it's murder . . ."

"Then it's even more murder?" Jessica added, her sympathy tinged with irony.

"Even the good and the innocent," exploded Terry sharply, slamming his palm on the mantle so hard it rattled.

Jess started back. She licked her lip, hesitating to push Terry on this tender point of Jessamyn Crane, but it was her life, and, yes, his, too, at stake.

"Terry, you can't keep going along with this," she said quietly, intently, stepping toward him again. "Not after what he did to Jessamyn. You can't let him get away with it."

Terry gave Jessica the strangest smile. He thought for a moment before finally saying, "Nice move, Jessica. You're almost as good as he is at pushing the right buttons."

"That's not fair," Jess protested. "Yes, of course, I want to get out of here, because you know as well as I do, once he's done with us, we're just two more loose ends that need to be snipped. Three, actually, counting Carolina. Terry, he does not deserve to get away with all this horror. Don't you want to stop him and make him pay?"

Terry only said, "He's not going to get the better of me. Don't worry about that."

Jess cocked her head and asked, "What's *that* supposed to mean?"

"It means enjoy the free trip to a tropical clime," Terry smoothly shut her down.

"Sure, but I'll probably be bunking with the horse the whole way. What a vacation! But, say, why his obsession with Blue? All this grief to get one horse out of the country to Chitzenega? What's the big deal? Who's at the other end of this cruise, anyway?"

"Ask me no questions and I'll tell you no lies," Terry warned. "The less you know, the happier you'll be."

"Add another cliché and you'll have a triple play," Jessica remarked sarcastically. Was she more annoyed or embarrassed by Terry's solidly blocking her attempt to fish for information? Jess didn't have time to think the possibilities through further. Another vehicle pulling up outside brought both her and Terry to attention.

Smiling grimly, Terry announced, "Sounds like the boss is here."

A sharp wave of fear reverberated through Jessica. She was glad Terry was too busy to notice, glancing out the door he'd now cracked open. For a fraction of a second, Jessica hopefully wondered if the car could be Hooley's. Would he drive up right out in the open? Terry quashed her hopes by turning back and saying, "I'm on the money. You sit tight in here while I run out for a chat. Don't even dream about trying to get away."

Jess quickly glanced at the sealed windows, then jerked her head back at the fireplace to retort, "Do I look like Santa Claus?"

Terry quirked a smile, then grew serious, even a little nervous, and warned, "Just remember, James is believed dead. I don't want my one good turn to get me in Dutch, fatally. Our lives depend on Georg not getting wise to my crossing him."

Jess gave Terry a quick nod and made a nervous swallow. The look in the usually smug Terry Clarke's eyes before he went out left her weak in the knees. Forcing herself to stay calm, Jessica moved back to the chair by the hearth. She couldn't afford to let Georg Zottigstrauch terrify her, even if it might serve her to make him think he had.

Taking a deep breath, Jess gripped the back of the chair till her knuckles were white. Her face, itself, became a white mask of stoicism in the gloom of the solitary lantern as she thought, *In a few minutes, I'm going to know whether Zottigstrauch is Nigel Cross or Nicholas Spenser.*

The door opened into her dark reflections, and Terry entered first.

Darn! she inwardly cursed–until Terry's companion stepped into the room. His features hid nothing now; his teeth were sharp and predatory in that cobra-cold smile of satisfaction.

Chapter Thirty-Two

Georg Zottigstrauch seemed to have it all. His dark eyes said as much with a chilling delight that would have given Boris Karloff the heebie-jeebies. Yet, Jessica felt just the tiniest relief that she was not facing Nigel Cross. As he took her in, coolly and satisfied, Jessica recognized the man she had known as Nicholas Spenser.

"Ah so, Mrs. Crawford," he began, "I'm delighted that you could join us on our little voyage."

"As if I had a choice," Jessica returned tightly, still careful to convey precisely the right degree of antagonism. She had to feel her way carefully through this chess match, and, unfortunately, her game of skill was mahjong.

"I know how attached you are to the horse, so I thought you'd enjoy taking a lovely Caribbean cruise with him," he said graciously. "I know you'd hate to be separated from him."

What's with the chit-chat? A glance at Terry: he was watching Zottigstrauch carefully. Something had happened outside to put traces of mistrust and resentment into his eyes. Until she knew what was going on, it seemed best to tamp down the anger and hide behind a screen of wit. Jessica offered, "You could keep Blue and me just as cozy by leaving us here. We'd be even cozier, actually, if you left us where my family and career are." Hoping to nestle a little probing into her smart talk, she finished, "What's so special about Chitzenega, anyway?"

Georg Zottigstrauch wasn't biting. Turning the tables on Jessica, he calmly tossed off, "Family, Mrs. Crawford? I understand Terence pulled up your strongest anchor behind the stables this evening, didn't you Terence?"

Terry abruptly shifted away, muttering something. She'd have to react convincingly to that heartless reference to James's "murder" if she were to keep Zottigstrauch in the dark about Terry's good deed. Fortunately, she could channel her horror and disgust at her antagonist's sheer malignity into her response.

"You bastard," she spat out, then leaned heavily against the chair before her, dropping her head, hiding her face behind the curtain of her dark hair. That wasn't enough, though; she had to keep out-thinking this creep, hit his weakness. His superior attitude suggested to her that as long as he thought Jess believed she had no allies left, she could use his ego and cruelty to blind, or at least distract, him. Jessica looked up, not acting when she glared her fury at all the cruelty and grief Zottigstrauch had perpetrated. Jess added just the right touch of desperation to declare coldly, "You have no idea how much I hate you."

"Now, now, Mrs. Crawford," Zottigstrauch "consoled" her, taking a cigarette from a silver case and lighting up, "this will never do. Animals can sense our distress. You wouldn't want the horse to become unsettled and injure himself. Should he need to be destroyed, it would be most inconvenient. I can't expect payment for damaged goods."

"That would put *you* in the hot seat, then," Jessica observed mordantly, tilting her head thoughtfully. "So, nixing your plans by refusing to help you with the horse would be payback. Your buyer in Chitzenega must be a demanding improver of the breed to put that kind of a frown on your puss. He must have some kind of hold over you . . ."

"Don't even dream of trying to cross me, woman," Zottigstrauch cut her off, tossing down his cigarette, then decisively, slowly crushing it out with his shoe as if he had far more on his mind than fire safety. His cold eyes underlined his next words, "Remember, you are alive now because I need you to ensure I can make my delivery. I have far too many plans riding on this transaction to tolerate any impediments. If anything happens to the horse, you have no reason to exist. Terence can attest to what happens to those who are superfluous, let alone obstructive, to my goals."

Jessica felt an icy rush up her legs, through her spine, and into her head. She didn't have to *act* scared now. The deadliness in her captor's eyes and words, the lantern light that gave his long sharp features and smooth-domed skull a death's head menace, all took care of that.

"Look," Terry cut in. "I don't see the need to bring me into this, anymore. You've gotten what you want out of me. Stop wasting time gloating."

Georg Zottigstrauch smiled a quiet, clever smile. Still watching Jessica, he told Terry, "Ah, dear boy, I never waste time. And I'm not merely gloating. You should know better on both counts. No, you see, we need to make Mrs. Crawford grasp that fully cooperating with us is in her best interest."

"I'm not fighting," Jessica replied bitterly. "I have no choice but to 'cooperate.' I'm entirely in your power. What more do you want from me—a smile?"

"Not at all necessary—though that gloomy expression doesn't become you. No, Madam, I could use a little more information. True, Terry has eliminated your husband as a threat, in and of himself. However, he was sent to capture me, most likely to stop my plans. Of course, I'm not afraid of a dead man, but I do need to discover how much he knew about me and what he'd told his superiors. I need to know exactly who may be after me, if they know whom I'm contacting, what their plans are. Of course, your husband was too dangerous to keep alive to get that information, but he most likely has talked to you. Just a warning to you, trying to ferret some of this information out of me a moment ago was not effective. I've been playing this game too long. Now talk."

"You're nuts," Jessica shot back, deciding that playing it dumb just might work on a guy who wasn't giving her credit for many smarts. "What's all this double talk about spy stuff? My husband is, was, a college professor. If you think anything else, you ought to have your head examined."

Zottigstrauch's words started silkily but ended leaving Jessica thinking she'd read the situation *all* wrong: "Really, my dear, I'd advise you not to take me for a fool. That ass of a professor clearly outed your late spouse. It was an unfortunate stroke of bad luck for him, but, again, the gods are on the side of the superior race. Even if they weren't, that revelation connects a collection of behaviors, innocent in themselves, into a context that can lead a man in my position to unfortunate suspicions."

Terry turned away and strode out the door. That left Jessica alone with Georg Zottigstrauch. A situation she didn't relish—at all.

He recaptured Jess's attention with: "So, I rather enjoyed playing with your husband through my little ploy concerning Nigel Cross, one to throw some suspicion elsewhere—at the very least tie him up trying to get himself out of trouble. Clever, no? Kept your late husband off balance, didn't I? He was no match for me."

"He was match enough to rattle you into making that move," Jessica retorted, immediately regretting confirming Zottigstrauch's assessment of James's mission.

Zottigstrauch smiled and replied, "It didn't do him much good, did it? With him ending up dead. Oh sorry, did I wound you? Then let us get down to business. What precisely did your husband know? Who else knows? What are their plans?"

Jessica swallowed hard. She didn't actually know as much as he wanted to learn. That was good for James, but not for her if Zottigstracu decided to get tough. She needed to do some fancy tap dancing to get out of this one. Still, if her earlier suspicions of James and Hooley's plans were on the money, she might be able to pull this off, if she could just stall.

"All right, you got me. Yes, James was in some sort of secret service. I discovered that he was looking for some kind of Nazi war criminal" (she enjoyed his annoyance at that term), "but that's all I knew. He didn't keep me up on his work. It's not the kind of thing you're supposed to blab to the little woman, you know. Beyond the fact he was looking for some depraved war criminal, hiding away, scared of being brought to justice, I'm in the dark."

Zottigstrauch didn't take her description of him kindly. Nothing obvious, just his mouth's corners slightly tensing, not quite masking the affront. *Good. Putting him even a little off-balance might open the door to his making mistakes.*

Though his tone was smooth, her captor sought to pressure rather than outsmart her with, "We do have ways of making you talk."

This time Jessica smiled, and she drove home her slight advantage by innocently replying, "You know one of the boys I talked to at the Stagedoor Canteen told me of a training film, *How to Resist Enemy Interrogation*, all about how you Nazis get people to give themselves away. I vote for the method where you wine and dine me, accompanied by sparkling, chummy conversation. Just a hint, I could really go for a steak about now. Cold air and a kidnapping really work up a girl's appetite."

His expression hardened for, "I helped develop some of those tools for making people loquacious, and I assure you that several of them are far less pleasant than a nice dinner."

"I can assure you," countered Jessica, leaning forward over the chair, "that a banged-up version of me isn't going to be much help soothing that savage bangtail you're trying to peddle to some fellow traveler in Chitzenega. We both know that you need me in good working order if you're going to complete your plan."

He started to glare at her, and it took all of Jessica's power not to wilt. Suddenly, though, he smiled. Jessica liked that even less. *What exactly did that smile mean?*

"Yes, Jessica Crawford, I do need you all in one piece. But I don't need what is mere superflux to me. That said, I brought someone to keep you company while I confer with Terence outside. Someone I don't need once we depart."

Zottigstrauch went to the door, leaving Jessica unnerved by the mystery of what he had up his sleeve. Opening the door, he called out, "Terence, bring in Mrs. Crawford's companion."

Jessica found herself digging her nails into the chair. She'd hoped for a moment to sink down into it, collapse, and regroup. Instead, her brain was battered by questions: *Who was it? Had Hooley been nabbed? Had James been discovered alive and snatched by Zottigstrauch?* Terry guided in the figure, hands bound, eyes blindfolded. This was worse than she'd expected.

"My Lord," Jessica breathed. "Alicia!" Turning on Zottigstrauch she raged, "What are you doing with this kid? Let her go! You've no right!"

Even as Jessica challenged Zottigstrauch, the young girl halted and managed fearfully, "Jessica? Minton? Is that you! What's going on? How do we get out of this?"

Zottigstrauch's wicked smile would have been the envy of any hungry shark. Jess realized that Alicia's terror and her concern for the girl played nicely into his plans.

He said, "Yes, I thought you might need some company, Jessica Minton Crawford, to calm you down and deflate some of that antagonism. And, yes, you're right. We do have many ways to make you talk, though they may involve what happens to other people–younger, more innocent people. Are you willing to take that responsibility?"

"Jessica?" Alicia almost whispered in terror, Terry's firm grip on her arm now seemed the mainstay holding her up. "Jessica, are they going to hurt me? Please, can't you help me?"

What pleasure she'd have scratching out Zottigstrauch's eyes, but she knew she had to play this scene just right.

Forcibly restraining her anger, Jess reassured, "Take it easy, Alicia. Don't let them get to you. They both know that if they try anything with you, I'll clam up tight, if I *did* have anything to say, which I *don't*."

Zottigstrauch smiled again and allowed, "Nice maneuver, trying to invert the *quid pro quo*. However, I'm not forgetting, and neither is this young lady, that she will have to suffer just to prove you haven't anything more to tell me. You must have extrapolated by now that I have no compunction about inflicting unnecessary pain, as long as it doesn't hamper my plans."

"Jessica?" bleated Alicia.

Before Jessica could formulate, let alone fire off, a reply, Zottigstrauch stated, "But why don't I leave you alone to build up your maternal bond with this child, Mrs. Crawford. She *is* a lovely child, isn't she Terence?"

Terry's mouth tightened into a grim line; however, he said nothing. He didn't even look at Jess now.

"Yes," reiterated Zottigstrauch, "indeed, a lovely child. It would be a shame if your recalcitrance were responsible for altering that condition . . ."

At those words and Alicia's trembling reaction, Jessica snarled, "If I could get my hands on you . . ."

"But you can't," Zottigstrauch calmly shut her down. "Now, Terence and I have some things to straighten out that you don't need to know. We'll step outside for a moment, while you two have a conversation about how your cooperation will preserve this child's loveliness. I know you won't attempt to escape. I designed the refurbishment of this cabin against such possibilities."

"You think of everything, except the fact that I can't tell you what I don't know," Jessica coldly insisted.

A quick, cruel smile and Zottigstrauch observed, "We shall see." Turning to Terry, he continued, "Put the girl in the chair." A nod toward the right of the hearth.

"Terry, please," Jessica pleaded, stepping forward. "You can't be a part of this anymore. Alicia's just a kid. You've got to draw the line here and now."

Terry hesitated. He hadn't looked happy with this part of Zottigstrauch's plan. It was clear to Jess that a lot was eating him, including, she suspected, fear that his boss would discover and punish him for his mercy to James. Her heart sinking, Jess gathered from Terry's next words that sparing James had been as far over to the side of the angels as he'd dared go. Forcing Alicia down into the chair, Terry looked Jess in the eye to warn, "Play it smart, Jessica. My hands are tied. Use your head."

"How can I play, period, when your Nazi pal over there holds all the cards?" she retorted.

"Clarke," Zottigstrauch commanded from the open door.

His back to his "master," Terry fixed Jess with an odd look, as if signaling something, then bobbed his head at Alicia and instructed, "Play it smart."

The door closed on Alicia and Jessica, leaving them alone in the pale yellow glow of the lamp. The rush of the ocean outside created a feeling of isolation, no, desolation. What had Terry's look meant? Knuckle under to Zottigstrauch to save herself and Alicia? Or was Terry hinting she might still be able to play for time? He knew James was down for the count. He'd have no way of knowing her suspicions of how Hooley might be able to track them. Would Terry risk being caught red-handed with Zottigstrauch, anyway? Was he counting on being able to parlay his sparing James into some kind of a deal with the Feds?

"Jessica!" Alicia's voice shattered her thoughts. "Where are you? Are they gone? What are we going to do?!"

"Oh my gosh!" escaped Jess as she whirled around to the girl. She rushed over to Alicia, saying, "Let me at least get rid of that blindfold and untie you! What was I thinking?"

In a jiffy, Jess had the blindfold off and was working on the rope around Alicia's wrists. Almost as much to distract Alicia from the horrible threat hanging over her as out of curiosity, Jess questioned, "How on earth did Zottigstrauch manage to grab you?"

Alicia was blinking even in this dim light and answering, "He went around under a fake name. He told me in the car. He told me a lot of crazy stuff."

That didn't sit well with Jess, Zottigstrauch letting the girl know too much about him. She knelt by Alicia to work on her bonds more easily, and asked again, "Okay, but how did he ever manage to get you?"

"It was crazy. I was at the fire with Lauren. Everyone rushed over. Lauren and I got separated in the confusion. Next thing I knew, this Spenser, I mean Zottigstrauch, came up and told me you had Blackie off in the paddock. You were nursing an injury he had, so you needed me. Halfway there, away from the crowd, he said he had to stop at his car. When we got there, he suddenly put this cloth over my mouth, it smelled weird, then I passed out. When I came to, I was tied up and blindfolded. Ooh, my head is still a little woozy. So, what is this all about, Jessica?"

Jess freed Alicia. Rubbing her wrists, offering a "thanks," the girl persisted, "Can't you tell me?"

How to answer that question without endangering Alicia further, without giving away her own hopes? Standing up, Jessica finally said, "What did Zottigstrauch tell you?"

"Well," the girl began slowly, "I was in a haze most of the trip. I don't even know exactly where I am–between being drugged and blindfolded."

Now *there* was some hope. If Zottigstrauch had planned to kill Alicia, he wouldn't have taken the trouble to keep her, literally, in the dark about his hideaway. Still, Jess needed to know more to decide exactly how much danger threatened the girl. She questioned carefully, "But it sounds as if he told you *something*. Think, Alicia. Anything Zottigstrauch might have said could give us a clue to his plans or how we might be able to outsmart him and get out of this tight spot. Think."

Alicia rubbed her temples, the lamplight bringing up the patrician structure of her face. She forced herself to recollect, "Yes, okay, all right. I, I do remember he got upset when I called him Nicholas Spenser, said he was tired of playing the *schwächling*. That's a German word, isn't it? And that name Zottigstrauch, that's German, too. Oh my goodness, Jessica, does that make him some kind of Nazi leftover from the war? Those guys were vicious! Oh God, Jessica, what will he do to us? And Professor Clarke, he's part of this, too? Oh, what can we do?"

"We can't lose our heads," Jess levelly warned, gripping Alicia's shoulders. "That's just what they want. We've got to hold on and think this thing out."

"Then, if Zottigstrauch is a Nazi, what he was saying about your husband, even you, is true?" Alicia pressed, incredulous.

"About James?" Jessica repeated, uneasily. "About me? Just what did he say?"

"It's absolutely out of this world. And, until now, I thought he was crazy; but with his actually being a Nazi, it makes sense," Alicia concluded. Incredulous, she continued, "After I came around, coming down the causeway, he told me that you and Professor Crawford worked for the Secret Service, that you were both trying to trap him. Is that true?"

Jessica couldn't help hesitating. How much could she tell Alicia? The cat certainly seemed out of the bag as far as James was concerned for Georg Zottigstrauch. So if she acknowledged to Alicia what he already knew to be true, he might be more accepting of the rest of what she said when he questioned the girl.

Reading Jessica's expression, Alicia exclaimed, "So it's true!"

"It's partly true," Jessica allowed. "I'm no agent. I had no idea of what James was up to; I just found that out. I'm only an actress. That's all. But it is true about James, and they killed him for it."

Alicia's expression collapsed and she said softly, "No, oh, I'm so sorry. How can you bear it?"

Jess turned away. She'd had to do a lot of lying on some of these cases, but it was hardly her favorite past-time. Nevertheless, she had no right to put Terry in jeopardy by betraying him. Just as important, she couldn't risk anyone finding out that James was still alive, just in case he could rescue them. Obviously, she trusted Alicia, but she couldn't chance that the girl would keep such crucial information to herself under duress.

Alicia interrupted Jessica's thoughts, persisting hopefully, "But if he was an agent, he might have some back-up. Someone could be coming for us this minute, right? Maybe he's not even dead!"

Jess wouldn't face the girl. *What if Alicia read the truth in her eyes.* She answered, "I saw Terry kill him. He's gone."

"Professor Clarke? Oh no, no. You have to be wrong. Not him, please," Alicia cried. "I thought they forced him into all this. Even he's that evil? No, no."

Jessica couldn't help turning anxiously back to the young girl's despairing outburst. Alicia's head of wavy black hair was buried in her hands. Sobs wracked her and she repeated, "No hope. No one to trust."

Jessica took Alicia by the shoulders, raising the teenager to face her with, "Don't lose hope. Terry didn't want to do it."

Alicia sniffed, her eyes brightening, and she managed, "Really, Terry isn't as bad as the rest? You forgive him? Maybe he might help us. Maybe he might turn on these creeps if we appeal to his conscience?"

Jessica hesitated. She didn't want to crush the poor kid, but she didn't want to give her false hope. And if Zottigstrauch got her to talk, such speculation about Terry would be a lousy reward for sparing James.

"Alicia, Terry is afraid of this guy; we can't count on him for anything. When push comes to shove, he's going to save his own skin. Remember, he didn't do anything after they murdered the woman he loved, Jessamyn Crane."

"They murdered Miss Crane?!" Alicia exclaimed. "How do you know that?"

Jessica cursed herself for letting something slip, after all. Getting up, she moved away, saying, "Does it really matter?" No, that was a lame response. She turned back and revealed, "Terry told me. He's bitter, but he's too weak to do anything about it. So, that's why I say we're on our own. We've got to use our wits to hold out."

"Hold out?" Alicia repeated, hope sparking across her features. "If we can hold out, there must be something to hold out for. Do you think your husband had people helping him? They might be on their way to rescue us right now!"

Jessica looked down. She hated to dash Alicia's hope, especially when she knew there was reason for it. Especially when she suspected that

James had hidden a homing device in Blue's halter, and that the car Hooley was bringing in was special for something more than standard transmission, special like tracking capabilities. But anything she told Alicia could fall right into Georg Zottigstrauch's lap.

"I don't know that," Jessica half-truthed. "But maybe I can convince old Zottigstrauch that I'll be more cooperative with you unscathed than scathed."

Alicia didn't seem all that satisfied. She shook her head, "I don't get why they want you, anyway. I mean, if your husband's dead, you aren't a bargaining chip to anyone, are you?"

Jumping at the chance to change the subject, Jessica explained, "That I can answer you. Zottigstrauch wants Blackie, who isn't really Blackie but a valuable Thoroughbred named Blue Warrior. He needs me to keep the horse quiet, so he won't fight and hurt himself."

Alicia asked an obvious question, "What does a Nazi want with a horse?"

"Not just any horse, *that* horse," Jessica corrected.

"Okay, then, why *that* horse."

Jess shrugged and managed to not quite lie once again: "That's the $64.00 question, kiddo. All I know is that the horse is worth a bundle, and my guess is that Zottigstrauch intends to collect it. For what end? From whom? Your guess is as good as mine. Remember, I'm no secret service agent."

"I wish you were. Then I could have some hope we'd get out of this alive," Alicia lamented.

Jessica's heart broke for the kid, but she had to set her straight: "We'll just have to figure out another way to hope, Alicia. I'm just a regular gal—and that's final."

The door opened and in came Georg Zottigstrauch, followed by Terry. Zottigstrauch instructed Jessica, "Time for you to earn your keep, Mrs. Crawford. We need to unload the horse *now* to depart on time. I need you to calm him down."

"Maybe he wouldn't be so hard to handle if you hadn't set his barn on fire—twice," Jessica coolly pointed out.

"I'm sure many people find your sarcasm amusing, Mrs. Crawford. I don't have time for it, and if you know what's good for you—and this child—you'll be less vocal and more compliant."

Jessica bit back a smart retort, though her hostility was no less evident. However, she knew better than to risk Alicia to this vicious man's displeasure.

Zottigstrauch was speaking, "Terry, tie up the girl again. You needn't blindfold her. Binding her hands and fastening her to the chair should keep her in place while I concentrate on the horse. I won't risk her escaping and alerting any intruders before we can get away."

Terry nodded, gave Jessica an appraising look she couldn't quite read, and went to work on the protesting, then frighteningly obedient, Alicia.

"Is that really necessary?" Jessica questioned Zottigstrauch, nodding toward her terrified fellow-prisoner's bonds.

Zottigstrauch ignored the challenge. Instead, pointing to the open door, he said, "Outside, Mrs. Crawford."

Jessica hesitated, looking at Alicia and Terry, calculating if she could parley Zottigstrauch's need for her into a gentler treatment of the girl. No dice. Zottigstrauch abruptly gripped her arm with a strength that belied his slender frame and propelled her out into the night, saying, "I have no time for games."

Behind her, she heard Terry call, "Play it smart, Jessica. Play it smart."

Chapter Thirty-Three

The evening was still frighteningly dark. The only illumination came from the taped headlights of Terry's car, pointed forward, and the sedan, with similarly altered headlamps, that Georg Zottigstrauch had parked at an awkward parallel to the first auto to illuminate the back of the van. Would that a little moonlight brightened the way. But, Jess supposed, if you want to heist a hot equine, a moonless night was just the ticket. This Zottigstrauch sure planned ahead. Yet he hadn't thought of everything. He'd underestimated Terry's moral fiber and James's added precautions. Had that miscalculation been enough to trip him up? At the moment, rescue appeared nowhere in sight.

With a vise grip, Zottigstrauch powered her down the steps. Jess tried to buck up her spirits with, "Hey, I'm cooperating. No need to get rough."

No response. Jess's captor pushed her toward the trailer, only speaking when they squeezed past his car: "You need to calm the horse so that we can take him out and examine him. You can tie him up at the porch railing, in the head lamps' illumination."

Jess could hear Blue snorting irritably, no uneasily, as they moved along the van to come around behind it.

"Open the trailer. Go in and bring him out," Zottigstrauch ordered, releasing Jess and giving her a little push forward.

At the sound of the man's cold, harsh voice, Blue jerked up his head and laid back his ears, straining to turn around, held in place by the secured lead shank and a second tie. He pawed the straw in front of him.

Much as Jess loved the horse, she didn't relish joining him in that narrow space right now. *And where was Carolina? Odd.* Maybe she could use this as a delaying tactic, till Blue calmed down a bit.

"Where's Carolina? You didn't leave her back at the top of the drive, did you?"

Zottigstrauch was concentrating so intently on getting the horse that he was a bit taken aback by both the question and her even speaking. Recovering quickly, he gave her the ghastliest of smiles to reply, "Let's just say that Mrs. Brent Clarke won't be making this trip, after all."

Jess didn't know why this man could still shock her, but the black delight he took in tossing off that sarcasm chilled her. She couldn't help gasping, "You've killed her, too? How could you?"

Now he looked bored, definitely irritated, when he shot back, "Use your brain. I contracted passage for only a limited number. With you along, there's no room for Mrs. Brent Clarke. You might even consider yourself responsible for her demise, since I had to liquidate her to make room you."

"I hardly asked to be part of your Caribbean cruise," Jessica retorted.

"Perhaps not, but here you are and there she is—was."

"Does Terry know? He won't let you get away with this . . ."

"No?" Zottigstrauch taunted, briefly succumbing to Jessica's playing on his delight in exerting power over others. "He certainly did nothing noteworthy after he realized that I'd had Jessamyn Crane, the woman he really loved, eliminated. No, he remained compliant to orders, not happy, but still compliant. He took his discipline like the minion he is. You know Terry Clarke far less well than you think. Now stop wasting time. The boat for the horse will be here soon, and I want to be sure all is in order with my equine treasure. Unhitch the ramp and get the horse."

Jessica narrowed her eyes, pretending she was resentful but defeated. Well, she wasn't acting the resentful part. She'd have to hide her satisfaction that Terry had proved Zottigstrauch didn't know him as well as *he* thought. Maybe that miscalculation would buy her and Alicia enough time for Hooley, if not James, to pry them out of this tight spot. Especially Alicia needed to be rescued, if Zottigstrauch's spiel about limited passenger space was on the level.

Unlatching the ramp, speaking soothingly to the defensive stallion inside, Jess was still trying to figure a way to save Alicia. Smart of him to figure out concern for the girl was pretty effective leverage over her. Smart in a malevolent, Third-Reich kind of way. So where were Tonto and the Lone Ranger? It was getting kind of late in the game.

"Stop standing there. You have the ramp down. Go in there and back the horse out," Zottigstrauch commanded impatiently, glancing at a watch on his wrist that glowed when he pressed a knob.

Jessica turned on her captor, warning tightly, "Keep your shirt on, buster. That's three-quarters of a ton of antsy horse in there. He *likes* me and his ears are back. With you here, it's harder to calm him down. I won't be able to do that if he takes those dainty little steel-shod hooves of his and stomps me into hamburger. I'll tell you, this would go a lot easier if you would back off and . . ."

"I hardly think, Mrs. Crawford, that either you or the horse is going out of my sight."

"Then eighty-six the threats. This horse doesn't like your tone, let alone you. Maybe because he knows you murdered his friend, Phil Novack."

"I didn't murder Novack," Zottigstrauch said, preoccupied with keeping to schedule.

"Then who did? Not Terry. Carolina?"

"Mrs. Crawford," Zottigstrauch silenced Jess, keeping his voice calm to avoid antagonizing Blue, "I'm losing patience. If you don't do as you are told and bring out this animal, I may be forced to have Terence drag that young lady out here so that you may see me 'treat' her in ways that will spur your cooperation."

The creep had her there. Seeing Blue had calmed a bit and cocked an ear back at her, Jess turned to the horse and soothed, "Easy, son. How about I get you out of this cramped old trailer? You look as if you could use some fresh air."

Blue scraped the floor with his right hoof, but not nervously. He turned his head as far as his ties would allow and gave Jessica a friendly whicker.

Jess cautiously entered the van, a gentle hand on Blue's haunches, keeping well clear of those rear legs. Talking calmly, stroking the horse, she made her way to Blue's head, squashing her fear of Zottigstrauch and even of the big horse unhappily confined in close quarters.

"It's okay, son," she whispered into his ear. "We'll be okay, soon."
She hoped.

Why she kept calling the stallion "son," Jess wasn't sure. It had worked for Fred McMurray in *Smokey* and Roddy McDowell in *Thunderhead, Son of Flicka. Son of a gun, it seemed to be working now!*

It was murder not to check the underside of Blue's halter for the homing device she was sure she'd heard James mention to Hooley. But no way would she risk giving away that one hope to Zottigstrauch. Or was she more afraid checking would reveal that one hope to be a delusion?

Jess crushed down her fear and concentrated on safely backing Blue Warrior out into the salty night air. Outside the van, the stallion took one look at the tall predatory man watching them, standing a safe distance, and flattened his ears again. If a horse normally growled, he would have. For a minute, Zottigstrauch looked nervous, then his grip tightened on his gun, and he seemed to take courage from the fact that he was armed, and the horse wasn't.

Jessica rubbed the stallion's forehead comfortingly. She couldn't help commenting, "He really doesn't like you much, does he? Blue's a nice judge of character."

Zottigstrauch was back to ignoring her barbs, instructing, "Take the horse around the far side of the van, away from the cars. Lead him over to the porch and secure him to the rail. You and Clarke will both inspect him there."

She really wanted to toss a pithy gibe at Zottigstrauch; however, his expression convinced her otherwise. She clucked to Blue and led him away as told. Out loud, Jessica sighed; but inwardly she shouted, "James! Hooley! Where the devil are you ?!"

Jessica was tying Blue up to the rickety railing when Terry stepped out, saying, "The girl's tied up. She shouldn't give us any trouble."

Jess looked from Zottigstrauch to Terry and pointed out bitterly, "I've seen how your boss keeps people from causing trouble, Terry. Do you really want that poor girl's blood on your hands?"

Terry's mouth hardened as Zottigstrauch said, "Terence knows which side his bread is buttered on. He's not about to risk himself."

Jessica sent Terry a pleading look and pushed, "Terry, you can't let him kill her."

"Let's check the horse," Terry changed the subject as he came down the steps. "We need him ship-shape for the buyer in Chitzenega, right, Georgie boy?"

Standing at an angle, off to Blue's right, and behind Jessica, the man with the gun said no more than, "Just make sure the animal is ready to travel. You, Mrs. Crawford, keep the horse calm while Terence inspects him."

"Sure," Terry smiled bitterly. He continued, "You really knew what you were doing when you hooked up with two people from horse country. Carolina's family being neighbors of the stallion's owner was sheer genius. Anything you didn't think of? Oh, yeah, that Phil Novack might develop a conscience, that Jessamyn Crane might learn too much or almost turn me human." Terry straightened up from examining Blue's legs. "That the U.S. government might get wise to you—and be downright cranky about your bumping off one of their own . . ."

"You seem to forget that was your responsibility. I didn't pull the trigger," Zottigstrauch dismissed Terry cruelly.

With Terry and Zottigstrauch on the other side of the horse, now, Jessica, from the cover of Blue's head, sent Terry a curious glance at his fib. He didn't acknowledge her, instead going on, "But you gave the orders for them all. That's a lot lives lost for just one horse. The buyer must be some kind of improver of the breed. He must have promised you a hell of a lot for delivery. You've been mighty hush-hush about the guy up to this point. I think after all the dirty jobs I've done for you, you owe me the whole story. Otherwise, there's been a lot of blood for a case of low-down, dirty horse thievin'."

"Ah, Terence, once more you're outsmarting yourself. As if any of those deaths matter. They're nothing compared to getting me what I want. I've got plans, plans to make this world over the way it should be, to put power in the hands of the people who deserve it. And all I have to do is turn over this horse to someone who has the money and influence to implement my network and keep it growing."

"Wait," Terry almost scoffed. "You're not trying to tell me a blue-blooded Chitzenegan improver of the breed is the head-honcho of some kind of Nazi resurgence plot? I don't buy that! We whipped you guys. You're all finished."

"It doesn't matter what you're willing to 'buy,'" Zottigstrauch sneered, his ego piqued. "This is too far above your comprehension. This is politics, war, international conquest. Whipped? Hardly. For simply turning over this horse, I'll be on track to create a new world order."

"Get off it," Terry scoffed genuinely this time.

Jessica's eyes flashed a warning to Terry, and she whispered, "Terry, lay off. If this guy thinks you know too much, he'll kill you, especially if you make him mad."

Terry ignored Jessica and demanded, "Hey, Zottigstrauch, I'm up to my neck in this for you, and now you're going on like some kind of a whacky megalomaniac. You want to keep me helping you, you better come clean about exactly with whom I'm mixed up and what's going to happen when we get to Chitzenega."

Those cobra-deadly eyes narrowed, and then Zottigstrauch smiled smugly, moving to face Terry. He sneered, "That's just how much cleverer we are than you. I received anonymous contacts with the offer: unlimited support in return for the horse. My benefactor is too smart to reveal his identity even when we deliver the horse. All I know right now is that he was shrewd enough to have an envoy present the offer. A Swiss account will be activated when I deliver the horse to a specified horse market on the border of Honi First Nation territory in Chitzenega."

"That's *it?*" Terry concluded doubtfully.

"That's it. You and I will be paid off, and, of course, we'll get new identities. No, my benefactor and I are far too shrewd to allow ourselves to become easy prey."

He stepped menacingly closer to Terry. His smile was confident, superior.

Jessica ducked under Blue's head and came between them, challenging Zottigstrauch, hoping to win Terry's support, "What about Alicia and I? Do we get new identities, too, or do we become stable girls for your mysterious pal? Or maybe," she looked at Terry, "we both end up members of the same club as all Zottigstrauch's murder victims. Terry, is that what you want? Do you want the initials of your new i.d. to be R.I.P.?"

Georg Zottigstauch stepped back and raised his weapon, saying carefully, "Curious list, Mrs. Crawford. You included everyone but one, your husband. I'd have thought he'd be at the head? Why is that?"

"Because Mrs. Crawford isn't a widow, yet!" came a voice from behind them, by the horse van. "Drop the gun, now, Zottigstrauch. I'm a good shot and I can read a twitching shoulder blade ready to fire like nobody's business."

James Crawford was edging carefully from around Terry's car. Before Jess's knees could give out, Terry pulled her around and away from Zottigstrauch's weapon. Jess tried to call out to her husband as Zottigstrauch dropped his gun, but the strange smile on their adversary's face as he looked up at the cabin, then turned to face James with arms up, gave her pause. But no more pause than Terry's seeming to realize something before he shoved her down, then shouted, "No" as he dashed up the stairs to the cabin door.

For Jessica, it all became an insane blur! A shot pierced the night from the cabin. To her horror, James hit the ground! *Shot or just dodging bullets?! Okay, he rolled away, under the car.* Yet through Blue's furious screams and rearing, she heard Terry gasping in pain. He'd dropped on the porch.

Blue was lunging, jerking, and pulling on his lead, trying to free himself from the old wood railing. Jessica half-rose, straining for sight of James, when she was jerked to her feet by Zottigstrauch's hard clasp on her left arm, his gun in his right hand. Blue was still fighting, and Jess just had presence of mind enough to twist her head to see Terry sprawled face down.

"My God, Terry!" she breathed. *How? Was Carolina really still alive? Had she sneaked into the cabin somehow and waited for such an emergency. She and Zottigstrauch had outfoxed Terry, disbelieving his obedience, after all? Was Alicia safe? Oh, poor Terry—after he'd tried to save James and me. James? Why hadn't I heard anything from him? But if Terry were hit and there'd only been one shot that had to mean James was . . ..*

Zottigstrauch jerked her closer and called, "All right, Crawford, the game's up. Clarke is dead, and I have your wife right here, with my weapon" (apparently retrieved in the commotion) "on her. Throw down your gun and step out with your hands clasped behind your head. You wouldn't want anything to happen to your wife, would you?"

Much as Jessica wanted nobly to tell James to forget about her, she took the practical route and kept her mouth shut, only pulling as hard as she could to the left, away from Zottigstrauch's gun and the plunging, maddened Blue Warrior.

"None of that, my dear," her captor warned determinedly, hauling Jessica back to clasp her in a near chokehold against him as a shield. "You wouldn't get very far at any rate, not with this weapon in my hand." Then he turned his attention to the hidden James and called, "Really now, Crawford, I'm growing impatient. I have a boat to catch. If you value your wife, you'll throw out your gun and come forward, hands clasped behind your head. Otherwise, it will not go well for her, I promise you."

"Jessica," James shouted above Blue's fractious commotion, "are you all right?"

She growled to Zottigstrauch, "Loosen the hold, bub, if you want me to answer." He did, and Jessica called out, "I'm okay for now, but Carolina shot Terry. He's not moving. I think he's gone. So, don't trust this guy. You see how he kills his own."

"No one's asking you to trust me, Crawford," Zottigstrauch called out. "I'm simply warning you that if you don't do as I've told you, I'll hurt your wife—badly. She will suffer now, whether or not you both die later. Throw out that weapon."

Blue seemed to understand the threat, for he pulled hard on the old wooden railing, which creaked but did not give, then. The stallion was making deep, threatening sounds. But James's gun flew out, and Jessica's heart sank.

Zottigstrauch called over his shoulder, into the cabin, "It is done. Kick out the panel in floorboards under the right window and get to the second landing below. Take the outboard to the waiting ship. I'll meet you there after the crew comes for me. I want to take care of these two myself." Turning back to the earlier direction of James's voice, he ordered, "I'm waiting, Crawford. Don't make me take my impatience out on your wife—and do remember, if you intend to use some kind of hidden gun, the bullets will have to pass through *her* to get to me."

Jessica couldn't catch her breath, whether from Zottigstrauch's tight hold or her terror for James. Blue's digging into the ground and tugging on the stressed rail only added to the nightmare. She prayed that James wouldn't come out, could outflank, outsmart this s.o.b. Then a thought came to her suddenly, through the haze of anxiety. She challenged, loud enough for James to hear, "You can't kill him now, Zottigstrauch. You know you still need him."

Her captor frowned above her, furious at the thought anything had gotten by him, and demanded, "What do you mean by that?"

"I mean just as you said earlier: you need to know what he knows, what he's passed on about you. You shoot him when he comes out—you'll never know. You'll always be looking over your shoulder, and maybe you and your Chitzenegan pal will find your plans scotched before you know what hits you. For a guy who prides himself on anticipating all contingencies, you're taking an awful chance if you nix my husband."

"She has you there," James called. "We're both more valuable to you alive than dead, and you still have the lady in your hands to make me cooperate."

Georg Zottigstrauch thought that over. Slowly he smiled before saying, "Yes, and if I keep you, and the lady, captive a little longer I may be able to pry out of you some useful information about this country's espionage system. Yes." He looked down at Jessica. "Good play. You've bought yourself some time."

Blue snorted and let out an angry call, one hoof smashing down and cracking the porch's wood.

"Damned beast," Zottigstrauch muttered. "If I didn't need him most of all, he'd be the first to take a bullet." Back to James, he relented, "All right. Out with you, now!" An unexpected twist of her wrist, painful and startling, forced a cry from Jessica, followed by Zottigstrauch's: "That's just to inspire alacrity."

James came out, hands behind his head, his eyes telling Jessica his feelings for her. In his confidence, Zottigstrauch relaxed his grip on Jess, letting her sink a few inches. James was almost by where his gun lay in the dirt, when she felt that shift in Zottigstrauch's stance. That move signaled Jess he'd changed his mind about sparing James. With all her strength, she rammed her skull up into the bottom of Zottigstrauch's jaw.

Jessica really did see stars, as his shot went wild. She was falling off to the left and somehow the cracking, splintering of wood and furious equine shrieks penetrated her dazed head. One minute Georg Zottingstrauch was above her, ready to fire, a huge black gun looming

441

over her, and then 80,000 psi crushed down on his arm. He was pulled up and away from her like the proverbial rag doll—a cursing, screaming rag doll.

The man was on the ground, and Jessica's vision cleared enough for her to realize that Blue Warrior's steel-shod hooves were enacting a brutal revenge for Phil, Terry, Jessamyn—everyone, She screamed and covered her eyes, then someone was yanking her away from the horror.

Jessica instinctively struggled, moaning she didn't know what, until her mind cleared enough to recognize James soothing her. He'd pulled her some distance away and was kneeling, holding her, calming her with, "It's all right. It's done. You're all right. I'm here. Don't look back."

Jessica shuddered into James's arms, murmuring, "It's horrible, horrible. I've never seen such . . ."

"Don't think about it," James finished for her. They could hear that Blue's pounding had tapered into pawing, then stopped. He released a triumphant cry.

When Jessica started to turn back again, James stopped her and said, "No. He's done for."

Blue gave a quiet whistle, signaling all clear, yet he sounded uncertain, as if bewildered now that his protective fury was spent.

Finally a bit steadier, Jessica asked James, "Is Blue all right?"

"He looks fine," James answered, watching the animal who stood trembling, lead dangling, finally moving uneasily away from what remained of Georg Zottigstrauch. James added, "But I'd steer clear of him till he calms down more. What about you? Are you hurt? Are you sure you're all right?"

"Yes, yes, I'm fine, all things considered," Jessica answered, "though I have a dilly of a headache-and a sore wrist." Then as her head cleared more, she straightened and cried, "Terry, they got Terry—and after he saved you. Oh, the poor slob! I was so hard on him, and he was even a hero at the end, or he tried to be."

"About time you admitted that," came a voice, followed by a groan, from the porch.

Startled, James and Jessica turned sharply in that direction, though the move was almost too much for Jess. A pale, wounded-in-the-shoulder, Terry Clarke was sitting up on the steps.

"Terry!" Jessica burst out, getting to her feet with James's help. Less woozy now, she moved as fast as she could, with her husband, to the weak but definitely alive Terry Clarke.

"You're alive!" she gushed. "Thank God! I was sure they'd gotten *you*, too!"

"They got me all right," Terry nodded toward his blood-soaked shoulder, wincing as James examined it, "but I elected for the better part of valor and played possum."

"Don't worry," James told him. "As they say in the flicks, 'It's only a flesh wound.'" He bound up Terry's injury, while adding, "By the bye, did you intend to keep playing possum while Zottigstrauch did in Jessica and myself."

"I saved you once tonight," Terry calmly noted. "And I hid you in the horse van, with *my* gun, for the ride out. Beyond that, I pumped Zottigstrauch for as much information as I could get out of him for you. That's sticking my neck out plenty. Anyway, I figured a master spy like you could come up with something when the chips were down."

Jessica regarded James with amazement to say, "*You* rode in the van with Blue? In those close quarters, on a bumpy road, when he was agitated? I don't believe it, the way you feel about horses!"

James shrugged and replied, "Let's just say all those visits to the stable with the carrots over the last week or so paid off. And a chap does what he has to do when the chips are down. Although after what I witnessed him doing to Zottigstrauch tonight, I'm not eager to hitch a ride back in the van with him. Ah, sorry, Jessica. I didn't mean to remind you of it. It's a bad business."

"Bad business or not," Terry snorted, "that horse saved your lives. Zottigstrauch had the drop on Jessica and chances are he would have gotten you, too, before you got to your gun. For my money, they ought to give that horse a citation, taking down Zottigstrauch after everything he's done, everything he planned to do."

"I won't argue with that," James agreed.

Jessica looked down, not sure what to say. Yes, there was strange satisfaction in revenge, but taking blood, that was something that didn't sit easily with her. She looked back at Blue Warrior. He stood by the van, watching them. Foam still flecked his neck, but his sides were no longer heaving. His eyes were alert, maybe a little scared. His ears pricked forward, listening to them, as if hoping for the comfort of familiarity—a return from savagery.

Jessica concluded, "I think he's calmed down now. I want to go over and—good heavens! How could I have forgotten?!" Her eyes shot to the cabin's entrance. "Alicia! We've got to see if she's all right!"

"Alicia?" escaped from a puzzled James.

"Yes," Jess answered, starting for the door. "Zottigstrauch brought her along as a hostage, to keep me in line."

Terry halted Jess with, "Wait, Jessie. Alicia's not there."

Jess spun around, crying, "Oh, no, Terry! Are you saying that Carolina took her away in the outboard? She's still a hostage?"

Terry shook his head, before answering, "You're still snowed, aren't you? Alicia's no hostage. She's Zottigstrauch's daughter."

James rose slowly, saying, "Yes, of course. They found the mother's body but never the daughter's. That's why he settled here, to be near his darling daughter."

"What?" Jessica blurted in disbelief.

Terry nodded, elaborating, "Yep, and a chip off the old block she was: Placed with some simpatico fivers, they raised her up to be a proper daddy's girl—if your daddy is a goosestepper. Sly like her old man, too. She figured out that working in the deeds and survey office would enable her to provide dear old Dad with this island for a hideaway. She just altered the records, so it looked to be uninhabitable.

"And she had you all eating out of her hand like old Blue Boy and his carrots. You thought you were protecting her from the big, bad seducer, aka me. That was her bright idea. All the while, she pulled the trigger on Phil Novack and drove off in Daddy's car, leaving Caro and me to clean up after her. She's probably even the one who put the bullet into my dearly beloved wife. I found out she sent Jessamyn a note to meet me in Cameron House, then murdered her." His voice was harsh, angry, bitter. "But she wasn't quite as adept as her old man at disposing of the body—used his method but didn't recalculate for the differences between a lake and an ocean. Old man gave her hell for that. She'd learned her lesson when it came to disposing of Phil. Me, I'd love to have seen *her* under that horse's hooves, too.

444

"As for what Zottigstrauch would have done with Jessica, or any of us for that matter, when he got the horse safely to Chitzenega? That's something I don't like to think about. Sorry I couldn't get more out of him for you, Crawford."

"You did your best, and I'm not going to be able to do any better, now that the horse has turned him into . . ." James stopped himself, seeing Jessica pale at his words. Instead, he finished, "He's no help to us now. My superiors aren't going to hand *me* any citations." Then he thought it over and decided, "But it might not be too late. If I can get to a phone, we can alert the Coast Guard. They may be able to nab Alicia and the transport. There's a chance someone in that lot has information or might be turned so that we can set a trap for the Chitzenegan connection. What do you say, Clarke? Up to taking a ride with Jessica and me back down the road to the nearest telephone?"

"Wait a minute," Jessica cautioned. "What about Blue? I don't know if he's settled enough to load in the van. We can't just leave him here— Zottigstrauch's connections are bound to show up while we're gone and take him. That rather defeats the purpose of your mission."

"Never mind that," Terry countered. "The three of us don't want to be sitting here when that little landing party shows up. They'll be armed; we'll be outnumbered. Hell, it'll just be you against them, Crawford. Jessie's no Annie Oakley, and I'm not up for a shootout, not with this shoulder."

That was when they heard the motorboat start up and peel off, away from the island.

"Damn!" Terry cursed. "Alicia must have waited out the shoot out in the boat, overheard all we said. She either took off to get reinforcements, or . . ."

"Escaped to signal a strategic retreat," James completed sourly. "All right, Jessica. You and I will see if we can load the horse. I'll help Terry into the back seat of the car, first. Damn, maneuvering that vehicle out of here will be no picnic!"

"But it won't get done if we sit around jawing about it," Terry added.

"Can't you clowns avoid SNAFUing anything when I'm not around?" came a familiar voice from the woods.

"Hooley!" Jessica called as Jeff Hooley's lanky form loped into view, careful not to come near Blue in his approach.

"I heard you people yapping all the way up the road," he continued. "What do you need . . . from me?"

His voice had trailed off a moment when he confronted what remained of Georg Zottigstrauch.

"This doesn't look good for you, Crawford," Jeff Hooley remarked, coming up to the porch.

"Never mind that," James ordered. "You used a radio car to track the horse here. Get on the horn to the Coast Guard. Put out an alert for the freighter in this area." Turning to Terry, James questioned, "Any idea how far out?"

Terry shook his head and explained, "Zottigstrauch was cagey about that, but my guess is that it would come in as close to the island as it could without running aground. Tell them to close in on Durgin Island."

James turned back to Hooley and ordered, "You got that? And don't forget to put out an alert for a small outboard craft piloted by Alicia . . ."

"Alicia? Who's that?"

"It's a bit of an eleventh-hour twist, Hooley," James replied quickly. "All I can tell you is that she's Georg Zottigstrauch's daughter–pretty, dark-haired fiend of a girl in her late teens. Now get on the ball. Maybe we can still salvage some part of this muck up. But be sure to return as fast as you can, in case we have to deal with an armed party looking for the horse."

"Yeah, sure," Jeff nodded, with the quickest of glances at Jessica. "I'll be back to help you get everyone out of here before you have any unwelcome guests." Then he was racing back up the road, his black trench coat flying witchlike around him, all before Jessica realized that his look had been a quick check to make sure she was still in one piece.

"James," Jessica began, "do you think it'll work? Will the Coast Guard be able to catch Alicia and the freighter?"

Her husband answered, "I don't know. We can hope. It looks as if I've made a botch of this."

"What do you mean?" Jessica protested. "You stopped the deal. Blue even finished Georg Zottigstrauch. He'll never hurt anyone again. Public Enemy Number One down for the count."

"Cut off the head of the Hydra," Terry pointed out, "and seven more grow in its place."

"Precisely," James agreed wearily. "Remember, Jessica, taking down this single man wasn't the ultimate end of my mission. I was supposed to set things up so we could see what exactly his plans are and who is supporting him. This is not going to go well for me."

"Well, that just stinks!" Jessica fumed. "I mean, even Georg Zottigstrauch didn't know who his contact was. You can't get blood from a stone."

"But we might have gotten his plans," James punished himself.

"There's still a chance that the Coast Guard will nab Alicia, or get their hands on the freighter," Jessica persisted.

James smiled wanly and agreed, "Yes, a slim one."

"Then she cuts herself a sweet deal and gets off scot-free if she sings like Ella Fitzgerald," Terry bitterly cut in.

Coolly amused, James observed, "It seems to me, Terry, that you cut yourself a deal back in the stable yard when you had Jessica out of earshot."

"It seems to me that that deal saved both your and Jessica's lives, at great risk to my own," Terry corrected James.

"*Touché*, Professor Clarke," James allowed. Then he put an arm around his wife and guided her down the steps and over to Zottigstrauch's sedan, to rest against it with her for a moment.

Jess said, "James, I've been thinking. What will happen to Blue? I mean, I know that they destroy killer horses. Will they, will they do that to him?"

James looked over at the horse, who was now calmly watching them, occasionally flicking an ear toward the intrusions of a foghorn. Finally, James said, "It seems to me that anyone who takes out a Nazi, as Clarke said, deserves a medal, not a death sentence. Leave it to me. Whatever influence I have, I'll keep him off the hook. At any rate, it sounds as if his owner is a man with clout. I predict that Blue Warrior will be sentenced to imprisonment in fields of bluegrass and clover."

"They don't actually have bluegrass in Maryland, I don't think. You mean Kentucky, but I catch your drift. That's good enough for me, though Lord knows I'll miss the big lug."

James squeezed her closer, his head resting against hers, but with a clear eye on Terry, nonetheless. Terry, however, had closed *his* eyes. He'd had enough for one evening. Jess wanted to ask James about how sweet a deal Terry would get. In fact, if it hadn't been for Terry's saving James, all of them, except maybe Blue, would have crossed over into the land of harps and clouds. But she was tired, so tired. She just wanted to close her eyes and give herself up to knowing that the worst was over, and she and James were safe together, finally.

Epilogue

Alicia's outboard had been found, washed up and wrecked in the same cove that had once held the hulk for Terry and Jessamyn's trysts. No Alicia, nor Alicia's body, had ever been found, though. Was she off plotting more mischief, carrying her father's banner? Or was she buried in Davy Jones' locker? Poetic justice considering the burial she'd given Jessamyn Crane and Phil Novack. Jessica hoped it was the latter and convinced herself that she didn't fear the former.

A freighter had exploded and burned out to sea, not far from Durgin Island, before the Coast Guard could reach it. All hands were lost. Had Alicia been aboard that freighter in its death throes or had she sabotaged it to cover her tracks? Maybe both were true.

These were Jessica's thoughts as she and Blue took their last gallop along the beach. Tomorrow, Hooley was in charge of vanning the stallion back to his owner in Maryland—away from Jessica, away from memories of Phil Novack, away from gallops on the beach—but also away from the memory of blood on his hooves.

The stallion's body moved with fluid grace, and Jessica delighted in posting in rhythm. For the last time. Kildeer, sandpipers, and plovers scattered before them. Yes, their last ride. True, Blue's grateful owner had made a person-to-person call, thanking Jessica for rescuing his beloved stallion, promising an open invitation to visit him in Maryland whenever she liked. Yet, it would never be the same; no more of the day-to-day relations they shared. Would he still remember her? Could he forget the human whose life he had saved? Would he miss her?

The stallion's neck arched; his ears flicked back to Jess as she told him again that their bonds could never really break. Did he understand, believe her?

Her cottage loomed into view above them. There was James, leaning on the balustrade, watching and waiting for her. He was back earlier than she'd expected. She couldn't read his face from here, but she could guess the text. Things had not gone well with the brass over the end of this assignment. They'd washed him out, and she hadn't seen him so relieved in ages. He was done. Richard Streeter had pushed to let him go, stressed his battle fatigue and drove home the case, but more for James's sake than anyone else's. She could have kissed the old hard nose for that. Truth be told, James probably could have, too. Maybe now he could begin to live. They both could.

Jessica smiled broadly as James waved to her. She pointed Blue up towards the slope, and James slipped over the balustrade, striding down to meet them, hands in the pocket of his windbreaker.

"Hello, there! You look chipper, Mr. Crawford," Jessica teased as she slowed Blue to a stop.

James surprised her by stepping right up to the horse and patting his neck.

"I was afraid you'd gotten shy of him since . . . since that night," she began, even more surprised at the twinkle in his eye as he pulled out a carrot and offered it to her eagerly accepting mount.

"I had a few bad moments," James admitted, watching Blue chomp away on the proffered treat, "but he did save my life—our lives. You know, you can get quite matey with a fellow when you share a lift in a horse van. Rather cozy."

"So now, you're not afraid of horses anymore?" Jess queried.

"Not this one anyway," James allowed, rubbing Blue's cheek.

Blue Warrior, finished with one treat, tried to lip James's pocket for more.

"Take it easy, old chap," James laughed. "That's all I have. You want to watch your figure, eh?"

"I think I'm going to faint," Jessica teased. "*You* making cute with a horse? You're certainly in a sunny mood. I guess being washed up in the cloak and dagger biz agrees with you."

"That and *not* being washed up in the 'biz' I truly love," James answered cryptically.

Jess tilted her head curiously. "Okay, buddy, what's the big secret? Spill."

"Maybe I will, if you come down off your 'high horse,'" he quipped.

Jessica rolled her eyes over the excruciating pun, but happily slipped out of the saddle and into her beloved's arms.

"Now, no more double talk, mister. What's with the cat-that-ate-the-canary expression?"

Blue's nose-butt to James's shoulder added emphasis to Jess's prompting.

"Well, I can't fight the two of you. I'm afraid as far as my teaching is concerned, we've gone from dearth to superfluity."

"In English, wise guy," Jess ordered with mock impatience.

"Of course. In plain English—on the one hand, I'm back to being Nigel Cross's fair-haired boy. He sees me as clearing him of suspicions by the authorities, and he has a rather sympathetic view of veterans under duress after his own experiences in the Great War. He's grateful, as well, for my role in bringing to justice at least one of those responsible for Jessamyn Crane's death. And I rather think he's more than a little pleased that I've gotten Terry out of his hair."

"What *has* happened to Terry? He disappeared after that dreadful night. Prison?" Jess was hoping that things hadn't gone too harshly for Terry. She owed him not just her own life but James's as well.

"Jessica, I don't honestly know. I'm out of that loop. However, knowing Terry Clarke, as I do now, I suspect that he's not suffering any more than he ought."

"That's certainly a cagey answer," Jess observed. "But since I can see that's all I'm going to get out of you, all right. Wait a minute, though. What about the college administration? I can't imagine the President would be too happy to find out her school has been the backdrop of a secret mission."

"True," James agreed. "If she knew. But none of my superiors want to breathe a word about this farrago, and Nigel's view is that what college administrators don't know won't hurt them, or us either. In short, he wants me to stay."

"Oh my gosh!" Jessica almost squealed, prompting Blue to shake his head and jerk the reins she held.

James gave the horse a calming hand. *Verily this was the age of miracles*, Jess decided. But then, she recalled James's earlier words and said, "Wait a sec. You said something about a superfluity. What's the deal?"

"Good memory," he smiled. "Remember the chap who reclaimed his slot at Washington Irving University, ousting me? He accepted a position at Princeton. Washington Irving has extended me an invitation to return to his old position. I'm good, but I can't fill two jobs at once."

"Oh, you dog!" Jessica teased. "I bet you just feel all smug and wonderful."

"Could it have happened to a nicer lad?" he queried mischievously.

"Maybe a more modest one," she teased. Then Jess hugged James close and told him, "Darling, this is unbelievable. But Lord knows you've earned this!"

"Well," he temporized, a bit embarrassed, "Let's just call it a delightful turn of affairs."

"It's about time. So, which do you want? I can keep my work either place you choose."

James tilted his head up, considering before answering, "At this moment, I choose to have a delightful summer day with my beautiful wife."

Blue snorted and interjected a throaty equine rumble.

"My beautiful wife and gallant steed," he amended.

Jessica found herself deep in James's arms; and the world *did* lie before them "like a land of dreams,/ So various, so beautiful, so new." At least for today.

Afterword

This is the part where the author tells you, "No, you didn't nail me on getting wrong some obscure fact! That was artistic license. So, there!" Well, here's where I put my license to work. If you read the country "Chitzenega" in the book and went scurrying to look it up, the reason you couldn't find it is that this delightful southerly country exists only in my head, invented so very long ago to populate years of amateur fiction, drawn from my love of cultural geography. It will make more appearances in forthcoming novels, including a less-than-relaxing vacation trip by Jessica and James - but that's all in the future.

And to those of you who ask, "How come a British SOE agent was carrying a .32ACP Colt, an American pistol?" Here's the answer. Lend Lease sent many kinds of weapons to England, including handguns, like the .32 Colt.

Sources:
- https://www.oldcolt.com/products/colt-1903-pocket-hammerless-32acp-sn-556545-mfg-1942-british-soe
- https://en.wikipedia.org/wiki/Special_Operations_Executive

Tattooing the inner, upper lip of racehorses for identification, to prevent illegal substitutions, is actually done. However, the procedure didn't come into practice until 1947, but it *was* driven by a plague of ringers in Thoroughbred racing across the U.S. There was no secret FBI program involved, but it would have been cool, wouldn't it? Aside from fifty years of following horseracing, my main research on the history and specifics of the ringer scandals and methods to prevent them came from the tremendously helpful *Ringer Rascals: The True Story of Racing's Greatest Con Artists* (David Ashforth). For information on lip tattoo identification, see also: https://washingtonthoroughbred.com/thoroughbred-terminology

Lou Smith, the President of Rockingham Park, was a real person. An extremely savvy and forward-thinking individual, he truly was the godfather of Thoroughbred racing in New Hampshire. He was responsible for all the innovations mentioned in Chapter Twenty-Seven, and more. The intriguing anecdotes are also true as well, and you can read more in *Rockingham Park: 1933-69* (Paul Peter Jesep). The following sources also provided solid research on horseracing in New England during the 1940s: *The Pilgrims Would Be Shocked: The History of Thoroughbred Racing in New England* (Robert Temple), "Heyday of the Old Rockingham Park" (Bill Dalton, *Andover Townsman*, March 8, 2012). Brass Monkey was a real horse who actually indirectly saved the lives of a few during the Coconut Grove fire in 1942. See "The Loser's Friend" (Richard Pritchett, *Turf and Sport Digest*, December 1974). However, stable hands Ceasare and Frankie are figments of my imagination.

Blue Larkspur and Equipoise were actual racing champs in the 1930s. Equipoise, the Chocolate Soldier, was inclined to take a chunk out of any equine who tried to pass him. Blue Warrior, alas, only exists in my head, an imaginative echo of Walter Farley's Black Stallion.

Lightning Source UK Ltd.
Milton Keynes UK
UKHW040017031122
411515UK00037B/52